BEHOLD THE SHINING MOUNTAINS

BY

Gary H. Wiles, B.A., J.D.
and Delores M. Brown

PHOTOSENSITIVE™
LAGUNA NIGUEL, CALIFORNIA

Gary Wiles & Delores Brown

BEHOLD THE SHINING MOUNTAINS
Copyright 1996 Gary H. Wiles and Delores M. Brown
All Rights Reserved.

This is Book Two* of our Talking History Series. It is an authoritative historical work based upon the extensive research in its Bibliography, the authors' interviews of historians and photographs of artifacts and natural sites.

For Information write to:

PHOTOSENSITIVE™
A Division Of
BIRTH OF AMERICA BOOKS™
P.O. Box 7008, Hemet, CA 92545-7008
or Call Toll Free 1-877-742-6241

PRINTING HISTORY
First Printing 1996

ISBN: 1-889252-00-X

PRINTED IN THE UNITED STATES OF AMERICA.

Library of Congress Catalog Card Number 96-68784

Other Books by these Authors

*PONDER THE PATH, Book One of our Talking History Series
HOW TO STOP SMOKING <u>WHILE</u> SMOKING

Please See Order Form Inside Back Cover To Order These Other Exceptional Books

TABLE OF CONTENTS

Continued on Next Page

TABLE OF CONTENTS

BEHOLD THE SHINING MOUNTAINS is dedicated to Mrs. Frances Koromy, my inspirational high school English teacher and life long confidant, who is now somewhere in the wilds of Oregon.

Gary Wiles

PROLOGUE

PONDER THE PATH[1], our Book One of this Talking History Series, featured the true exploits of the Sublette family and their legendary cohorts, battling Indians, grizzlies, bad whiskey and each other for the West's vast beaver fortunes between 1808 and 1830. *PONDER* begins in 1808 when the United States was a 17-state postage stamp on the corner of North America fighting four powerful foreign countries and 50 Indian nations for the rest of the continent. *PONDER* blares the big news stories and political fireworks of the era. It's the very human story of how eight year old William Sublette's grandfather Whitley inspired him to open the Oregon Trail to wagons from Independence, Missouri to the Rocky Mountains two decades later in 1830. In its 1996 Review *Muzzleloader* Magazine said, "*PONDER THE PATH* is inspiring, informative and just plain good reading."

BEHOLD THE SHINING MOUNTAINS is Book Two of our Talking History Series. In Talking History, the people talk instead of just being talked about. *BEHOLD* is a free-standing sequel, rejoining the lives of *PONDER'S* real life people in 1830. *BEHOLD* begins after William Sublette and his partners send their 1830 letter to Secretary of War Eaton about their wagons crossing the Great American Desert from Missouri to the Rockies. They say wagons can reach the fertile West. This shocking letter's read to the U.S. Senate. Reprints hit the nation's newspapers, firing imaginations from religious zealots seeking savages to save to farmers lusting for virgin soil. The letter unleashes the American dream of owning your own land upon hordes of city people.

Like Book One of this Talking History Series, *BEHOLD THE SHINING MOUNTAINS*[2] combines the true tales of many

---

[1] Published in 1994 and now available from PHOTOSENSITIVE™ by using the Book Order Form inside this book's back cover or through your local book store.

[2] The name *Shining Mountains* [for the Rocky Mountains] is in John Jacob Astor's 1794 journal & was later popularized by Thomas Hart Benton's September 25, 1819 *St. Louis Enquirer* article.

I

epic people, weaving them into a grand tapestry of the times without losing sight of the main characters. *BEHOLD* entwines the lives of Mountain Men, Missionaries and Native American Tribes, in rousing adventures on land that was, or became, 36 states. The intrigues, epidemics, and shenanigans of 1830s life in eastern U.S. cities occupy half of this book, including 27 chapters on early day New York, where inhabitants feared the bears would eat their pigs, rather than merely destroying a bull market. Powerful dramas play out in the primeval splendor of the West in the rest of the book's 57 chapters.

Opening the rest of the Oregon Trail to wheeled vehicles from the Rockies to Oregon's rich-soiled valleys will be attempted in 1836 by the most quixotic group imaginable.

BEHOLD THE SHINING MOUNTAINS laminates in the valiant struggles of Dr. Marcus Whitman, his new wife Narcissa and other Missionaries to spread the Gospel to the heathen -- red and white. Mountain Men often greet God's minions with curses, rotten eggs and brutality. The heart-wrenching dramas of these Missionaries are highlighted by a marriage of convenience that becomes a passionate love story in spite of the spurned suitor along on their honeymoon from hell!

Scottish nobleman, Captain William Drummond Stewart, tries to lose his creditors in the wild west and finds himself.

Nathaniel Wyeth, a New England inventor hungry to capture the western fur trade, learns luck can make or break a man.

Economic genius General William Ashley reshapes the fur trade, makes a fortune and goes off to Washington as a Congressman to tangle with President Andrew Jackson, formidable Senator Thomas Hart Benton and the richest ogre in America, John Jacob Astor.

To break Astor's monopolistic stranglehold on the western fur trade, backwoodsman William Sublette goes nose to nose with Astor in New York City in a gut-wrenching duel of wills none of them would ever forget!

Chronological headings supply each chapter's time frame. Three vintage maps list key locales to help you follow the stirring adventures.

BEHOLD features quotes from letters, journals, diaries and periodicals, which were also used to shape the dialogue and attitudes of its real life Talking History characters, all of whom are listed in our Index of Persons [with Identifying Data] at the end of this book.

In *BEHOLD's* turbulent years from 1830 to 1836, America defines itself as a world power, expands its western horizons, fights Indian wars, suffers killing cholera epidemics, wrangles over slavery and stares into the chilling chasm of civil war. One of the earliest generations born free of the autocratic straight jackets of their fathers, these Americans recklessly challenge destiny for control of their own fate and fortune.

Join us in the misty hills of history! Share high adventure with your forefathers in the robust young America of the 1830s! Live frontier life on the edge with death ever your constant companion.

Despite its historical precision, *BEHOLD THE SHINING MOUNTAINS* is a three hanky book with a dozen belly laughs.

Gary H. Wiles, B.A., J.D. and Delores M. Brown

ACKNOWLEDGMENT

For our earlier book of this genre, *PONDER THE PATH*[3] , covering the period from 1808 to 1830 we annotated 151 books, drove 10,000 miles to the principal sites involved in the book and took 1,600 research photos at pertinent locations and in museums in Oregon, Washington, Wyoming and Louisiana. We thanked helpful historians in *PONDER's* ACKNOWLEDGMENT, but since we relied on their contributions for this book as well, we again express our gratitude to:

Gary Wilson, Director- Museum of the Mountain Men at Pinedale, WY.

David Hansen, Park Curator of Ft. Vancouver at Vancouver, WA.

David Hunsaker, Director - Oregon Trail Interpretive Center, Baker, OR.

National Park Rangers of Yellowstone Park in northern Wyoming

Tribal Councils and Indian Schools in Idaho, Oregon and Wyoming

and Dr. Fred R. Gowans of Brigham Young University.

BEHOLD THE SHINING MOUNTAINS is a sequel to *PONDER THE PATH*. *BEHOLD* spans America's chaotic years from 1830 through 1836 and was done with the aid of many generous people!

We thank Librarian Joanne R. Euster and Assistant Johanna Christensen of the University of California at Irvine for access to their 1,200,000 books and 16,000,000 more through their computer. [*PONDER THE PATH* is in the Academic and

---

[3] Published in 1994 and now available from PHOTOSENSITIVE™ by using the Book Order Form inside this book's back cover or through your local book store.

A

Research Collection of UCI, where we have been privileged to lecture.]

Our deepest appreciation to Dr. Charles Hanson Jr., Curator of the Museum of the Fur Trade at Chadron, NE for his interview and allowing us to photograph hundreds of cherished artifacts in his temple of our American heritage.

Our thanks to Robert A. Clark, owner of the Arthur H. Clark Company, for his fine tuning of our Bibliography and his permission to use his map of the Fur Country of the Far West.

Hats off to Lawrence L. Dodd, Archivist/Curator of Whitman College at Walla Walla, WA for his assistance in locating maps and hymns and furnishing a compendium of physical descriptions of the Whitmans.

Thanks to Chief Ranger Roger Trick of the Whitman Mission National Historic Site west of Walla Walla, WA for valuable site data.

Our gratitude to Librarian Emily Miller, Assistant Edna Smith and Archivist Martha Clevenger of the Missouri Historical Society at St. Louis for helping in our quest for original documents and data.

We thank Ilona Walker of Fort Laramie, WY for helping us acquire books with data on the Fort, building of which appears in our Chapter 29 with other visits later in the book.

Our appreciation to Mary Lee Lein, Director of the Bannock County Historical Museum and Wayne Rickard, Director of the Fort Hall Replica near Pocatello, ID for historical data and for allowing us to photograph maps and artifacts depicting the building of Fort Hall in our Chapter 33 with visits in subsequent Chapters.

Thanks to Anna Belle Cartwright, Curator of the National Frontier Trails Center at Independence, MO for furnishing key documents.

Our sincerest appreciation To Reverend Daniel Merrick of Raymore, MO, Editor of *The Chalice Hymnal* for locating the 1832 hymn, *Missionary Farewell*, enabling us to include it in Chapter 48 of this book!

Our special thanks to Ray Glazner, esteemed historian and consultant to the entertainment industry, for his insights on nitty gritty details such as how the first pencils were made by rolling a bullet into a pointed lead stick in the late 1700s.

Arlene Padilla of State Records Center and Archives at Santa Fe, New Mexico gets our thanks for her helpful data on early day Santa Fe.

Our appreciation to James Corsaro, Associate Librarian of Manuscripts and Special Collections, of the New York State Library in the University of the State of New York at Albany for the 1830 map of his state.

Texts relied on for intimate detail of this period appear in our accompanying 223 volume Bibliography. We gratefully acknowledge the contributions of each of these worthy author-historians to our nation and to our vibrant living history of the 1830s.

Gary H. Wiles, B.A.,J.D., and Delores M. Brown

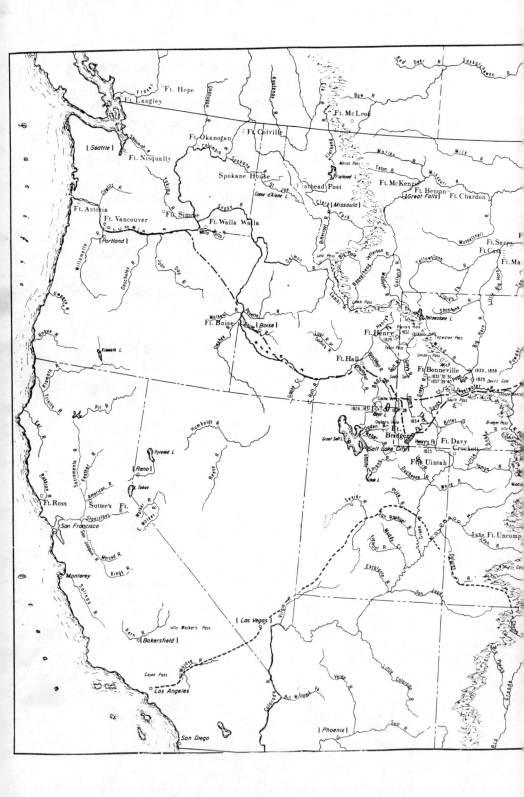

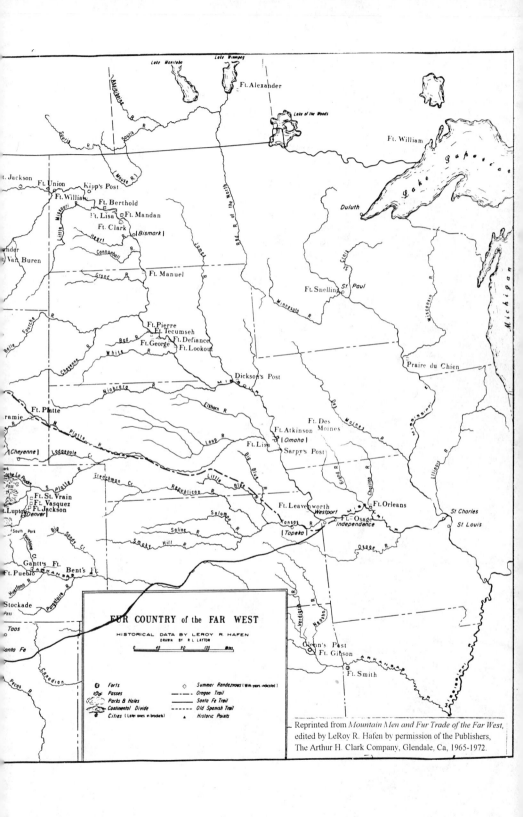

FUR COUNTRY of the FAR WEST

HISTORICAL DATA BY LEROY R. HAFEN
DRAWN BY R L LAYTON
0   45   90   135   Mls.

	Forts		Summer Rendezvous (With years indicated)
	Passes		Oregon Trail
	Parks & Holes		Santa Fe Trail
	Continental Divide		Old Spanish Trail
	Cities (Later ones in brackets)		Historic Points

Reprinted from *Mountain Men and Fur Trade of the Far West*,
edited by LeRoy R. Hafen by permission of the Publishers,
The Arthur H. Clark Company, Glendale, Ca, 1965-1972.

CHAPTER 1

A GOD FORSAKEN PLACE TO DIE   SPRING 1831

      St. Louis' Franklin Street wagon lot reeked of hot mule apples and whiskey vomit in the dawn mist. Wagonmaster William Sublette laid on his back under one of the 23 assembled wagons to inspect its wheels for grease and check for a full grease bucket on the rear axle. A dark figure walked up, shook the box he was carrying and dumped a buzzing rattlesnake in Sublette's face. Sublette yanked off his floppy felt hat, caught the rattler's strike inside its crown and clamped down on the snake's head. He catted to his feet with a yard of rattler hanging from his hat, bellering, "I oughta feed ya this head first!"

      A swarthy Frenchman in a heavy cloak tossed away his box to poise his hand above the dueling pistol in his belt. He squinted at Sublette's long wavy blond hair and inch-long scar gouged into the left side of the chin. "You are *Cutface* Bill Sublette. Your brother Milton destroyed my brother. I came to destroy you as a matter of family honor!"

      Shaking with anger, Sublette growled, "There ain't no honor in nis snake!"

      "I would not expect the illiterate like you to understand the gentleman's honor."

      "Not yer kind. Honor ain't about killin'. Honor's about keepin' yer word an' payin' what's owed. No life oughta be tuck over a card debt er a fool's insult."

      "Milton Sublette seduced *la épouse de mon frère*. Instead of dueling on the field of honor, he stabbed Caton in the buttocks with his own *couteau*. Caton wears a diaper to keep from staining himself! A Sublette must die for that!"

Seizing a pistol from his boot, Sublette cocked it grating, "That was five years back! Ain't nothin' ever over with you Frenchie Gumbos?"

A roguishly handsome young fellow with dark hair down to the shoulders of his buckskins weaved through the wagon lot's wispy fog, singing *Old Rosin the Beau* in a drunken tenor:

"I've traveled this wide world over and now to another I'll go.
I know that good quarters are waiting to welcome Old Rosin the Beau.
Get four or five jovial fellows and let them all staggering go
And dig a deep hole in the meadow and in it toss Rosin the Beau.
And in it toss Rosin the Beau!"

Sublette snarled,   "Feller in his cups is little brother Andrew. He's 23 -- an' he ain't gonna duel you. We got work ta do!"

William Sublette yelled back over his massive shoulder, "Drew, some Frenchie Gumbo's here a fussin' because o' Milt." Sublette dropped the rattler between the Frenchman's feet and blasted its head off.

The Frenchman coughed in the gun smoke, astonished to find himself intact.

Sublette growled, "I scairt ten dollars-a-head off'n every mule on nis lot to save yer garlic-stinkin' life.   Yer honor satisfied now?"

"Not until I meet a Sublette on the field of honor!"

William motioned to brother Andrew.   "Drew, Uncle Solomon raised ya on high toned talk. Explain ta this Gumbo why he oughta strut on home while he still can. Then kick his butt outa this wagon lot. We're burnin' daylight!"

Andrew Sublette towered over the dazed Frenchman. His dark tresses shunted his whiskey breath into the Frenchman's face, and his curly beard split into a fierce grin.

"What is funny?" the Frenchman gasped.

"That a cockroach like you would tackle a bull grizzly like Bill!"

The Frenchman hissed, "This Bill is more uncivilized than Milton. At least Milton draws blood. There is no honor in shooting the dirt."

Andrew rasped, "Bill's the *only* civilized Sublette. Milt woulda dumped that snake back in the box and shoved your face in it! I'm about to strip you buck naked and whip you all the way home with the bloody end o' that snake!"

The Frenchman clawed at his waistband for his family's sacred dueling pistol. Andrew tore the pistol from the dainty fingers, broke it over his knee and tossed the pieces into the fog. He tapped the man's forehead. "I see you one more time, I'll put an extra eye right there!" He drew back his boot, but the man scrambled into the fog as lawyer Borradaile dodged from his path.

Jedediah Smith spied the spindly lawyer, L.V. Borradaile in the dawn's orange light. Jedediah's blue eyes were pale in his bronzed face. His black hair hung down his forehead, but not enough to hide the white lightning scars flashing from his hairline to the corner of his left eye. Only 32, but looking a decade more, Jedediah stood ramrod straight at six feet with squared shoulders and legs that barely filled his slim buckskins. Jedediah asked in his *R-less* New York accent, "You bring the Will for Jedediah Strong Smith?"

"No sir, Mr. Smith. Jist your passport and papers on your two-wagon share o' this expedition. Your Will's still bein' writ. Courier'll bring it to ya at Lexington. It'll pass your St. Louis house and lot, your servants and personal effects in equal shares to your brothers Ira, Austin, Peter and Ralph."

"Quiet. Three of them are here in the fog. I'm relieved the Will's not here. A Will rubs a man's nose in his own mortality. Makes death a fact of life."

"Been a pleasure draftin' yours, Mr. Smith! You and Mr. Sublette are the only famous men I ever met. Read about your two California explorations, Mr. Smith. Newspapers called you the *Knight in Buckskins*!"

"Eastern papers called me *The Disciple of Death* because only seven men lived of the thirty-three who persevered through those two odysseys with me. You'll find me a humble, God fearing man behind a welter of newspaper hyperbole."

William Sublette drifted out of the fog, dwarfing Smith and Borradaile. Sublette's hook nose and piercing eyes were like a huge Andrew Jackson-faced eagle. "Got my papers?" Sublette asked, wondering if this sprout lawyer could see through eye glasses no bigger 'n pennies.

"Yes, sir. Here's the Passport General Ashley sent from Washington."

Sublette strained in the dim light and read, *Height, six feet two inches; forehead straight and open; eyes blue, light; nose Roman; mouth and chin common; hair light or sandy; complexion fair; face long and expressive; scar on left of chin; thirty-two years old.* He shook his head. "Close, but I ain't turnin' thirty-two till September."

"Here's Governor Miller's Trade Recommendation to Governors of Santa Fe, Chihuahua and Sonora."

Sublette scanned it. Governor Miller said he'd *been acquainted with the reputation of Mr. Sublette ...that... his character and standing is that of a high minded honourable man, fair and generous in all dealings and punctual in his contracts & engagements.*

"Thought Henry Geyer Esquire was gonna git the Governor ta write all this palaver bout my partner David Smith. *Sublette* ain't a name tuck kindly in Santa Fe since Milt's shoot-out with them Mexican soldiers three-four years back."

"Henry asked the Governor ta write this about David Jackson, but you know politicians. Here's your deed to the 446 acres of Sulphur Springs you bought in March for $3,000, Mr. Sublette."

"Hang onta that deed an' tell Henry to buy me the adjoinin' 333 acres with the water, but don't go over $4,000 fer it. Zat about it? We gotta git!"

"This's your Will needin' to be signed with requisite formalities."

"We been th'owed off schedule. I'll sign it at Lexington," Sublette proclaimed, thumbing lawyer Borradaile out of the meeting.

Jedediah mused, "Bill you're becoming a man of property."

Sublette grimaced and turned away.

4

"What's wrong, Bill?"

"That Frenchie Gumbo we buffaloed this mornin' was dead right about me bein' a illiterate."

"An illiterate is someone who can't read, Bill."

"Dammit, he's right, Jedediah!"

"Don't be profane, Bill. You know how that offends the Lord."

"Sorry, Jedediah. I wanta be *respectable* like my Grandpa Whitley! I'll never git respectable talkin' like a backwoods fool!"

"Bill, you amaze me! You're the quickest man with figures I ever knew."

"Been thinkin' on numbers since I's weaned."

"Then start thinking on how to talk. I've learned my words from the scriptures. Read the Holy Book. Listen to me and just talk like I do."

Sublette's back began to retch. Jedediah was embarrassed to think his frontiersman friend could be sobbing. He urged, "You *can* change the way you talk, Bill."

Sublette turned around chuckling wildly. "I don't know if'n it's worse ta sound like a down-home fool er a New Yorker!"

*   *   *

After crossing most of Missouri, Jackson and Sublette's 23 mule drawn wagons lumbered into the Aull Brothers' muleyard in Lexington, their dust stretching half a mile behind them. Wranglers shunted their herd of horses and braying mules into a corral.

William Sublette swiped the mosquito-infested dust with his floppy hat, hollering, "Davie, let's ditch these bloodsuckers!"

Davie Jackson slouched toward Sublette like a hound with a busted tail. Davie's brother Judge George Jackson had just died of TB. Davie still had a wife and four kids, but looked pitiful lonesome. Sublette could hardly swallow that Davie was only 44. The lines netting his partner's kind face were deep cracks in brittle rock. Davie'd looked older than dirt even before they'd bought out General Ashley's fur business five years ago.

Sublette dropped a thick arm around Jackson's shoulders and steered the smaller man into a dark smithy where the forge's glowing manure fire choked the mosquitoes. Davie muttered,

5

"Fitzpatrick's a month late picking up Rocky Mountain Fur's supplies for the Rendezvous at Cache Valley. Fitzpatrick's dead."

"Naw, Fitz'll ketch up. I brung their goods. Lookie this." Sublette pointed at a hulking wagon.

The squared lines of the oak-framed freight wagon looked like their others. But this wagon smelled of gun oil. The forge's firelight reflected in tiny crimson fires on its shiny hickory wheel spokes.

"What's so different about this wagon, Bill?"

Sublette grinned, "Don't never say them Aull brothers ain't got a sense o' humor. You'll find out if we git jumped by hostiles."

"I don't catch your drift Bill, but I got a shaky feeling about this trip."

"So do I. We're headin' inta 800 miles o' prairie an' fryin' pan desert, an' there ain't one of us ever been on the Santa Fe Trail."

"I thought Senator Benton's bill for a well-signed public road from Missouri to Santa Fe passed in 1825."

"Jim Aull says Comanches burnt all the road marker's fer firewood. Jim says even if we don't git lost, crossin' them deserts in July's gonna kill us to a man."

"Everybody said you couldn't take wagons through the Great American Desert to the Rockies last year, including me! You proved us liars to a man."

"Davie, I done that route six times with mule trains fore I tuck them wagons on it. Coulda done the wagon trip dead drunk with a bucket over my head."

"If that's what it takes, Bill, lets get a bottle and a bucket!"

*   *   *

Now heavy with supplies purchased at Lexington, the wagon wheels bit into the damp spring dirt. The lead wagon's mules charged into their harness to ford a grassy-banked rill where reckless tadpoles darted between the spokes in the roiled water.

"Hey, you divels hold up there!" shouted Thomas Fitzpatrick, loping his winded pinto along side the wagons.

"Where'd Bill Sublette be keepin' hisself?" Fitzpatrick queried in a brogue born of County Cavan.

The teamster, swathed in blankets against the merciless mosquitoes, pointed to a small rise. "Scoutin' over there! Thought ya was dead, Fitz!"

The slender 32 year old, sharp featured Fitzpatrick raised his thick eyebrows and nodded, "I am. Been kilt a hundred times, but only wounded once." Fitzpatrick urged his lathered horse up the rise to where Sublette sat his mule.

Sublette wiped sweat and mosquitoes from his eyes with a red and white trade handkerchief. "Me an' the World's Smartest Mule Bluegrass, is glad yer finally showin' yer ugly face, Fitz. Gotcher RMF supplies in nat wagon. How's Milt?"

"Left heel's still painin' Milt somethin' fierce. But that aside, I'm scratchin' me head how ta get these supplies up to Cache Valley."

"Hook onta some outfit at Independence er go to Santa Fe with us, then ketch a caravan north to Cache Valley. Needja ta sign a note fer Rocky Mountain Fur on them goods either way. Milt send word fer me?"

"Nary a word, Bill. Nary a word."

*   *   *

William Sublette leaned back on the World's Smartest Mule Bluegrass and watched the wagons rumble through grass with the wind sweepin' waves through it like the ocean. He'd lived on one trail or another for a third of his life. He treasured the trail routine with sentinels wakin' the daylight with a rifle shot at four A.M. The smell o' meat sizzlin' inna pan. Men eatin', wavin' their butcher knives, crackin' gleesome jokes an' wipin' their greasy hands down their buckskins. Shoulderin' cold mules into the traces - an' smellin' worse'n they do. He wondered if he could ever give this life up to become respectable. He wanted to, but could he?

William Sublette read every track and blade of grass. He'd fer sure know the way back! They made good time from Independence to Council Grove across flower strewn prairies blessed by misty spring rains and endless buffalo herds. After Council Grove they hit plains with rocks that struck sparks from the wheel rims, choking caravaners with red dust. Game got hard to come by.

God had made the hilly ford of the Arkansas River for ambush. Milton'd told William about Comanches stealin' 600 of Colonel Marmaduke's horses here three years back. William saw no *Comanch*, but dispatched ten armed men on fresh horses to swim the muddy water with orders to dismount on the far bank, lay their mounts down an' fort up behind 'em. William sent the wagons across the swirlin' Arkansas in six tight ranks of four abreast so they'd be a movin' fort.

Once across, the wagons formed three sides of a square with the river as the fourth. They camped and waited with the hobbled stock inside the square. Hungry prairie wolves worried the stock with yips and howls, but it was peaceful until first light.

May 8th dawned with hundreds of vermilion-faced Comanche warriors, feathers wafting in the wind, sitting their horses just west of camp.

Out numbered three to one, Sublette's 86 men huddled with scared eyes. Sublette comforted, "I know some o' you never kilt anything bigger'n a chicken. Dyin's no worse'n gittin' a tooth pulled and killin's a site less painful. Crawl under yer wagons an count off. Don't open fire till I wave my hat er git struck down. Then *odds*'ll shoot while *evens* load. *Evens*'ll shoot while *odds* load. If ya all shoot together, they'll overrun us while yer reloadin'."

Sublette steered Davie Jackson to the Aulls' mystery wagon. "Davie, you wasn't spoofin' bout bein' a cannoneer fer Andy Jackson at New Orleans, was you?"

Jackson retorted, "Ran two gun crews."

Sublette motioned to several ex-soldiers to join them. Sublette cranked a lever down on the wagon's side, releasing a heavy stand into the dirt inside the back wheels. He grasped the tail gate, and pulled the back wheels out as a gun carriage sporting a cannon.

The closest Comanches had trouble getting their horses to hold still at sight of such a thing.

Sublette ordered, "Unload enough powder and four pounders fer ten volleys."

Davie loaded the canon expertly, then asked, "Shall I aim the first round at the Chief."

"Ya could, but they's so many tryin' ta look important I cain't tell which one that be. Drop a blast in fronta them. I'm hand signin' that all our wagon's got a thunder gun that'll kill 'em if they don't go way. Now I'm signin' nat I hope the Great Mystery makes Sunrise in their hearts. Davie, make 'em a loud noise one time!"

KA BOOM-OOM-OOM the cannon shattered dawn's stillness with a grand rolling smoke ring, panicking all but a half dozen Indian ponies into a dead run, then *BLAW-WOOM* the exploding shot spooked the last six ponies past some that had a head start. The ground trembled till the stampeding horses were dots in the distance.

Sublette muttered, "I guess the *Comanch'* ain't waitin' to see if the sun comes up in their hearts. Now all we gotta hope is some greenhorn under the wagons don't shoot us by accident."

*   *   *

On May 27th the caravan sank into suffocating sand. They lashed blankets to the wheel rims to keep from sinking. Rope tethers on the blankets broke. They tried leather thongs and shouldered the wheels, paying a sweaty price for every yard.

Fitzpatrick scouted for water within rifle shot of the stalled caravan. He spied an Indian in the sage. Fitz pulled his pistol and charged. The foe was a 9 year old boy with tear stained cheeks and a tongue swollen by thirst. Fitz wiped the Indian child's tears away and carried him back to the Rocky Mountain Fur Company wagon. He shared a stale bread crust and two swallows of water with the scared boy. He soothed, "I vow to keep you till I find a body to care for you. Today is Friday, so I'll call you Friday like Robinson Crusoe's desert island friend."

Friday didn't know Fitzpatrick's strange tongue, but knew the man was a great Chief. He hugged the Irishman's leg until his small dirty hands slipped down the ragged buckskins and joined the napping boy at Fitz's feet.

Thirst maddened mules and men. Fitz and Jedediah Smith lead water scouting parties.

But the water holes were hot sand pits, tormented by withering winds and scorched by the sun. Fitzpatrick clawed for water in a dry river bed till his hands turned bloody. Soon, men dug about him in a frenzy of flying sand.

Jedediah went on alone, his horse chewing its tongue and swallowing its blood. He searched for "deeps" where pools had once lain in the Cimarron River's parched course. The "deep" looked dry, but Jedediah dismounted and scooped a hollow in the wrathful sand. A steaming slurry dribbled into the basin. Jedediah looked up to find himself surrounded by a Comanche hunting party with murder in their faces.

Jedediah rose and whispered, "*The Lord is my shepherd; I shall not want. He maketh me to lie down in green pastures; he leadeth me beside the still waters.*"

As his cracked lips moved dutifully through the 23rd Psalm, Jedediah pulled his pistol and butcher knife. The Comanches charged with lowered lances. He grated, "This is a God forsaken place to die."

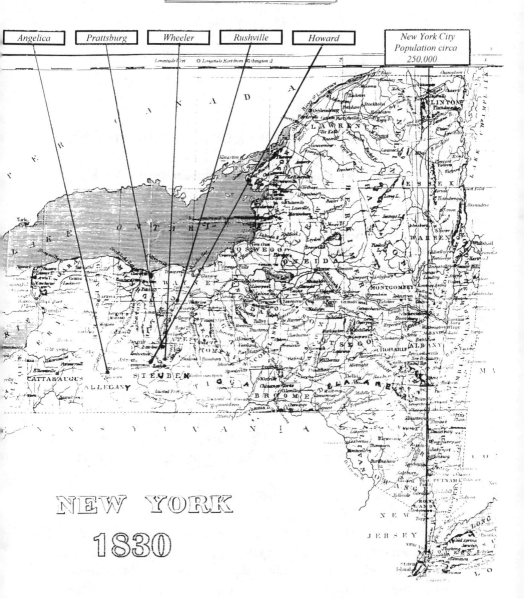

This Map of New York in 1830
Is Reprinted by Permission of
The New York State Library,
University of the State of New York

Angelica   Prattsburg   Wheeler   Rushville   Howard   New York City
Population circa
250,000

NEW YORK
1830

CHAPTER 2

BY THE GRACE OF GOD AND A MOUNTAIN MAN   MAY 1831

Narcissa Prentiss's heart savored each New York spring as more glorious than the last. But at 22, her head asked her the frightening question, "Narcissa, will you ever marry?"

She selected a serene place on Franklin Academy's grounds to meditate -- to assess herself through the noon repast under the bower of flowering vines beside the lilly pond. Narcissa leaned forward on the creaking bench to study her reflection in the greenish pond's gently undulating surface.

Her auburn-blond hair framed her alabaster face like gentle fire. The tiny row of freckles across the bridge of her nose didn't show in the water, but her wide blue eyes did. "Are my features too large? Is my look too direct?"

Tall as most men, Narcissa was 5'7" and weighed a buxom 136 pounds. Her neck was chastely hidden by her full dress's high collar. As a proper lady, she never showed her ankles except when she lifted the hem of her dress to rush to a lecture.

Henry Spalding peered down the path toward the frog pond. That full bodied Narcissa Prentiss sat brooding there. Though she laughed far too much for piety's sake, she dominated his thoughts, occasionally making him blush. At 27, Henry knew he ought to be more worldly. But prurient thoughts should not sully the mind of a man who'd some day be called *Reverend*. Like a mindless leaf whirling down a vortex, he was drawn to this tempting vixen.

Before Narcissa could ferret the flaws that forestalled her wedding, a head bloomed beside hers in the reflection -- that vexing disciple of Socrates, Henry Spalding! Henry's forehead bulged. His blazing brown eyes crackled. His expression was sterner than ever.

Henry asked in his clarion voice. "Have you become your namesake?"

"What's that mean, Henry?" Narcissa asked eyeing his skinny form in the lilly pond and angering again at his snide attack on Abolitionism outside chapel this morning.

"Where's your ancient Greek! Narcissus fell in love with his own reflection in a pool, and was transformed into a flower."

"How addlebrained! Do you see me a flower?"

"No, but you are fragrant as Lavender."

"Henry Spalding, how can you say Slavery is a *natural institution* of mankind?"

"Slavery's existed since man began. It's found in Babylon's *Code of Hammurabi* from 1800 B.C. Ancient Egypt lived by slave labor."

"That was before slavery was made wrong by the Bible, Henry!"

"The Bible even lists rules how Hebrews shall treat their slaves," Henry argued.
"Here read *Exodus* Chapter 21, verses 2 through 6!"

Narcissa read the verses. He was right. "Henry, your Bible's as hard as your heart! My Bible's joyous as spring. This is *Isaiah* 55:12.
"For ye shall go out with joy, and be led forth with peace; the mountains and the hills shall break forth before you into singing, and all the trees of the field shall clap their hands!"

"What's that got to do with slavery, Narcissa?"

She wanted to explain, but his tirade would not be interrupted.

He railed, "Article 1, Section 9 of the U. States Constitution ratified in 1788 provides for continuation of slavery!"

"Whites have trapped enough Negroes in Africa!"

"Your history's deficient as your Greek, Narcissa! Africans had other Negro slaves from the dawn of time -- mostly their war prisoners. When the New World slave trade started in the 16th century, it was Africans who sold their kin to the Arabs, Portuguese, French, English and Dutch!"

"You are a slaver, Henry Spalding!"

"I am a Colonizationist. I believe the Negro should be hauled back to Africa and given freedom in his own colony. He'll never be free here!"

"That's hidebound thinking, Henry! Have you read William Lloyd Garrison's new weekly, *The Liberator*? He brands the American Colonization Society as the handmaid of Slavery."

"Garrison's a radical without the faintest hope of helping those he seeks most to serve."

"John Greenleaf Whittier calls Garrison a champion of those who groan beneath oppression's iron hand. I myself say, one who has no noble dream has nothing!"

"Oh, you do, do you? Pray tell what noble dream you have for yourself, Narcissa?"

Narcissa clasped her hands to hide their trembling. She bit her lip to keep from revealing her thoughts to this man who never forgot anything, but she just boiled over. "I will be the Lord's minister to heathens beyond the Shining Mountains."

Henry laughed, "Narcissa, if you minister to anyone, it'll be in your father's grand home in Prattsburg, New York! You will never go west of this town. Where'd you get such a fool notion?"

Her lip trembled. Too angry to heed her inner cautions she replied, "When I was 16, I had a vision. The Lord God told me I would save heathen souls beyond the Shining Mountains."

"And did the Lord God tell you how a white woman would get to a foreign land where no white woman has ever set foot?"

Narcissa shook her head, tears streaking her white cheeks. "Not then, but He has since shown me the man who can deliver me there!"

"Your delusions will be the death of you! For all your misguided sass, you are a noble and comely woman." He laid his hand softly on hers. "Narcissa, you could do worse than a man like myself. I'd free you from your suicidal cause. You could be my wife, and we'd save the hordes of sinners abounding here in New York!"

Narcissa was shocked at a proposal invading this nasty clash. Henry Spalding wanted her for his wife, but her revulsion for this self-righteous, shambling man was too strong. "Thank you for your generous proposal, but we could never be man and wife, Henry -- never."

"I suppose that's because I was born on the wrong side of the blanket and cast out by a drunkard -- while you are the daughter of *Judge* Stephen Prentiss, a founder of this very academy!" Henry shouted.

"Henry, control yourself. Your humble beginnings have nothing to do with my feelings. This *Judge* Stephen Prentiss you envy so, is a *carpenter* who supports nine children and once served ever so briefly in a minor judicial job. *Judge* Prentiss is a founder of Franklin Academy -- who contributed $50! My answer is based on the chasms between our hearts and souls."

Henry gripped her hand. "Don't turn your back on me! I'm a worthy man."

"Henry, you're crushing my fingers! We cannot be! We just cannot!"

"You are like your namesake. You're a vain woman in love with yourself! You've spurned me wretchedly. I shall hate you till you die!"

"How can you propose to me in one breath and despise me to death the next?"

"And just who is this fool who'll lead you to your death across the Rocky Mountains?"

"I've never met him. But his name is William Sublette."

"You've what?"

"God lead me to read of his daring exploits in the Boston paper. Last year he proved wagons can cross the Great American Desert. One day, I will ask him, and he will guide me over the Shining Mountains to save heathen souls floundering in darkness."

"You know nothing of this William Sublette. If he's one of those savage Mountain Men, he'll only despoil you in the wilderness!"

"Leave me now, Henry Spalding!"

"You'll regret this eternally, you harlot!"

Narcissa sensed someone passing on the pathway, but could not identify the person. "Oh, Merciful God, I pray they did not hear you! My reputation will be ruined by your cruel lie."

Narcissa sobbed as her only marriage proposal, now her mortal enemy, shambled away down the pathway. She looked skyward through the flowered trellis. A spring rain pelted her face. God was cooling her molten anger, but not her dream. She placed her hands together in prayer, "By the Grace of God and a Mountain Man I shall save heathen souls beyond the Shining Mountains."

CHAPTER 3

MEXICAN STAND OFF   SUMMER 1831

Thirsty caravaners with salt etched faces bunched around William Sublette while Jedediah Smith's brother Austin pleaded, "We can't quit looking for Jedediah, Mr. Sublette!"

Sublette cleared his raspy throat. "Them unshod pony tracks inna Cimarron's bed says Jedediah's been tuck by the *Comanch* -- er worse."

"Jedediah could be staked out with coyotes eating at him, Mr. Sublette. We can't leave now."

"Caravan don't go till you Smith boys is satisfied."

Big Samuel Flournoy growled, "I talk fer ten wagons. We ain't waitin'. Men and mules is goin' mad."

Sublette stretched to his full 6'2" and searched the troubled eyes of each haggard man about him. Then he spit. "They ain't that mad."

Peter and Austin Smith hobbled off over the scorching sand with six riflemen. Exhausted men sprawled in the shade under their wagons. Thirsty mules brayed and stomped the sound-smothering sand.

William stripped Bluegrass' saddle and bridle off. "You claim ta be the world's smartest mule. Find water. Now git!" He whacked her hip with his floppy hat. Bluegrass honked and kicked out her heels. She looked accusingly at Sublette, her huge ears laid back. He raised his hat again, and she plodded off. "Drew, grab a extry rifle! We're gonna find out if Bluegrass kin smell water!"

After half an hour, Bluegrass sidled up another rocky hill. Andrew snorted, "Ah, Bill she's just going to higher ground to cool off."

"She's aimin' fer that cave up there inna rocks with all that cactus below it."

"How'll we get to the cave through chest high cactus?"

"That's what rock slides is fer, Drew."

The cave's artesian spring water was laced with alkali, but it filled all the canteens and barrels and still dripped water to boil beans for supper.

As dawn's sun spiked the sky with hot gold, the Smiths called off their search for Jedediah. The caravan rolled west out of the desert. William Sublette was sad as the day the Sublettes buried Papa Phillip in St. Charles. Jedediah lived on inside every man o' the troop. Come Sunday, they'd share a empty mornin' with no Jedediah sermon to remind 'em how rotten they was.

Jedediah'd live on for William another way. William'd study Jedediah's Santa Fe Trail journal. From the grave, Jedediah'd teach William Sublette to talk *respectable*!

Throughout June the caravan rolled, camping nights at Middle Spring, Willow Bar, Upper Spring, Cold Spring and McNees' Creek.

Where the Trail was wide enough, they moved four wagons abreast to stave off Indian attack. At Rabbit Ear Creek, William figured the caravan'd covered about 600 miles.

Tempers got ragged. After a dirt-mean day fighting up grades to about 6,500 feet at the *Rio Colorado,* two red necks took bull whips to each other. Former Constable William Sublette hollered, "One o' you boys is gonna lose a nose or a eye, but I ain't gonna stop ya!" So they quit.

At *San Miguel,* they saw their first Mexican corn fields -- crooked rows of dry stalks guarded by a three-legged dog. It was July 2nd. Sublette figured they were almost to Santa Fe.

July 4th was a glorious day! Surrounded by snowy peaks, Santa Fe stretched below them across a valley so winsome it made them forget how they hated the Cimarron Desert. Since its founding in 1609, Santa Fe's streets wandered from a central public square like tree roots with no pretense of regularity. The *Palacio* on the public square was the only big building. A Rio Grande tributary meandered lazily through town.

Caravaners cut each other's hair. Shaved beards left light skinned chins under bronze-black cheeks. Buckskinners donned their best. Farmers unfolded clean cotton shirts and dark corduroy breeches last washed by women in the U. States.

Tradesmen pulled on hard wool suits with no room for new trail muscle.

William Sublette grinned as brother Andrew approached in bright new buckskins. "Drew, you fixin' ta climb up one o' them balconies inta some *señorita's* arms?"

"You're really wondering if us Sublettes'll be hung from a balcony over brother Milton's past indiscretions in Santa Fe."

Their wagons squawked their brakes down the grade behind stiff legged mules. Dark skinned boys in ragged muslin shirts ran beside them. Yapping mongrels joined the excitement. Mexicans yelled, "*¡Los Americanos!*" "*¡Los carros!*" "*¡La entrada de la caravana!*" Most women wore a chemise and bright flannel *enagua* over their shapely bodies. Their black eyes and bright smiles brought hoots and howls from the caravaners. *Un caballéro rico* on a spirited black stallion pranced beside the caravan. His blue jacket glinted with gold thread. A crimson sash girdled his slim middle. He threw a small salute, reared his steed and vanished into a side street.

An American about 40 in a spectacular *sombrero* loomed over the crowd, shouldering his way to William. He extended his huge hand up to William. "I'm Ewing Young. You look enough like Milt to be his brother."

William took the hand, crushed its crushing grip and grinned. "Know Milt Sublette, do ya?"

"Well enough to go to jail for his crimes after he lit out of here in '26. I'm a friend of Davie Jackson's, so I'll help you boys anyway. I talk the lingo. Don't toss the name *Sublette* around, hear? I'll get your customs duties set. What's your cargo?"

"Mostly dry goods. Bout half is bolts o' cotton cloth-- silks, calicoes, velvets, drillings, shirtings. Smatterin' o' hardware."

"They pay most for red. They're used to buying goods freighted all the way from *Vera Cruz*, so don't be bashful about gouging on your prices. It'll pay for some of the *mordida*."

"What's *mordida*?"

"When your gold's gone and you got nothing, that's *mordida*!"

18

"Ain't interested in gold. Jist beaver peltry an' buffalo hides. They want our goods, they kin buy hides and trade."

"Most traders'll take specie -- gold or silver."

"Not me. We got enough trouble in the U. States over valuin' our own shinplasters an' specie. Furs is hard currency. Bankers cain't shrink 'em or sew 'em back on the critters they come from. Speakin' o' value, I see yer wearin' yer scalpin' insurance."

"Whatta you mean?"

"That's the broadest beaver *sombrero* with the heftiest gold band I ever seen. Indian gits that, he couldn't want no more. Yer hair's gotta be safe!"

Ewing young doffed the enormous *sombrero*, exposing a bald head beaded with sweat. "Hair's already gone! You even talk crazy like Milt."

"Wait'll ya hear Andrew. He was raised up smart by our uncle Solomon whilst me an' Milt was a kissin' the b'ar."

*   *   *

Magistrado Chavez recognized the foul Sublette name on Governor Miller's Trade Recommendation to *El Jefe Politico of Santa Fe, Jose Antonio Chaves.*

Magistrado Chavez with *una escuadra del soldados,* arrived at William Sublette's wagon to arrest him as the *bandido* named Sublette. Sensing trouble, the men of Sublette's caravan surrounded him. *Soldados* fixed bayonets on their muskets.

William Sublette told the interpreter, *"Sublette*'s a common name in Missouri like *Chavez* is in Santa Fe. If his nibs here hollers the name 'Sublette' to these *Americanos,* more *Sublettes* is bound to answer."

The *Magistrado* yelled, "Sublette."

Andrew sidled forward, "I am Andrew Sublette." Then Andrew lied brazenly, "Our five other Sublettes are praying in the cathedrals of Santa Fe."

"¡*Da me su pasaporte!* *Magistrado* Chavez snapped at Andrew.

Andrew handed his passport over with a deep bow.

Smiling, the *Magistrado* observed in English, "What fine manners, Mr. Sublette."

Andrew replied, "All the Sublettes I've known have been mannerly men save one criminal -- Milton Sublette. Milton was banished to the Green Tree Saloon long ago."

"These Sublettes are truthful. I know all of them will spend *mucho dinero* in *nuestra ciudad* beginning with a *regalo* of 100 *doubloons por cada gente* from you two Sublettes and the other five. I will take these 700 *doubloons* now for our hungry orphans. Welcome *Hombres* to -- *Tierra del enderezar ponerse de punta Mexicano* -- the land of the Mexican Stand Off."

*   *   *

Andrew Sublette absorbed enough *Español* to impress *Señorita Peña*. He felt easy and happy in her company. Her delicate frame was clad in mysterious black with gracious lace over some of her features he was most interested in. Their flirtations seemed unlikely to lead to more -- until they did the *fandango*. It was a mix of waltz, cotillion and other amorous movements that made this night a history of the world for him. From the scarlet flower in her hair to her delicious smile, she enthralled his senses.

Andrew and *Señorita Peña* left the *fandango* to engage in Santa Fe's other grand vice -- inveterate gambling! It took 15 minutes for the *monte banco* gambler to turn his $60 for three months trail wages into the *caballero's* plunder. But *Señorita Peña* consoled Andrew so sweetly that he staggered back to his wagon singing *raucously* through a smile that would not die.

William put his Rendezvous trading skills to good use. Despite sizable profits, by late August William Sublette lost his zest for trading.

So did Davie Jackson. "Bill, my heart's not here. I'd like to dissolve our partnership and go into the mule trading business in California."

"Godspeed, Davie. I'm bout through here, myself."

Davie Jackson smiled and shook William's hand. "I can't go back home with my brother George and Jedediah both fresh-dead, Bill."

The next day David Jackson entered into a partnership with David Waldo and Ewing Young and set out for Monterey California with letters of introduction to Captain Cooper.

Jedediah's brother Peter and Samuel Parkman joined Jackson's company for their grand California adventure. William hoped they'd do better in California than Jedediah did. Jedediah'd been jailed there as an illegal alien in 1826 and again in 27.

Sublette's trading amassed 55 packs of beaver and 806 buffalo robes. William wished Santa Fe's 3,000 friendly citizens farewell and headed his caravan for home by way of Taos.

*   *   *

William Sublette was sure Taos had ten times the Indians in Santa Fe. Most were gaunt and hungry. He spent two days finding Fitz and Friday a caravan headed north toward the Cache Valley Rendezvous for which they were long overdue.

William shared buffalo humps around the evening fire with the caravaners taking his friends north. One was a jovial little fellow that matched Andrew drink for drink with *tequila*. His name was Kit Carson but he called himself the "One Cent Man."

William asked, "Where'd ya git a fool name like 'at?"

Carson dug in his possibles bag and pulled out a tattered newspaper clipping. "Name was give to me by a admirer. Here, you read it. I can't read."

William read the five year old clipping from the October 12, 1826 *Missouri Intelligencer* aloud:

"Notice: To whom it may concern: That Christopher Carson, a boy about sixteen years old, small of his age, but thick set, light hair, ran away from the subscriber, living in Franklin, Howard Co., Mo., to whom he had been bound to learn the saddler's trade, on or about the first day of September last. He is supposed to have made his way to the upper part of the state. All persons are notified not to harbor, support or subsist said boy under penalty of the law. One cent reward will be given to any person who will bring back the said boy.
David Workman, Franklin, Oct. 6, 1826."

When the laughter died away, William slapped Kit's shoulder. "I do like a man who tells jokes on hisself! When ya see Milt Sublette up in Cache Valley, give 'im a kick inna butt fer me an' tell 'im I headed fer St. Louie!"

CHAPTER 4

A TRULY MODERN PLACE   FALL 1831

Though Narcissa Prentiss and Henry Spalding attended Prattsburg, New York's Franklin Academy after she spurned him, they never spoke nor let their gazes touch. Thoroughly revolted, Henry fled Franklin in the summer of 1831, but not before one Mrs. Orman Jackson wrote Eliza Hart on Henry's behalf.

Meeting by mail, Henry and Eliza corresponded for months. Both shy, they bared themselves in letters beyond anything they could have imagined in person. They traded secrets about God, their souls and their futures. Henry'd study until ordained, then minister to heathens somewhere. Eliza's devotion to God and her talent for languages might fit her for the missionary life, but their letters stopped short of the committal word "Love."

Rashly they agreed to meet on the Village Green near Eliza's home in Holland Patent, New York. Henry was en route to Hamilton College in Clinton, New York with the $150 he'd earned at 6¼ ¢ per hour in a print shop. The thought of actually seeing each other was petrifying. They'd left no room for the usual deceptions nor even innocent artifice. It was like meeting naked.

Eliza fidgeted in the morning sun. She had no idea Henry'd been watching her since she'd arrived in her best black Sunday dress and lace gloves 30 minutes early. Her black bonnet wasn't her best, but her dearest, because her mother'd made it.

Henry was not discouraged that Eliza was a plain mousy young woman of small stature and nervous manner. Her sad face evinced no lack of piety as Narcissa's had with her flaunted gaiety. He was torn between charging onto the Green to hug this sweet Christian woman and fleeing to save his soul from being mutilated again.

He kerchiefed his forehead. Stay or go? He turned to run, but his loneliness demanded Eliza be met. He was going on 28. He couldn't be a bashful boy forever, but he strode toward her in child's steps -- all his serious reservations would allow.

Startled, Eliza's heart fluttered inside her ribs like a darting dove. It mattered not that Henry was stoop-shouldered with a high forehead full of wrinkles or that his beard was scraggly. He had compassionate brown eyes. He was a dominant figure radiating piety -- an eloquent writer who'd actually built his own wagon.

Although fluent in Latin and Greek with the classics foremost in her mind, Eliza had no idea what her first words to this sacredly important man would be.

Henry bowed slightly. "Upstate New York's become such a truly modern place."

Eliza nodded, put her hand to her lips and replied in her scratchy voice, "Oh it is! The bears don't eat our pigs any more!"

*   *   *

Never bashful about anything, Reverend Samuel Parker hammered the door of Fairfield Medical College's Infirmary. The preacher's thin face was crimson. He rued not bringing his buffalo coat to Fairfield, New York on such a frosty night.

The door parted a crack. Candle light flickered eerily under the rugged face of a sleepy fellow about 30 in a flannel night shirt who yawned, "I'm Dr. Marcus Whitman. State your business." His deep baritone words were swathed in his foggy breath.

"You a Thomsonian Doctor?" Reverend Parker yelled, endangering the candle's flame.

"*Puke Doctors* are charlatans!" Dr. Whitman replied. "Inducing vomiting with *lobelia* and cayenne pepper makes a sick man sicker."

"Right! I'm Reverend Samuel Parker, Pastor of the Presbyterian Church at West Groton, afflicted with chills and ague. Open up."

Dr. Marcus Whitman admitted the purse-mouthed old man. Cold air clustered on the skinny stranger like a cloak.

Dr. Whitman raised his tired wool greatcoat to put his arm in it, but Reverend Parker wrapped it about himself. "How much you charge?"

"College charges 25¢ same's a practicing physician. That includes your medicine," Dr. Whitman rumbled, wrapping his shivering body in a threadbare blanket. "Sit, Reverend."

"Raw board's hard. Have a softer seat?"

"This's not a sitting room. Bare your arm, so I can bleed you. You have too much blood. Here's a spoonful of calomel."

Hissing at the metallic taste, Reverend Parker bared his left arm. Treated by *Mineral Murderers* before, Parker gripped his dainty hand and forced up the artery inside his delicate elbow.

Dr. Whitman tightened the ligature strap around the *bicep's brachial* artery to control blood drainage, then lanced the *bleipital fascia*. Scarlet blood trickled down Parker's fish-belly white arm into the blue porcelain catch basin.

Reverend Parker's eyes swept heavenward at sight of his own blood.

Waiting for the bleeding to be done, Dr. Whitman asked, "What brought you to Fairfield?"

"Conducted a revival -- saved sinners! You a sinner!"

"I'm a Presbyterian like yourself, but we're all sinners in the Lord's eyes. Longed to be a minister myself, but couldn't afford the education."

Parker beamed in the candle's yellow glow.   "Brother Whitman, the American Board of Commissioners for Foreign Missions wants Doctors. You experienced?"

Seeing how sparingly Parker bled, Dr. Whitman loosened the ligature. "Began ridin' with Dr. Ira Bryant in 1823. He was cousin to William Cullen Bryant and a corker of a physician!"

"A *corker?*"

"Ira could saw an arm off in three minutes -- a leg in five."

24

"I guess that's tolerable -- if they needed to be cut off."

"They did -- bear maulings -- putrid flesh. Quickness is next to Godliness for a surgeon. No way to soothe pain but hard liquor. I'm a staunch temperance man like Ira. Many's the Sunday we harangued agin liquor at the logging camps."

"No formal medical training, Brother Whitman?"

"Come here to Fairfield College in 1825 after ridin' two years with Ira. Got licensed to practice in the next year when I was 24."

"Why're you still here?"

"I'm not *still* here."

"Sure you are, Brother Whitman!   My blood's drippin' into your pan. You're here all right, and I don't feel no better yet for all this gore!"

"Hung my shingle in Pennsylvania, then practiced in Ontario. Come back here for my M.D. degree first o' this year. It'll be conferred after this term. I'll practice in Steuben County."

Reverend Parker sized up Brother Whitman. Shaggy hair. Deep fiery blue eyes. Aquiline nose with a hump like it'd been broken. Broad shouldered, muscular. Near six feet. More like a logger than a Doctor. "Well Brother Whitman, you're rude in speech and careless in appearance, but you got the soul of a Saint shining through -- just the man I need for Oregon."

Peeved by the Reverend's rudeness, Marcus argued in his *basso profundo*. "Nobody goes to Oregon. No road."

Reverend Parker shook his finger.   "Mountain Man named Sublette took wagons from Independence out to the Rockies and back last fall. I'm fixing to find some mission sites out there. I could use a Doctor -- with a strong back and pure heart -- to tend me. I give God my all -- leaves me feeling poorly."

After reconciling the shock of such impossible wagon travel, Marcus muttered, "I can't go."

"Wife have you tethered?"

"My wife's my studies on Asiatic Cholera. Cholera's piling up corpses in Bengal -- Russia -- Berlin. I'm studying the disease. I'll make a stand against it right here in New York."

"Only a fool fights a myth! Cholera slays non-Christians! It dare not invade Christian New York -- I'm making your fight for you -- saved 17 sinners from perdition today!"

"Cause of cholera's a mystery, Reverend. Most Doctors think it rains from the atmosphere. Me, I think it's something like smallpox that Edward Jenner stopped with cow pox."

"Cow pox? Cholera is *evil*, Brother Whitman. My fight -- not yours. *Evil* cannot swim the Atlantic! Make yourself ready for *Oregon*!"

"Before tonight, I knew wagons couldn't reach the Rockies. You say they been there n' back. When I'm certain cholera can't swim, I'll consider Oregon."

Wily Sam Parker wasn't about to let a new convert to *Oregonism* slip away. "I'm running a revival next Sabbath at Stephen Prentiss's grand home in Prattsburg. He has five comely Christian daughters. Join me!"

"London lecturer on cholera's comin' to New York City. I'm helping him."

Parker tried a new tack. "I'll hold this strap. Run your candle by that picture on the wall. What is that?"

"A sketch of my father Beza Whitman's tombstone reciting a riddle."

"What's it say?"

"*Stop here my friend and think on me*
I once was in this world like thee
This is a call aloud to thee
Prepare for death and follow me."

Marcus lowered the candle. "I've always wondered what hidden meaning lies in those words."

Reverend Parker leered, "Come to Oregon with me and I'll tell you."

*   *   *

Henry Spalding matriculated at Hamilton College for ever so short a time before Eliza Hart moved to Clinton, New York to be near him. They were safe in the arms of Jesus, though they longed to be in each other's. Eliza was in love -- both with Henry and their mutual destiny. Together they would serve God -- perhaps in India or the Sandwich Islands. Of course Henry had to be ordained first.

Henry's path to ordination became impassable at Hamilton. Though he worked two jobs to supplement the aid he received from the American Education Society, the aid made him an outcast. No one said anything to his face, but with a lifetime of practice Henry knew when he was being shunned. He agonized over how to tell Eliza he had to retreat to far off Ohio. What if she would not leave New York? He couldn't stand losing her. But he couldn't tolerate haughty Hamilton's mean spirit either.

Eliza met Henry outside the print shop where he inked the presses from six till midnight in a blotchy apron. His eyes spelled doom. She said nothing, but awaited disaster in the drizzling rain freezing into snow.

Henry's brow was more furrowed than ever. "Eliza, I can't take any more of their muddleheaded hostility at Hamilton over my AES aid. I've been accepted at Western Reserve College in Hudson, Ohio. What will become of us when I leave here?"

Eliza wanted to blurt that she would crawl to Tibet if she had to, but wiped the mist from her glasses deliberately with her monogrammed linen handkerchief.

"What are your intentions toward me, Henry?" she asked in her scratchy voice.

"Why honorable, of course!"

"How honorable?"

"Massively honorable." He extended his arms to show the girth of his honorable intentions.

"What will I tell my parents, Henry?"

He knew what he had to say to save their precious love. He didn't want to say it because it would create such a distraction from his slavish regimen of study and work. The way she wiped her glasses was so noncommittal. He felt Eliza slipping away as he watched her pious face. "Tell them we're engaged -- purely spiritually, you understand."

Eliza didn't look up from polishing the now crystalline lenses. "Does that mean we will be married -- no subterfuge?"

Henry clenched his inky hands into fists and jammed them into his apron. Airy snow flakes stuck to his sweaty face.

"Of course, Eliza. There can be no subterfuge in a matter of this magnitude."

She exploded into his face and kissed his thin lips hard, pinning his hands in his apron with her fervent embrace. She released him, and walked into the falling snow. Without risking a change of his mind by looking back, she screeched, "I will write home at once."

Realizing that her father would rant that she was compromising herself shamelessly by pursuing Henry unwed, Eliza decided not to write home until she was already in Ohio -- a small, but necessary female subterfuge.

*   *   *

Henry and Eliza had so few worldly possessions, the move to Hudson, Ohio was actually more spiritual than of the flesh. But what looks handsome from afar is often hideous close up. Henry found Western Reserve ablaze over abolition, though he gave no hint of it to Eliza so soon after their wrenching move. He worked in Western Reserve's manual school, again earning 6¼ ¢ per hour. He took on a second job at the same wage in the Seminary's printing plant, abstaining from the abolition turmoil splitting faculty and students. He had no money to move again. Besides, no college relished a divinity student flitting from school to school like a fickle butterfly.

Henry was a member of the American Colonization Society -- for orderly repatriation of the Negroes to Africa. He hadn't mentioned this allegiance at Western Reserve, but it infuriated him to hear others damn this noble organization as the handmaid of slavery. He prayed for the fortitude to remain aloof from the fray no matter the insults.

Eliza enrolled at one of Hudson's two girls' schools and found her new school opprobrious. She was force-fed un-Godlike algebra and astronomy. Astronomers even pretended stars had existed longer than the 4,000 years since God created Earth. She was eager to switch to the other school until she met its tyrannical head mistress and realized algebra and astronomy were infinitely less abominable by comparison.

Eliza finally decided to let her parents know her whereabouts, and that she and Henry were engaged, writing:

"... *I presume you do not question the object which induced me to break away from your fond embrace and consent to accompany a stranger into a land of strangers. If I am not deceived respecting the motive which led me to take this step -- it was to seek those qualifications which are requisite in order to become prepared for usefulness in the service of my Redeeming Lord.*"

During Henry's third week in the Seminary, Beriah Green, pastor of Western Reserve College church and professor of Sacred Literature, ended his sermon with a tirade making William Lloyd Garrison sound tame. Green shouted, "NO MAN AGAINST ABOLITION CAN BE A CHRISTIAN!"

Amid disbelieving gasps, Henry Harmon Spalding stormed out of the church, slamming the cathedral door so hard he shattered its glass.

CHAPTER 5

COMING TO GRIPS WITH RESPECTABILITY   FALL 1831

In Taos William Sublette linked his wagons to a larger caravan headed for St. Louis. Night camps at one spring after another gave William time to study Jedediah's journal for April and May by lantern light. Sublette was astounded how different Jedediah's impressions of the outbound trip from St. Louis were from his own. Knowing words changed a man's viewpoint. May 27th was blank -- Jedediah'd disappeared without writing his own epitaph. William would use Jedediah's journal to teach hisself how to talk gradual like -- so's nobody'd notice.

William decided to start by givin' up *ain't*. *Ain't* was a friendly down-home word. He loved it, but it had to go. For the last time he mouthed the word lovingly as he announced into the night wind, "I *ain't* gonna say *ain't* no more. *Ain't* that right, Jedediah?" William waited, gazing at the shotgun blasts of stars twinkling in the inky sky, but Jedediah didn't answer. It wasn't right that a powerful man of God who'd ridden 17,000 miles through Indian country could go so quiet like -- and just be gone like a ordinary man.

                *   *   *

On October 30th, Sublette's caravan rolled into the wagon lot on Franklin Street in St. Louis. Men and mules were gaunt. Muleskinners collected their wages and galloped for the grog shops and brothels.

William and Andrew checked into E. Town's *City Hotel*. By the time William finished his first bath in two months and headed downstairs to meet General Ashley in the Dining Room, Drew was singing *Billy Boy* in the Bar.

As William approached Ashley, the General pulled his spare frame up to his full 5'9" and donned the stern look he used to start every meeting. Facing 50, the long gray hair the General combed over his bald spot was more tousled than when it was black. He gestured toward their table with his very prominent chin. "Table's ready, Bill." They exchanged back slaps, then sidled between tables of conversing guests to theirs in the corner.

The chair creaked under Sublette's 220 pounds. He wore his new buckskins. His fresh-washed long hair kept flaring over his bronzed face, so he locked it in his fingers behind his head. The waiter buried their table with smoldering roast beef, steaming mashed potatoes, crisp collard greens and fresh baked bread that woke up Sublette's spit.

Not one for niceties, General Ashley inquired, "Profitable venture?"

"Mebbee. Tuck in 55 packs o' beaver and 806 buffalo robes, but had to dish out 700 doubloons in *mordida*. Whole load'll run about three ton before we pack 'em in the casks. Like to warehouse 'em with you till you kin sell 'em back east. With the $3,500 you expressed to me at New Franklin, I'm gonna owe ya serious money -- at least till you sell my peltry."

"You're good for it, Bill. I read about Jedediah. Death's caused quite a stir. What happened?"

"Jedediah scouted the dry Cimarron River bed fer water. Never come back. Comanche brave sold Jedediah's pistols to a *soldado* in Santa Fe. Here's his Will. You're Executor," Sublette said hoarsely. He kept his head down and ate the good food around the lump in his throat. "What's goin' on here in the States?"

"Andy Jackson's hell bent on destroying the U.S. Bank. Nicholas Biddle's arrogance has Andy killin' mad. You'd think Biddle was President of the U. S. instead of the U.S. Bank. Bank thing's spilled blood here in St. Louis! It could change my life, Bill."

"How?"

"Being a staunch Jacksonian Democrat, Congressman Spencer Pettis reviled the Bank at every turn. Major Thomas Biddle -- Nicholas Biddle's brother -- would tolerate no more. Major Biddle broke into Pettis' hotel room and horse whipped him. Pettis challenged Biddle to a duel. Nearsighted fool Pettis chose pistols at five feet."

"Five feet?"

General Ashley nodded. "They met on Bloody Island August 26th. Both lay dead in three days."

"How'd you git into it?"

"I've been nominated to succeed Pettis in the U.S. House of Representatives! Election's tomorrow."

"You'll win in a walk, General!"

"You said I'd win when Miller beat me for Missouri Governor in '24. The *Missouri Republican* just endorsed me. James Aull thinks he can swing Lexington voters to me. But the *Missouri Intelligencer* says my campaign is run by small squads of meddling politicians and a collection of obscure, beer-heavy hacks."

"You been a Jackson supporter long as I knowed you. There --- *isn't*--- no problem!"

"What?"

"There *isn't* no problem."

"I don't know what's got into you Bill, but I'm a Director of the U.S. Bank's St. Louis branch. My opponent Robert Wells is a solid Jackson man with no sullying bank history. Believe me -- there *is* a problem!"

"The Sublettes never let a friend go b'ar huntin' alone, General."

William Sublette got up and hollered, "The Sublette brothers is buyin' drinks in the bar fer every feller smart enuff to vote fer General Ashley in the mornin'!"

Friend and foe joined the crush of men into the bar. General Ashley excused himself around midnight, but no one noticed. William and Andrew shoved Ashley's pre-election victory celebration through two fine hotels into the *Wayward Woman* on the levee, making howling Ashley converts by the score.

A couple of hours after daylight, William hocked his boot pistols toward the bar bill at the *One-Eyed Dog*. The Sublettes herded their reeling Ashley crowd through the wind lashed rain toward the Courthouse polls with Andrew singing:

> *"What can we do with a drunken sailor?*
> *What can we do with a drunken sailor?*
> *What can we do with a drunken sailor*
> *Ear-lie in the mornin'?*
> *Way, hey and up she rises*
> *Way, hey and up she rises*
> *Way, hey and up she rises*
> *Ear-lie in the mornin'!"*

*   *   *

A few days after General Ashley triumphed over Robert Wells by a scant 212 votes of the 10,000 cast, the rains slackened. William's men casked his Santa Fe furs and hauled them to Ashley's warehouse on the levee.

Even though Ashley'd gone to Washington, he acted as William Sublette's agent to sell the Santa Fe furs. The beaver market slumped in the east as the result of over supply and early indications of a horrifying invasion of London by the silk hat. Allison & Anderson in Louisville and Frederick Tracy in New York accepted fur consignments but didn't offer much hope in the sluggish market.

After Ashley's $300 commission and $1,200 in interest, the dissolved firm of Jackson & Sublette closed its books on their Santa Fe venture owing Ashley over $7,100 before any eastern fur sales.

Putting his cash worries aside, William Sublette rode the World's Smartest Mule Bluegrass to his new Sulphur Springs acreage outside St. Louis. He couldn't clear all 779 acres alone, but hoped to prepare a building site and sink some fence posts in the ground before it froze. He'd do all he could at Sulphur Springs before putting the 1832 Rendezvous caravan together in the spring.

William loved the feel of a fine honed ax biting the trunk of a solid tree. He stripped his shirt and worked off a little camp-fat. The tree toppled noisily into the marshy spot where he'd aimed it.

Sublette jerked around toward the sound of a whip. A caravan of a dozen Negro slaves crested a rise 50 feet away. The overseer wielded his whip from a bay draft horse. Sublette bellered, "No slave'll be whipped on my land!"

"And just who would you be?" the overseer sneered.

"William L. Sublette"

"*Little Bill*! Zat you?" yelled a muscular black woman in filthy rags.

Stunned, Sublette stared at her.   It *was* Artemis. "Whatta ya doin' there? Yer free!· C'mere!"

"Cain't Little Bill."

Carrying his ax, Sublette loped toward the dear woman who'd raised him from a tadpole. The overseer grasped the big bore rifle lying across his saddle. "Bill o' sale on that nigger wench says she's property of one Thomas G. Berry of St. Louis. Lay hands on her -- an' die!"

Sublette eyed the chain along the ground from slave to slave. It threaded through a loop on Artemis' leg iron. Sublette cleaved the chain with one blow of his ax. The overseer's whip notched Sublette's ear.

"Little Bill, I cain't go wit ya. Angus Peabody -- he one crazy slaver. He gun you down."

Grasping his bleeding ear, Sublette remembered he hadn't redeemed his boot pistols from the bar man at the *One-Eyed Dog* yet. Sublette growled, "I'm the son of Judge an' Isabella Sublette. They freed this Negro at their death in 1822. As Constable of St. Charles Missouri, I give Artemis them papers myself near ten years back. She's free."

"Bein' Constable, you know that there's fer settlin' in Court, not in some field with a bunch o' niggers lookin' on." Peabody raised his rifle. "Step aside. We're passin' through to St. Louis."

"Member we used ta bust them punkins Little Bill? Peabody got a punkin busta on his pommel. Let's talk ta him bout dat."

Sublette took her cold arm with the "R" branded deep into her shoulder. "Got sumpthin' here you'll want ta see, Mr. Peabody."

They walked toward the overseer. "Artemis, you'd a tanned me sumpthin' turrible, if ya ever caught me stinkin' bad as you do. Been sortin' skunks?"

"Rotten punkins, Little Bill," the graying woman grinned, showing the gap between her front teeth he'd always wondered about.

Reaching Peabody's horse, Sublette ducked under the rifle barrel. "See the *R* burnt inta her shoulder? That's our family mark."

"What kinda fool ya take me fer? *R* 's fer *Runaway.*"

Sublette snatched the horse pistol from the holster on Peabody's saddle. He wrenched away the man's rifle and whip. "When I was a tyke, me an' Artemis busted punkins with pistols. She shoots better'n me, so she's gonna cover you while I write a note to the man who claims ta own her. Git down an' gimmee pencil an' paper."

Peabody dismounted. "Ain't got none!" His ruddy face blanched as he looked at the .71 calibre pistol held by the nigger wench he'd given lashes yesterday -- and last Tuesday -- and twice before that.

"Then tell the owner Artemis was a free black as of January 22, 1822. William Sublette will pay him a compromise of $100 in gold or 1¢ in lead."

"Little Bill, I cain't go off an' leave these otha folks."

"Artemis, I got no say over what happens to them."

"You right Little Bill, you *ain't*," Artemis said, picking up Peabody's rifle. "We'll be goin' now. You an' Peabody git right good acquainted cause you *ain't* comin' along." Artemis splintered the rifle stock on Peabody's head, dropping him at her feet.

"Artemis, I wish you'd learn not to say *ain't,*" Sublette said, sitting down on the newly cut tree trunk to wait for the overseer to come around.

CHAPTER 6

YOUR OWN WATERLOO   EARLY 1832

Captain William Drummond Stewart paced between two gnarled trees on Birnam Hill. His valiant 15th King's Hussars who'd routed Napoleon's legions at the Battle of Waterloo had been mustered out in 1821. Like all warriors after wars, Captain Stewart'd become expendable. With a chest full of medals, he'd been retired on a pittance. So he'd conquered the Inns and bawdy houses of England and Europe.

His royal fathered grudgingly honored the bills until his death five years ago. Now outraged creditors from six countries had the warrior himself under siege. Captain Stewart must convince his haughty brother, Sir John, to release his trust funds or suffer leg irons in debtor's prison.

"Sure now, you didna expect Sir John The Tardy to be here at first light to foretell your future, didja Billy Boy?" chided Jamie the Dwarf.

At 5'11", Captain Stewart towered above the misshapen man whose stubby legs and great feet spraddled like a fowl. Jamie alternated between servile tasks and being Murthly Castle's impudent jester. Jamie'd tended the Captain since they'd climbed these same two trees as boys three decades ago. But the Dwarf could nettle him when he played the fool too well. "Jamie, I've serious business afoot here. Surprised you're not off despoiling a chamber maid."

"Leave such things to my betters, Billy Boy! Or have you forgotten Christina and little George?"

When Captain Stewart lost his temper, the proper British accent acquitting him so well in Wellington's Army burnt away. "Wee devil! Dinna touch them wi' your foul tongue!"

"Billy Boy, if you'd heeded ma foul tongue, you wouldna be yearnin' ta taste your pistol, now wouldja?"

Captain Stewart turned to watch the bleak morning sun singe the mists from Murthly Castle where he'd spent his boyhood. Murthly wasn't like the Stewarts' other two castles, Grandtully and Edinburgh, built as fortresses against the robber barons of the Highlands. Murthly's 17th century architects had crafted a gentle repose with a mile of lawn between it and the placid flowing Tay.

Serfs had manicured this lawn every three days until his father George's death.

Now knee high grasses waved in the morning mist as if saying good-bye. Since brother John had taken title to all 32,000 Stewart acres by primogeniture, he'd squandered all the estates' cash constructing yet a fourth lavish castle for John's new wife, Lady Jane.

Since the Stewart lands were entailed, Captain Stewart would never own one clod as long as brother John remained free of the lead coffins entombing their ancestors in Grandtully's chapel.

Jamie the Dwarf shouted from his windy perch in their old tree, "What'll it be, Billy Boy? Feedin' fleas in debtor's prison or the fiendish clever murder of brother John that cheats the gallows and brings you the Stewart estates?"

Captain Stewart spied John ascending Birnam Hill astride the elegant Arabian stallion Whitelock. "Never mention murder of a Stewart again!"

Whitelock's flowing mane flashed in the new sun as John rode the arch-necked stallion up out of the shifting mists. William steeled himself for the most critical meeting of his life.

John reined Whitelock in. He looked down his bulbous nose at his profligate 37 year old brother. "Luring me to Birnam Hill was frivolous. We could've had this one word discussion passing each other in the hall. The answer is *no*!"

"*No* to what, John?"

"No to squandering your £3,000 trust fund father left in my charge."

"No discussion. It's just *no*?"

"Discussion? You're pathetic! You spy some hand maid tromping blankets in a tub at the Atholls' farm, part her legs, then dishonor our dead father by naming her foul bastard George! Did you discuss that with me beforehand?"

Captain Stewart responded icily, "I married Christina and put her and the boy up in Dunkeld village. My son is a Stewart, and he'll be educated as one."

"You'll rot in debtor's prison before you fritter away funds of our noble lineage on your whore and her bastard! Keep them on your Army pay!"

"Seven shillings and six farthings a day willna board this horse! Gi' me my £3,000!"

"Father deemed you wise in war and a fool in all else. He swore me to saving our family from your vulgar profligacy. I'll not betray a nobleman's oath for a rogue like you. Find a war or admit you've begotten your own Waterloo. Do the honorable thing for the sake of our noble name." John galloped Whitelock down the hill toward the once serene Murthly castle.

Jamie chortled, "There goes a Stewart who finds murder palatable -- even if he must do yours by your own hand! How kin a mon who kills for a livin' refuse killin' to save himself an' his family!"

"I'm a *soldier*, not a cutthroat. I vow I'll never sleep under Murthly's roof again."

"Billy Boy, you kinna withstand your suing creditors to the east. Ya kinna fly up an' you mustna go down in your grave -- as your brother begs. Ya must go west an' gi' your creditors the slip in the wilds of America. If I act the fool enough, your mother'll gi' your wife an' child money ta tide 'em over."

"Had I more fools like you by my side, Jamie -- we'd tame the earth."

*   *   *

Captain Stewart's first view of New York in June 1832 was unimpressive. Its tallest buildings stood four stories. It's bedraggled wharves bore hastily painted signs like facial sores quarantining them because of cholera, so his ship anchored in the

38

harbor. As an influential passenger, he was rowed ashore with his considerable baggage.

Streets near the docks were idle and eery. He was wrestling his luggage up town, when a well waxed carriage halted. Occupant J. Watson Webb graciously urged him to accept a ride to the *City Hotel*. Bags stowed, except for one the Captain carried inside, the carriage's docile blacks clip-clopped over the cobblestones toward the hotel. A dress sabre in a silver sheath graced the tapestried wall over one of the leather seats, and a scarred field sabre in a dented scabbard hung above the other.

Webb and Stewart introduced themselves. Webb added, "I'm editor of two New York papers." Stewart wiped his sweaty hand on his trousers before taking the other man's hardy grip. Though only 31, the wiry J. Watson Webb was nearly bald. His small regimental mustache with its turned up tips was identical to Captain Stewart's.

"I daresay you've soldiered some," Captain Stewart observed.

Webb nodded smartly. "Ten years as an officer on our western frontier. My father's General S. B. Webb. Your luggage names you Captain in the 15th King's Hussars. Your unit helped bring Napoleon to his knees at Waterloo. What'll you do in America, Captain?"

"Hunt in the west. My Manton rifles ride atop your coach. I have letters of introduction to Hudson's Bay Company officials."

"Where'll you start, Captain?"

"I'll see your country from horseback all the way to St. Louis." Captain Stewart left his intent to leave his creditors baying in America's wilderness unspoken.

"Here's my card. Come by just before lunch tomorrow. I'll provide letters of introduction to influential St. Louis gentlemen -- General William Clark of the Lewis and Clark expedition, Congressman William Ashley and my good mountain friends, William Sublette and Robert Campbell."

"Sublette. Name sounds French," the Captain mused.

"If he's French, Bill's forgotten it. But I wouldn't go on about the War of 1812. Bill's Grandfather, Colonel Whitley, died in the Battle of the Thames after killing the great Chief Tecumseh."

"I'll not *whisper* to Mr. Sublette about the War of 1812. My former commandant, Sir Edward Pakenham, and 2,500 of his finest died at the Battle of New Orleans. Andrew Jackson sent Sir Edward home to England *butt-up* in a keg of rum!"

After their smiles died, Captain Stewart asked, "Streets always this deserted?"

"Cholera's paralyzed the city. Thousands have fled. Frankly, I rather prefer this calm to the riots and looting that followed initial upper class flight."

"What's that foul odor, sir?"

Covering his lower face with his handkerchief, Webb answered, "*Corporation Pie.*"

"What's in it?"

"New Yorkers call city government *The Corporation.* Even before the epidemic, *The Corporation* spent all the refuse collection funds on graft. So our 250,000 people pushed their uncollected garbage to the center of the street. The city turned out thousands of pigs to eat this filth. Except for the stench, there was a certain utility to it -- until cholera came. Now rotting corpses're piled up faster than the hogs can eat them, so we have *Corporation Pie!*"

"What's being done about it?"

"I'm smearing *The Corporation* with printer's ink several times a week and praying for relief from the scourge of cholera. Most people contracting cholera are dead by night fall. It's killing over a hundred a day."

"Doctors found a cure?"

"Captain, they don't know the cause. With their insane overdosing of calomel, Doctors're killing as many as the plague!"

Captain Stewart changed the subject. "When I come for your kind letters of introduction, may I buy your lunch sir?"

"No, but you can help me serve it!"

"But of course. To whom?"

"New Yorkers are too terrified to go out for food. Relief parties pass out bread throughout the city. I've drawn the starving whores at Five Points again. They're a hopeless conundrum. We discovered they sell their bread to buy liquor the minute we leave. Any thoughts on that?"

"Two. Tear the loaves apart. When they can't sell the pieces, they'll have to eat them!"

"What's the other?"

"Pestilence walks in death's tracks, so battlefield dead are buried with dispatch. Your city's laid siege to itself. Purge your streets of *Corporation Pie!*   You're begetting your own Waterloo!"

CHAPTER 7

RENDEZVOUS AT PIERRE'S HOLE   SUMMER 1832

Sublette offered his huge square hand as General Ashley entered St. Louis' Green Tree Tavern. "Any news on them Santa Fe furs, General?"

General Ashley waited for his eyes to get used to the dimness. He shirked Sublette's bear-trap handshake and sat down, smoothing his hair over his bald spot. "Allison sold your beaver at $4.50 the pound. Tracy had no market, so I reconsigned that peltry between Siter, Price in Philadelphia and Janvier in Baltimore.Your buffalo robes are off the market till hot weather's over."

Sublette nodded, tossing his long blond hair. "Black Hawk War's hiked prices on corn, bacon, flour an' mules.I was countin' on that fur money fer Rendezvous."

"Bill, I'll stake you as usual. Your furs will sell. But you better pray this bad market doesn't hold and bury the furs you bring back from this 1832 Rendezvous. Any trouble getting men to go Up the Mountain?"

"Naw. I've hired 41. Bobby Campbell's got five ta handle his goods. Fitz took on four fer Rocky Mountain Fur Co. You seekin' re-election ta Congress?"

"You helped elect me for the rest of Spencer Pettis' term. I'm seeking a full term -- still a Jacksonian -- supporting the U.S. Bank!"

"Senator Tom Benton says supportin' the U.S. Bank after Jackson vetoed its recharter makes you a *counterfeit* Jacksonian. How ya answer that, General?"

"To this day Andy Jackson bears a bullet in his shoulder from his gunfight with Tom and Jesse Benton. That bullet tells you who's the *real* counterfeit Jacksonian!"

      *   *   *

Rain-sopped underwear, shirts and pants draped every tent in Sublette's camp as the sun shouldered past the thunderheads. Even tethered mules had steaming clothes drying across their backs.

Clad only in buckskin breeches, William Sublette walked his camp perimeter to stop evening defections to Independence. The town rode a high bluff with a smattering of log houses around six stores and a few tippling taverns. Sublette grinned as a score of greenhorns in odd uniforms of pantaloons, striped shirts and high boots marched into his camp with shouldered muskets tipped by bayonets. The newcomers halted and ordered muskets to their sides.

A slender man about 30 stepped forward. A scraggly beard fringed the lower edge of his jaws. He removed his billed cap, revealing a forehead that reached the peak of his head. Looking up at Sublette, he barked in a New England twang, "I'm *Captain* Nathaniel Jarvis Wyeth," extending his slim hand.

Sublette crushed it. "*Captain* William Lewis Sublette. Whatta ya want, Mr. Wyeth?"

Wyeth massaged his numbed fingers. "To talk in private."

Sublette looked from greenhorn to greenhorn, then growled, "Git!" They scattered except for one tear-drop bodied man in his 50's. Sublette asked, "Now whatta you want?"

"This's my brother Doctor Jacob Wyeth."

Sublette asked, "What's on yer mind, gentlemen?"

Wyeth's blue eyes blazed. "Hall J. Kelly of the Oregon Colonization Society read us your letter about your epic wagon journey to the Rockies in 1830. It fired the combustibles of my imagination! I trained these men near Boston. I mortgaged my home and my pond-ice cutting patent to finance this expedition. I've transported them all this way to join forces with you for the trip to Rendezvous."

Sublette asked, "You jist git off the steamer *Otter* at Independence?"

Nathaniel Wyeth nodded. "What do you say, sir?"

"From here on, we got no steamers. We got one *Captain*. Me. Discipline day an' night by my rules."

"Why can't we share leadership?"

"I been Up the Mountain since 1823. I never seen you there."

"Nat, *Captain* Sublette's quite right," Doctor Jacob Wyeth intervened.

"That'll do for now, Jacob,"Nathaniel grunted.He turned to Sublette. "I trust you'll pass all orders through me."

"Will if you're handy, but there's a lotta trail out there," Sublette waved toward the brilliant rainbow dancing on the prairie, "It's all yers if my bein' in charge don't set well."

"It's agreed. We'll be here at dawn."

Robert Campbell emerged from his tent. The mountains had been good to Campbell and bad for his TB. Fair haired, above medium height, at 28 Campbell'd filled out the cadaverous body he had when he met Sublette in 1826, but he still trilled his R's like a Scot. "Mr. S, I think you'll have more'n a wee bit o' trouble with Mr. Wyeth. He's a man in charge o' everythin' he sees."

"Might be, Bobbie, but Wyeth unloaded 15 head o' sheep an' two yoke o' oxen at Independence. They'll eat real good fore we reach Grand Island."

"Aye, an' high priced meals they'll be, Mr. S!"

At dawn on May 13th William Sublette headed the combined party of 86 men in double-file military order with their pack mules and stock onto the Santa Fe Trail. Andrew Sublette hazed caravan stragglers, yelling "Catch up or feed the wolves."

Each night, they camped in a hollow square changing guards every four hours. Each dawn William Sublette rode Bluegrass through camp shouting, "Turn out!"

The caravan headed northwest off the Santa Fe Trail to the Kansas River Agency near the village of Topeka. By the time they forded the spring-glutted Kansas River, three of Wyeth's men had deserted, including Wyeth's cousin Thomas Livermore.

When they reached the Platte near Grand Island, William Sublette told Wyeth's men, "The Platte's too muddy to drink an' too thin to plow. Leave it be." Some drank it anyway and fell sick with diarrhea. Wyeth countermanded Sublette's order that the sick men walk instead of riding. Wyeth refused to make his cousin John Wyeth walk for falling asleep on guard.

Robert Campbell said nothing about Wyeth to William, but loaned him a popular novel, *The Scottish Chiefs*. Somehow, Campbell knew William wanted to improve his talk and thought the book would help.

The last of Wyeth's sheep and oxen were slain before buffalo herds suddenly stretched for miles along the Platte. William grinned, "Drew, take *Captain* Wyeth on his first buffalo hunt. He needs some Mountain Man Cider ta improve his judgment." Andrew tossed his brother a little salute.

At the herd's edge Andrew cautioned Wyeth, "Buffalo's hard to kill with one bullet. The closer, the better."

Wyeth downed a grazing cow. "I've got the hang of it! I'm ready for a redskin now. Where'll we find one?"

"They trail the buffalo, but you can't order one like a roll of ribbon." Andrew cut the fallen cow's throat. "Plenty hunters been mangled by a half-skinned *kill*."

Andrew split the cow's gut open, exposing her twisting entrails in a cloud of hot choking odors. "You baptize your first buffalo with Mountain Man Cider." He knifed her paunch and caught its green, gelatinous fluid in a small pan. "Your cider, Captain. Drink it down!"

Wyeth looked stricken, then clamped his eyes shut and gulped the pan dry.

"Want more?"

"Plenty for now," Wyeth gagged, then lost his cider on the prairie.

*   *   *

Timber remained scarce and food was low by June 12th when the caravan halted at Laramie Fork where Kit Carson and 20 other trappers waited among the willows for Captain John Gannt.

Glad to be off the World's Smartest Mule Bluegrass for a while, William joined the bedraggled trappers. "Gannt's bankrupt in St. Louis."

"Real gooda him ta leave us a sittin' here forever!" Kit snarled.

"Thought you's workin' fer RMF Kit," William said.

"Was. Went with Gannt after Fitz left an' Rockaway Bill Gray stabbed Milt so bad fer triflin' with Gray's woman."

William poker-faced it. "Milt all right?" he asked as Fitz joined them in the cool of the willows where the flies hovered soundlessly.

Kit Carson shook his head. "Dunno. Jim Bridger left Joe Meek to tend Milt er bury 'im."

Fitz stepped in front of William. "When would this stabbin' be, Kit?"

"Last winter."

Fitz thought a minute, then said, "Kit, RMF'll be buyin' your band's peltry. You can cache 'em here, an' ride along to Rendezvous." The trappers war-hooped. Fitz turned to William. "I'll dash ahead on a fast horse an' let them at Rendezvous know the caravan's on its way."

William nodded, "Take two horses, Fitz. Find out what's become of Milt. Meet us at the foot o' the Three Tetons' western slope."

After filling everything that'd hold water, the caravan snaked into Wyoming territory's Black Hills, watching for grizzlies in the greasewood between towering red sandstone escarpments. Scaling the Snowy Range Mountains, they camped at the thaw-swollen Laramie River.

William ordered the building of Mandan bull boats. He showed Wyeth how the mountaineers stretched buffalo hides over a framework of willow cuttings and waterproofed them with buffalo tallow. Wyeth scorned the flimsy bull boats, muttering, "Men need a solid deck under their feet." He ordered his men to build a raft and pull it across the river on a rope.

Sublette's men were offloading their bull boats on the far shore when Sublette turned to see what was keeping Wyeth. Just then, Wyeth's raft snapped its rope and catapulted his blacksmithing tools and gunpowder into the Laramie's raging currents.

After pulling two drowning men ashore, a wet William Sublette confronted Wyeth. "Some times it's hard to tell a leader

o' men from a half-broke jackass. This is not one o' them times.
Yer on yer own after Rendezvous, Mr. Wyeth."

*   *   *

Fitz's pony was picking its way down the rocky western
slope of South Pass when he spied the band of Gros Ventres.
They charged, startling his spare horse so bad it tore free. Fitz
galloped his horse back up the hill till it was winded. He slid off
and slapped the wheezing pony's hip to make shod tracks going
away from him.

He ran backwards into heavy brush, found a cave and
crawled in it, stacking rocks in its mouth. He prayed to the
Blessed Virgin that he hadn't sealed himself in a grizzly's lair.
Fitz heard triumphant yells as the Gros Ventres captured his
horse. Footfalls approached, then died away.

At nightfall, Fitz found his pursuers camped just outside
his cave. A dog yipped but didn't stop their snoring. He
replaced the rocks silently, blinded in the dark by his own sweat.

Yells jerked Fitz awake. He cracked his knees crawling
for his rifle and pistol, but the rocks remained in the opening.

*   *   *

The second night, Fitz inched around the Gros Ventres
camp to a creek where he sucked in all the icy water he could
hold. Something brushed his leg -- a fleeing animal as scared by
him as he was by it. He waded the freezing water till dawn and
covered himself with brush. Voices woke him during the day,
but no one attacked.

Weakened by hunger, he reeled through the darkness.
By morning's light he ate berries and roots but was still afraid to
shoot the doe he saw.

At an unfamiliar river he fashioned a crude raft to keep
his clothes and powder dry. The raft broke up on a rock, letting
his rifle, pistol, shot pouch and powder horn plummet beneath
the swirling froth.

With only his butcher knife, Fitz pushed on toward
Pierre's Hole. While digging for a root, he was jumped by
wolves but escaped up a tree with two bites. He clung to the
tree all night, realizing he'd lost track of how many days he'd
wandered.

Like a gift from God, Fitz found a wolf-killed buffalo carcass. He made fire by rubbing sticks together and cooked the maggoty meat. When Fitz could no longer walk, he crawled. Finally, he lay awaiting the Angel of Death.

*   *   *

Failing to find Fitz at the foot of the Three Tetons' western slope by July 6th, William Sublette lead his caravan into the glorious valley known as Pierre's Hole. Some 30 miles long and 15 wide, Pierre's Hole stretched in emerald meadows crazy-quilted by fields of red, yellow, blue and purple wild flowers. To the east rose the snow mantled Three Tetons, the tallest of them towering over 13,000 feet into stormy clouds.

Wyeth's men straggled back down the trail, most too sick to do more than hobble. Not wanting to mix Wyeth's sick crewman with his hardy Mountain Men, Sublette told Wyeth where to camp. Wyeth gladly accepted autonomy.

Pierre's Hole teemed with friendly Flatheads, Nez Percé and trappers -- about a thousand in all with over two thousand mules and horses. Each time William met a friendly face he asked if they'd seen Milt Sublette or Tom Fitzpatrick -- to no avail. After William set up his camp, he searched afoot for Milt and Fitz. Before he'd gone a hundred yards, William glimpsed George Nidever lugging a skeleton of a man and broke into a thundering run.

Fitzpatrick tried to smile through the tears drenching his sunken eyes. His hair'd turned pure white. Sublette hoisted the sobbing man and lumbered toward his camp yelling, "God A'mighty, these shanty Irish're hard to kill!"

After talking with trappers, William learned Jim Bridger hadn't brought his men in. If Milt was alive, he'd be with Jim.

Indian belles in buckskins adorned with shells, feathers and beads flirted with interested trappers.

Sublette told Andrew to start selling goods and mete out their 450 gallons of alcohol by the pint. Merriment ensued, grew to frenzy and turned to rioting. Feats of horsemanship and personal strength gave way to wide scale drunkenness, singing, loving, fist-fighting and puking. Nathaniel Wyeth's men gawked till they figured it was time to dive in.

Jim Bridger's men came in led by handsome 6'4", raven haired Milton riding a chesty white horse. Arms about Milton's trim waist, *Umentucken Tukutsey Undewatsey,* his exquisite Shoshone wife, rode behind him. Milton signed to her to pitch camp and found his brother William.

After their back slapping and hollering was over, Milton groaned, "Rocky Mountain Fur's in serious trouble."

"Over the stabbing?" William asked quickly.

"Joe Meek got me through that. My heel still feels like it's been b'ar chawed from that Apache bullet back in '26, but them wounds is small potatoes."

"What's wrong?"

"American Fur Company dogs us every place. They steal our catch, bust our traps, hire our trappers! Ruin our tradin' with the Indians by payin' more an' lyin' bout us. We met Vanderburgh and Drips up on the Bear River an' offered ta split the Rocky Mountain trappin' grounds with 'em.   They jist laughed an' tole us their owner John Jacob Astor's the richest man in the world. They don't hafta divide nothin' -- cause they're gonna take it all jist like they done the Upper Missouri country!"

William Sublette's eyes flashed as he growled, "Before I'm done with them American Fur Boys, they'll beg to divide the Rockies trappin' territory with you, Milt!"

CHAPTER 8

WHEELER'S SAVIOR?   SUMMER 1832

Marcus Whitman's new medical office occupied the choice spot on the main crossroads in Wheeler, New York. The nearest M.D. was six miles away in Prattsburg! Wheeler was not founded until 1800, but it'd grown to 200 people, counting close-by farms. Then cholera came like vipers striking townspeople down. Survivors fled. Marcus knew unless he worked a miracle, Wheeler would vanish -- like it'd never been there at all.

Never pretty, Marcus resembled a prisoner escaped from a dungeon. Riding the countryside every night tending the stricken gave him a skull's black holes for eyes. His mysterious, chronic pain gnawed his side incessantly.

He napped on a rumpled cot in his office instead of retiring to the Aulls' boarding house.Journals and newspapers freighted with cholera news littered his floor. American cities were under siege. Commerce was paralyzed while arguments raged about what cholera was.

Just as Reverend Parker had railed against Marcus last fall in the Fairfield Infirmary, clergymen across the nation denounced physicians for meddling. Cholera was God's Will. God inflicted cholera upon the unworthy, and only God could undo it.

Although President Jackson and New York's Governor Enos Throop refused to bow to the clergy's demand for a declared day to seek God's forgiveness, 12 states and scores of communities designated one. Arguing in Congress for such a

Holy Day of Deliverance, duelist, drinker and gambler Henry Clay provoked the July 9th *Hartford Times* to jeer:

"Could Clay gain votes by it, he would kiss the toe of the Pope and prostrate himself before the Grand Lama."

But labor radical George Henry Evans countered in the *Workingman's Advocate* that men, not God, permitted filth, wretchedness and poverty. Evans demanded a graduated income tax to make recurrence of cholera impossible. Marcus disputed the income tax cure, but was struck by Evans' claims that Irish workers living in squalor suffered the highest death rates. It could be that liquor weakened the Irish, making them easier victims of cholera.

Cholera treatments abounded in the literature under Marcus' cot. Conservative remedies like bleeding, laudanum and calomel were extolled. A Louisiana physician boasted in the *Boston Medical and Surgical Journal* that he'd drawn ". . . blood enough to float the General Jackson steamboat and gave calomel enough to sink her,"* but made no mention of curing patients.

New York State Medical Society's president prescribed the practical solution of plugging the rectum with beeswax or oilcloth to stop the diarrhea. Newspapers claimed this remedy caused many cholera sufferers to disclaim any knowledge of their affliction.

The *Cholera Bulletin* trumpeted that Doctors and cholera were combatants for the right to kill the public:

"Cholera kills, and Doctors slay, and every foe will have its way!"

Samuel Thomson, the New England farmer who'd become rich selling his Botanic Physician kits in pulp magazines, included Lawyers and Priests in his condemnation:

> *The nest of college-birds are three,*
> *Law, Physic and Divinity;*
> *And while these three remain combined,*
> *They keep the world oppressed and blind.*
> *On Lab'rers money Lawyers feast,*
> *Also the Doctor and the Priest;*

The Priest pretends to save the soul,
Doctors to make the body whole;
For money, Lawyers make their plea;
Save it all and dismiss the three.

Much as Marcus despised *Puke Doctor* Thomson as a fraud for making people vomit senselessly, he was more annoyed by the addled efforts of the clergy to cure cholera. Cholera was perhaps the only thing that could not legitimately be blamed on lawyers.

Plattsburg, New York's elders had sent Dr. Kane to Montreal, where North American cholera struck first, to investigate the killer. Dr. Kane reported cholera was not contagious, ". . . *for it had descended in many parts of the city simultaneously like a shower of hail.*"

If Marcus was right that cholera had a worldly cause like smallpox, instead of a miasmic malady from the vapors as Kane and most other doctors said, he must fight it with a real weapon instead of praying, taxing, bleeding or plugging someone's behind with beeswax.

Marcus was scorned by other Fairfield Medical College doctors for boiling lances, scalpels and amputating knives after use. His colleagues wiped theirs off and talked of "laudable pus" being a healing agent for wounds. Marcus didn't like the stink of rotting flesh and blood on his tools, especially after pulling a scalpel covered with mold out of his bag in front of a Quaker woman that near fainted. At least one doctor whispered that Marcus' ancestor John Whitman had been consigned to the flames and died without recanting the devil. Some raised brows and confided that Marcus Whitman was either a witch or a religious fanatic given to "notional doings."

His fellow physicians would have muttered all the more about witchcraft had they caught him poring over the English translation of Italian Girolamo Fracastoro's ancient 1546 book about sicknesses carried by little beasties he called "seminaria," although he never saw one. Maybe these tiny beasties were what Antoni van Leeuwenhoek saw with his close-lens in 1676 or what Christian Gottfried called "Bacterium" of late in his classifications.

What did Marcus have to fight little beasties his eye couldn't see? His meager supply of calomel? His pliers for pulling teeth at 10¢ each? He was a knight with no sword! Then the ugly brown bar of lye soap beside his operating table caught his eye. Cleanliness next to Godliness? Prayers hadn't vanquished his enemy. Maybe his soap would.

Marcus scribbled his thoughts in two columns on a sheet of paper on his rough operatory table.

"1. Cholera in New York City, Baltimore, Cincinnati, Philadelphia, New Orleans, St. Louis, Chicago & etc

1. Cities with cholera on water ways. Water a contaminator? Sewage? Wriggler or poison in Water?

2. Symptoms - diarrhea, vomiting, blue cold puckered hands, chills & cramps

2. Same symptoms as arsenic poisoning.

3. Sickness

Cholera is a little killer beastie like smallpox or poison like arsenic -- or hard use of liquor.

3. Remidies

Clean water of sewage, filth, poison or pond scum. Boil drinking & bath water. Bathe patient with lye soap. Dry well & keep warm. Give hot broth for viger. Pour out liquor. Scrub rooms with lye soap & wash blankets & etc. in same or burn. Pray to Almighty God you have finally done something to save your fellow man."

CHAPTER 9

THE BATTLE OF PIERRE'S HOLE   SUMMER 1832

William Sublette prowled the Rendezvous camps on July 15th's dawn. Pierre's Hole named for old Iroquois Pierre Tevantigon had never seen a Rendezvous hellacious as this one. Sublette hadn't, and this was his eighth. Rowdies still howled and fired their guns upward into falling snow. Somebody'd set a whiskey-soaked trapper afire "ta git better drinkin' light." Drunks sprawled as snow-frosted "corpses."

Robert Campbell fell in beside Sublette, stepping on a fallen drunk. Sublette grunted, "If Blackfeet come a' killin' like they done at Bear Lake in '27 an' '28, God hisself couldn't rouse these men ta fight, Bobbie."

"Aye, but Blackfeet'll na raid in a snow storm. Where ya goin', Mr. S?" Campbell's breath hid his question.

"Ta see Milt. Them American Fur Company boys is gettin' his goat."

"They'll have all our goats and everythin' else we got er hope ta get if we let 'em, Mr. S. John Jacob Astor's the greediest man ever God put upon this pitiful planet."

"Milt's wife *Umentucken's* gonna teach Drew some Flathead, so's he kin trade better here."

"Saved back soom o' mah trade goods. Be more dear than last week. I'll get to tradin' now, Mr. S."

Trappers stumbling back to their own camps set dogs to barking among the Flathead lodges. In the Nez Percé village women in bright blankets struck sparks with flint and steel into hoarded dry grass. Several young fires sizzled snow off the buffalo chips. Hollow sounds of chopping echoed in the dimness.

William pulled the flap back and squeezed into Milt's smoky lodge where the sleek Shoshone woman in beaded white buckskins had just made a fire. Drew sat cross-legged, wrapped in a blue trade blanket. Milt was gone.

In the musky golden fire light, the woman's skin glowed like the idol in the Catholic church in St. Louis. Her almond black eyes flashed danger. William greeted her in Shoshone, "*Ha gunni hanch*!" and began to sign to her. He raised his right index finger in front of his nose, then laid both index fingers side-by-side on his chest. Finally, he thrust his right hand on edge away from his body.

She extended the first two fingers of her right hand, raised the back of that hand to her eye, then moved the hand away quickly several times.

Andrew grinned, "You asked where her husband went, and she told you he's hunting."

William nodded, "But with Milt you gotta wonder whose lodge he's huntin' in."

"No say dat!" *Umentucken* hissed like an angry cat. "Milton only gone little minutes!"

"Sorry. Din't know you talked our *Tab Aboo* tongue. What's your *Tab Aboo* name?" William asked.

"*Umentucken Tukutsey Undewatsey* in *Tab Aboo* is Mountain Lamb."

"Mountain Lamb! Kinda thought that second word'd be *Lion!* Taught you any Flathead yet, Drew?"

"How to count to a hundred. *Inco* is 1. *Asale* 2, *Tchat les* 3, *Mose* 4, *Tsuel* 5, *Tacan* 6, *Seispel* 7, *Haine* 8, *Hay noot* 9 and *Open* 10. *Asale-Open* is two times 10 -- that is 20 -- and so on repeating the number followed by *Open* up to *Open-Open* for 100."

William clapped his younger brother on the back. "Right smart, but most Flatheads use *In-kaw* fer 100. Them Flatheads an' Nez Percé is the most honest men you'll ever meet. Treat 'em right."

Drew smirked, "Bill, you talk a little Flathead, Chopunnish, Shoshone, Absaroka and sign with the best of 'em. When you gonna learn to talk *Tab Aboo*?"

"Drew -- yer tasked ta teach me *Tab Aboo* on our way back ta the U. States!   When we see them Aull brothers in Lexington, I wanta sound like Jedediah Smith!"

"How's Jedediah, Bill?" Milt asked, thrusting the head of a two point buck through the lodge flap with dirt on its leathery eyes.

"Same's that buck, Milt.   *Comanch* done Jedediah in down on the Cimmarron in May o' '31."

"Then Jedediah's the one shoulda learned ta talk better. *Comanch* are sittin' ducks fer a sad story."

"What was ya tellin' them *Comanch* when they tuck them 600 horses o' Colonel Marmaduke's offa you at the Arkansas River, Milt?"

It galled Milt plenty when Bill showed him up.   Milt motioned to Mountain Lamb to come out and dress the buck, then he limped into the lodge.

"That old heel wound hurtin' ya, Milt?"

"Donchu worry bout it, Bill!"   Milt asked Andrew, "What's our li'l brother Solomon doin' these days?"

"What every 17 year old's doing -- telling everybody how to run the world, unable to earn a living -- and living off our fat uncle Solomon in St. Charles."

"When's Solomon comin' Up the Mountain?" Milt asked, sitting down to get the weight off his pain-shot heel.

William grated, "I brung Pinckney Sublette up here in '27 when he weren't no bigger'n a baby bird.   Now his scalp's hangin' in a Blackfoot lodge up on the Portneuf River. I'll not bring the Blackfoot another Sublette."

"Well now, Bill that's fer Solomon ta say, ain't it? Bill, you cain't run ever'body's life, no matter how they's blood related now kin ya?"

"Things don't change -- do they, Milt?"

"Guess not. Stayin' fer venison? Thought we was gonna talk about the AFC."

William bulled out into the icy air, waving to Mountain Lamb as he bolted past her. She waved back with her bloody hand, then made the unseen sign to stay away.

*   *   *

The American Fur Company camp's 90 men had given up on Lucien Fontenelle's Rendezvous supply train by the time William Sublette was ready to leave.   Captain Benjamin Bonneville's pack train hadn't made it to Rendezvous either. AFC was low on everything and more surly than usual.   Neither AFC's William Vanderburgh nor Andrew Drips offered so much as a nod to Sublette or his men.

Wyeth's camp was even more riled.   Wyeth's men demanded a New England town meeting.   Nathaniel Wyeth read the roll, calling for a *yea* or *nay* vote as to who would go on to the Columbia River with him or return to St. Louis with Sublette. Wyeth jerked with each *nay* vote as though it'd pierced his heart.   He wilted at brother Jacob's *nay*, followed straight away by cousin John Wyeth's.

Left with only 11 of his 18 men, Nathaniel Wyeth cautioned his brother.   "Not too smug, now Jacob.   I'm leaving this Rendezvous with William Sublette's brother, Milton.   It seems in these lofty climes that blood grows thinner than water."

Milton and Wyeth's 11 man party wended north. *Umentucken* rode her white horse regally in blue broadcloth skirt and bodice with scarlet leggings, her saddle and bridle ornamented with fine cut glass beads and tinkling hawk bells. Like most Shoshone women, she had a war tomahawk on one side of her saddle and a peace pipe on the other.

William located Jim Bridger's lodge in the Rocky Mountain Fur camp and hailed Jim.   Jim crawled out and stretched his fatless frame to its full six feet in the warm sun. His gray eyes were ever so direct.   "What's on your mind, Bill?"

"Wanta talk with you an' Fitz bout AFC an' next year's supplies."

"Fitz's been sleepin' sunup till sundown.   Man's near dead.   Let's talk bout AFC.   Ketch Fitz bout supplies inna mornin'."

"Milt tole me AFC's doggin' ya bad an' ruinin' ever'thin'."

"They is."

"AFC's stickin' to ya cause they don't know where ta trap."

"Zactly."

57

"Mebbee ya oughta leave 'em on the Blackfeet's front porch, Jim, so's they kin tell them shriekin' savages how rich ole man Astor is."

"Sounds like one o' my big lies that I ain't got around ta tellin' yet. I like it, Bill."

*   *   *

Having camped only eight miles from Rendezvous, Milt and Wyeth readied their men for the July 18th march. Iroquois Antoine Godin galloped in shouting, "Two hunnert Blackfeet comin' down the pass -- be here quick."

Milton barked at Wyeth, "Blackfeet'll 'tack a small outfit like iss right quick! *Umentucken,* git help from Rendezvous! Godin, you an' Dorian stall them Blackfeet till we fort up. Sign an' talk Iroquois till I whistle, then hustle back here!"

Umentucken cut the hobbles on her white horse and leapt astride its bare back. Kicking it's flanks, she loped off with a fistful of flowing mane in one hand and her sacred tomahawk in the other.

Antoine Godin and Iroquois Baptiste Dorian hand-signed for a parley and rode toward the Blackfoot Chief who wore a shimmering red blanket on his bony pinto with eagle feathers festooning its mane and tale.

Antoine recognized the Blackfoot Chief as the slayer of his father, Thyery Godin. Antoine growled, "He plans treachery! Shoot his face. I'll count *coup* and grab his blanket!"

Milton gaped in disbelief as Dorian's gunshot blasted the Blackfoot Chief's head apart. The dead Chief's escort party thundered through the grass with rifles booming. Godin and Dorian raced ahead of them, jumped down and cut their horses' throats for shelter from the lead hornets and arrows cutting the air.

The trappers fired and reloaded three times for every shot Wyeth's men got off, but the bayonets on the New Englanders' muskets seemed to mystify the Blackfeet, who withdrew to regroup. Dorian lay lung shot, spewing red froth from his chest beside his dead horse. Godin crawled to Milton's line and waved the trophy red blanket in Milton's face. Milton stripped the blanket from Godin and belted him out with a bone-busting punch, as the Blackfeet bunched for another charge.

58

Umentucken's horse pounded over the crushed grass circles that had been Rendezvous lodges to Sublette's camp. "Blackfeet killing Milton!" she screamed.

William yelled, "Stay here! You may carry Milt's baby." He left Bluegrass hobbled and saddled a fast horse.

Robert Campbell rode up on a prancing bay. "Mah men're ready! Alexander Sinclair an' his 15 Arkansas boys're comin'! Your Flathead an' Nez Percé friends are headin' down the valley now!" Campbell wheeled his horse and joined the race behind *Umentucken*, who'd just stolen William's best black thoroughbred.

Seeing the dust darken the sky and feeling the ground tremble beneath them, the Blackfeet retreated into a willow swamp, forted it with buffalo hides and lodge parts.

William remembered what he'd told the trappers when the Blackfeet attacked the Bear Lake Rendezvous in '27. They needed remindin'. "Boys, them Blackfeet're gonna kill Rendezvous if they git away with this raid. We gotta show 'em they can't come between a Mountain Man an' a good time!"

The men roared.

As the trappers, Flatheads and Nez Percé war-hooped into the swamp, William and Campbell told each other their wills and made each other executor. Then they bellied toward the Blackfeet, rifle balls busting willow branches and arrows screaming from the sky. Sinclair crawling beside Campbell took a ball in the eye and fell dead. William's rifle blasted the head off Sinclair's assassin; he rose and charged the Blackfeet. Leaping the first barrier, William blew down a brave with his boot pistol. Campbell shot down the massive Blackfoot charging him.

Blackfeet scattered before them. William knifed one who stopped, then another rose inside a buffalo robe and broke William's arm with a bullet that punctured his side and came out under his shoulder blade. William sat down hard, yanked his other boot pistol and blasted the Blackfoot that shot him.

Flatheads and Nez Percé chased their ancient enemies, amazed to see the Blackfeet fleeing for a change.

Campbell stuck his neck under William's good arm and staggered back toward the creek. "Mr. S, we're leavin' this frolic, so ah kin count the holes in yee. Over ten, you're doon fer the day!" William grinned, then passed out. Campbell stuffed bullet patches in William's side and back wounds to stop the bleeding, hoping Dr. Jacob Wyeth could finish bandaging back at camp.

Milton, Jim Bridger, Joe Meek and Robert Newell tried to burn out Blackfoot stragglers in swamp thickets, but the willows smoked and went out. The Blackfeet slipped away.

Milton carried in wounded trappers, Flatheads and Nez Percé. They buried Alexander Sinclair and six other dead trappers. With William, they counted 13 wounded. Between the Nez Percé and Flatheads they suffered 25 dead and 35 wounded. Some 27 dead Blackfeet braves and one grieving Blackfoot woman lay in the swamp. *Umentucken* buried her tomahawk in the woman's head, freeing her spirit to join her dead brave's.

*   *   *

On July 25th William got up and negotiated contracts with Fitzpatrick providing that William Sublette would supply goods at the next annual Rendezvous and would freight RMF's 7 tons of furs to St. Louis for 50¢ a pound. The contracts set RMF's debts to William at $17,764.44. They acknowledged RMF's debts to the late firm of Smith, Jackson & Sublette of $15,532.22 and to the late firm of Jackson and Sublette for $3,135.75 all sums bearing 8 %. interest. William agreed to pay $10,318.47 owed to RMF men going to St. Louis, for which RMF would reimburse William.

On July 30th, William's pack train left Rendezvous with 169 packs of furs and his arm in a sling. When they stopped at the top of Teton pass, William looked back at Pierre's Hole below now trampled and abandoned -- its memories already beginning to fade. Old Pierre hisself'd been killed by the Blackfeet and forgot years ago. William knew there'd never be another Rendezvous like this one. And if the fur market was still in the ditch, the fight and all the work had been for nothing cause he'd gone bankrupt in the bargain.

William Sublette took a painful breath of pure mountain air and muttered, "Aw what the hell! Busted or not -- this Rendezvous was worth it!"

CHAPTER 10

WOUNDS IN THE BACK   SUMMER-FALL 1832

On July 24th Milton Sublette and Nathaniel Wyeth lead their men from Pierre's Hole, following the Portneuf River to the Snake River Valley. Each day Milton's excruciating heel pain worsened his limp from the day before. Milton forbade *Umentucken* to mention it. Milton drank to smother the pain but never enough to make him crazy drunk. At the Snake River, Wyeth asked, "How long can you walk with that lurching gait?"

Milton glared down at Wyeth, "Long as it takes. St. Louie papers called me *The Thunderbolt of the Rockies* because I was faster'n any man inna country -- an' I still am!"

They trapped the Snake River for three days, but took no beaver. Wyeth was awed by the Snake's majestic water falls and its wall of a thousand springs where springlets released shimmering trickles into the churning waters below.

Wyeth and Milton gnawed at rabbit morsels around the fire at Milton's lodge. *Umentucken* never cooked the meat enough for Wyeth, so he ran a stick through his bloody piece and sizzled it over the flames. Milton chased each gulp of rabbit with a pull off his whiskey flask. "Hudson's Bay's trapped the Snake dry. Water's cursed. Gotta find virgin streams."

Wyeth bit into his smoking rabbit thigh again, searing his lips. Even as he waved cool air onto his blistered mouth, his face was serene. "It beguiles me, Milton."

"Hot rabbit meat?"

"The Snake River. It makes me dream grand dreams."

"Like what?"

"Even as our brothers Jacob and William lug the fur spoils back to St. Louis, I'm spirited upward by the notion that we could supply your Rocky Mountain Fur Company's Rendezvous with the same quality goods vastly cheaper than your brother does. Your company'd like saving money, wouldn't they?

"How?"

"William charges you criminal prices for the goods he brings to Rendezvous, because he's paying top dollar for them in St. Louis. You and I could buy quality goods in the east -- New York, Boston, Philadelphia -- eliminating several layers of mark up. Besides, we'd break your brother's financial stranglehold on you and your partisans.

Milt savored Wyeth's dream and capped it by emptying his flask. "That there's one dream that's gonna come true. Me an' my boys'll head down the Owyhee whilst you take yer crew on to Fort Walla Walla on the Columbia. Come next season, we'll git with Fitz, make a deal an' show ole Bill Sublette the hole inna doughnut."

*   *   *

On their fall hunt along the Dearborn River, Jim Bridger still couldn't get used to Fitzpatrick's white hair. "Whatta you spose done that to your hair, Fitz?"

Exasperated at hearing about his hair, Fitz reined up his horse and motioned for Jim to lean closer. "An elf, Jimmy Boy. A leprechaun he was. Tapped me head with his little spatula and said, 'Now them Blackfeet'll think you're your own grandfather - - an' leave you plumb alone outa respect for their elders.' "

Bridger grinned, but went serious. "See if yer elf'll shake off them AFC boys. They're stuck tighter'n burrs on our butts."

Fitz nodded, "We left 'em in Pierre's Hole with no supplies. They must've found Fontenelle's caravan, then cut our tracks. They got double our 60 men. Nothing we can do."

"Bill Sublette said we oughta lead 'em inta Blackfoot country."

"It'd do my heart good to see Vanderburgh and Drips with white hair, Jimmy Boy."

"Better with none a'tall! Let's head fer the Three Forks o' the Missouri."

A Mexican named *Pablo Loretta* and his Blackfoot wife, were the best scouts Bridger'd ever had. *Loretta* knelt at Bridger's blanket while the crescent moon was still up. "Jeem. Beeg Blackfoot war party comeen down dee Madison Reeber!"

Bridger lead the Rocky Mountain Fur men into the Gallatin River valley as false dawn brightened the edges of the sky. They whispered and walked their horses through the dark trees, clearing dead branches from the pine needle beds under foot.

*   *   *

AFC's William Vanderburgh and Andrew Drips were furious that RMF'd ducked them in the dark. Vanderburgh snarled, "Drips, take the mules and half the men. Cut the gullies to the west. Fire twice if you find their trail. I'll take the rest and head up the Madison. We'll catch those toads, if it's the last thing I ever do!"

Vanderburgh's anger overwhelmed his West Point training and his guile of many years Up the Mountain. He rode recklessly through the dewy grass, turning occasionally to beller, "Close it up!" Nettled by their timidity, he decided to put Warren Ferris, Auguste Pilou, R.C. Nelson and the first four men behind them out in front. "Scouting party move out!"

Vanderburgh's scouting party galloped ahead through Alder Gulch, then pulled up at an Indian buffalo kill. In cooler mien, Vanderburgh would have spotted the carcass as ambush bait, but not this windy day. He ordered, "Dismount!"

Thundering over the brow of a low hill 200 feet away, the Blackfeet charged, firing their rifles in white puffs. Head shot, Vanderburgh's horse toppled, pinning his leg. Pilou fell dead, leaking red into the rough sand. Ferris and two others were hit, but could still run. They paid no heed to Vanderburgh's shouts, "Stand firm! Stand firm!"

Kicking free of his fallen horse, Vanderburgh raised his rifle and blasted the closest warrior off his pony. But another circled and lanced him through the back. Vanderburgh grasped the lance head protruding from his chest, crumpling into the tall grass as his scouts escaped amid the confusion of milling horses.

*   *   *

Jim Bridger rode up a gully ahead of his column toward a hill where he could get the lay of the land. From nowhere, Blackfeet filled the gulch ahead of Bridger. Bridger laid his rifle across his pommel, called for *Loretta's* Blackfoot wife to interpret and signed for a parley. Just as *Señora Loretta* arrived, the Blackfoot Chieftain wrested Bridger's rifle away, throwing Jim from his horse, and fired it into the dirt beside Jim.

As Fitz and the others returned fire to save Jim, the Chief seized *Señora Loretta* and rode off with her, bellering at her in Blackfoot.

Arrows zipped through the whoops and yells. One pierced Bridger's foot. Another *thunked* into his back, lodging by his spine.

Many Blackfeet swung their horses from the fight, following the Chief to their camp less than a mile from the battle. The remaining warriors sniped with rifles and arrows till dark, then left calling to the spirits of the nighthawks.

Fitz shoved the arrow through Bridger's foot, then marveled at it, "Head's three inches long. Eagle feathers make it wail like a banshee -- fiercer than a bullet!"

Bridger moaned, "What about the one in mah back?"

"Slants downward. Can cut off the shaft, but it's too dark to be diggin' out the head." As Fitz spoke, *Pablo Loretta* rode past with his whimpering baby son *Marfil* in his arms -- heading for the Blackfoot camp. "Where you goin', *Pablo*?"

"Thees baby weel die weethout hees mother's meelk."

"You know you're goin' to your death to give life to the child?" Fitz whined.

Loretta rode into the twilight.

"What if his mother's already dead?" Fitz yelled.

"*Entonces* we shall all be together," *Loretta's* solemn words drifted back.

Bridger raised on his elbow. "Bust off that shaft an' ketch me up a horse, Fitz."

"Aw, Jimmy boy! Have ya lost yer mind?"

"He ain't goin' in nere alone, Fitz."

"Aw, Jim -- Jim. Now we'll all die."

CHAPTER 11

MYSTERIES OF THE BLACKFOOT MIND   FALL 1832

Hoback Canyon had a bad reputation.   Blackfeet had massacred Mountain Men and enemy tribes in the canyon narrows for years.   With his left arm still splinted and a pain like a burrowing rat eating at the bullet hole in his shoulder blade, William avoided Hoback.   His 60 men and their heavily packed mules braved a fording of the Snake River, hugged the Gros Ventre River's bank and struggled upward into Union Pass -- only to find over a hundred Blackfeet sitting their ponies near the crest.

Robert Campbell rode his horse up beside Sublette's mule.   Instead of grabbing a boot pistol, Sublette raised his good right arm and showed his empty hand.   The Blackfoot in the tattered British Officer's red coat raised his hand.   He turned and motioned his braves down the hill.

The only noises came from a few rocks rolling down the steep trail as the sullen-eyed Blackfeet rode past the pack train down Union Pass.   Dumbfounded, Sublette and Campbell looked at each other with raised eyebrows, then rode upward over the crest.

*   *   *

Jim Bridger, his foot bloody and a broken arrow shaft protruding from the back of his buckskins, hunched over in the saddle ahead of *Pablo Loretta* and baby *Marfil*.   He fought dizziness.   He wanted to see the Blackfoot who killed him. As the warm smells and camp sounds surrounded them, Jim Bridger struggled to sit up straight.   Man oughta look like a man when he meets his maker.   He wanted to shout out his pain, but he bit into a smile and froze it.

The infant had been crying, but his father soothed the cries away with gentle strokes on the tiny brow. He loved this boy *Marfil* more than his own life. If the dear Blackfoot wife he knew as *Alma* still lived, she would give the sweet life of her breast to *Marfil*. He proudly held his son up high for all the mystified Blackfeet to see. He would tell the Blackfeet how he had saved *Alma* from death by torture when she was a captive of the Crow. Surely *Alma's* blood kin would see the beauty of this boy and release her.

His white hair twitching in wind gusts, Fitzpatrick rode behind *Loretta* and his tyke.Fitz fingered the Rosary about his neck, silently reciting the simple prayers he'd learned as a boy in Ireland's County Cavan. In his heart Fitz heard Angel voices singing more powerfully with each footfall as they rode deeper into the Blackfoot camp.Each delicate *Ave Maria* began with a single clarion soprano, blended into a full rich paternoster then resounded in a thousand voices roaring a ground shaking *Gloria!*

Alma sprawled on her side in the moist black dirt outside the Chief's lodge, her arms bound behind her.Her eyes were swollen black.New bruises blotched her body from the squaw beating she'd endured in silence. She gaped at sight of the three riders with her child. "¡*Escaparse!*" she shrieked.

The Blackfoot Chief peeked through his lodge flap. He gasped then beckoned to his other two wives. Their heads crowded into the lodge doorway beneath his.

Pablo said, "*Marfil tiene hambre, mi Alma.*" and held the child out toward his fallen wife. *Marfil* thrust his thumb into his eager mouth and cooed.

The fattest squaw squeezed past the others in the Chief's lodge flap as Blackfeet brandishing knives and tomahawks swarmed about the invaders. The squaw seized a knife from a snarling brave and cut the rawhide bindings off *Alma's* wrists. The rotund woman grabbed *Marfil* from his father and thrust him into *Alma's* hands.

Marfil fretted, but *Alma* soon quieted him with her breast, the blood from her wrist splotching her baby's face. *Alma* wanted to cry with joy, but kept her smooth coppery Blackfoot face impassive.

Bridger's agonized smile turned real, but the fat squaw wasn't having any of that. She stuck her jaw out, slapped Bridger's pony on the chest and gestured emphatically for Bridger to go. "*Pablo*, you done whatchu come fer. Le's go!"

"Dey must release *Alma* and our child."

The fleshy squaw smacked *Pablo's* leg, then pointed for him to go.

Bridger and Fitz closed their mounts around *Pablo's* horse. Fitz grabbed the Mexican's reins. They sidled their three ponies carefully through the crush of grumbling warriors.

Once clear of the Blackfoot camp, Bridger lamented, "I jist lived my biggest lie, an' nobody'll ever bleeve it. I don't even bleeve it."

Fitz groaned, "I believe it. So do the Angels flittin' about our heads. But we can't tell a soul or nobody'll ever believe us about anythin' again. Unless ya want mates for that arrow in yer back, Jimmy Boy, you'll light out right behind me!"

CHAPTER 12

A DIFFERENT KIND OF WAR   FALL 1832

By the time Sublette's pack train neared Independence, Missouri in the third week of September, William was sick of Andrew nagging him to put "ing" on the end of words. "Drew, I remember when talk*ing* used to be fun. Let me be fer a while."

Andrew fell back to haze stragglers up.

At the edge of Independence, several city clad gentlemen lounged beside the trail eating cold fried chicken and other delicacies. One rose, walking toward the caravan.

Sublette got off Bluegrass, rubbing his aching arm in the sling. "Lost?" Sublette asked the little flower of a man with overlarge eyes and a rosebud mouth.

"Why no. I'm Washington Irving. I'm writing on the West. Come have some chicken. We can talk."

William took care not to crush the porcelain hand Irving offered. He signaled his caravan to keep moving, then accepted a plump chicken breast and small goblet of wine. Irving and Sublette walked toward the creek.

Irving asked, "Have you been waging war on the Indians?"

"Some. Lost seven good men to the Blackfeet at Pierre's Hole."

"I suppose you slaughtered the Blackfeet."

"Not so's you'd notice. Got my arm busted by a bullet that tore through my side an' out my back."

"What do you think of Black Hawk?"

"Never met the man."

"I just interviewed him as a captive at Fort Jefferson. This Black Hawk who's such a menacing figure in our newspapers is upward of 70, enfeebled by his sufferings. Has a well-formed head -- aquiline nose -- good expression of eye. Though he's accused of many cruelties in the Black Hawk War, I see his brother-in-law as fomenter of that disturbance. I always favor the red men and find it difficult to get the right story of these feuds between them and the whites -- even when I'm *this close* to the seat of their actions."

William Sublette eyed the little dandy and downed his last drop of wine. "Yeah, when you're *this close* to a Indian War, you oughta be able ta tell who's in the right. Thanks fer the vittles. I gotta go."

Irving took that as a compliment, adding it to his notes as the evil smelling mountaineer trotted off on his odoriferous mule to rejoin his comrades.

Sublette's outfit stopped in Columbia. He borrowed money against Ashley's account for expenses to St. Louis, arriving there October 3rd.

St. Louis was closed down by a cholera epidemic, so William took Andrew and Campbell to his ramshackle cabin at Sulphur Springs.

Sublette was peeved to learn Thomas Berry'd sued him for two lost slaves over the incident at his farm last fall. But once Sublette's lawyer Henry Geyer checked the whip nick in William's ear and assessed the facts, he assured William he'd blunt Berry's suit with counter charges of Trespass *Quare Clausum Fregit,* and assault and battery by an agent.

William Sublette respected Bobbie Campbell as a man in good standing with white and Indian traders alike, deciding to go into partnership with him. Together, they vowed to fight the American Fur Company's take over of the Rockies. Both knew they needed General Ashley's help.

Sublette entered Ashley's office in the toughest part of the St. Louis levee and found it stripped of furnishings. "Almost looks like nobody's home, General!"

Ashley stroked his prominent chin, "Had two break-ins this year. No sense baiting thieves with more plush furniture."

"Heard ya won yer Congressional seat agin!"

"By a whopping one per cent majority. Wells carried 19 of the 33 counties, but I beat him big in the Boonslick Trail counties and buried him in New Madrid County with 97%."

"Gonna give the Missouri Governor's chair another whirl?"

"That's my *real* goal, but I'll wait till the time is right and run a better campaign than I did in '24."

"How's things in Washington?"

"Desperate! Andy Jackson will likely bring down the U. S. Bank, and there's nothing to replace it. That'll precipitate a depression. Even more dire, Congress passed the Textile Tariff Act and South Carolina's threatening secession from the Union. That'll mean civil war, Bill!"

"You mean some states at war with other states? Never happen, General!"

"South Carolina's outraged over the hundreds of abolitionist societies blossoming in New York and New England. Civil war's inevitable. We can only postpone it. Another old mountaineer, Congressman Davy Crockett, is helping me cool down South Carolina."

"Anything good ever happen in Washington?"

"I championed the Bill creating Major Dodge's Ranger Battalion and attended the Ranger outfit's commissioning at Fort Gibson in Arkansas Territory. Ran into your old friend Jim Clyman. He's a 2nd Lieutenant in Captain Jesse Bean's Company. Clyman introduced another junior officer, Abe Lincoln -- not much of a military man but he sure can spin a yarn. Now that rabble-rouser Black Hawk's in jail, the Rangers'll be relegated to herding Indians out of Illinois and Wisconsin."

"Never forgit Jim Clyman sewing Jedediah Smith's scalp an' ear back on after that Grizzly tore 'em off." Sublette's eyes misted over. "Can't forgit some men, General. Jedediah's good as ever a man born."

"As you say -- the best of the great. You stand beside him in my eyes, Bill."

"I'm honored, General. Just went inta partnership with another fine man -- Bobbie Campbell. How do I stand on yer books?"

Ashley sneaked his smudged spectacles from his vest and turned up the wick in his smoke blackened lamp. He examined his ledgers and letters while Sublette's palms got clammy. Finally, Ashley grunted, "Looks grim, Bill. Income from your Santa Fe furs is only $14,500, half of which is not due from John Halsey till December. You still owe me $7,100 from your Jackson partnership's dealings. Since then I've paid out a little over $20,000 to merchants in New Orleans, Philadelphia, Pittsburgh, Cincinnati and Louisville for the trade goods you took to Pierre's Hole. With my 6 % annual interest on cash advances and 2½ % commissions on fur sales, you owe me $27,500 and change."

Sublette sighed, then said, "I hold Rocky Mountain Fur Company's notes and indebtedness totaling $46,750."

"They're into you too deep. What makes you think they're good for it?"

Sublette smiled, "Look who's talk*ing* General!"

"Say that again, Bill."

"Look who's talk*ing*?"

"You taking diction lessons, Bill?"

"Some."

"Good thing. You got RMF collateral?"

"I'll be paid out of the sales of seven tons of furs we're hauling to your warehouse. Once they're receipted, I get another $7,000 in transportation fees. I got the contract to supply RMF's Rendezvous next spring."

"Bill, I'd be leery of giving RMF more credit if this fur market doesn't crawl out of its grave."

"They're honest men, General. I know they'll pay me jist like you know I'll pay you."

"Bill, my dear dead wife Eliza told me, you're the solidest man she ever met. She was never wrong about people."

"Since Eliza sold them blooded carriage horses to finance my wagon trip to the Rockies, I worshipped her like a Saint. Like to killed me when I -- came -- back an' found Eliza'd passed away."

"Bill, you can live without a wife. I can't. I'm going to marry a doctor's widow, Elizabeth Moss Wilcox -- daughter of Dr. James Moss of Boone County."

"When?"

"This month. Elizabeth's queenlike, charming and possessed of exquisite tact -- exactly the woman a Congressman needs! Her two little daughters'll give me the family I always wanted."

"General, you may not want me at your wedding, when you find out what I'm up to."

Ashley tried to mask the alarm in his eyes. "What's up, Bill?"

"American Fur Company's hounding my brother Milt and his boys, stripping traps, hiring men away, lying to the Indians. Milt offered to split the Rocky Mountain territory with 'em, but Vanderburgh told him Astor'll take it all jist like he took the Upper Missouri. We're gonna fight 'em. I know it'll cost big money an' you don't wanta hear that when I owe you so much now."

"No I don't, but I'm already fighting AFC. A bill creating the Department of Indian Affairs came to the House floor. An amendment prohibited hard liquor in trade with the tribes. Astor demanded I knock out the liquor prohibition because the British use liquor putting Americans at a hopeless disadvantage. I refused. Liquor amendment passed in July. Pierre Chouteau, AFC's agent here, shipped a thousand gallons of liquor up the Missouri. Fort Leavenworth officials confiscated it. Now Chouteau refuses to buy your furs and tells me AFC's going to bury us."

"Whatta ya know about AFC, General?"

"I have a detailed file in Washington, but here's the profile. Astor chartered AFC in New York in 1808. Astor's motto was *Rule or Ruin*. AFC bought the competitors it couldn't crush and crushed the rest. Never in the history of the U. States has any corporation marched more ruthlessly over the corpses of its opponents to maintain a monopoly than AFC. Secretary of War Lewis Cass received a *birthday present* of $35,000 in cash from Astor back in 1817 when Cass was Governor of Michigan Territory."

Sublette rose and stalked to the window. "People never been Up the Mountain think Indians're Mountain Men's worst enemies, but they're not."

"Who is?"

"Every critter's got more to fear from its own kind than any other. Elk'll maim each other in mating season. So do eagles an' badgers. A prairie dog'll kill her neighbor's pups if she feels they're crowding her territory. Vanderburgh says Astor an' AFC will bury us like all the rest!"

General Ashley rose. "Jesus will run for President of hell before Astor buries us! But this time it'll take brains instead of brawn. John Jacob Astor's brilliant and brutal, but he must have a weakness -- commercial, political or personal. It's there. Our job is to find it."

Sublette got up to leave. "Will I be a guest at yer Wedding, General?"

"No, Bill."

Sublette spun around, "No?"

"No, Bill. You'll be my best man, and I'd like to know who's got her eye on you, so I can get ready for yours."

"General, if some woman out there's got me in her sights, she must feel I'm jist too worthless to skin out."

CHAPTER 13

THE PRISONER OF PRATTSBURG   OCTOBER 1832

Narcissa Prentiss poised on the edge of her chair, perspiration gathering around the edges of her finest black bonnet. Any moment Reverend Rudd would finish his bombastic sermon and direct her to sing her solo. She knew the words to *Rock of Ages* like the beat of her own heart. But she was always jittery till she sang the first few words and the Lord launched her voice on the flight of Angels.

Narcissa blotted her damp palms on her long skirt. Prattsburg, New York had hosted Revivals, but nothing like this. Reverend Rudd's Revival was so blessed by God's bounty, it overflowed from the new Prentiss home's vast hall onto the Village Green, then cascaded into the surrounding countryside like a flooding river.

People no one had ever seen before rolled up in creaking wagons, braving October's rains to set up housekeeping with the women sleeping inside and the men on India rubber cloths underneath. This new Holy clamor -- lowing oxen, barking dogs, squalling infants, wash tubs vomiting murky waters -- commenced at dawn and went on long after God fearing folk should have been asleep.

This Revival was out of control inside the Prentiss home! Instead of signaling Narcissa to sing as scheduled, stern-faced Reverend Rudd surrendered the pulpit to Reverend Higby.

Reverend Higby's fiery hair rose like rampant flames, increasing his height to a full 5'5". He read William Lloyd Garrison's tirade against Gradual Abolitionism in a tremulous falsetto, launching the words at the audience like avenging mosquitoes:

"I determined, at every hazard, to lift up the Standard of Emancipation in the eyes of the nation, within sight of Bunker Hill, and in the birthplace of liberty. That Standard is now unfurled; and long may it float, unhurt by the spoliations of time or the missiles of a desperate foe; yea, till every chain be broke, and every bondsman set free! Let Southern oppressors tremble; let their secret abettors tremble; let their Northern apologists tremble; let all the enemies of the persecuted blacks tremble. . . .

I am aware, that many object to the severity of my language; but is there not cause for severity? I will be as harsh as truth, and as uncompromising as justice! On this subject, I do not wish to think, or speak, or write, with moderation. No! No! Tell a man, whose house is on fire, to give a moderate alarm; tell him to moderately rescue his wife from the hands of the ravisher; tell the mother to gradually extricate her babe from the fire into which it has fallen; but urge me not to use moderation. I am in earnest. I will not equivocate -- I will not excuse -- I will not retreat a single inch -- AND I WILL BE HEARD. The apathy of the people is enough to make every statue leap from its pedestal, and to hasten the resurrection of the dead!

Reverend Higby stood down to the strident cheers of some and the total dismay of others fearing the divisive passions such talk unleashed upon an infant nation. But Garrison's words demanded Narcissa's freedom too -- a fiery demand that like others in bondage -- she be freed to do the Lord's work beyond the Shining Mountains. She was 24 with so little time left.

Narcissa readied herself to rise in song, but Reverend Rudd pointed instead to Narcissa's father, blocky Judge Prentiss, to have his choir sing, mouthing the words "Judge Me, O God."

Eight Prentiss children and the other two members of the choir rose in their rumpled robes. Judge Prentiss with his ever-perspiring brow gave the key with a toot on his battered pitch pipe, and the choir sang:

"Judge me O God and plead my cause against a sinful race.
From vile oppression and deceit, Secure me by thy grace.
From vile oppression and deceit, Secure me by thy grace."

The choir's flat tone irked Judge Prentiss. He tooted his pitch pipe again, but before they could render the second verse Reverend Rudd motioned them to sit, his eyes branding their effort unworthy.

Narcissa took a deep breath, but Reverend George Rudd was incensed. Having spied snide smiles during the choir's dreary rendition, he attacked sinners guilty of gaiety -- smiles were a sin on the Sabbath! Laughter on the Lord's day was a slap to the very face of God! Narcissa was certain he meant his bludgeoning for her. Constantly rebuked by her mother Clarissa for her excessive smiles and laughter, Narcissa had practiced looking glum. But her natural buoyancy of spirit constantly broke through. She bowed her head and prayed she might be as naturally glum as the others.

As Narcissa looked from one "oatmeal" man to another among the throng, her heart screamed a silent entreaty, "Where are you, my Mountain Man? You needn't love me as a woman -- nor even as a human being -- nor feel the need to touch me nor want to have my young. You need only lend me your name for a marriage of convenience, so I may spread His Word to the heathens! I beseech you to free me. I am the Prisoner of Prattsburg."

Narcissa knew nary a single word of that plea could ever pass her lips, for these words -- meant so purely -- would brand her as a heartless wench. Instead of demonstrating her abject love of God and His Work, they would incite the American Board of Commissioners for Foreign Missions to bar her from ever serving God in the West. She wondered how her pure heart could be so debased with impurity. Was she actually praying for a vile loveless marriage just to escape from Prattsburg?

Reverend Rudd implored,"Narcissa.*Please* begin. *Please Narcissa!*"

She rose and peered into the strange faces packing the grand center hall of her home. Her hymn's words were gone -- like the Mountain Man who wasn't there to free her as Mr. Garrison would the slaves.

"Narcissa, PLEASE!"

Judge Prentiss tooted his pitch pipe vehemently, then sweetly.

Narcissa rose and heard her own voice like a tiny chime:

"Rock of ages, cleft for me,
Let me hide myself in thee;
Let the water and the blood,
From thy riven side which flowed
Be of Sin the double cure,
Cleanse me from its guilt and pow'r."

Narcissa's intensifying soprano unfurled above the great room's silence like a brilliant blossom in bright morning sunlight:

"Not the labors of my hands
Can fulfill thy law's demands;
Could my zeal no respite know,
Could my tears forever flow
All for sin could not atone;
Thou must save me
And Thou alone!"

Narcissa's voice diminished to a whisper. Suddenly she knew the man God would send to save her was not among these people. She raised her voice to reach out to him wherever he was:

"Nothing in my hand I bring,
Simply to thy cross I cling;
Naked, come to thee for dress;
Helpless look to thee for grace;
Foul, I to thy fountain fly:
Wash me, Savior, or I die!"

Her soul said the man would come for her. She sang passionately knowing her salvation was at hand:

"While I draw this fleeting breath,
When mine eye-lids close in death,
When I soar to worlds unknown,
See thee on thy judgment throne --
Rock of Ages, cleft for me,
Let me hide myself in thee!
A-men. Am-men. A-men."

Narcissa finished knowing that her voice was free, searching heaven and earth for the man to release her from bondage. The awed silence that followed Narcissa's hymn gave way to sobs of joy -- Christians melted to tears and hardened sinners wept bitterly. Reverend George Rudd stood, his head bowed, tears flowing so welcomely down his face. Men and women charged forward and fell to their knees, yelling "Hallelujah!" "Praise God!" and begged, "Brother Rudd, cleanse me with the Blood of the Lamb!" The collection basket burgeoned. This Revival was done!

CHAPTER 14

THE TIME, THE TERMS, THE TERRAIN   OCTOBER 1832

After surveying Sulphur Springs' 779 acres on horseback, William Sublette curried and rubbed down his sleek black stallion. Now he lived in a log shack, and his ramshackle barn had only two stalls, but his mind brimmed with sites for his mansion, barns and the race track he'd build if he ever got out of debt. He remembered Grandpa Whitley telling him on Sportsman's Hill near Grandpa's race track in Lincoln County, Kentucky that a fine horse should never be rode hard and put up wet. He wondered if he'd ever get so respectable he didn't fancy the honest smell of horse sweat.

Sublette loved this chesty thoroughbred that Milt's wife had stolen to ride to the Battle of Pierre's Hole. He'd even named the horse after her. *Umentucken* was favoring the right front foot. He cradled the hoof against his knee and dislodged a rock from its frog with his knife. *Umentucken* whinnied as another horse approached.

The rider didn't roll with the motion of his heavy bay horse like a Mountain Man. He rode ramrod straight. Sublette had checked his Hawken boot pistols before his ride this morning. Both were charged and ready to fire.

"Capital thoroughbred!" the dismounting stranger complimented in clipped English words with a hint of Scottish brogue. "I'm Captain William Drummond Stewart. Do I have the pleasure of meeting *Cutface* William Sublette?"

Sublette nodded, sizing the man up as several years older than his own 33, just under six feet, a muscular frame and a small mustache with upturned tips. His gentleman's riding habit had seen better days. Their fierce handshake popped all their knuckles.

"Heard yer name before, Captain. Can't think where, but it'll come to me."

"Here's a letter of introduction to *Cutface* from your New York friend J. Watson Webb."

While Sublette read Webb's letter, Stewart tied his bay stallion's reins and inspected the teeth of Sublette's horse. The cups in the lower teeth surfaces were worn smooth from the central teeth a bit over half way out toward the incisors. "Stallion's around five years old," Stewart observed absently. "Bought horses from the peasants on the Peninsula in Wellington's campaign against Napoleon. Teeth wear smooth by nine and don't reveal the horse's age after that. Joke was the gray-muzzled horses for sale were all nine. What's this stalwart's name?"

Sublette handed the letter back. "*Umentucken Tukutsey Undewatsey.*"

"What on earth is that?"

"Shoshone for Mountain Lamb." Sublette opened his stallion's mouth again. "With our horses, after they're smooth mouthed -- cups gone -- you can read the stars on these teeth surfaces till they're about 12."

"Useful tip."

"I'll stall these horses and grain 'em up," Sublette said, leading the snorting, wild-eyed stallions together into the crude barn.

"Ever so generous!" Captain Stewart followed into the barn. "They get on famously for a couple of stallions! Hope we do as well."

Sublette patted his own forehead, "Jist remembered where I heard o' you," and pulled his left boot pistol.

"See here! There's no call for that!"

Sublette butt-firsted the pistol to show the silver *W* inlaid in its handle. "Bought a brace o' these at Hawken's in St. Louis the spring o' 1827. Jacob Hawken said they made 'em fer you. I's leaving for the mountains that day. So he said they'd make you another set. I jist got 'em back. Hocked 'em fer a bar bill at the *One-Eyed Dog.*"

"Remarkable memory! I ordered them from Dunkeld village in Scotland. Duplicate pair's in my luggage in St. Louis."

Captain Stewart laughed, "I've run up a tab or two in my day. Once left a sodden French wench to secure my tab in Paris as I dimly recall."

"Was easier remembering your name than where I hocked them pistols. I was somebody else by the time I parted with 'em. See you don't carry a Hawken rifle."

Sublette pulled the bridle off of Stewart's horse and dumped air fogging bran in the feeder boxes. The stallions crunched contentedly, occasionally swishing their tails at the flies.

Stewart eyed the sky through the barn's rickety roof, then removed his elegant rifle from its tooled boot under his stirrup. "I prefer this big bore Manton. Cost me 40 guineas in London."

Sublette hefted the Captain's immaculate weapon. "Dandy fer buffalo. Don't it git a might heavy?"

Stewart nodded, "But worth it. I actually have two of them. Before I left New York City in June, I shipped everything to St. Louis. All I carried were two sets of clothes, a blanket and this Manton. It shoots a trifle flatter than my other one."

Handing the jewel-smooth rifle back, Sublette grinned, "Inna mountains they say 'Travel light. Live fast. Die young.' How'd ya git from New York City to St. Louis?"

"Horseback across New York to Niagara Falls. Southwest along Lake Erie through Pennsylvania and west across Ohio into Indiana. Then over into Illinois and down to Missouri."

"Inns purty scarce after New York?"

"At first I sheltered in settler cabins. Your barn's luxurious compared to most o' those. I slept on dirt floors alive with ravenous fleas and wild children. When I tired of scratching, I decided to shoot squirrels or pigeons, roast them and tuck myself into the forest undergrowth."

"What's yer plan now?"

"To marry America for better or for worse!"

"Where ya staying?"

"*Mansion House* at Third and Vine."

Sublette whooped, "Making up fer yer tough trip quick! Mansion'll skin out yer wallet fore ya feel a thing! Might wanta stay where my partner Bobbie Campbell rooms now."

"My attorney in Scotland managed to extract some money from my trust fund. I'll squander that before I seek modest quarters. I'm hoping to join your caravan to the spring Rendezvous in the mountains."

"Gonna become a fur trapper?"

"Just like to learn my new bride's darkest secrets."

"Can't figure why anybody'd go Up the Mountain fer no reason. Indians, grizzly b'ars an' blizzards'll make yer trip from New York seem like a shave an' a light trim."

Stewart's face grew ruddier, but his smile didn't fade. "My service under the Duke of Wellington in the Peninsular War began when I was 19. It ended at an insignificant village named Waterloo between Dinant and Mons."

Stewart's eyes rolled up as he continued, "Wellington made the French attack first. Pire's Lancers stormed us. Our grapeshot took many o' them. We rode forays against the rest till their bodies filled the rolling plain. Horses wandered riderless. Men dying in the mud begged for *le coup de grâce*. By nightfall the dead were heaped upon each other till the difference in uniforms no longer mattered. Napoleon's armies were decimated. I received this."

Stewart withdrew a silver medal on a red and black ribbon from his left shirt pocket. On one side it displayed the Prince Regent's head and on the other Wellington's with an eagle and the words, "*Waterloo, June 18, 1815.*" Around the edge it was inscribed, "*Lieutenant W. Stewart, 15th King's Hussars.*"

The Waterloo Medal was still warm with the body heat of the man who'd won it. Having fought in the three greatest Indian battles of the fur trade -- the Arikara twice in 1823 and the Blackfeet this summer -- Sublette understood war. He handed the medal back respectfully. This was no cocksure Nathaniel Wyeth. This was a soldier.

"It's the only medal I carry to remind me of the iron discipline necessary to win any campaign. I take discipline like a man. I dish it out like a demon."

"Why'd Wellington go after Napoleon at Waterloo, so close to home? Isn't it better to string out yer opposition's supply lines before ya fight 'em?"

"Good commanders do that, because it's by the book. The great commander selects *the time, the terms, the terrain* for the battle. The more of three he dictates, the better his chances for victory. Attacking the foe's home ground changes everything. On far flung battle fields, your enemy can retreat, abandoning land for which he cares nothing. But fighting from his own doorway, he makes desperate decisions. That -- in a nutshell -- is why Wellington defeated Napoleon."

Sublette's eyes shone bright with new light.

Stewart grinned, "How about it? I'll even pay to ride along to Rendezvous! We'll become Lords of the Mountains together!"

"Be honored ta have ya in our spring caravan ta the Rockies Captain, but my partner Bobbie Campbell'll be in charge."

"Where'll you be?"

"Most likely in New York."

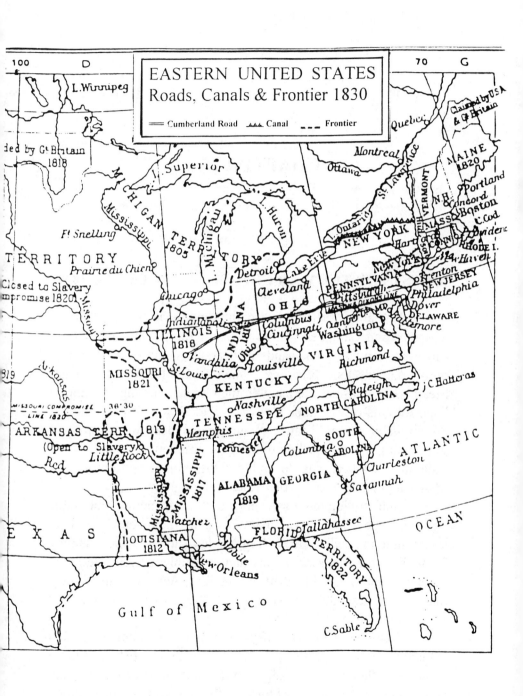

EASTERN UNITED STATES
Roads, Canals & Frontier 1830

═══ Cumberland Road ▲▲▲ Canal ▬ ▬ ▬ Frontier

100   D

70   G

L.Winnipeg

ded by G.Britain
1818

Superior

Ottawa

Montreal

Quebec

MAINE
1820

MICHIGAN

Mississippi

Ft Snelling

TERRITORY
1805

L. Michigan

L. Huron

S. Lawrence

VERMONT

NH

Portland
Concord
Boston
C.Cod

TERRITORY
Prairie du Chien

Closed to Slavery
Compromise 1820

Chicago

Detroit

L. Ontario

Cleveland

OHIO

NEW YORK

Lake Erie

New York

Hartford
MASS
CONN

RHODE I.

N.Haven
Providence

Indianapolis

Columbus

Pittsburgh

Wheeling

Baltimore

PENNSYLVANIA

Trenton
NEW JERSEY

Philadelphia
Dover
DELAWARE

ILLINOIS
1818

INDIANA

Ohio

Cincinnati

Washington
MD

819

Arkansas

Vandalia

St.Louis

Louisville

VIRGINIA

Richmond

MISSOURI
1821

KENTUCKY

Raleigh

C.Hatteras

MISSOURI COMPROMISE
LINE 1820

36°30

Nashville

NORTH CAROLINA

ARKANSAS TERR
(Open to Slavery)

819

TENNESSEE

Memphis

Tennessee

SOUTH
CAROLINA

Columbia

ATLANTIC

Red

Little Rock

Mississippi

MISSISSIPPI
1817

ALABAMA
1819

GEORGIA

Charleston

Savannah

E X A S

LOUISIANA
1812

Natchez

Mobile

FLORIDA
TERRITORY
1822

Tallahassee

OCEAN

New Orleans

Gulf of Mexico

C.Sable

CHAPTER 15

QUEST FOR THE WAR CHEST   DECEMBER 1832

William Sublette relished the din of the St. Louis levee where he and Campbell waited to board the steamboat for their trip east. Rowdy dock hands in bearskin coats muscled cargo onto the decks, bragging who'd be drunkest soonest. Steamboats smashed the air with their horns, cursing in calliope lingo for cuts-offs or dock blocking. Paddle wheels pounded the brown water white. Teamsters shouting, "Make way!" rammed their mules between milling passengers. Sublette wanted to dive right in -- to take charge and get the work done before the Mississippi froze over for the winter.

Sublette lugged a satchel of old newspapers about Astor and the American Fur Company. He eyed Bobbie Campbell, sweating in the chill air from dragging luggage. Bobbie was only 28 with a few thousand to his name. Sublette was five years older and mired in debt. With his millions, Astor was the richest man in America. Sublette laughed, "Bobbie, we're two bugs out to bag a grizzly b'ar!"

Campbell chortled, "If ya remember *The Scottish Chiefs* I loaned ya last spring, ya know after the British murdered William Wallace's wife, Wallace let down his blond tresses -- like yours -- cut off a handful of locks with his sword and proclaimed that God armeth the patriot's hand. Would ya like a wee haircut before we charge into battle?"

"Can't even afford a trim, Bobbie. We'll be lucky if Astor don't take our scalps!"

They boarded, got their state room and went on deck, crowding between the cigar smokers along the rail. Charging before the current, their steamer swept past Ste. Genevieve on the western bank, blowing Sublette's hair back from his shoulders.

"Feels like we're flyin' doon't it, Mr. S."

"We are. That artist George Catlin told the *Missouri Intelligencer* last July he rode the AFC steamer *Yellowstone* up to AFC's Fort Union on the Upper Missouri. He come back down a *hunnert miles a day*! I'm creeping 20 miles a day on the World's Smartest Mule Bluegrass whilst AFC's flying a hunnert a day with 10,000 buffalo tongues on board!"

"Lucien Fontenelle left Fort Union last June for the Pierre's Hole Rendezvous with AFC's supply caravan an' never got there at all! That's why we did all the business oop there."

"We can't count on Lucien swallering the cork every trip, Bobbie."

"The mon's dog even slurs his barks."

"I'm going below to study up on Astor, Bobbie."

About midnight, the steamer swung hard to port at Cairo, Illinois. The engine shuddered against the Ohio's current, shaking Sublette awake. He laced his fingers across his massive chest and let his memory meander back to his Grandpa Whitley's uphill fight on the Fourth of July in 1812. The old man gathered a thousand guests around his Liberty Pole and singed 'em with a hell fire speech to give 'em the guts to fight the British. Hecklers shouted the British had 900 warships to America's 12, but in the end Colonel Whitley shut them up yelling, "Now the freeborn sons of America must fight to preserve this land their fathers won with their blood. Americans will prove to the world that we have not only inherited liberty but the power and the will to maintain it!"

Colonel William Whitley died at the Battle of the Thames after slaying the great Chief Tecumseh. William knew Grandpa'd be proud of him now -- even if this hopeless fight killed the last family member bearing the old man's name.

William drifted off and slumbered till the steward rapped on their door at sunup.

Engines laboring, their steamer thundered up the Ohio, arriving on December 5th at Louisville, Kentucky. Huts, carriages and heaps of pig iron vied for space on the rickety dock. Sublette and Campbell supped ashore with their fur merchants Allison and Anderson. In spite of William's urge to bring up the coming donnybrook with AFC, he didn't. Neither did Campbell. But they did finesse the check letting the merchants buy their odd tasting fare.

They docked December 10th in heavy sleet at Wheeling on a narrow strip of land below the river bluffs. Its buildings, dingy with soft coal soot, huddled along two main streets paralleling the river. Their hotel was drafty, with occasional "gunshots" as it shrank in the cold that had Sublette sleepily pawing his long johns for his boot pistols.

Next morning they boarded a swaying stage that sickened Sublette. Campbell mused, "Do ya na find it queer that the first man ever to take wagons to the Rocky Mountains o'er hillocks a goat couldn't climb, kinna ride a stage coach doon the Cumberland Road wi'out getting seasick?"

Their stage rumbled through Uniontown, Pennsylvania and into Cumberland, Maryland. William found himself conquering his seasickness near the end of each leg of the journey and dreading reboarding for the next.

Drifting snow smoothed the road from Hagerstown, Maryland to Frederick, where William bought two tickets on the marvel of the age, the Baltimore and Ohio Railroad. Their car, deliberately designed like a stage coach, swayed and jerked along iron rails riveted to granite blocks for 73 miserable miles to Baltimore. Both viciously ill with *mal de mer*, they repaired to their rooms at the *Tavern Beltzhoover* without supper.

Boarding without breakfast, Sublette was pleasantly surprised by the gliding run of the Phoenix Line's heavy coach behind six pacing Friesians through the rolling farm lands of Maryland.

Arriving in the afternoon, they registered at the *Indian Queen Hotel*, a mere six blocks west of the nation's capitol, in time for a hot bath and shave before meeting General Ashley in its fashionable dining room.   Sublette concluded St. Louis had a lot to learn about how thick a carpet should be and how soft a seat could get before you died of pure joy.

General Ashley arrived punctually at 6:30 and ordered prime rib around, insisting they be his guests and mercifully saying nothing about their fashionless suits.

"Most kind o' you, General -- not only ta feed us, but ta sit with us, when everbody in here thinks we look like yer down-home hounddog."

"Bill, you misapprehend what a treat it is in this town to see real men instead of fop politicians whose association they possess far beyond their needs."

"Whatta ya think he meant by whatever he said, Bobbie?"

"The General's tellin' us that we're really not taken for the scavenger boozards we appear ta be, Mr. S."

Their rare prime ribs came on delicate china plates beside mashed potatoes dented with pools of brown gravy, candied carrots and pre-sliced bread.   They ate with a vengeance. General Ashley tacitly demonstrated how to dab their lips with a napkin every now and then, whether they needed it or not.

The General confided, "Ever since Andy got re-elected with the Little Magician -- Martin Van Buren -- as his Vice President, we've expected him to quit his deranged assaults on the U.S. Bank.   But Andy disappointed us, demanding that Congress withdraw its $10 million deposit of public funds and sell all its U.S. Bank stock. Congress didn't disappoint Andy. It refused. Andy ordered Secretary of the Treasury Duane to do it, but he refused. Now everybody's scratching their heads trying to remember who refused to do what first."

"You was fretting about civil war last time we talked, General. Where's that got to?" Sublette asked before sinking his startlingly white teeth into his third slice of yeasty bread.

"Southern states know Britain's about to outlaw slavery throughout the empire.   They think Congress will follow suit because of northern pressures from anti-slavery societies. Congress won't go that far, but it may not matter.   South Carolina's declared the U.S. Tariff on Textiles null and void. Andy's threatening to overturn their nullification with troops, making war imminent."

"You know we're here to git yer blessing fer our partnership and to see if you still wanta square off agin the American Fur Company."

"Should I tell you I already think your partnership's a sound move, or would you like to convince me of it?"

"No need to recook a roasted apple, General, but ya might wanta know the terms. Partnership'll be fer three years. We'll each put up $3,000. Go equal on everything. Firm name'll be Sublette & Campbell, doing business as the St. Louis Fur Company. Right, Bobbie?"

"Precisely, Mr. S."

"Now that you're partners, I think Bill oughta let you stop calling him Mister."

"Oh, but I like callin' him Mr. S. They always give him the check when we're doon with dinner."

"Gentlemen, when Astor finds out what you're up to, this partnership's a death pact. If you've the stomach for that, be in my office at 10:00 tomorrow. We'll go over where to buy on your own credit, how to bargain with each firm and the personal guarantees I'm willing to give on your debts with merchants I trust. I'll loan you my dossier on John Jacob Astor. If you're not there by 10:15, I'll assume you've regained your sanity and gone home."

"General, Bobbie an' me know how to say Thank You -- and we do. But you're gonna be in a snot-flying brawl once this gits going! Yer new family could git hurt. Sure you wanta risk getting them bloodied?"

"I've developed a taste for carnage in Congress. I'm in. All I require is don't drag my name into it if the liquor situation goes awry."

"Liquor situation?"

"I'll crawl out on your limb, but I won't shinny up the cross with you if you get caught with hard liquor in Indian country."

"Is trade liquor that dangerous?" Sublette asked.

"The *Washington Globe's* Andrew Jackson's mouthpiece. It's after Astor because he's backing the U.S. Bank. *Globe* charges that Astor gets Indians soused to defraud them. And incidentally, when the American Fur Company started handing out medals to the Indians with a bust of Astor like the British do with their Kings, the *Globe* dubbed him 'King Astor the Ghastly.' One of New York's Democrat papers demanded that Astor be guillotined so the medals'll be a perfect likeness."

William put his ham-sized hand over his heart. "We won't give up your name if we're dipped in brandy and set afire, but you know the fur trade won't work without alkyhol, General. You invented Rendezvous in '25."

Ashley flagged the waiter. "Bring a magnum of black label champagne on ice." The champagne arrived in a silver ice bucket big enough for a 50 pound beaver. The waiter popped the cork like a small caliber gunshot and brimmed their glasses.

"Gentlemen, *wine* is not prohibited by the 1832 Law or my Amendment and is therefore *legal* in Indian country. My toast -- may we all develop an insane belief in miracles, for we shall need millions of them to best John Jacob Astor at the game of greed."

CHAPTER 16

HITTING WHERE IT HURTS   WINTER 1832-33

William Sublette's room in Washington's *Indian Queen Hotel* was littered with newspapers and files on Astor's empire. William sprawled in his overstuffed chair wearing only his bearskin coat. Robert Campbell sat cross legged on the bed in his dress shirt with a red muffler around his neck. Their plan for attacking Astor's operations had to be perfected before they bought anything in the East.

William muttered, "Astor's cozy with Vice President Van Buren -- holds Senator Benton's halter rope an' owns Secretary Cass. But Andy Jackson hates Astor cause he's a U. S. Bank director an' tried ta derail Andy's re-election."

"Aye, an' Astor oons New York City's prime real estate. Has ships plyin' the China trade, business firms in world's big cities and a stranglehold oon the Oopper Missouri fur trade wi' his line o' forts. Astor's son William estimates their annual fur trade income at $500,000."

Sublette mulled over Captain Stewart's advice about picking the time, the terms and the terrain. "Astor's 70. He's midstream in handing command ta his son. Now's the time ta attack."

"Mister S, mah Scottish relatives are misers, but John Jacob Astor makes 'em look like trappers squanderin' ten years pay oon a night wi' a Hidatsa squaw! Wi' Astor everything is *mooney*--squeezin' men for *mooney* till the blude runs. The only way ta hurt Astor's ta make the mon see he's *losin' mooney*!"

Sublette nodded, "Inna mountains, we're grizzlies. Inna big city we're grub worms. Gotta make our fight in fur country. Astor's got nothing ta lose inna Rockies, but he's invested heavy in forting the Upper Missouri. We build a fort next ta every Astor fort, he's gonna lose money."

"Aye, but we better na mention the Oopper Missouri ta General Ashley now! He thinks we'll take Astor on in the Rockies where we know every rock."

Sublette laughed, "If anybody's ahead o' General Ashley, it's cause he wants 'em there. Let's dress an' pack!"

Uneasy in the city's strange noises, Sublette and Campbell boarded the stage back to Baltimore. They rode a steamboat into Chesapeake Bay. At Frenchtown they braved the Newcastle Railroad, rattling along the Delaware River to Newcastle. They ran shouting with their luggage to catch a steamer upriver to Philadelphia, arriving late in the day.

Robert Campbell'd visited his brother Hugh's home town before, but Sublette never had. T.W. Dyott's picturesque Glass Works on the Delaware was the most handsome factory he'd ever seen. After registering at the *Congress Hall Hotel*, they gawked around Philadelphia all evening. Spotless sidewalks lead to sturdy brick buildings with marble steps. Shiny-buttoned police patrolled the cobblestone streets. Side streets harbored four story brick homes. "Aye, and they have water closets in all their baths," Campbell marveled.

At U.S. Bank headquarters on Chestnut Street, Sublette mused, "Like a Greek temple you'd see in a book."

"Aye. A structure o' rare beauty -- built less than ten years agoo."

"Hard ta see Andy's corrupt monster when ya look at this Bank."

"Bad blude between President Jackson and Bank president Biddle. Biddle was President Monroe's darlin'. Biddle's made soospect loans ta Daniel Webster and other directors. Bank's printed millions in drafts for five and ten dollars payable to bearer. Jackson says the Bank's usurpin' government's right ta print currency."

"Let's hit the sheets, Bobbie."

Next morning they took cabs to Siter, Price & Co., Ferguson, Jones & Co. and Gill, Campbell & Co. All three companies wanted to do business, but nobody had three-point Mackinaw blankets, light flintlocks, scalping knives or beads and everybody wanted cash for gunpowder. Sublette fumed, "Philadelphia's beautiful, but you can't buy nothing here!"

"That's why there's a New York City, Mr. S! Short on looks. Loong on business!"

After a wretched stage ride, they registered in the *City Hotel.* Sublette asked, "Where's the refuse piled in New York City's streets we read about?"

The dapper clerk cracked, "Cholera's better'n soap! Cleaned up City Hall!"

Thanks to Ashley's guarantee, hardware dealers Wolfe, Spies & Clark sold them $4,000 worth of goods on credit.

Campbell returned to his brother's in Philadelphia to see what Hugh could do for them.

Sublette brought Riddle, Forsythe & Co. in to sell off their 1832 furs. Their man Danner not only talked like Jedediah Smith, he moved most of Sublette's Pittsburgh furs at over $4 a pound, and showed Sublette where to drink in New York City without getting his throat slit. Sublette asked Danner," Is New York all one big city?"

"No. Pastoral countryside upstate. Ought to barge up the Erie Canal. When you reach Steuben County, you'll think you're out west again! Comeliest women this side o' Paris."

"No time ta frolic. Gotta tie up loose ends here -- then I'm heading west ta find forts that need new neighbors."

*   *   *

William discovered doing business in the East was like hammering a nail in hardwood -- one lick wouldn't do it. He hit the same companies time and again. After checking into Philadelphia's *Congress Hall Hotel*, he met three comely sisters waiting in the lobby outside the dining room. He was taken by the shapely one with the amber eyes the others called Cathryn.

"You may call me Cat!" she purred from her plush lobby couch.

"An' you may call me Cutface Sublette!" he retorted, whooshing his 225 pounds into the leather couch beside her.

"You're obviously not of this world, Cutface Sublette. Is that a dueling scar on your chin?"

"Wild hog bit me when I's eight years old."

"Dueling scar's romantic," Cat whispered. "You must learn the art of the polite lie. What do you do, and where do you do it?"

Sublette flashed his very white teeth. "I'm a Lord o' the Shining Mountains. Spend my time being dev'lish clever an' trying to stay under all this yellow hair."

"Stay under your hair?"

"Blackfeet -- are dead set on lifting it."

Cat covered her sensual lips with her fan. "Isn't that novel? Whatever would they do with your hair?"

"They'd dangle my scalp on a lodgepole next to my little brother's, so's they have a matched set."

Cat's sisters aborted dinner. The plumpest grabbed Cat's hand, squeaking, "We must pack to leave on time for Baltimore in the morning!"

Sublette rose and kissed Cat's hand. It was the first time he'd tried that, and it wasn't bad -- even through the satin glove. Cat held the hand to her lips as she was dragged away.

William'd looked forward to Cat's company for dinner. The food was even tastier than at the *Indian Queen* in Washington, but the chairs at his table were plumb empty.

As he left the dining room biting a toothpick. Cat rose primly from the sofa and held out her delicate hand. He took it with two fingers and she led him, his heart hammering, along the first floor corridor. She unlocked her room, pulled his head down, extracted his toothpick and kissed him long and hard on the mouth. Cat nudged her door open with her foot. "You see Cutface, I don't really care if I'm late to Baltimore in the morning."

*   *   *

By the time Sublette arrived in Washington on January 29th, Robert Campbell was marshaling summer Rendezvous goods in Pittsburgh. Sublette read Washington Irving's book excerpt in the *Washington Globe* about a pack train Irving'd met last fall in western Missouri:

". . . *their long cavalcade stretched in single file for nearly half a mile. These mountaineers looked like banditti returning with plunder, their bold leader with his arm in a sling. On top of some of the packs perched several half-breed children of the Trappers. Seven of their number had fallen in combat with the Indians. . . .*"

William had read his exploits in St. Louis papers, but seeing these poetic words here by the little man who'd shared his chicken near Independence, warmed him through.

William reached the stable as Ashley returned from his morning ride. "General, mind if I curry that horse for ya? Smell o' fresh horse sweat puts me in mind o' the mountains."

"Groom can, but your face tells me your serious."

Sublette's huge hands kneaded the geldings chest, then his shoulders and barrel. "General, this horse's tight. Don't git rode enough. Be chewing his stall first thing ya know."

"Already is. I'll have the grooms ride him regularly."

"I'm kinda chewing my stall too, General. You been Down the Mountain since '26. How long's it take fore a man stops aching fer the high country?"

"Men like us won't live long enough to find out, Bill. Civilization will kill us off first."

"Mountain Men say a man shouldn't own more'n he kin carry. Mebbee they're right. When a man gets too much to carry, he stops owning things -- and them things starts owning him."

The General rested his arms on the fence rail with a far away look. "Remember when we wrestled those keelboats -- *Yellowstone Packet* and the *Rocky Mountains* -- up the Missouri in '23?" Ashley confided, "Sometimes a man needs to go back where he's been -- to find himself again."

Sublette flashed the General a dazzling smile, "You got the Mountain Fever worse'n me! Let's talk business. Our 1832 beaver's selling at $4 the pound, and we think we bought enough trade goods for Rendezvous."

"Buy more scarlet and blue cloth. They're fetching the highest trades on the Upper Missouri."

"Figured out where we're headed, have ya?"

"Only place to hit Astor's where it hurts, Bill. What about the keelboats?"

"They'll go 25 tons apiece and seem like a hunnert going up the Missouri. Let's eat. I gotta go back up ta New York."

Sublette skirted the ice blocking some inland water ways in early February, returning to New York to supervise shipping of his goods to St. Louis. The Camden and Amboy Railroad was open, so he puffed back to Philadelphia on the train. But the *Congress Hall Hotel* wasn't the same. As he walked past the room Cat'd had, a Jewish family filed out. Sublette's forlorn look was lost on them as their children scampered down the hall, leaving him so deathly alone.

On February 20th, Sublette penetrated Pittsburgh by stage coach and took a room at the *Griffiths Hotel*. It was a triangular city near the cliffs of the Monongahela River with steeples rising like picket fence tips above the leaden coal smoke.

Next morning he met Robert Riddle and signed papers for the two keelboats. Sublette was more at home on the keelboats than anywhere he'd been on the trip. He improvised rigging and stowed his accumulated goods aboard the well seasoned boats. Sublette attached towlines to the steamer *John Nelson*. At sundown on February 22nd the strange flotilla headed down the Ohio for Louisville.

At Louisville, William bought a ton of tobacco, 100 kegs of alcohol to fortify 25 kegs of legal wine and switched the keelboat's sodden hawsers to the *Chieftain*. Their trip to Cairo, Illinois was tame. The *Chieftain* swung hard to starboard and shuddered north against the Mississippi's current.

Winter still had March by the throat when Sublette docked in St. Louis on Andrew Jackson's Inauguration day. Elated to be home, William hired a crew of drunken roustabouts to moor his two keelboats.

He picked up a *Missouri Republican* on the way to the Greentree Tavern. Spreading the paper in the Greentree's cool gloom, he laughed at the line begrudging Jackson's re-election luck, asking, "Is Jackson found in the Old Testament or the New?"

William rued the day last July when he'd swore to brother Milt he'd make Astor's American Fur Company boys beg to divide the Rockies. "This newspaper oughta be asking 'Is William Sublette the biggest fool in the whole world -- or jist Missouri?' "

CHAPTER 17

BURNED ALIVE ON THE UPPER MISSOURI   SPRING 1833

William Sublette banged on Bobbie Campbell's door at St. Louis's *City Hotel*, yelling, "Even a blind hog gits a acorn once inna while!"

Campbell whipped his door open, "What?"

"See this draft fer $47,612.13 for the 1831 an' 1832 furs! I'm solvent agin!"

Campbell muttered, "A good omen! Now ya won't die broke on the Oopper Missouri!"

"I owe Ashley $32,500 and a little to Davie Jackson on the Santa Fe furs, but it's honey sweet ta be back in the black!"

"Grubbed up soom mooney mahself! Captain William Drummond Stewart showed the gentry he may be new ta St. Louis society, boot he's na new ta poker. Captain paid us $500 ta take him to Rendezvous. He says General William Henry Harrison'll pay us a thoosand ta take his son Dr. Harrison aloong for his health."

"Thought General Harrison's stomping grounds was up Ohio way."

"Aye, General Harrison says he may roon fer President when Andy Jackson's doon. Captain Stewart's his guest now."

"We oughta ask Captain Stewart ta bring Doc Harrison down here from Ohio."

"Aye, I have. And how's the keelboat riggin' business?"

"Be ready fer the Upper Missouri by middle o' April. I gotta meet Davie Jackson at Sulphur Springs. We're winding up our old partnerships since I got my money."

William saddled *Umentucken* in the hotel livery and pranced toward Sulphur Springs. He missed the World's Smartest Mule Bluegrass. Becoming respectable cost plenty. Bluegrass was pastured at Sulphur Springs. He'd scratch her ears and lie to her a little today.

Spring had been bound up by winter, but was escaping in bursts of wildflowers and whirring birds. Fluffy thunderheads castled upward. A damp wind rustled the bushes. Sublette thought it'd rain before he got to Sulphur Springs, but the thunder only made *Umentucken's* ears flick. Davie wasn't there yet.

Sublette got *Umentucken* stabled before round-bellied drops splatted on its rough shingles. Now that he had some cash, he'd roof the barn an' cabin.

Davie Jackson rolled up in a buggy, got out and the buggy left. Sublette grinned. Bluegrass would be going back to St. Louis tonight after all unless Davie's buggy returned.

Sublette bellered from the barn, "Go on inna cabin, Davie! I'm wrapping the partnership account books in my saddle blanket."

"Forget the books! Whatever you say's good enough fer me, Bill!"

Sublette wet-catted through the downpour into his cabin. Davie Jackson huddled on the driest part of the dirt floor with roof leaks plinking around him. Sublette was ready to b'ar hug his old friend, but Davie looked so poorly, he got him the oak chair with the bark on it. Sublette lit a candle, dragged his stool over and plopped on it. The tallow candle flickered in the wind piercing the cabin walls, ghosting yellow flashes across their faces.

Davie'd looked old when Sublette named Jackson Hole for him back in '26, but the ditches lining Davie's face had turned to canyons. "Davie, you bout 45 now?"

"Just turned 46 and look twice that old."

"Now yer bragging. Mountain Man never sees 50. How'd yer California mule deal turn out?"

"We left Sierra Ranch on the Santa Ana River last May with 600 mules and a hundred horses. Took us 12 days to ford the Colorado River below Yuma. Ewing Young turned 6½ bales of beaver over to us to smuggle through New Mexico. We stashed the beaver outside Santa Fe and did the monkey dance with the Mexicans over how many furs and mules we had till we bribed *Magistrado Chavez* with 10 mules."

"Crossed that feller's palm with 700 doubloons myself when we was down nere in '31. *Chavez* is like the Crows. He won't kill ya, cause he wants ya ta come back so's he kin steal from ya agin."

Jackson coughed hard, checked his lips with his fingers, then said, "Lost 47 mules and 16 horses to desert heat before we got to Fort Gibson in Arkansas Territory. Met an interesting little fellow there, Washington Irving."

"World's no bigger'n a pea. Met Irving myself near Independence. Read some clever lines he wrote about me inna *Washington Globe* couple months ago."

Jackson shifted his chair from under a persistent drip. "My TB got worse, but I got the mules, horses and beaver into St. Louis in February. Deeded my dead brother George's property back to his son. I'm in bad shape, but I'm better off than old Hugh Glass."

"What's old Hugh up to now?"

"Hugh had the hardest luck of any Mountain Man I ever knew. Remember when Ashley split our trapping parties after that peculiar war with the Arikaras in August of '23?"

"Sure, Davie. I went with Jedediah Smith, Ed Rose, Jim Clyman -- Tom Fitzpatrick -- mebbee Tom Eddy. You went with Major Henry, Hugh Glass, Johnson Gardner, Jim Bridger an' a couple other fellers."

"Right. Hugh got grizzly-ripped and left for dead. Bridger and Fitzgerald were left to watch over him till he died, but lit out when Hugh was still alive. Took Hugh's guns and food. Then old Hugh crawled 300 miles to Fort Kiowa and spent the next year tracking down Bridger and Fitzgerald. Well Hugh lived through that, but last winter the Arikaras finished what that sow grizzly started."

"Hugh dead?"

"Way I hear it, Hugh Glass, Ed Rose and a trapper named Menard were hunting grizzlies near Fort Cass on the

Upper Missouri.   Arikara ambushed all three.   Trappers got scalped, butchered and burned alive."

"Hate like hell hearing this about Hugh!   But Ed Rose swore to kill me in '24, an' tried it a time er two since.   How'd this story turn up?"

"Some German nobleman, Prince of Weid, got it from Johnson Gardner on a boat trip down the Missouri after the ice broke up."

"Prince o' Weid's dickering with Bobbie Campbell about taking an artist -- feller named Karl Bodmer -- out to the summer Rendezvous with our outfit.   I wanta ask this Prince bout Ed Rose.   May hafta send them Arikaras a *billet-döux* if they done Rose in."

"But that's not the end of it, Bill."

"Well, finish 'er off, Davie.   Ya got my tongue hung out like a winded hound."

"Prince says Gardner and 20 trappers tracked the Arikaras.   One night two Arikaras waltzed into Gardner's camp, trying to sell Hugh's powder horn and that pewter cross Hugh always wore.   Gardner's boys scalped and burned both Arikaras alive.   Gardner give Prince Wied an Arikara scalp.   Now those Arikaras'll never stop till they scalp and burn more Mountain Men alive!   Revenge is a wheel that never stops turning."

William got off his stool and stretched.   "Really makes a feller wonder why anybody'd be blind-mule-ignorant enuff to hit fer the Upper Missouri, don't it, Davie?"

CHAPTER 18

BLOOD MOON OVER RENDEZVOUS   SPRING-SUMMER 1833

The steamboat *Otto* bearing down on the wharf between Missouri's Lexington and Liberty Landing, towing two keelboats, fascinated Captain William Drummond Stewart. The *Otto's* chimney swirled smoke, and its foaming bow waves fanned through the foliage below the dock. He mused, "Seldom does a prosaic labor saving device fail to rob society of the poetic. The steamboat is the noblest exception."

Brawny deckhands tossed uncurling lines to men on the dock. Captain Stewart intercepted a wrist-thick hawser and snugged it to the dock with a copied knot. He was extracting a sharp fiber from his finger when big blonde Bill Sublette materialized on deck and shouted, "Captain Stewart, ask Bobbie Campbell ta send me 20 men ta unload these keelboats!"

Before Captain Stewart could speak, Campbell stormed past with a gang of men scaling the keelboats like pirates. Sublette catted down the steamer's gangway yelling, "Good ta have ya with us, Captain!" then hollered, "Bobbie, we got a change o' plans." Captain Stewart discreetly slipped away.

"What's that, Mr. S?"

"Here's yer manifest. After you unload yer $15,000 worth o' Rendezvous supplies off the forward keelboat, jury-rig the rudder and send it back to Drew at my warehouse in St. Louis. It crawfishes inna water. Tell Drew to fix it, then sell it. I'm going up the Missouri with the other keelboat behind the *Otto*."

"Overland party o' 45 men stands ready, Mr. S."

"Remember yer 125 kegs are *wine,* but pack 'em outa sight. Who's here besides our crew?"

"Ya saw Captain Stewart -- and a fine mon he is! General William Henry Harrison's son Dr. Benjamin Harrison *and flask* aloong wi' Fitz's boy, Friday the Arapaho."

"How'd it go with that German?"

"Prince Maximilian of Wied-Neuwied -- the mon's an *ologist* o' every variety. Speaks all languages fluently -- boot English! His mon Driedopple translates easy words and his artist friend Karl Bodmer helps with the hard ones. Prince has stoodied the Indians o' South America and wants to compare 'em wi' the aborigines o' North America. When ah told the Prince if he crossed the prairie wi' us, he cood be fightin' Indians instead o' stoodyin' 'em, he decided ta take AFC's steamboat *Yellowstone.*"

Sublette asked, "Did the Prince mention Hugh Glass an' Ed Rose gittin' scalped an' burnt alive?"

"Nah, boot yesterday we heard from a half breed John Gardner got skinned and cooked alive by the Arikaras. The Oopper Missouri's in an uprisin', Mr. S."

"How'd they know it was Gardner instead o' Rose?"

"They found scraps of an American Fur Company hoonting agreement Gardner signed wi' his X in July of last year."

As Sublette climbed the *Otto's* gangplank he yelled, "Man's gotta be careful what he eats up river -- could be a ole friend!"

*   *   *

After their cargo was off-loaded from the faulty keelboat, Campbell rounded up the mountain crew laced with greenhorns and guests. He gazed them quiet, then spoke loudly, "Each mon'll have three mules -- one ta ride and two wi' packs. No two mules're alike and every one is smarter'n you are. Treat 'em good and get there. Treat 'em bad and get nowhere."

Campbell pointed to the items laid out around a jenny mule. "Each mon'll receive equipage of two halters, one saddle, one saddle blanket, one bearskin ta coover the pack, one pack strap ta bind the pack and a bridle for his riding mule."

The men crowded in to see where Campbell was pointing. "Step back so all kin see. One o' the halters is dressed beef hide. The other halter's tarred rope. Tarred rope rein for each halter's 16 feet loong fer the trail and connects at night ta the iron loop on this two foot hard wood stake. Drive your stake deep and firm. Each mon losin' a mule will carry its burthen. All equipage and each item in your pack are charged oot ta ya now and booked in when we reach Rendezvous. Same routine if ya come back from Rendezvous wi' us. Ya'll be coomin' out o' yer blankets at four tomorrow morning. Those still here'll be ridin' ta *Rendezvous!*"

On May 7th Campbell was up at three. Though it was spring, he could see his breath as he did the nettlesome job of apportioning goods by lantern light with his small, spare, wiry clerk, Charles Larpenteur. They made separate mule pack piles in four rows of ten with a mixture of butcher knives, blankets, gunpowder, lead, pistols, beaver traps, woolen capotes, bacon, salt pork, tea, coffee, sugar, vermilion, beads, mirrors, hawk's bells, ribbons, awls, bright silk handkerchiefs and bolts of blue and scarlet cloth. "We'll set out the *wine* kegs after each man is here ta sign for 'em, Charles."

Larpenteur smiled in the darkness, *"Monsieur* Campbell, I have smelled these *wine* kegs of yours. I was born five miles from Fontainebleau in France. I know and cherish the grape. Vines producing that concoction would have left a smoking crater wider than the English Channel. What do you call your potent vintage?"

"Panther fizz *du maison.* Yer contract specifies oonder no circoomstances will ya groomble over hardships. Are ya groomblin'?"

"No, I'm merely intoxicated by your *wine's* enchanting *bouquet.*"

*   *   *

Campbell's caravan snaked across Kansas and Nebraska territories, driving 11 cattle and 20 sheep to the Platte. Captain Stewart took responsibility for Dr. Benjamin Harrison's well being in the austere circumstances of the trail. Dr. Harrison was sharp for one who kept his brain pickled with an endless supply of secret bottles.

As a former Royal Cavalry officer, the Captain couldn't stomach riding a mule. He rode ramrod straight on his spirited chestnut gelding with its ears permanently at attention. He eased beside Dr. Harrison's mule. "May I escort you across the Platte, Doctor?"

The tall emaciated Doctor turned his head like an owl. "If there's anything that brings on my need for moral support, it's the sight of a large body of water."

The Platte's spring flow had subsided to its usual shallow, muddy oozing. A few of the cattle and several sheep sucked up the putrid water. Ropes laid across their backs hazed them into the line of march.

Stewart made another gentlemanly effort to converse with Dr. Harrison. "Is it true your father's girding to run for the presidency?"

Dr. Harrison's sardonic smile showed sallow teeth. "If he were, I'd be the last person he'd tell. He deems me a blatherskite."

"I know your father was a Major General in the War of 1812, a War I seldom feel called upon to mention since my side lost, but have you had other family members in government?"

"My grandfather signed the Declaration of Independence. I'm the sixth of ten children, and I was a human being before demon rum turned me into the shambling wreck you see before you. It's not necessary to patronize me, just because you helped the General exile me from my usual haunts, Captain."

"I saw it more as arranging a gentleman's outing, Doctor. And please don't feel you have a monopoly on being at cross purposes with a family member. My elder brother John was sly enough to beat me through life's portal by a scant 14 months, so he could take all titles and estates upon my father's death. Now John and I would gladly behead each other, but great distances deny us that delight. I long to see John in his coffin that I may know where to spit and ready myself to exchange my gentile poverty for the boundless riches John's death will afford me!"

"May I offer you a drink, Captain Stewart?" the Doctor grinned, extending a dented silver flask with an heraldic *H* embossed on its shiny side.

"My pleasure!" Captain Stewart exclaimed and drained the flask.

"Don't worry, I keep its brother near and dear to my heart -- unlike yours!" Dr. Harrison laughed dryly and would have toppled from his mule but for Captain Stewart's quick grasp.

Dr. Harrison asked, "What do you think of your current King William?"

"I was most gratified by his initial ascendance to the throne, Doctor!"

"And how was that, sir?"

Well King William has been portrayed as a royal ninny because his head resembles a turnip with tufts of hair, but he was in his finest hour the morning King George the Fourth passed away in 1830. William was awakened, summoned into the corridor at five in the morning, told he'd become King and was asked if he wanted to commence plans for his coronation."

"Whatever did the fledgling King say, Captain?"

Captain Stewart mustered his haughtiest British accent. "Heaven's no. I'm going back to bed straight away. I've always wanted to sleep with the Queen!" And this time the Captain couldn't stop Harrison from tumbling off his mule.

*   *   *

William Sublette remembered his first time up the Missouri on Ashley's keelboat, *The Yellowstone Packet*, exactly ten years ago when it'd been hauled inch by inch by cordelle men on the banks. Now the steam-powered *Otto* towed William's keelboat a thousand times faster.

The *Otto* steamed past the mouth of the Platte, ascending into the Upper Missouri. The *Otto's* Captain James Hill, a crusty fellow who sucked noisily on his carved ivory pipe, peered through his smoke at Sublette. "Didja know all the great rivers of the fur trade rise within a hundred miles o' the Grand Teton in the Rockies?"

Sublette sipped his tin cup's bitter coffee and shook his huge blonde head.

American Fur Company's Missouri rises there. Rocky Mountain Fur Company's Green River has its head waters up there. Hudson's Bay Company works the Columbia's watershed that rises west o' Grand Teton. Santa Fe traders operate along the Arkansas and Rio Grande. Rivers is everythin' to the fur trade."

Sublette winked at the *Otto's* Captain.

"What's wrong with what I said?"

"It's all changing. American Fur Company better hitch itself up an' move over. Rocky Mountain Fur Company an' Sublette & Campbell are taking over the Upper Missouri."

"Now that's a pipe dream, young feller." He puffed out another cloud. "Recognize a pipe dream right off, cause I've had so many myself. The only thing mightier 'n the American Fur Company's the Missouri herself."

"Know the Missouri, do ya?"

"Been my first an' only wife. Mrs. Missouri rises at the head of Red Rock Creek -- some say Jefferson Fork. She trickles almost due north to the mouth of the Marias River where she runs wild through the Gates of the Mountains between them vertical cliffs. Then she tumbles 150 miles to the Great Falls -- 8 miles o' cataracts an' rapids -- the Lower Great Fall is called the Niagara of the West. About 37 miles further, she gits nice n' navigable and flaunts herself 2,285 miles to the Gulf o' Mexico."

"Aren't you having her swallow the Mississippi in nis pipe dream o' yours?"

"Well if ya take away her dirty laundry from the mouth o' the Mississippi south, then my old lady loses 1,276 miles, but bleeve me, Bud -- she kin spare it!" Captain Hill puffed quietly, then added, "You think you're up agin principled men here. You're not. The AFC'll do anything it takes to keep the Upper Missouri fur trade - absolutely anything."

At Bellevue in Nebraska territory, the *Otto* took on fresh supplies, then hummed and thumped north.

News of William Sublette's entry into the Upper Missouri beat the *Otto's* July 17th arrival at Fort Pierre where the Bad River empties into the Missouri in Dakota territory. William Laidlaw, the American Fur Company's surly agent, muttered, "All you'll do is drive up the price o' beaver and help the free trappers."

Having already dispatched his party to cut trees for his post near Fort Pierre, Sublette grinned at Laidlaw, "Nothing wrong with either o' them things. We'll jist build up stream o' you, so free trappers an' Indians'll see our place first."

Laidlaw bared his own big teeth. "We already done returned the favor. Lucien Fontenelle lit outa here with our supplies fer the Green River Rendezvous on the edge o' the spring thaw. You take a biscuit from AFC here, an' we clean yer plate at Rendezvous!"

"Last year Fontenelle never even made it to the Pierre's Hole Rendezvous. If ya listen close now, AFC'll hear Upper Missouri trees falling -- all the way to New York City!"

*   *   *

On the first of July, Robert Campbell dispatched Louis Vasquez ahead to find Fitzpatrick's camp on the Green River. Campbell's caravan moved up the Sweetwater River and over South Pass. Big German Henry Fraeb of the Rocky Mountain Fur Company met Campbell's caravan and guided it to the Rendezvous site on July 5th as the first supply outfit to reach Rendezvous.

About 50 lodges of Snake Indians and 300 trappers gathered around Fort Bonneville, built the previous August, but now standing abandoned.

Campbell assessed the fortification. It stood on a rise about 300 yards west of the Green River with a commanding view of the plains. Its 15 foot picket wall was set in the ground with rough hewn block houses at diagonal corners. It yearned to do business. Campbell yelled to Charles Larpenteur, "Set up our *wine* tent right there in the middle o' this fort and start selling it -- $5 a pint -- right now. What do they call this place, Charles?"

"Fort Nonsense. Very soon it will be Fort Insanity! And I'm not grumbling. I'm making a prophecy!"

Larpenteur's prophecy came true within the hour. Gleeful shouts, gunshots into the fort's empty bastions and fist fights at the gate followed like nothing the young Frenchman could have imagined before. Then it got rowdy.

In the midst of the saturnalian chaos, Tom Fitzpatrick approached his foundling Arapaho boy, Friday, who'd come out from St. Louis with Campbell. They looked at each other uncertainly, Tom with the white hair Friday had never seen, and Friday in his regular schoolboy clothes from the settlement. Fitz rushed to the boy, picked him up and hugged him. "Would ya be gettin' too smart to be seen with your old friend Tom?"

Tears streaming down his dark cheeks, Friday shook his head, "No sir. You are my father now, but how did you get old so fast?"

Fitz put his boy down and knelt beside him, "Jist from worryin' if I would get to see my boy here today!"

"Worry no more, sir. I am no longer called *Warshinum*. I am Friday Fitzpatrick in my school and at all places -- especially here in my heart."

They walked hand-in-hand through the reeling, screeching drunks toward the sparkling Green River, as serene and deep as the bond between them.

Moses "Black" Harris's hunting party came into Rendezvous on foot with seven packs of beaver and thirsts to go with twice that many pelts. Just under six feet, Moses was broad across the back and big in the arms, but lean in the legs. His mahogany skin made his teeth flash extra white, except for the gap where his upper left dog tooth was missing. He wore a badger skin cap with a sea captain's leather bill above his eyes, and his head was never still for a second.

Welcomed by wild drunks he'd known as trappers for over ten years, the grinning Negro Moses bellied up to the bar and told how the Arikaras had stolen his outfit's horses. A few believed that story because it was true, so Moses asked, "Hab ya ebbah tried -- argh -- to shoot one a dese Green Ribbah antelope?"

Nobody answered, so Moses went on, "Well sabe yo'self a bullet, boys! Dem Green Ribbah antelopes is de fasest tings alibe! I done shot at one las yeah -- argh -- by dem big trees. When I come tru deah dis mahnin mah bullet -- argh -- was still aftah dat antelope an it was losin ground!"

When his drunken friends fell to the ground in hysterical laughter, Moses drank their untended pints as fast as the antelope in his yarn.

On July 6th, Campbell set up trading, using 400% of his cost of goods as his retail price. Once trading got brisk, the prices would be raised with the demand. Horses thundering across the plain in boundryless races dampened early trading, but by noon most were too drunk to ride.

Dr. Harrison ogled the snot-flying drunks about him. He announced to no one in particular, "I can't say I truly understand the theory of this treatment for my alcoholism, but I'm deeply moved by the therapy."

Lurching trappers bearing beads, bright handkerchiefs and bolts of scarlet cloth wandered into the Snake village seeking feminine companionship. Twilight settled over the plain. The moon rose red as running blood, alarming the Shaman, who'd already had a vision of a mad wolf attacking from the forest.

Moses "Black" Harris tried to focus his eyes on the blood moon. He didn't like it. It was an omen. A chill iced his back as a nearby wolf howled louder than any Moses'd ever heard this close to a huge camp before.

CHAPTER 19

VILE LUCK OF WOLF CAMP   SUMMER 1833

Lucien Fontenelle's 60 man American Fur Company caravan trudged into the Green River Rendezvous confronting two ugly situations. Fontenelle dismissed the Shaman's vision that a mad wolf stalked the Rendezvous as Shoshone superstition. And he couldn't believe Campbell's outfit was already trading -- but it was. Fontenelle's only chance for business was to camp at Horse Creek and trade with different trappers.

Fontenelle's swarthy face grew darker as he drove his exhausted men toward Horse Creek. Arriving here late was the same vile luck that'd plagued him from birth. A hurricane had killed his parents and demolished their New Orleans plantation, orphaning him at eight.

Foul luck had dropped Lucien in the lap of his caustic Aunt, who pronounced him too sensitive to reach manhood. He fled her hostile house, but bad luck stuck to him like Satan's tail. Now 33, he'd squandered his life on the fur trade with nothing to show for it but an Omaha wife who wouldn't leave her people, offspring he didn't know and bottles he did.

At Horse Creek, Fontenelle told his men to camp while he rounded up trappers for trading. The men knew that meant they wouldn't see Lucien Fontenelle sober for days.

*　　　　*　　　　*

Reduced to traveling from Fort Vancouver to the Rendezvous with only two of his original men, Nathaniel Wyeth found safety with the Hudson's Bay Company brigade under Francis Ermatinger.

Unable to keep pace with HBC's trappers, Wyeth fell back with the Nez Percé drifting behind them. He wondered how these Indians could be so carefree in this cursed country. Wyeth's own luck had gone from bad to abysmal.

After the Pierre's Hole battle last year, Wyeth'd gone to Fort Vancouver, then on to the Pacific estuary with towering expectations for the ship he'd sent around the horn before leaving Boston in 1832. But the brig *Sultana* had struck a reef and sank with its cargo, its crew barely surviving in long boats.

Upon overtaking Ermatinger's HBC brigade again, the sweating Wyeth learned that American trappers were camped on the Salmon River. Hiking to the American camp, he found men lounging around their fire with no shirts -- a breach of decorum.

A stocky fellow in buckskins about 35 with a walrus mustache and an air of authority approached Wyeth, "I'm Captain Bonneville. How'd you get here?"

"I'm Nathaniel Jarvis Wyeth of Cambridge, Massachusetts," he answered gripping the Captain's strong hand."

"I meant how'd you reach our camp?"

"From Fort Vancouver with the Hudson's Bay people beyond that hill."

"Like to hear more about your journey with them. Won't you join us?"

"Of course!"

After Wyeth choked half-raw elk meat down with coffee that would have killed the elk, Captain Bonneville knelt beside him. The fire's embers popped glowing trails into the evening.

Wyeth asked, "Are we near the Rendezvous site?"

"It's not far."

"You sure, Captain?"

"I should be. I built the fort there."

Realizing Captain Bonneville was a man of substance who should be cultivated, Wyeth asked, "Long ago?"

"Last year, but I'd like to know the details of your trip."

"From Fort Vancouver?"

"Yes. How'd the British treat you?"

"Quite civilly. Dr. John McLoughlin's a consummate gentleman."

"How has Hudson's Bay Company consolidated their trapping territories?"

"I don't know. I'll gladly introduce you to Mr. Ermatinger who's in charge of HBC's fur brigade."

Annoyed by Wyeth's naiveté on gathering intelligence, Captain Bonneville replied, "Tomorrow perhaps. I'm going to turn in."

"Your accent intrigues me, Captain. Is it French?"

Pleased at somebody taking a personal interest in him, Bonneville smiled, "Suppressed -- but quite French. My name's a dead give away."

"What is it?"

"Benjamin Louis Eulalie Bonneville, born in trouble near Paris."

"Trouble?"

"My father was an anti-monarchist *journaliste*, living in the shadow of the gallows. Our situation grew untenable when Thomas Paine took up residence in our household, so we moved across the Atlantic to his home in New Rochelle, New York around 1803. My father joined us there a year before Thomas Paine died in 1809, leaving us much of the Paine estate."

"You have a military bearing."

"I'm a West Pointer. My French accent was rejuvenated in 1825 when the Marquis de Lafayette took me back to France for 18 months."

"When did you complete your Army service?"

"I'm still in. Just took leave from 1831 to this coming October, to reconnoiter the west and engage in the fur trade. We've been dogged by beastly luck from the beginning. We've been thwarted by other trapping companies, Indians and worked-out beaver streams. After a year's Herculean labors, we've amassed 23 packs of beaver -- less than 20 skins to the man."

Wyeth'd heard of a U. S. Army spy posing as a trapper. If this be him, he was none too circumspect. Perhaps Bonneville sought to make secrecy seem irrelevant by appearing overly candid. Bonneville was either dashedly clever or a fool.

"And your luck, Mr. Wyeth?"

"Loathsome, sir. My organization disintegrated. Yesterday, I found the bones of my employee George More with his empty powder horn. His skull was shattered, and so was I. It's devastating to hold the head of a man you knew when he had eyes and hair and dreams. Though my only crime was luring George More to these barbaric lands by insinuations of riches, I felt I was his murderer. I buried his bones fast as I could, but I will always carry them with me."

Not wishing to absorb another man's pain, Bonneville rose muttering, "We will reach Rendezvous by mid-July. Won't you join us?"

"Gladly."

*   *   *

On July 18th Captain Stewart rode up to the bower of branches he shared with George "Beauty" Holmes, an extraordinarily handsome fellow. The Captain was followed by a stunning Shoshone woman on a brown and white paint mare.

Captain Stewart had obviously favored the shapely Shoshone and her pony with every bauble to be bought at Rendezvous. A scarlet kerchief adorned her shiny braids. Blue ribbons festooned her buckskins, beads circled her neck and cheap rings sheathed all her lithe brown fingers. Her obsidian eyes stared icily. Silver hawk's bells jingled with every step of her horse. He asked, "How about sleeping outside tonight, Holmes while I entertain this nubile maiden?"

Holmes grumbled, "All them gewgaws don't make her no Guinevere, but I'll do it."

"My bride for the night and I thank you!" The Captain dismounted and lifted the Shoshone from her horse, savoring her softness before carrying her into the bower of pine bows.

Holmes dragged his blankets to a grassy nook and drifted off to sleep. By midnight the moon faded white. Dogs yapped -- then growled ferociously. Holmes rose on his elbows. The hulking wolf's hairy body flattened Holmes. Slobbery fangs ripped his face from his jaw to his ear.

Holmes shrieked and beat the beast with his fists. The wolf snarled, baring its fangs, its fiery amber eyes glowing. It bunched to spring again.

Men waving guns charged, but Captain Stewart yelled, "Don't fire! You'll hit each other!" A naked Stewart smashed the wolf with his shovel, stunning it momentarily before it darted into the shadows. "Get Dr. Harrison -- no matter his condition!"

Surprisingly sober, Dr. Harrison had been playing the Old Sledge card game with Moses "Black" Harris. "Captain, if the animal was mad, I can only clean his lacerations and stay by his side." The Doctor tended Holmes, while Moses "Black" Harris ripped his own new red shirt into bandages. The Doctor confided to Moses, "Before dawn, we must find the stone talisman in the Shaman's incantation. Modern medicine has no cure for this."

Captain Stewart returned in his pants on horseback. "I'll rouse the other camps!" But the drooling wolf flashed through the moonlight, blasting through the bushes, running without fatigue. By the time Captain Stewart's lathered mount labored the five miles to the American Fur Company encampment, the wolf had bitten nine men and a red bull and vanished.

Captain Stewart leaped from his wheezing horse, shouting, "Don't shoot. We mustn't injure more men!"

Lucien Fontenelle, clad only in a loin cloth, brandished his pistol in one hand and a feathered tomahawk in the other. Enraged, he ranted, "Vile whelp of hell -- you shall die by the hand of one of your own kind!" Fontenelle stormed into the darkness.

In moments, a shot boomed through a yelp. Fontenelle dragged the dead wolf by its tail into the fire light and cast it across the fire. He buried his tomahawk in the wolf's still brain and stalked through the stench of its burning fur toward his lodge without another word.

CHAPTER 20

POSTING THE UPPER MISSOURI   LATE JULY 1833

Building a dozen trading posts on the Upper Missouri before the fall freezes was a job for a surveyor, logger, carpenter, Indian fighter and magician. William Sublette was all of those every day. The American Fur Company hired his men away, got them too soused to work and fired shots into his new forts. But Sublette's toughest job was getting cast offs and renegades to do something foreign to their nature -- work. Every day was a new challenge.

Sublette gathered his dozen men in the chill dawn air beside the Missouri River at the Yellowstone's mouth. He pulled his buckskin shirt off. At 6'2" and 225 hard-muscle pounds Sublette was formidable. "Instead o' working on the fort today, we're gonna gamble!"

The scruffy men in their tattered buckskins grinned at one another suspiciously.

"We'll head up to that stand o' trees. We'll all pick a tree a foot thick, but me. I get two of 'em. When I make the first axe cut, you all go after your tree. Every man who fells his tree fore I drop both o' mine, wins $5 cash an' sits out the day at full pay. Any man I beat owes me five trees down before noon and a good day's work till dark."

"What about a man don't wanta gamble?" asked a bear sized brute with a fur patch over his eye.

"Me an' him'll have a fist fight."

"And if nobody wants ta gamble?" One-Eye barked.

Sublette scratched an "X" with his axe handle in the dirt. "That line starts right here. You wanta be first, One-Eye? Gotta tell ya my first punch's gonna close yer good one."

The men burst out laughing and slapped each other's backs. Everybody knew William Sublette's nickname from St. Charles, Missouri. A skinny boatman with a salt and pepper beard said, "*Constable One Punch*, you make wood cuttin' sound like a thing o' beauty and a joy forever. Grab yer axes boys!"

CHAPTER 21

A GENTLEMAN'S AGREEMENT   SUMMER 1833

On July 18th of a listless Rendezvous, Nathaniel Wyeth wrote to Francis Ermatinger of Hudson's Bay Company. After divulging his plans to probe the Upper Missouri where Sublette was building posts opposing American Fur Co., Wyeth closed, *"There is here a great majority of Scoundrels."* After reflecting on that phrase, Wyeth wondered if he was one of them.

Near Wyeth's tent, Edmund Christy and Fitzpatrick squatted in the humid grass. Christy said, "My dear departed sister Eliza urged me to follow the trail of her prosperous husband, General Ashley. Having seen the potential for profit in this fur business, I'm of a mind she was right. Let's form a new outfit -- call it The Rocky Mountain Fur Company & Christy."

Fitz eyed the St. Louis greenhorn warily. "What be your terms?"

"I've come into $6,607.82½ from another venture. I'd invest that into the new company."

Debt-ridden Fitzpatrick beamed, "RMF partners be meself, Milt Sublette, Jim Bridger, Henry Fraeb and Jean Gervais. Your handshake'll do till the papers be done."

"I'll want to trap the Snake River country."

"Plenty o' beaver on the Snake!" Grinning broadly, Fitz figured his 62 packs of furs to be worth around $21,000. Campbell'd haul them to St. Louis for 50¢ a pound. That'd cut RMF's gross to about $18,000 -- all owed to Bill Sublette. Beyond that, RMF'd still owe Sublette over $15,000. RMF's 55 man payroll had to be met with money it didn't have. Fitz had to break Sublette's choke hold on the Rocky Mountain Fur Co.

*   *   *

Hobbling worse than when Rendezvous fizzled out July 24th, Milt Sublette joined Campbell's mule caravan with Fitzpatrick, Wyeth and Captain Stewart. Milt couldn't believe his best friend Joe Meek had lit out for California with Joe

Walker. Maybe Joe'd taken a shine ta *Umentucken,* an' wasn't ready ta risk a killin' over the squaw. Maybe Joe Meek left with Walker just cause Steve Meek did. Lotta brothers stuck together. It was a sorry thing that his own brother Bill'd never asked Milt to be his partner. Bill Sublette'd live ta regret that.

Bobbie Campbell's caravan headed for the Bighorn river, skirting narrow canyons where Blackfeet had ambushed many a trapper. Arriving at the Bighorn, Campbell set his men to building Mandan bull boats to haul the Rendezvous furs to his meeting place with William Sublette on the Upper Missouri.

While Campbell's boys built the willow frames, sewing and tallowing their buffalo hide covers, Milt Sublette waited edgily in a swamp for Fitz and Wyeth. Long legged birds stilted the marsh grass beaking minnows and tadpoles.

As Fitz and Wyeth wended down the hill, Milt wondered if Fitz would go through with it. Milt stretched his leg out and took several hot gulps off his whiskey flask to cool the fire in his heel. Milt didn't look up. "I don't wanta read the contract, Nat. Jist tell me what it says -- leavin' off the frills."

"It bears today's date -- August 14th."

"Fergit the frills!"

"Milt, you and I'll select the goods in the East, then bring them to Rendezvous within 200 miles of the Trois Tetons by July 1, 1834. Rocky Mountain Fur pays my $3,000 cost of goods and $3,521 with beaver at $4 per pound. Agreement's void if Rocky Mountain Fur sells out or I can't get financing. Each party fulfills the bargain or forfeits $500."

"Say in nere it's ta be kept quiet?"

"No. This is a Gentleman's Agreement. I'm not ashamed of it."

"I am, but I'm signin' it." Fitz fumed. "Pacts o' this ilk are for back alleys in dark o' night."

Hearing frantic shouts, Fitz sprinted up the hummock with Wyeth scurrying behind him. Milt limped after them.

George Holmes, calf deep in the river, shrieked in his rabid madness, "Git away! I'll bite!" He tore his buckskins off, leapt about the icy water naked and clawed himself bloody. As Captain Stewart and the others watched helplessly, Holmes howled, then exploded from the water into the forest.

Captain Stewart groaned, "My remorse for my part in this shall never leave me. I owe Holmes the *coup de grâce.*" He grabbed his heavy Manton rifle, his shovel and trotted after him.

A veteran of bloody sabre battles, Captain Stewart was astonished at tears welling in his eyes. Of all the things he'd done in pursuit of debauchery, putting Holmes out of their bower while he pleasured himself with the squaw was the most heinous.

When he spied Holmes crouching in the brush, Stewart murmured, "Peace for you old friend," and exploded the man's skull with his Manton's massive bullet. His tears sank quickly into the black dirt as he buried the bloody hulk once called "Beauty" by admiring comrades.

*   *   *

Fitzpatrick watched the burdened bull boats skidding into the Bighorn's swirling waters. Fitz never understood how anything so flimsy could hold so much and work so well. Returning to his hunting party, Fitz was startled to see Captain Stewart among his 30 Rocky Mountain Fur men. "Sure now Captain, I thought you'd be gallivantin' back to St. Louis."

Captain Stewart replied, "I'll make meat for the trip with my rifle."

"Glad I am to have you and your fine gun, Captain."

Fitzpatrick and Stewart rode in silence at the head of the pack train. Not wishing to make camp and eat in the dark, Fitz halted on a plateau before five. Among the shadows swallowing the valley below, Fitz pointed out 40 lodges.

"What tribe?" Captain Stewart asked.

"We call them Crows. They call themselves Absaroka."

"We camping with them?"

"We be campin' here. I'll go down and smoke with the Chief before dark and see if their squaws are along. They're like us -- twice as wild if they've left their women ta home!"

Fitz selected a blue blanket with a small tear in one corner and some trade baubles for the Chief. He put Stewart in charge. "Not likely the Crow'll come up here except to steal our horses."

Friday pleaded with Fitz until the Irishman took the boy along. "If the Crows ask, you are a Creek."

"You have told me never to lie. I am Arapaho."

"Crows have no wars with eastern tribes. Their enemies among western tribes change from day to day. My boy, we call this a *livin'* lie."

"What is a *living* lie?"

Fitz smiled down at the bright black eyes in their honest little face, "That's a lie ya tell ta keep on *livin'*, Friday."

Fitz was alarmed when the Crow Chief refused to hand sign his own name even after he took Fitz's presents. Fitz signed to smoke with the Chief. There were no squaws. Something was wrong. Knowing the Crows made slaves of their prisoners, Fitz clasped Friday's thin shoulder. The Chief circled behind them, then kicked them into the darkness.

Stewart had posted sentries around the perimeter of Rocky Mountain Fur's camp, but 60 young Crow warriors surged into the camp from all sides before a shot could be fired. A pantherish Crow in his teens with a black face and pug tracks painted across his chest confronted the angry Captain. When Captain Stewart did not return hand signs, they lashed him to a tree with a rawhide rope. Hovering over the Captain, they slashed the air with their butcher knives. Stewart looked unflinchingly until the warriors spit in his face and left him to pillage the camp.

The whooping band kicked stew pots over, hissing the fires out, then slashed several of the tents. Loading RMF's beaver skins on the company's best horses, the Crows galloped howling into the night.

Making their way back to their RMF camp after their puzzling encounter with the Chief, Fitzpatrick and Friday were overrun by the Crow warriors.

Fitz hand signed to them, "Kill me if you have no choice, but do not hurt my son."

Fitz expected to die when the Crows pressed in upon him, but they knocked him down and stripped off his shirt. He crawled over Friday and shielded the boy as the warriors kicked and spat upon them.

Suddenly they vanished. Fitz asked, "Are you hurt, boy?"

"My body is not hurt by their women's blows and my spirit is not lame, for I told them no lies."

Fitz growled, "Run to our camp, boy. I have business with that black hearted Crow Chief."

Shirtless and unarmed, Fitz stalked into the Crow camp. He returned to the Chief's lodge where the whooping raiding party gathered to divide their plunder.

Furious, Fitz signed to the Chief, "I have many winters here and never see these Coyote ways by the great Absaroka nation. I give honor to your nation and receive it before your bad puppies are outside their mothers. Why is this evil put to me and my men?"

The Chief looked at Fitz with shame in his eyes.

The angry Irishman signed, "You stole our goods and shamed us for the American Fur men, did you not?"

The Chief nodded and gave the *Yes* sign by extending his right forefinger, moving it to the left and downward.

Fitz signed, "The Absaroka are not dogs of the American Fur men. Give our goods back." He showed the Chief the small RMF brands on the skin sides of the 43 beaver taken and pointed to himself. The Chief waved Fitzpatrick away. Rough hands grappled Fitz past the edge of the firelight.

Angry words zipped the air like flaming arrows between the Crows, then Fitz was thrown onto one of his horses. Sullen young Crows herded him back to his own camp. Reaching the perimeter, Fitz heard two rifles cock and yelled, "Don't fire!"

As Fitz dismounted in the darkness, rifles, beaver traps and a few shot pouches thumped to the ground around him. The surly Crows left them a dozen horses and most of their mules, then vanished.

Still enraged from his own Crow encounter, Captain Stewart stepped forward. "Why'd the Crows attack us?"

Fitz growled, "The American fur Company put 'em up ta all this. Indians treat a man well or they kill him. Spitting on a man be no part o' the savage mind. Spitting's for civilized people."

*   *   *

Campbell's bull boats swirled and darted down the Bighorn to the men's whoops and shouts. Lurching around a sharp bend, Campbell's bull boat capsized. Unable to swim, Campbell floundered under several times before the river's current swept him gasping onto a sand bar. With precious beaver packs sinking, Campbell gagged out the water, then shouted for help. Following boats beached and bull-dogged most of the beaver bales.

Campbell took stock of the disaster. He'd lost his rifle, saddle bags and four packs of beaver. He knelt in the gravelly sand and thanked merciful God for allowing him to breathe through the balance of the day. He began to reload his wet boat.

Crows suddenly surrounded Campbell on the sand bar. He finished reloading his boat while the Crows eyed him in awe, having seen him raised from the waters by the Great Spirit. Campbell signed, "The Great Spirit saved me and I go."

Campbell waved farewell to the Crows. The warriors did not wave back, nor tell Campbell the American Fur Company had a bounty on his head that the Great Spirit would not let them collect.

The bull boats reached the Yellowstone, then hurtled into the Missouri. landing near the end of August at William Sublette's camp two miles below the Yellowstone.

Campbell found William Sublette lying alone on the dirt floor in one of the huts, his face a near skull and his breath coming in racking wheezes. He raised up on one elbow. "Been a long summer, Bobbie."

Trying to mask his alarm, Campbell asked, "Did ya build a fort or two, Mister S?"

William coughed and spit out a mouthful of phlegm. "We built a fort north o' Fort Union, a Mandan trading house near Lisa's Fort, a scamp of a post near Fort Kiowa and started this one right next ta Fort Union. Built nine more forts Bobbie, but jist now I can't recollect where they are." Sublette flopped onto his back too exhausted to say more.

Campbell covered him with a blanket and uncorked his canteen. "Doona worry, Mr. S. Lost forts are easier to spy than hypocrites in the front pew."

CHAPTER 22

A GRAND MILESTONE   AUGUST 1833

Despite Henry Spalding's shattering of the door glass in Hudson, Ohio's Western Reserve College Church during his irate flight from Reverend Beriah Green's abolitionist declaration, it was not Henry Spalding who was expelled from the campus.

The Board required Henry to replace the door glass and write Reverend Green a letter of apology. Henry replaced the glass, but delayed his letter until after Green's departure for the abolitionist climes of Oneida Institute of Science and Industry.

Western Reserve students' consensus was that Henry's bold revolt had clinched Reverend Green's dismissal. Their surprise was that Green's abolitionist ally, Professor Elizur Wright, had not been sacked as well.

Since Henry Spalding didn't have Reverend Green's precise new address, he was forced to rip his apologetic letter into 84 pieces and drop them into the waste can at Western Reserve's printing plant. But Henry did mail a letter about Green. In his letter to fiancée Eliza Hart's parents, he wrote that Beriah Green had "about ruined this college" and would likely do the same at Oneida. Henry also confided that he was tutoring "Sister Eliza" in algebra and astronomy.

Henry's graduation day from Western Reserve arrived August 28, 1833. Attired in a new suit and high collar that cancelled his print shop earnings of 6¼¢ per hour for the past three months, Henry reached the podium to read his essay, "The Claims of the Heathen on American Churches."

He had no parents to perspire in the packed hall or clap for his eloquence, so his glance found his adoring Eliza. She radiated her blank look of piety that Henry cherished so. This graduation ceremony was the crowning achievement of his life.

Henry's collar seemed to have a screw that tightened as he began reading his essay in quavering words. He worked a finger inside his collar and stretched it, then launched once more into his treasured essay.

Pandemonium erupted! Henry realized his work was well crafted, even inspired, but this outcry surpassed all his dreams -- until he looked up. Portly Professor Elizur Wright, who'd survived at Western Reserve only through God's benign neglect, paraded down the aisle arm-in-arm with a Negro barber in a defiant pantomime of the graduation processional! The audience milled out of the hall in high dudgeon at such blasphemy.

A lesser orator would have faltered, but Henry Spalding read on -- to the occasional spirited applause of his sole listener, Eliza Hart. Her hand-claps ricocheted small echoes off the dark rafters of the vacant hall.

Realizing his audience lacked an essential participant, Henry paused. His imagination placed Narcissa Prentiss with her impious smile in the rear of Western Reserve's hall. At first Narcissa's apparition just sat. But Henry was no longer the pitiful bastard of Rice's school -- nor Narcissa's rejected suitor of pathetic Franklin Academy -- so he forced Narcissa to clap and cheer his grand milestone. Henry raised his stentorian voice and read on battering Narcissa with each powerful word, while soothing Eliza all the while.

When Henry Spalding exhausted his text, including the footnotes, he stepped down into Eliza's embrace -- banishing the chagrined Narcissa forever.

"Henry, you were transfixing in your premise and transcendental in your culmination!" Eliza screeched.

He kissed her forehead, trembling as he held her. His sense was that they should be married at once! He ferreted his degree from those on the platform and they strode triumphantly from the hall into the warm evening air.

The crickets chirped frenetically. The humid summer air hung heavy. At age 30 with his bachelor's degree clenched in his fist, Henry Spalding had overcome another insurmountable obstacle. This graduation assured Henry's acceptance into the Lane Theological Seminary of Cincinnati, Ohio. Eliza was beside him and life at Lane lay before them.

CHAPTER 23

CORN LIQUOR, MEDALS AND POLITICS   FALL 1833

Ice like brittle butterfly wings spanned the puddles on Sublette & Campbell's unfinished fort site below the mouth of the Yellowstone. Robert Campbell shattered a puddle's sheet ice with his boot and muttered, "Ah Christen thee Fort William in honor o' William Sublette."

Bundled in a woolly capote, Milt Sublette hobbled up to Campbell,"What're you up ta?" his misty breath hung like smoke.

"Ah'm goin' ta finish this fort. Ah hope you'll take your big brother back ta the settlements before he finishes killin' himself for yee."

Milt argued, "Bill's tole me he kin take care o' hisself since we was knee high to a lizard. I'm gonna let him!"

"Have ya forgot how ya started all this last year at Pierre's Hole? Ya goaded Mr. S into sayin' he'd make the American Fur boys beg ta divide the Rockies trappin' territory wi' ya. The mon's built thirteen forts on the Oopper Missouri this summer! He's coughin' blude. Kin ya na' take 'im home before we hafta poot the pennies oover his eyes?"

"Yer so damn worried, why donchu take him home, Bobbie?"

"AFC's Fort Union's joost oop the Missouri. It's AFC's bell cow. Ah moost finish Fort William and roon it till this fur war's doon. And Milton -- only mah friends call me *Bobbie*."

*   *   *

Nathaniel Wyeth had heard much, and believed little, about majestic Fort Union and it's "King," Kenneth McKenzie. He'd debunk these myths before returning to the settlements.

Fort Union squatted on the Missouri above the Yellowstone's mouth like a giant stone frog. Cumbrous cannon crouched on either side of its double gated entrance. Stone bastions stood in the corners of its picket-pole stockade walls.

It was indeed the most regal fort he'd ever seen -- rivaling Dr. John McLoughlin's palatial Fort Vancouver. Fort Union's interior was orderly -- except for a shed spewing smoke and strange rumblings that piqued Wyeth's curiosity.

Comparing Fort Union to the primitive huts he'd just left at Sublette & Campbell's embryonic Fort William made Wyeth sneer. Fort William was a larval insect under the nose of the world's fiercest frog. Though Sublette & Campbell would soon become Wyeth's open rivals, Fort Union's monstrous conceit made Wyeth fume.

Wyeth was hustled inside the biggest building by a uniformed official. A stately table stretched the length of the cavernous room. Sumptuously set, the table was bordered by stiff-backed men in formal coats sitting like surreal puppets in the candelabra's flickering glow.

A powerfully built man in his early thirties, wearing a white colonial wig and a uniform befitting a European Field Marshall, rose at the head of the table and lifted his wine glass. "I'm Kenneth McKenzie. You are my guest, Mr. Wyeth." His British accent seemed forced. Men scrambled to insert a chair for Wyeth where McKenzie pointed.

Wyeth resented being ordered to the table before he could wash his hands, but McKenzie's commanding mien allowed no nuances. The moment Wyeth sat, McKenzie plopped down and resumed a heated exchange with his clerks as if Wyeth'd vanished.

McKenzie eyed the stumpy man seated to his right. "Laidlaw, did our horses survive the Arikara attack or not?"

"The men excaped. Be that not enough, even if our horses were lost?"

"Damn the men! If the horses had been saved, it would have amounted to something!" McKenzie snorted. The stolid faces around the table shook their heads as one. His business concluded, McKenzie resurrected Wyeth from the grave of his indifference. "What brings you here, Nathaniel Wyeth of Boston, Massachusetts?"

"Cambridge, Massachusetts, sir," Wyeth corrected, forking a bite of aromatic buffalo meat to go with his thick white bread and steaming vegetables.

McKenzie snapped, "Boston -- Cambridge -- twaddle -- same as two dumplings on a platter. What do you want?"

"To trade my bullboats for a pirogue to sail down the Missouri to the settlements."

"If it's a good trade, I'll do it. Glad you have the sense to abandon those twerps below us on my river. American Fur Company's labored hard to make trading respectable on the Upper Missouri. Hundreds of our hunters probe the streams for beaver and the plains for bison. Thousands of Crow and Shoshone bring their peltry mighty distances to trade at Fort Union. No room here for gimcrack gypsies like Sublette & Campbell."

"I've heard you called King of the Missouri -- even Emperor of the West. Which do you prefer?"

McKenzie's laugh was humorless. "Neither. I'm King of the U.M.O.!"

"What's the U.M.O.?"

"The Upper Missouri Outfit, Mr. Wyeth." He hoisted his Madeira. His subordinates joined his unspoken toast to himself and his vast fiefdom. McKenzie glowered at Wyeth's wine glass and jerked his eyes upward until Wyeth raised his glass. Instead of the ritual sip, McKenzie and his men drained their glasses.

McKenzie wiped his thick lips with a linen napkin fluttering like a small ghost in the candle light. "These fools think history will respeak itself."

"I don't catch your drift, sir," Wyeth answered.

"When my Columbia Fur Company held sway over the Upper Missouri, the American Fur Company built posts adjacent to all of ours -- just like Sublette & Campbell are doing now. American Fur couldn't loosen our grip, so they bought Columbia Fur at a hearty profit to myself. Tell those fools, we will not buy their pitiful posts."

"Why not and end this fur war before everyone loses money?" Wyeth asked.

"This is why!" McKenzie sprang up, dashed his wine glass on the carpet and ground the shards under his boot heel.

Wyeth was incensed, but his curiosity would not let him depart the table till he got his maddening question answered. "You clearly have the means to pulverize them, but I beg you to satiate my inventor's curiosity about your smoke-belching building."

McKenzie chuckled, "The 1832 Law prohibits transportation of liquor into Indian Country, not *making* liquor in Indian Country. We buy maize from the Mandans and distill corn liquor by the barrel!"

Wyeth said, "If you had your glass, we'd surely toast your ingenuity, sir! In passing, what's that medallion hanging from your neck? Is it a bust of yourself?"

McKenzie snapped his fingers. A waiter chimed a new wineglass into his hand and stilled the crystal's ringing with iced wine. The King of the U.M.O. would not talk until his corn liquor inventiveness was duly toasted. "Obviously, the elderly gentleman on this medal is John Jacob Astor. We honor Indian chiefs with these medals just as the Hudson's Bay Company does with likenesses of its British Kings. We've used them to forge trading status with the Blackfeet tribe -- something no others have done."

"May I, sir?" Wyeth asked as he approached McKenzie.

McKenzie nodded and Wyeth examined the silver medal. A couple of inches across, it displayed the left profile of a beaky, scowling man with hair like Caesar's surrounded by the words *"THE PRESIDENT OF THE AMERICAN FUR COMPANY."*

"I imagine you've created quite a stir with these, sir -- quite a stir."

That afternoon, Wyeth traded his bullboats for a battered pirogue and sailed clumsily down the Missouri. He'd planned to sup at Sublette & Campbell's hovels, but recalled the wineglass under McKenzie's heel and thought better of it. Wyeth, did not however, think better of Kenneth McKenzie.

When Wyeth's 20 foot sailing canoe reached the U.S. Army's Fort Leavenworth in late September, he reported Fort Union's illicit distillery to the Colonel in charge, turning the officer's face crimson. The crimson swelled turgid when Wyeth confided that the American Fur Monarchy was awarding king-like Astor Medals to the Indians, usurping the governmental function of the United States.

Feeling far better about Kenneth McKenzie, Nathaniel Wyeth continued his trip to Boston. There he'd raise enough capital to give another domineering swell-head, William Sublette, his comeuppance -- if there was anything left after McKenzie finished with him. The West demanded a fresh hand at its helm, and Nathaniel Wyeth knew he was the man to provide it.

*   *   *

Maintaining a truce between bed-ridden Mr. S and his limping brother Milton, Robert Campbell spurred the crew into finishing Fort William. They cleared its 130' x 150' plot about 300 paces from the Missouri with a view of both the Missouri and the Yellowstone. They laid out plots for 10 houses, located a well site and commenced erection of an ice house.

William Sublette had been up for several days when skim-ice edged the Missouri. On his first voyage up this river on Ashley's keelboat in '23, he was sure the bullet hadn't been made that could kill him. Now he felt privileged to live through each coughing fit.

He hoped Bobbie could survive when winter froze the Upper Missouri into a glacier. William knew he couldn't. Milt walked like his leg was broke. William'd promised Mama Isabella on her deathbed in '22 he'd take care o' his brothers and sisters. He had to take Milt home to Sulphur Springs so they could get well.

With the Missouri turning to ice pudding, William boarded the keelboat with Milton and *Umentucken*. She was madder than a wet cat at being dragged to the settlements. William bunked in the main cabin. That night *Umentucken* sliced her palms and rubbed blood all over her face.

"Does that mean in Shoshone she's peeved?" William asked sour-eyed Milt.

"Means the next thing she cuts ain't gonna be hers," Milt said dourly.

Milton dragged *Umentucken* on deck, foisted her sack of belongings and four gold coins on her and dumped her at a trapper's shanty village. *Umentucken* stung Milt's face with the gold coins before she stormed into the snow-feathered mist. Milton hobbled below deck. He slumped on his bunk with his head in his hands, remembering how beautiful that wildcat was when she wasn't out of her mind.

On November 2nd, they docked the keelboat at Fort Leavenworth. Holed up below deck in a black mood, Milton wouldn't come ashore. So William waded drifting snow to the U.S. Army Commandant's quarters alone.

William slapped the snow off his floppy hat, and stood wheezing while a skinny Private looked for the Officer Of the Day. The orderly room's pot-bellied stove glowed orange, setting the roof to smoking around its bonking chimney stack.

The O.D. was inspecting the guard, and the Colonel was abed with the croup. Finally, the adjutant, who'd mustanged from the ranks, sauntered from the officers' quarters to the orderly room in his underwear top with his galluses hanging on either side. "Lieutenant Parsons. State yer business."

"I'm Bill Sublette. It's hot enough in here ta roast buffalo on the run."

The Lieutenant laid the stub of his right forefinger beside his nose. "Betchur gonna tell me McKenzie's makin' Blue Ruin outa broom corn at Fort Union."

"Well he is, but that isn't why I come ashore."

"You wanted ta leave yer liquor with me 'fore I hafta kick holes in yer boat lookin' fer it?"

Sublette's laugh lost itself in paroxysms of coughing. "Ole hound like you knows better! Who the hell smuggles liquor *down* river? I'm looking fer a Doctor ta git sumpthing fer my peemoany."

"Our Doctor fixes busted fingers like this stump. You don't wancher chest hacked off, you'll git back on yer scow an' drift south." He slapped Sublette on the back and poured him some scalding coffee from a decrepit pot. "Two things I gotta know, fore you go, Sublette."

"Asking me don't mean I'll tell ya."

"Howdja gitchur teeth so white?"

"Mama Isabella made me scrub 'em with salt and soda on a rag. Still do it now and agin. What's the other thing?"

"Didja know John Jacob Astor's dishin' out medals with his bust on 'em like Limeys do with their king?"

"No, but I figure I oughta git one!"

"Why's zat?"

"I'm gonna take his scalp, an' I wanna git used ta it gradual like!"

*   *   *

On November 5th, William keelboated past Independence, Missouri where wagons thick-wheeled swampy streets heading out onto the Santa Fe Trail. William wondered if Jedediah's ghost was out there on the Cimarron pining to come home. Unlikely, cause Jedediah was the wandering knight in buckskins -- a brother of the wind. No telling where he'd got to.

The keelboat docked near Lexington, like it had last spring. William got the Aull brothers to prepare pork and salt for shipping upriver to Bobbie Campbell when the ice broke up.

William sold buffalo robes at Arrow Rock, Jefferson City and St. Charles, reaching St. Louis by mid-November.

General Ashley'd left a message for William in St. Louis that beaver was bringing good prices in the East. The note added that their old compatriot Major Andrew Henry was found dead on his own front porch. Sublette had Drew's boys pack his furs in casks at his warehouse and ship them east, splitting them between Ashley and Tracy.

The carpenters had caulked the cabins at Sulphur Springs, but the cold still probed hidden holes. William's cough petered out, but Milt's heel stayed bigger'n a ham hock. Milt mooned over *Umentucken*, and near picked a fight with anybody who mentioned her. William changed the name of his black stallion from *Umentucken* to Hellfire, so her name wouldn't set Milt off agin -- and the meaning staid the same.

William's friend Dr. Bernard Farrar, physician to General William Clark, tended Milt's heel with smelly poultices and occasional gory lancings, but sat William down alone just after Thanksgiving. The kindly graying Doctor confided, "Milton's foot -- maybe up to his calf -- has to come off, Bill. Shall I wait till after Christmas?"

"Wait forever, Doc! Hang the cost! Jist save Milt's foot! Always was the fastest runner anybody ever saw. Gotta save it, Doc!" William bolted before Dr. Farrar could reason with him.

Gloom and snow suffocated Sulphur Springs until Moses "Black" Harris and his inseparable companion Dr. Benjamin Harrison rode in with expresses from Fitzpatrick for Milton and

General Ashley. While Moses padded silently about in his wet moccasins searching for William, Dr. Harrison delivered Fitzpatrick's letter to Milt.

Milt mused, "Doc, you look sober's a new preacher an' yer burnt blacker'n Mose. All the liquor go bad up in B'ar Country?"

Dr. Harrison grinned, "Moses says my singing off-key annoys him when we're crawling past the Pawnees like a pair of reptiles."

"Doc, what kin ya do fer a foot that looks snakebit, but ain't?"

"I'll take a look at it after I reacquaint myself with the notion of food."

"Cook'll scare you up sumpthin'. Come back soon as ya can, Doc."

Milton upped the lamp's wick and squinted at Fitz's letter. After complaining about being robbed by the Crows, the letter's unsteady hand went on, "I have been uneasy ever since we parted about our arrangements with Wyeth. However it may terminate well but still I dread it."

Milt growled, "Bill Sublette ain't no God to be bowed to. Wyeth's 1834 Rendezvous goods'll be cheaper'n Bill Sublette's, so RMF'll buy 'em!"

Moses "Black" Harris found old friend Bill Sublette entering neat numbers in the Sublette & Campbell ledgers. After swapping backslaps, Moses handed Bill the letter from Fitzpatrick to General Ashley. "Dis express -- argh -- come open on accident, but you best read it, Mista Bill."

Fitz's letter said the Crow Chief admitted robbing Fitz for the AFC.

William Sublette grinned, "AFC's making corn liquor in Indian Country, passing out medals like a foreign government an' now they done robbery. General Ashley'll have Astor dancing the Polka on the floor o' Congress."

CHAPTER 24

BATTLES IN THE EAST   WINTER 1833-34

Miserable weather, impassable stage routes and Milton's ailing leg tormented the Sublette brothers all the way to Philadelphia. Arriving bone tired, William put them up at the *Congress Hall Hotel*, scene of his magical tryst with Cat. Cat was gone and so was the Philadelphia that'd been so peaceful. A stomped-hornet's nest buzzed in its place -- streets bustling with harangues over slavery, the U.S. Bank debacle and Pennsylvania's funds being frittered away on turnpikes instead of commercial canals.

Still wondering why Milt'd made this rotten trip east, William asked, "Gonna try yer cane today, er should I gitcher crutch?"

Milton grunted, "Crutch'll do. Whatsa flashy room like iss costin' us?"

"Not costing you a nickel, Milt -- so think o' sumpthing else to grouse about."

"Ain't we touchy!"

"Milt -- " William choked off the ugly things he wanted to yell. "Let's git breakfast an' let the morning ease by. Bobbie Campbell's brother Hugh'll be over. Might ask us fer Christmas with his family 'fore we meet Ashley in Washington."

"We ain't chained together, Bill. Campbells ain't no friends o' mine. I'm headin' ta New York City ta see what I kin see."

"When ya leaving, Milt?"

"Right now." Milt lurched from the room, leaving only his sullen anger behind in the roiled silence.

William read a newspaper over his congealing eggs and side meat. Britain wasn't paying full value to owners of the empire's freed slaves -- only £20 apiece for the 78,000 slaves freed July 31, 1834. Slaves'd still serve six more years to ease economic pain.

William Lloyd Garrison's new National Anti-Slavery Society had a convention across town. William scanned Garrison's *Declaration of Sentiments*, then lowered the paper. He'd freed Negro slave Artemis twice -- once the day his mother died and two years ago at Sulphur Springs. The second time had got William sued, but old Henry Geyer'd backed slave owner Tom Berry outa the Courthouse with his countersuit.

But the slavery brawl wasn't over fer the country. General Ashley was right. War between Slave and Anti-Slave states was coiling to strike. It raised William's hackles to think of Americans massacring Americans -- to think of brothers butchering brothers. Would him and Milton be Cain and Abel? Milt's story about going to New York as a tourist stunk like maggoty fish. Was Milt in cahoots with the American Fur Company?

*   *   *

William spied Ashley strutting through the *Indian Queen's* bar with his chin out a foot as usual. "First time we've met in three years when I haven't owed ya money, General!"

"That's what I get for keeping a straight set of books, Bill!" General Ashley wisely ignored Sublette's mutilating hand shake, and they slipped onto lavish leather stools.

After confirming strong sales of Sublette's beaver and buffalo robes, the General ordered a brandy. "As you know, I got re-elected to the House in the fall. Missouri Senator Alex Buckner died of cholera right on the Senate floor. Governor Dunklin appointed Dr. Lewis Linn to fill Buckner's seat. Linn's a leech on Senator Benton, so American Fur Company's got another Senator."

William glimpsed his own tense face in the bar mirror and went poker-faced. "How's the AFC war going, General?"

"AFC's made bad blunders. Right after we strengthened the Indian Liquor law last year, Pierre Chouteau shipped 1,000 gallons up the Missouri and the Army confiscated it at Fort Leavenworth."

"I knew bout that."

"Secretary Cass smothered most of that scandal. Then old J.P. Cabanne, who was with AFC's shipment when it was seized, caught P.N. Leclerc with liquor and confiscated it. Marched Leclerc in chains to the Indian Agency at Bellevue. Leclerc got home, screamed to the newspapers and sued AFC. General Clark took testimony and sent it to Judge Herring, Indian Commissioner here in Washington. *Washington Globe* and other Jackson papers are mauling Astor."

"What about them Astor medals an' Fitzpatrick's letter bout the Crow robbery done fer AFC?"

Ashley held up his hand. "All in due course, Bill." The mustached bartender thought the General was ordering another round and brought them new brandies in globe goblets.

"The Astor medals had the political cartoonists doing nip-ups -- and Congress is outraged -- even though Cass had approved the medals. I read Fitzpatrick's letter in open session of the House. Papers called Astor a brigand -- said he should be brought before the bar of justice in chains like Leclerc. I've reported Leclerc's $9,200 judgment against AFC to the Commission. But I haven't mentioned AFC's biggest blunder"

Sublette checked his now grinning face in the bar mirror. "What's that?"

"McKenzie's corn liquor still at Fort Union. McKenzie, who styles himself *King of the U.M.O.* wrote Judge Herring that the distillery was only intended to promote the cause of botany! McKenzie admitted Fitzpatrick's 43 *robbed* beaver skins with RMF brands turned up at Fort Cass and will give them back -- *if Fitzpatrick pays for them!* Newspapers went berserk. AFC's Chouteau assured the Indian Commissioner that McKenzie's being exiled to Europe and that no cause of complaint against the company shall ever exist again."

Sublette's guffaws turned heads in the bar to see who the bumpkin was.

"Putrid publicity doesn't mean Astor's going broke -- or giving up AFC's fight with you. He's still the richest man in the U. States."

"Agreed, but I read everything you give me. When this ole German's cornered, his weapon o' choice is money. Bought out ever'body who bulldogged him."

"Could be, but nothing's written about dead men dumped at the end of some trail. If there was ever a time to negotiate, this is it."

"Will Secretary Cass be able ta sweep all Astor's troubles under the rug?"

"Eventually. Cass is sweeping away."

"What's Cass's first name?"

"Lewis."

"With that $35,000 bribe you say he got from Astor, his first name oughta be *John*."

"Why's that, Bill?"

"Most fellers named John is called *Jack*."

"I don't get it, Bill."

"Jist think on it. Even if ya don't git my jokes, I'm plumb pleased yer on my side.   After Christmas at Hugh Campbell's place, I'm gonna sidle up ta New York an' peddle some barely broke-in forts.

"Watch yourself!   Astor could buy and sell you ten thousand times."

"Only happens to Negroes nowadays, General -- an' even that's gonna stop. William Lloyd Garrison's not gonna put up with it. Neither's this country."

*   *   *

Nathaniel Wyeth'd just returned to the icy streets from the cozy Boston offices of Messrs. Tucker and Williams where he'd induced Henry Hall to finance his 1834 Rendezvous Contract with Rocky Mountain Fur Company and other ventures. At first, Hall'd given Wyeth the same story everyone had -- they'd get back to him.

Wyeth slipped his freezing hands under his armpits. Carriage should have been waiting on the cobblestones, but wasn't. You couldn't count on people these days. Christmas carolers in red woolen caps and gaudy mufflers had stopped down the street to sing of glad tidings. Wyeth's tidings upon returning home in November had been anything but glad.

Disaffected members of Wyeth's original expedition had gone public. His witless cousin John Wyeth had published *Oregon; or a Short History of a Long Journey* in which he derided Nathaniel's ability to lead an expedition. No doubt John was manipulated by Dr. Benjamin Waterhouse, whose sole aim in life was to slander schemes for western migration. Henry Hall had handed this odious opus to him a half hour ago. Wyeth recalled characterizing his kinsman's book as "little lies told for gain." Hall'd liked that enough to proceed with their deal.

They'd signed papers organizing the Columbia River Fishing & Trading Company and deposited the investors' $25,000 and $2,500 of Wyeth's own money in the new company's Boston bank.

Nathaniel met Milt Sublette in Boston, then went to New York. Together they chose the goods Wyeth would need to fulfill his contract with Rocky Mountain Fur Company at the 1834 Rendezvous.

Nathaniel hired Captain James Lambert to command the brig *May Dacre* for its voyage around the horn to the Columbia River's Pacific estuary in time for the 1834 salmon season. Wyeth dismissed Milton's reminder that Captain Lambert was the same man who'd lost the *Sultana* Wyeth sent on the same route. Wyeth and Milton picked out 20 men for his land expedition to Rendezvous in the spring.

Wyeth knew the fur trade was out there just waiting for the conqueror with guts enough to seize it all. Wyeth realized he was that man and dreamt of his next homecoming to crowds and fanfare.

*   *   *

On January 22, 1834 backwoodsman Bill Sublette was admitted to the American Fur Company's New York City board room of polished walnut and brass. John Jacob Astor's 40 year old stoop-shouldered son William B. Astor, accomplished monopolist and second richest man in America, headed the AFC contingent of eight other financiers.

Sublette asked, "Where's the boss?"

William B. Astor growled, "My father's in Europe, so I'm boss. Let's get down to business."

Sublette's eyes did not betray the panic in his gut. Stripped of all his plans designed to beat ole man Astor, he'd have to bare-knuckle it with nine strangers till he plain, flat knocked the slobber outa all their heads. "Fine. I got thirteen fur posts on the Upper Missouri ya don't want in yer lap. Yer losing business an' they're costing ya money. Yer paying $12 a pound fer beaver. That's three --maybe four -- times what you kin sell them plews for here in New York. My posts're fer sale at the right price, if AFC gits outa the Rockies."

"Gets out of the Rockies? You propose we buy posts we don't want and we still get out of the Rockies?" the squinty-eyed William B. Astor asked unemotionally.

"Right."

"Why don't you get out of here?" William B. Astor rasped.

"Come a thousand miles ta talk. Ya want me outa here in two minutes, you throw me out. Nine o' you plush-butted sow-bellies oughta be up ta tossing out one ole boy from Missouri."

William B. Astor clicked open a box inlaid with rainbow mother of pearl at his elbow. He extracted a chrome plated pistol, dropped it noisily on the polished hardwood and muttered, "One New York .45 is all it takes. Get out, Sublette."

Sublette leaned forward and pulled both his boot pistols. He aimed them under the table at William B. Astor's paunch. Sublette grinned, showing dazzling teeth. He cocked one of his Hawken pistols, then the other. "You put one finger on nat fancy paper weight, yer gonna have three belly buttons. Tell yer boys to bust out them pens an' git ta ciphering. Business'll be done here, er you won't be around ta brag why it weren't."

Sublette had each of his 13 fort's building costs itemized on a separate sheet. Since they were going businesses, he demanded three times their original cost as a selling price. By ten o'clock that night, many alternatives had been explored and all mention of shootings had dissipated. They agreed to meet at nine the following morning.

Sublette's razor'd been left at Hugh Campbell's, so bright blonde stubble covered his face through the second day of haggling.

The stubble fit the hairy situation, so Sublette gave up all notions of shaving the third day. They got close to a deal around noon, but the American Fur men pulled back. The nine men took turns haggling with Sublette over every penny of his recorded costs for each fort, but none had the guts to call him a liar.

Sublette realized they were playing him like a fish, so on the fourth day, he brought a bed roll and some jerky. He dozed on their big leather couch that night till he heard voices in the hall and saw light flickering under the door.

Three brawny roustabouts tip-toed into the board room and bunched in the dark near the couch. Sublette, sitting cross-legged in his undershorts on the board room table, growled to the man still outside, "Bring that lantern in here, Suzy." As the lantern light flickered over the men with clubs poised around the couch, Sublette stabbed his foot- long bone handled knife into the parqueted table, then leveled his boot pistols at the intruders. "How many o' you boys're gonna be at work inna morning?"

The men peered at Sublette's massive muscular body, the murder in his eyes and scrambled out the door.

The fifth morning, Sublette put only his pants on and waited till one of Astor's financiers appeared in spotless clothes. "Tell Astor and the boys ta git in here."

When they filed in, Sublette grinned, "Me an' the girls had a great shindig here last night, but I lost my sense o' humor. Yer already in bad odor with the gov'ment an' crucified by the press. Them notes I send out ever' day tell Congressman Ashley how things're going. Agreement'll be made, er I'm gonna lay myself open with this b'ar knife an' git the press up here ta show 'em what you done ta me."

William B. Astor muttered, "Your stone age behavior's amusing, but will avail you nothing." With that disclaimer, negotiations got serious. Sublette refused to wear a shirt by day, camped in the board room by night and his bathless body grew gamier as the days crept by.

On February 1, 1834 a bearded William Sublette and a limp William B. Astor signed an agreement selling AFC all the Upper Missouri Sublette & Campbell posts at two and a half times their original cost, a handsome profit. The American Fur

Company also agreed to refrain from all fur operations in the Rocky Mountains for one year.

There were no handshakes, but William B. Astor said, "I demand two more things."

"Ya wanta dicker another fortnight?" Sublette asked in annoyance.

"Leave your knife stuck through our table, as an example of tenacious negotiation for our executives."

"What else?"

"Your word you'll take a bath down the hall before you leave, so civilized people won't think New York's got *Corporation Pie* back again."

"Trade ya both them things fer yer answer ta one question."

"What's that?"

"Is yer middle name really Backhouse?"

William B. Astor nodded in disgust.

*   *   *

William Sublette left his Agreement at Ashley's office in Washington, then returned to Philadelphia and slept three days straight on the top floor of the *Congress Hall Hotel.* An odd note came from General Ashley:

"I've christened your AFC agreement - Bill's Miracle! It looks like the partitioning of Poland.

I've just heard something that makes me think you should read the last line of Micah 7:6 in the Good Book."

On February 13th, Milton, using only his cane instead of his crutch, rejoined William at the hotel. Surprised at Milton's boyish mood, William asked, "Get medical treatment?"

Milt answered, "Right nice trip. How'd yers go?"

"Sold all our posts to AFC an' they agreed to keep out of the Rockies fer a year."

"One year? Hell, that's one trappin' season, Bill. What good's that gonna do me an' the Rocky Mountain Fur Company?"

CHAPTER 25

SPEAK FOR YOURSELF, JANE SPRING 1834

Dr. Marcus Whitman listened raptly to Reverend Parker's sermon at the Presbyterian revival meeting on Wheeler, New York's soggy village green. Lively for a man in his mid-fifties, Parker had started his sermon an hour ago, skinny arms at the sides of his great coat, his purse-lipped face pallid under his stove-pipe beaver hat. Parker'd spoken softly of a kind God that nurtured his children with infinite love.

"But then God discovered your hideous shortcomings!" Parker's voice shrilled, "God is sickened by your greed, your ceaseless animal desires of the flesh -- and -- your stingy offerings to pay for God's Work!" His veins swelled to ropes as he shrieked, "It was God's own whip -- the dread cholera lashing the unworthiest among you to death!!" Finally, he hugged himself feebly as he recounted, "And in the end a most merciful God saved you from the blue-faced death of sin!"

As Parker's voice fell to a whisper, Dr. Marcus Whitman and a dozen others dashed forward to kneel in the melting snow around the perspiring old man. Reverend Parker opened one eye and asked, "Marcus, does this mean you're going with me to Oregon?"

Tears streaking his cheeks, Marcus replied in his deep baritone, "It does if the American Board'll have me."

After Reverend Parker's stove-pipe hat was a quarter-full of money, he leaned over Marcus and whispered, "Reverend Strong will write the American Board today, urging them to dispatch you west with me."

As a piercing spring wind whipped them with winter's memories, the steel-eyed Reverend Strong got Marcus's assurances that his chronic spleen ailment was mended enough to make the journey. Strong agreed to report on his progress to Marcus at the revival in the Prentiss home at Amity, New York. Not one to abandon his fate to others, Marcus launched his own letter to the American Board, advising that he'd resumed his active practice after developing skill in treating cholera and that he wished to do the Lord's Work in Oregon.

For some baffling reason, the Board wanted to send Marcus to the Marquesa Islands. Marcus wrote back he feared the effect of the tropical climate on a man accustomed to brisk autumns and frigid winters.

The American Board's reply raised again the specter of Marcus's missing wife. Marcus admitted in his response that he presently had no arrangement for marriage.

*   *   *

Although he was only 41 and suffering from a chronic, racking cough, Dr. Wilbur Fisk was admittedly the most powerful Methodist in New England. Each day, upon returning to his sanctum in Middletown, Connecticut from presidential duties at Wesleyan University, the bespectacled Fisk ritually read newspapers and periodicals.

Fisk knew the Nez Percé had requested "black gowns" from the Methodists, unaware that Methodists were not the Catholics who wore those raiments. He worried that these simple Indians would inadvertently bring down a swarm of Catholic Priests upon their naive heads. Now the *Christian Advocate* announced that the Presbyterians' Parker was mounting an expedition to the heathen tribes in Oregon.

Rankled, Dr. Fisk knew the Methodists must be *first* in the West, as they were in the East. Wilbur Fisk would not stand idle while Presbyterians picked the plums, relegating refuse to the Methodists! Reverend Fisk's tiny, graying wife wearing her permanent smile, tip-toed in with more newspapers. Wilbur Fisk rose, and thrust open the double stained glass windows, coughing as the wind whisked papers off his desk, and announced, "My dear, the Methodists shall have the *first* mission in Oregon."

Latching the window, she muttered "Must stay out of drafts with that cough." She returned wind-snatched papers to his desk. "Dear, your health's far too delicate for such an ordeal as that trip."

"True, but my former student, Jason Lee can go. He's barely 30 with the body of a bear and a black beard that would be Lucifer's were Jason not so pure in heart and deed."

"Pure in heart or not, you know Jason's a Canadian who's already applied to the British Board for missionary duty."

"Providence is moving a finger here! I'll write Jason Lee a letter and have it posted within the hour."

Without mentioning his newspaper source, Dr. Fisk's letter confided that New Englander Nathaniel Wyeth was outfitting his second expedition to Oregon. Fisk urged Jason Lee to accept immediate Methodist ordination and join Wyeth's troop. He reassured Lee the unstinting Methodists would raise the trip money with rousing revivals. He closed with the exhortation:

"Our movement is the most potent intellectual force ever liberated in the U. States. A mixture of Methodist religion with democracy and frontier spirit propels us West with explosive force. Jason, you must join us. Our time is upon us!"

*   *   *

Dr. Marcus Whitman found the Prentiss family's imposing clapboard home in Amity, New York awesome as he rode past the structure to put up his horse in their stable. The wiggle in the front curtains convinced him to wait with his snorting, stomping horse instead of barging into the Prentiss barn without knowing their wishes.

Marcus perceived a lovely vision of womanhood in her early twenties descending the back stairs with a smile that warmed him head to toe. She was tall, blond, well rounded and dressed in a bright blue gown that caressed the ground around her. Her graceful walk rippled her skirt like a gentle wind. She extended her hand, forcing Marcus to swipe his sweaty palm down his rough pants.

She made the stranger out to be about six feet, husky and shaggy like their Irish Wolfhound *Shamrock,* who'd died the day after Christmas. The stranger had *Shamrock's* humped nose and powerful stance. He had the brute body of a logger, but his deep blue eyes were gentle with a respectfully lowered gaze. "And who would you be, sir?" she asked melodiously.

"Dr. Marcus Whitman here for the revival," he replied in a voice so deep it sounded like it came from the Prentiss well.

Their hands clasped gently for a moment that was over too soon for him. She fluttered her eyelids like butterfly wings and said, "Well, you're several hours early, Doctor. You can put your horse in the second stall on the left."

"Thanks, but who are you?"

"I'm Jane Prentiss."

Marcus unlatched the barn door and led his heavily shod horse clopping across the planked floor. He marveled at the barn's massive beams so perfectly pegged together. "Never seen such stout construction in an out-building," he remarked as he unsaddled his horse. He toweled off his horse's wet back, then began to curry its moist hide.

"Now you see why we had to move from Prattsburg, Doctor."

"Don't follow you, Miss."

"My father, Judge Prentiss, builds structures that endure eternally. His indestructible buildings eventually run him out of town to find work -- a sort of perpetual self exile."

"Went from Wheeler to treat Prattsburg patients. Always wondered why their wooden houses had the feel of stone."

"Aren't you the Doctor who's becoming a missionary to the heathens in the West?"

Amazed at how fast news traveled between small towns, Marcus muttered, "I'm hoping to. But the American Board wants married missionaries."

"That has my elder sister Narcissa frustrated. She fancies serving the Lord in the Far West, but the Board's bypassed her because she's unmarried."

"Is Narcissa here?" he asked, removing his new Bible from his saddle bag.

Jane Prentiss entered the barn from the dazzling sunlight, her rustling skirts stirring the flecks of bran on the barn's floor. As she spoke, her eyelids fluttered momentarily. "No she teaches at Butler, and their term's in session. You'd enjoy

Narcissa.   She smiles too much for piety's sake, but she's a delight and honest to a fault.   She uses the truth like my father uses lumber."

Marcus finished rubbing down his horse and draped the towel over the stall.   If this Narcissa finagled her sister into making these bold overtures, Narcissa must be mud ugly.

Jane took the Bible from Marcus's hand and said, "Let me favor you with Narcissa's most treasured verse, *Isaiah* 55:12: *"For ye shall go out with joy, and be led forth with peace: the mountains and the hills shall break forth before you into singing, and all the trees of the field shall clap their hands."*

Touched by the verse's singing prophecy, Marcus asked, "Does Narcissa sing?"

"Oh she sings," Jane laughed at some private joke. "Perhaps you'd like to hear her?"

"Perhaps, but mannerless as I be," Marcus met her gaze, "I hafta ask, why don't you speak for yourself, Jane?"

CHAPTER 26

FUR COMPANY FUNERALS   APRIL 1834

In spite of the slavery crisis in the East, Andy Jackson's war with the U.S. Bank and South Carolina's Tariff war with Andy Jackson, St. Louis seemed to William Sublette to wear the garland of prosperity.

Business in St. Louie was done blood rare with a go to hell and a fiddledeedee. Dozens of steamboats bobbed on their hawser lines, eager to move cargo. William could tell their cargoes from how low they rode in the Mississippi. Foods and bar lead seemed to be the mainstays today.

Traders, boatmen and Indians mingled in muddy streets where ragamuffins floated toy boats in puddles. Settlers ganged the land office, while well dressed locals pretended not to smell dead animals rotting in gutters. Western parties outfitted with leather that was still light tan hauled overloaded mules through the coarse crowds.

William watched two parties outfitted for Santa Fe heading to muster in the old wagon yard. A company of Army Dragoons passed with the jingling and clanking civilian outfits never had, making Hellfire's ears flick nervously.

What made William Sublette happiest was the article in the St. Louie newspaper about American Fur Company's funeral. Old man Astor'd retired. American Fur Company's New York charter expired. Ramsey Crooks bought out AFC's Northern Department, and the Western Department remained under St. Louie's Pratte, Chouteau & Co. Astor claimed he'd abandoned the fur trade because it was doomed by the silk hat. Sublette hoped he'd had a part in the old German's decision to quit.

Though Sublette couldn't put words to it, being out of debt'd set him free. He'd taken debts serious as his Grandpa had told him to. He still remembered saying good-bye to his Grandpa Whitley in the stable as a boy of 12 in Kentucky's cold dawn. The Colonel'd cut such a figure in his blue uniform with the gold braid standing beside the ebony stallion -- that looked jist like Hellfire. The old man'd pinned him with those eagle eyes and told William his recipe for living: *"Be true to your country and yourself. Be courageous even when you have nothing left to give to the fight. Be honest in all things. Keep honest accounts and pay your debts even if it costs you your supper!"*

That recipe'd become a religion for William. He hadn't forgotten the rest of it either! The old man'd winked and said, *"But the two most important things to remember are never hit a man without your bullet pouch inside your fist and always carry a double loaded pistol in each boot!"* Then Colonel Whitley'd thundered out o' the stable with his stallion's shod hooves clanging sparks off the stone floor. The Colonel'd died at the Battle o' the Thames after killing Chief Tecumseh. To this day, William carried a double-loaded stubby Hawken pistol in each boot. That he lived proved the old man right.

After riding to his warehouse, William asked Andrew Sublette to watch Sublette & Campbell's eastern fur sales and got another English lesson on verb tenses. If William kept this up, he'd talk good some day like Grandpa Whitley. A man needed to sound *respectable* -- even if he wasn't. William shook his head. Needed to *be* respectable too.

Spring roosted at Sulphur Springs. Quail tracks in the mud had littler tracks behind. Bright green shoots pierced melting snow. William'd worked all his life to own this place. His new buildings would stand here some day. He needed one more strong season. Even if Astor was right that the fur trade was done in, it had to have one more season left. After that William'd be a merchant -- or a banker. He'd cut loose from the beaver growing scarcer every spring. Future was buffalo robes -- still a million o' them critters on the prairies.

No sooner'd William'd put his horse up than Moses "Black" Harris and happy Doc Harrison rode into Sulphur Springs. The cook scared up bread and cold beans to quiet their bellies, till the beef was roasted.

When Doc Harrison left them to wash his clothes, William asked, "What didja do ta Doc Harrison? Acts like a man fulla pee and vinegar!"

Moses set his boots out to dry on the hearth. "Nobody ever let Doc -- argh -- do nothin' fo hisself. Now dat his-- argh -- hand is on de tillah, he steer hisself -- argh -- a good coahss."

"Mose, you wouldn't take credit fer doing nothing good if ya had nail holes through both hands an' feet."

"Well ah -- argh -- gonna do sumpthin' right -- even if it's wrong, Mista Bill. Got expresses here from Fitz -- argh -- to General Ashley and yo brothah Milt. De one from Fitz to Milt -- argh -- done fell open an' you bettah read it!"

Fitzpatrick's remorseful letter carried all details of Rocky Mountain Fur's back-stabbing contract with Nathaniel Wyeth for their 1834 Rendezvous goods. So this was what Ashley's note meant about the last line o' *Micah 7:6* -- "*A man's enemies are the men of his own house.*" He lied, "Known bout it fer months."

Moses grabbed Sublette's chin and looked into his eyes. "Sho yo has, Mista Bill."

Sublette exploded, "Near kilt myself backing Astor off Rocky Mountain Fur's trapping country! RMF still owes me big money! By God, they're gonna honor them debts! An' this Wyeth -- the fool I wet nursed to the '32 Rendezvous -- thinks he'll beat me packing goods ta the mountains? I don't think so!"

Moses Harris slapped his thigh and whooped, "Ah ain't heard so many words -- argh -- outa yo mouf at once since I knowed ya!"

William yelled, "Eat hearty, Mose an' sleep good. Gonna see my lawyer in St. Louie!" then loped out the door toward the barn.

*   *   *

The following afternoon, William entered his warehouse that reeked of dank furs and salt. Andrew Sublette was singing something at the far end when William waved some papers. Andrew sauntered toward him looking too much like Milt for his own good. "What's up?" Andrew asked.

"Got papers fer ya to give ta Bobbie Campbell."

"What'll I tell him?"

"This's the Sublette & Campbell agreement selling our trading posts to AFC with a letter to Bobbie on it. I want ya ta take these by steamboat ta the Upper Missouri. There's a map here. Dig up our goods cached near Fort Cass and sell them to

AFC under this agreement. Be careful of them AFC whelps and the Arikara."

Andrew smiled, "Glad to, brother Bill! Must feel good about kicking AFC's butt."

"Purely tickled," William grunted as he left for the Green Tree Tavern. William checked Henry Geyer's office to see if the papers William'd discussed with him yesterday were done yet, but they weren't. He wondered why lawyers charged for their time, but never got anything done on time.

William reined Hellfire onto Church Street. The sky darkened. The air smelled damp. As William neared the Green Tree, a spring rain let go. He loped Hellfire around to the barn in the rear wagon yard, stalling him to cool down out of the downpour.

Sublette slopped through the rain to the back door. Nobody was supposed to go in through the kitchen, but he'd been Up the Mountain for years with owner Thomas Eddy. The orange bearded Eddy met William at the back door.   Before Eddy could tell William again that his new wife Margaret didn't brook back door entries, William grabbed him by the shoulder. "Tom, I need a favor."

"Aye, you've got it. Mind tellin' me what tis?"

"Gotta git up bout forty men fer a supply train -- real quiet like."

"How soon?"

"Yesterday!"

"My job?"

"Hire 'em from the first o' May through August, usual wages, to go Up the Mountain. I don't wanna use a regular wagon yard to muster 'em. Need ta use yours."

"Aye. Ya want a banner wi' a skull and cross bones fer this boonch o' footpads?"

"No but I'll pay ya $10 bounty fer every good man, an' be back in August to kick yer butt fer every bad one."

"Where ya goin'"

"Snake hunting."

CHAPTER 27

HELLBENT FOR RENDEZVOUS   SPRING 1834

The expedition Nathaniel Wyeth was assembling south of St. Louis in late March made the locals laugh. They called it "Half o' Noah's Ark -- cause it's got one o' everything." Truth was, to finance the expedition without obliterating his new Columbia River Fishing Company's bank account, Wyeth had a bizarre assortment of paying guests.

Pious Reverend Jason Lee, Daniel Lee and three lay assistants were going to establish the first Methodist mission in Oregon.

Thomas Nuttal, recent Curator of Harvard's Botanical Garden, and bespectacled ornithologist John Kirk Townsend paid large stipends to study and preserve species of western flora and fauna with Wyeth's assurances they'd be given a free hand in their studies. They'd decided to hike to Independence, gathering specimens along the way. Wyeth wished these pedants would get lost now that he had their money.

New England Sea Captain Joseph Thing would measure distances and map the country by celestial navigation with his sextant. As Wyeth's second in command, Thing would be handy to captain the return voyage of Wyeth's ship now sailing round the horn if need be.

Cripple Milton Sublette shared command with Wyeth. In April Wyeth's expedition moved to a St. Louis wagon yard and prepared to depart. But Bill Sublette sat his mule like the bull grizzly version of Napoleon barring their path.

"Ride him down!" Wyeth commanded, but nobody dared. "All right, what do you want?" Wyeth shouted up at William.

"Milt Sublette's not leaving St. Louie till he pays Sublette & Campbell his $500 note that's past due."

"That's solely between you and Milton."

"It's your problem if ya think Milt's ducking out without paying up!"

Wyeth prided himself on not losing his temper in public. "Highway robbery's no way to collect a debt!"

"Milt pays er stays."

"Ah Bill, we're brothers. Whatta ya doin' here?"

"Fer once, Milt, yer gonna pay yer debt."

"Here's your blood money!" Wyeth yelled, flinging gold coin and wadded specie in the dirt, startling William's mule into braying raucously.

William's eyes locked up with Wyeth's. "Put $500 in my hand, Mr. Wyeth." Sublette's demand brought rumblings from Wyeth's men. Somebody cocked a rifle.

Wyeth knew a St. Louis killing would stall him for months. He picked up the dirty money and counted $500 into William's massive callused hand. "There, I've paid the ransom! Stand aside."

"You paid a legal note," William growled. He scribbled *Paid without Interest* across the note and handed it to Wyeth. "Throwing my money inna dirt's bought you boys a race to Rendezvous."

Wyeth grated, "You're bluffing! You've got no expedition. You want things so legal -- better not break my supply contract with Rocky Mountain Fur Company, or you'll be getting sued."

"What supply contract'd that be, Milt?" William asked, his eyebrows arched above his piercing eyes.

Wanting to avoid openly murdering his own brother, Milt spurred his horse past William, leading his glowering men around his redic'lous relative.

*   *   *

William Sublette stormed into the dim Green Tree Tavern. Thomas Eddy slapped a roster of 37 names in his hand. "They're ready and rearin' ta Rendezvous," Eddy grinned. "I've earned meself $370 without riskin' a single red hair o' my head!"

"Nathaniel Wyeth jist paid you, and here it is!" Sublette rasped, counting out $370 on the damp oak table. "Like always, I'm quick pay."

"Aye and I got a surprise fer ye! Yer gettin' most o' yer mooney back!"

"Why?"

"Read this."   He handed William a bulky envelope addressed to W.L. Sublette from the Army's Jefferson Barracks near St. Louis.

"Dear Bill:

Lawyer William Marshall Anderson's my grand nephew. Last year when he was 26, I agreed to his riding w/ Dragoons to quiet Pawnee-Picts this spring. He's here, but health's gone -- weighs 135 -- maybe less. Can't take Army campaign.

My $300 draft's to take Marsh to mountains & right health like you did General Harrison's son. Not drinker! Had cholera, then Yellow Fever. Clever command of words. Been aide on Kentucky Governor Breathitt staff since 1832. Can chronicle expedition. Mustn't know of $, & work as rest of men if able.

Yours & c.

Henry Atkinson, General U.S. Army"

Sublette was secretly cheered to have a lawyer chronicling every move if Wyeth did sue. "You read this letter addressed to me?"

"Aye, but I didna cash the General's draft yet. Want the mooney fer the trip?"

Sublette nodded.

"Take $300 of Wyeth's cash back. Know it moost have sentimental value ta ye! General's kin's waitin' at the bar."

*   *   *

Wyeth was relieved to get his 70 men, 250 horses and missionaries' horned cattle out of Independence and it's odd war on April 28th. Before leaving, Wyeth'd heard that a fanatic sect called Mormonites had been ejected from Independence and taken refuge across the river in Liberty. Independence folk, fearing they'd soon be put to the sword, had sentries pacing the levee and militia training in the square. The bloodless war'd ballooned the price of Wyeth's horses.

But the Mormonite War wasn't Wyeth's strangest obstacle at the outset of his mountain odyssey. In spite of Wyeth's need to scurry ahead of any interference by William

150

Sublette, Boston botanist Thomas Nuttal stalled the expedition for 40 precious minutes right after nooning to pick untrampled plant specimens from their path. Wyeth'd given his word the scientist wouldn't be disturbed, so he fumed, wondering how he could minimize this pedantic insanity.

After finding a night camp site, Wyeth laid down the law as swooping bats and Nighthawks foraged for insects. "Divide into messes of eight with an old hand in charge to allot rations of pork, flour and the like. Each mess has its own tent." It worked out to nine messes, though Wyeth's only had four men -- if he counted Milton Sublette, who drank so much to kill his heel pain he was absent most of the time.

Wyeth rode about the camp's hollow square with a sputtering lantern pointing with his saber where each tent should be pitched. Then he ordered, "Horses shall be unloaded, and their bales of goods placed for perimeter defense. Horses shall be hobbled, then firmly staked in the center of the square to graze through the night."

Wyeth formed the guard of six men, to be relieved three times each night, with each watch to serve on alternate nights. The watch captain was the mess commander. It galled Wyeth that he'd learned this camp routine from William Sublette on his 1832 trip to the mountains.

But he'd gone Sublette one better on the guards. Wyeth ordered, "The captain shall cry the hour and *all's well,* and so on every 15 minutes. Any guard not repeating the cry shall be visited. A guard found asleep will walk three days instead of riding."

Wyeth recalled countermanding Sublette's punishment order two years ago when Wyeth's cousin John slept on guard -- but there'd be no leniency this trip. As Wyeth recollected how cousin John'd betrayed him in Boston with that lying book, he wished he'd made John *crawl* three days!

April 29th was born in a deluge, dousing any hope of hot breakfast and sending them forth in wet clothes that were soaked by noon. Then it hailed ice musket balls, panicking several pack horses into bolting across the plain strewing goods in the mud behind them.

Wyeth was forced to camp early in the open, assembling the remnants of his shattered command. Night had fallen by the time his muddy horses and goods were back in camp, with but a few miles to show for the day's effort. Wyeth shouted repeatedly, "You must keep control of those horses! That's an order! We've lost precious time!"

Someone shouted back, "It'd help if we could git some sleep 'thout them loud mouth fools hollerin' all night."

Wyeth was livid. "Who said that?" Only the rain answered, so he retreated to his soggy tent and ate sodden bread till he fell asleep in his sopping clothes.

On May 1st, Wyeth's desertions started with three men skulking off in the night, purloining food, rifles and horses. By nightfall, the rain turned to icy winds and Wyeth set up camp with canvas whipping on a branch of the Kansas River near a Kaw village of six lodges.

The Kaws called themselves the Kanza, and immediately began begging from Wyeth's brigade. They wore little paint, but their ears were full of trinkets and old gashes. Most wore baggy woolen pants cadged from the whites with their naked upper bodies wrapped in blankets. The squaws knew their begging would fare better if their blankets fell open.

Both of Wyeth's scouts returned from their all-night rides to assure him there wasn't a hint of a Sublette expedition behind them. Wyeth relaxed and let his men spend May 2nd cleaning their filthy equipment and drying their clothes near the Kaw village. He did his best to shield the Methodists from some of the things being bartered there. At least he knew now how the Kaws came by all those pants.

The expedition got off to a rousing start on May 3rd, and nooned on the Kansas River. Indian lodges of saplings driven in the ground and tied together at the top covered with buffalo skins dotted both sides of the river. Indians shuffled out with yapping dogs and squealing children to welcome Wyeth's band. None had heard of William Sublette or any expedition.

Wyeth ordered, "Unload the horses and drive them into the water. Put them in that fenced lot on the other side and guard them." The unladen horses swam the river easily and accepted penning.

After considerable dickering, Wyeth's chief hunter Richardson, a skinny Connecticut Yankee who hadn't been home in 12 years, bought a big flat-bottom Kanza boat for 5 pounds of tobacco and 20 vermilion sticks.   They ferried the rest of the men and goods across the Kansas River with the help of these Kanza Indians, who appeared well fed and did not beg.

White settlers tending their cattle and corn fields surrounded distant frame houses.   Wyeth decided to forego travel to trade with Indians and whites, stocking up on toothsome corn and potatoes.

Throughout May 4th, Wyeth traded for food and clothing with these handsome Kanza Indians who wore only buckskins in spite of their neighboring whites.   Their canoes were buoyant and strong.   With flat prairies and rich grass before them, Wyeth knew they would go far on the morrow with good graze and fine fortune ahead.

*   *   *

At dawn on May 5th William Sublette led twin columns of his 37 men with 95 horses and mules out of Independence, Missouri at a brisk walk. Skinny young Marshall Anderson rode his 14 hand thoroughbred Black Hawk beside Sublette on the World's Smartest Mule Bluegrass. "Shouldn't we be at the dead run, Captain Sublette? Aren't you in a Brobdingnagian hurry to catch Wyeth's caravan?"

"No an' yes."

Tiring of waiting for Captain Sublette to elaborate, Marshall asked, "Aren't your answers inconsistent?"

"No,"Sublette snapped, then turned yelling,"Catch it up!Catch it up!"

"Sir, if I wanted to catch people with a week's head start, I wouldn't be chasing them at a walk."

"Then you wouldn't be catching 'em neither. Steady 25 to 30 miles a day wins the long race."

"When do you figure reaching Rendezvous on the Green River?

"Bout June 15th."

"That's 41 days."

Sublette shook his head, "Nope. Got all day today, May 5th. Add 27 days in May to 15 in June. I make that 42."

"People in Independence said Wyeth's caravan left April 28th -- 7 days ago. You're handing Wyeth 7 days out of 42. You don't want a tie, so you need to beat him by another day, meaning your've spotted him 8 days. That's over 19% of total trip time, Captain Sublette."

"Forgot ta throw in nat I also need a day or two to lay out a new fort at the Laramie Fork."

William Marshall Anderson laughed," We add two more days to what you're giving away. That makes 10 days or almost 24% of total trip time. How in God's world can you win?"

"Admire yer ciphering, but ya made three mistakes," Sublette said holding up three broomstick sized fingers.

"Three mistakes?" Anderson repeated incredulously, "I'm well versed in mathematics."

"First's figuring our miles per day same as Wyeth's. Second, ya didn't lop off his time fer losing the trail. Third, the man doesn't have the common sense God gave a goose."

CHAPTER 28

DEVIL TAKE THE HINDMOST MAY 1834

On May 7th Nathaniel Wyeth camped before dark at Red Vermilion Creek. Black-bearded giant Reverend Jason Lee spied whiskered catfish in the creek. After the tents were pitched, the men fished with Reverend Lee. As a Canadian frontiersman, Reverend Lee fit in with the Mountain Men. He gave sermons on Sunday, but made no effort to reform them. They liked that. The catfish liked kernels of corn.

Milton Sublette, himself a huge man at 6'4", joined Reverend Lee beside the creek, but he didn't fish. He knelt on a rock slab overhanging the gently rolling water and razored slits around his left boot ankle, then eased his boot off, exposing his fiery leg with its mutilated heel. He eased his agonized leg into the soothing icy water and stifled a sigh of relief.

Reverend Lee landed a flopping footlong catfish, killing it with a whack to the head with his knife handle. "How'd you come by that leg?"

"Coyotero Apache shattered my heel with a rifle ball in 1826. Plucked bone splinters from it with a bullet mold fer months. Use ta put my foot on the bar in Taos *Cantinas* and make diggin' out splinters the entertainment. Healed over, then swole up agin. St. Louie Doc says leg's gotta come off jist under the knee."

"You can't cross a continent in all that pain, Mr. Sublette. The Lord forgives you. Go home."

Milt ripped his leg from the water and lurched toward his tent, nearly trampling ornithologist Townsend who was enraptured by the ravens cawing raucously throughout their camp.

Townsend startled the camp by shooting a raven with his toy-sized pistol. He marveled at the spectral colors glinting on its ebony feathers. He dismembered the raven and immersed its body parts in crocks of alcohol on his pack saddle where he'd also stored specimen spiders, lizards and snakes. Townsend was unaware the Mountain Men'd dubbed him "The Fool," slyly siphoned off his alcohol and gobbled his "pickled vittles."

*   *   *

When shadows grew gangly on May 7th, William Sublette camped on the Kansas River beside General Marston G. Clark's Agency that served the few lodges of Kaws. After supper, William sent word he'd be privileged to meet the Kaw Chiefs.

Sublette conferred with Moses "Black" Harris, his second in command, and young Marshall Anderson, who spoke French, in his tent. "Marshall, we wanta show these Chiefs we're men o' good will. Find out whatchu can bout Wyeth's outfit an' have a right good time. Learn from these Kaws. They been out here since God made dirt."

The first Kanza Chief into Sublette's tent was the oldest man any of the whites had ever seen. Stooped, blind, sparse snowy hair, weals of wrinkles with a voice like grinding stones, Chief *Vieil* muttered, "*Bon Jour, mon ami*," showing both his teeth. The lean, pockmarked interpreter helped *Vieil* sit, then joined him cross-legged on the tent floor.

The younger Chief nodded, held up his right hand with two fingers extended side by side in the "friend" sign and settled beside his cohorts. The Indians smelled of cooked dog, hot peppers and unwashed bodies. Their blankets were rags.

Sublette led the whites in sitting on the floor. He gave each Indian a large twist of tobacco and several trinkets. Pouring tin cannikins of brandy, he passed them around.

Vieil smelled his cup, then passed it to the interpreter. Sublette raised his cup and toasted, "We honor this Chief the Great Mystery has given so many suns in Kansas." Sublette sipped his brandy. The others tossed theirs down.

The tent became "the tower of babble." Few understood, but talked anyway. Both of the seeing Kaws touched the bearded face of Moses "Black" Harris, making the hands to ears sign for the bear. Moses made them laugh by making the sign of the fox for himself. The interpreter spoke of Wyeth's outfit. *Vieil* admitted to Marshall in French that he was 106. Sublette gave wrapped salt pork to the younger Kaws and a small red pot of waxed-over honey to *Vieil* to prove even the bees loved the oldest Kaw of all. When *Vieil* fell fast asleep, Sublette toted the snoring Kaw home, making the "friend" sign to the blind Chief's sleeping eyes.

*   *   *

At dawn on May 8th, Milt Sublette couldn't pull his left boot on over a foot swollen into a ham. He swathed his leg in a nubby blue blanket, tied thongs around it and packed for the settlements.

Nathaniel tagged along beside Milton's horse to the camp perimeter. "Can't you persevere for me?"

"Cain't even persevere fer me, Nat. Gotta go home an' shuck this swoll-up foot er die." Milton Sublette hung his head and rode south through a dawn so glorious he floated on the pain.

*   *   *

On May 8th, Marshall Anderson had fresh eggs with his kinsman General Marston Clark at the Agency. They reminisced about Soldiers' Retreat, the magnificent Kentucky stone fortress and place of Marshall's birth in 1807. The General recalled meeting guests there -- faithless Aaron Burr, fearless Andrew Jackson, James Monroe, Henry Clay and Chief Little Turtle of the Miamis. He especially savored the banquet for General Lafayette in 1825 where Marshall's father, Richard Clough Anderson, claimed to be the third ugliest man in the Army and played classics on his violin. Marshall didn't tell General Clark how the creditors dismembered Soldiers' Retreat after his father'd died in his arms in 1826.

Sublette's cavalcade of men, mules, horses, cows and sheep forded the Kansas River, plodding relentlessly through trampled prairie grasses. Sublette laid his cheek to the ground to see how much the grass had sprung back. He figured they were four to five days behind Wyeth. He spit and got back on Bluegrass. He'd expected more of himself.

Marshall fired his little Tryon rifle at a Kawsie dog for trying to steal their sheep, but missed. Sublette raised his rifle to blast the dog, but realized it was jist doing what it'd been trained to. He sent it scurrying with a shot that dashed dirt in its face, then yelled, "Catch it up. Catch it up!" They trudged on with Moses "Black" Harris distantly repeating these cautions from the rear of the caravan.

*   *   *

May 9th meant more prairie to Nathaniel Wyeth, but the 10th was a curse. They got lost in low hills that all looked alike. Their maps were so barren of landmarks, Captain Thing's celestial sextant fixes were only suggestions. May 11th was a nightmare. While still trying to find the trail, Wyeth found that the three men deserting last night had thieved the prized rifle he'd carried across the country two years ago.

While Townsend savored the mating calls of grosbeaks, thrushes and buntings, Wyeth's caravan forded a creek with a quicksand bed. Pack horses toppled, cursing men and squealing horses floundered in the deep ooze. Townsend began to cackle out loud. Wyeth would have shot him -- if that other coyote hadn't stolen his rifle.

*   *   *

May 9th found William Sublette's boys breakfasting on the Soldier River. By noon they reached a village where a few Kaws guarded the lodges while others hunted. They nooned at village edge, sparing morsels to the Kaw sentries and their rib-showing dogs. Midway of the meal, William Sublette spotted a dot on the horizon and got to his feet. "It's Milt. Tell from how he rides. Hope Wyeth hasn't got the rest of his men kilt."

Though Marshall Anderson suffered pleurisy pains, he asked, "Want me to bring your glass for a better look?"

Sublette shook his head and strode to the other end of the village. If Wyeth was alive, Milt'd be going home because of his heel. With all this ruckus over Wyeth's supply contract, they'd forgotten they were brothers. He directed Yancy the Cook, "Heap plenty o' hot food on yer biggest platter an' bring it when Milt gits here."

Milt Sublette rode up glumly. William grinned, "Got hot vittles, Milt. Set a spell an' show the boys how ya got sa big."

William wanted to help Milt off his horse, but knew better. Milt hobbled over, snatched the food from Yancy the Cook, sat well away from his brother and wolfed it. Finally, he grunted, "Buy a lotta grub fer $500, cain't chu Bill?"

"Enough to fill yer plate as often as ya can empty it. Want a whiskey chaser ta give yer leg a breather?"

"Take more grub, but I only drink with my friends."

"Fine, we'll give ya a jug ta nurse till ya git back among 'em."

Milt took the whiskey jug and a well-provisioned pack horse. He rode south into the hot golden afternoon, tears streaming down his face.

William pushed the men hard during daylight and camped on a small creek.

Throughout May 10th Marshall Anderson held his painful side and swept his spyglass for buffalo as the caravan ground relentlessly onward.

May 11th brought a smile to Sublette's bronze face with its blonde stubble. They crossed Cannonball Creek on Sublette's trace.

Marshall asked, "Captain, how'd this bridge ever get way out here?"

Moses "Black" Harris chuckled, "Mista Bill built it for -- argh -- dem ten wagons he brung out heah foah yeahs ago when he open de Oregon Trail!"

While the caravaners ogled the crumbling bridge, William filled his buffalo coat with wet and dry grass. Hoisting the bulging coat onto his shoulder, Sublette ran down the creek to where a great tree buzzed with bees. After setting fire to his dry grass, Sublette scattered the wet grass over the blaze, smothering the tree in pungent white billows. Wrapping his coat about his head and shoulders, he clambered up the tree to a dark runny hole in it's side.

By the time Marshall Anderson got there, Captain Sublette was standing down from the tree, with great gobs of honey in hand and sticky smears around his gleaming grin "Captain -- you're a boy inside a bear's body!"

Sublette stuffed another waxy glob of honey in his face and muttered, "We'll make metheglin at Rendezvous!" Dazed bees circled, but Sublette scaled the tree and clawed honey comb into his vat. Finally, he descended swatting bees from about his head as he lumbered off booming laughter.

Marshall found Sublette washing honey off in the stream and asked, "Did you know bees out here came from hives early settlers brought from Europe?"

"No an' I hope them bees don't find out."

"Why?"

"No metheglin if they go back."

Stuffed with honey, Sublette strolled to his caravan, mounted Bluegrass and became Captain Sublette. "Mount up, we're gonna skin past Wyeth's boys tonight!"

        *   *   *

Grizzled Mountain Man Richardson frowned at Wyeth the morning of May 12th. Richardson dipped snuff then groaned, "Big trail o' whites. Come outa nowhere an' slicked by us in the night. Sublette's been out here since before the Bible was writ. He's one sly ole dog, he is."

"Well, you're right about the last part. We'll hop to today and return the favor tomorrow night."

Richardson grumbled, "Hop to where? Sublette's a eagle racing bullfrogs."

Wyeth scurried to his tent and wrote to Thomas Fitzpatrick:

"Wm Sublette having passed me here, I am induced to write to you and hope you will get it. You may expect me by the 1st of July at rendesvous as named in your letter to Milton which you sent by Dr. Harrison who opened it and I presume told Sublette all. I am not heavily loaded and shall travell as fast as possible and have sufficient equipment of goods for you according to contract. . . . Milton left me a few days since on account of his leg which is very bad. . . . P.S. I have sent a vessell around the Horn with such goods as you want and would like to give you a supply for winter rendesvous for next year on such terms as I know would suit you."

Wyeth eyed his courier mounted on a trim paint horse. "Get this express to Fitzpatrick before Sublette reaches Ham's Fork on the Green River! If you run into Sublette, ingratiate yourself, then ditch them before you reach the Green. I'd delight in Sublette helping you deliver my letter to Fitzpatrick." Wyeth slapped the horse's hip and yelled, "Devil take the hindmost!"

Wyeth drove his men hard to recapture his lost lead.

*   *   *

The change from the plains of May 12th to the rugged hills of May 15th brought wild game. Marshall Anderson tried out his rifle. He missed the ghostly antelope. His stray shots only spooked some elk, but he crushed a rattlesnake's head with an empty boot beside his bed. "Finally hit something," he grunted, whacking the twitching rattler again.

While Sublette's caravan nooned beside the Blue River, a man on a paint horse wandered up to them. "I'm half starved," he groaned.

"Get down and eat," Sublette said, eyeing the man. "Whatta ya doing out here alone?"

"Went antelope hunting, got tangled in my mind. Been lost two er three days."

Sublette left the man eating noisily and cornered Marshall between two boulders. "That's Wyeth's man. Spy or courier. Watch 'im like he's your best girl on payday night inna Army camp. He takes off, let me know."

"Right, Captain. Anything else?"

"Find Moses Harris. Tell him I wanna know ever' time that jasper breathes. You got that?"

"Right," Marshall snapped, elated at being in the intrigue.

Sublette lead the caravan at a hard walk on the World's Smartest Mule Bluegrass. Realizing they were leaving Otoe land and entering Pawnee country, Sublette camped on high ground that would be easier to defend.

Dawn didn't disappoint Sublette. Dust clouds towered into the fiery sky. Sublette ordered, "Strike them tents and pack the mules. Move them horses from the top of the knoll ta that box gully over there! Hobble and picket 'em on deep stakes." He helped the men throw bales around the brink for breastworks. If they were lucky, the Pawnees'd settle for tribute. If not, there'd be a battle. Sublette wanted to be done with the Pawnee before Wyeth got ahead of him again.

Sublette grabbed Charley Lajeunnesse, who talked Pawnee, by the shoulder. "Go down the hill with this American flag.   Halt them dust raisers about 200 yards out, so they're still in rifle range. Bring the Chiefs back up here."

Charley grunted, then crabbed down the hill with his odd, side-swinging gait and palavered with the Pawnee. Finally, four war bonnets headed up the hill, leaving over a hundred, standing their ponies "in a string of fight."

One of the Chiefs in a breechcloth was tall, broad shouldered and tapered down to the waist of a woman above shiny muscular legs flexing in the sunlight.

Sublette asked the Chiefs what they wanted in sign.

The muscular Chief signed, "Plenty tobacco, powder, balls, ochre paint and beads."

Marshall asked, "You aren't going to give them anything are you?"

"Sure am."

"Isn't that a sign of fear?"

Placing the goods they'd asked for in a pile before the Chiefs, Sublette answered, "My pa ferried people across the Mississippi. Charged a toll. That's what this is. They're charging us fer passage over their land."

When the pile was completed, the biggest Indian signed that this pile was for the Grand Pawnee village. Another pile of same size must be made for the Republican Pawnees.

Sublette growled to Charley, "They're all Grand Pawnee."

"No doubt o' that. Now it's jist whether you wanna double the goods er die."

"They'll know we're scared if I double 'em. Translate what I say."

"Start, an' I'll foller along," Charley said, "Go light as goose down."

Sublette eyed the powerful Chief, "I lived 11 summers in the Mountains. I killed many Blackfeet an' Arikaras -- never Pawnee, for I say truth to the Pawnee an' they say truth to me. I know the four Pawnee tribes." Sublette held up four chair-leg fingers, tapping one for each tribe as he spoke, "The Grand, the Loup, the Republican an' the Noisy."

Charley finished parroting in Pawnee, "*Chauis, Skidis, Kitkehahkis -- Tapages.*" Charley whispered to Sublette, "They outnumber us three to one. Ain't gonna translate it if you call 'em liars. They'll scatter our guts all over this hill."

Sublette watched the Pawnees eye each other, then went on, "The Grand Pawnee are a great people with much honor in their fathers. I know the Grand Pawnee will not sell their fathers for one pile of goods. Take the big pile of goods we give. Go back to the Grand Pawnee nation in peace." Sublette laid four more twists of tobacco on the pile. "Smoke the calumet for us, your friends. We will meet in peace and give more goods another day."

The Grand Pawnee Chiefs stood with chins dropped against their chests as Charley sweated through translating Sublette's words. Sublette knew he could kill two of the Chiefs quick with his boot pistols. His rifle lay in reach. That meant he had to cut the big one's throat *first*.

The Chiefs nodded. They snatched up their pile of plunder and trotted down the hill. Only their dust wafting in the breeze and the crushed flowers at the base of the rise said they had ever been there at all.

Charley muttered, "Are they gonna go home an' smoke them extry twists er come screamin' back up here with all them braves an' take it all?"

CHAPTER 29

FIRST OUTFIT AT RENDEZVOUS   SPRING 1834

Right after breakfast on May 17th, Sublette's caravan pulled up at the Platte south of Council Bluffs. Sublette shielded his eyes from the river's glare, then told Marshall Anderson, "Platte's a mile wide and a inch deep. Too thick ta drink and too thin ta plow." Marshall chuckled and waded into the shallow brown water. Sublette hollered, "You kin wade across without getting yer knees wet."

Marshall came ashore to scribble in his diary:
"The Indian name Nebraska means the flat river. . . In appearance, the Platte is like the Mississippi, broad, boisterous and deep, capable of bearing the navies of the world. But it's an infernal liar and hardly able to float a canoe. . . . The ground hereabouts is covered with a white efflorescence, a feathery substance, resembling dry snow looking lovely, and yet it is nothing but the very bitterness of beauty -- the unfulfilled promise of earthly happiness."

                    *   *   *

At the Platte on May 18th, Wyeth mustered his men for the long wade across it. Townsend noted in his journal the presence of *Antelope furcifer,* wolves (*Canis lupus),* sandhill cranes (*Gruidae canadensis*) and great herons (*Ardea heroidas*).

Townsend was fascinated by the soda flats. He tasted the crusted powder that stretched along the sandy banks, analyzing it as a combination of sulphate and muriate of soda. The soda water in puddles was so bitter it made him spit violently. Chief hunter Richardson grabbed the ornithologist's arm, "Don't none o' them books tell ya, ya cain't put ever'thing ya find in yer mouth?"

Townsend absently jerked his arm free to discuss distance computations with Captain Joseph Thing. Townsend wrote in his journal:

"Our observed latitude is 40°, 31' and our computed distance from the Missouri settlements is 360 miles."

*   *   *

Young Marshall Anderson viewed May 18th as an eerie day the moment Sublette's caravan halted at the Pawnee ceremonial site. On the way to investigate a circle of red stakes festooned by hair and scalps, Marshall spied a bleached human skull. He lowered his cheek to the ground and peered into the long vacant eye socket that had become the loom house for a spider's gossamer threads. An abandoned mouse nest occupied the shattered brain case.

Marshall heard the skull's former occupant say, "Like you, I rejoiced in the wonder of the mountains and savage forests until I relinquished the domicile of my mind to a family of mice." Marshall felt the chill of death and arose, but the grinning skull moaned its lament in Latin, "*Memento homo tu es pulvis, et in pulverem reverteris.*" The skull now revolted him. Marshall recoiled from it to investigate the ritual site where Captain Sublette knelt. "Why the bloody swamp?" Marshall asked.

"Glad I missed iss party. Squaws sing revenge over the scalps, then pluck out their enemies' eyes. That brown eye's likely Sioux -- born enemy of the Pawnee. Eye shoulda gone inna a charm bag to be et. Gives all sights ever seen ta her that eats it. Mount up. Gonna rain."

"Why're those six buffalo skulls lined up with their noses down river?"

"Pawnees bleeve where the ghost herd points, live herds will follow."

On May 19th, a vicious wind whipped the rain drops sideways. Sublette rode beside Moses Harris. Marshall Anderson's arms shielded his face from the horizontal hornets. Sublette turned and said, "*Arra-raish -- the straight walking rain.* That's what the Crows call me!"

Moses Harris shook his head, water drenching his drooping fur cap. "Don't you bleeve it, boy. Crows calls him -- argh -- *the straight walkin' pain* cause he bahgain so hahd it huhts!"

*   *   *

May 19th began with two Grand Pawnees dancing their horses through the heat waves of Wyeth's spyglass. Wyeth and hunter Richardson rode out to meet them.

Richardson asked, *"Chaui?"* The Grand Pawnees nodded.

The Indian with the deformed hand signed that their war party of 1,500 was camped close by and would come for tribute.

Townsend poised his pencil over his Journal and asked fellow scientist Nuttal, "Don't you think these savages are fatter than those who accosted us last time?"

Nuttal wrestled the question, then threw up his hands in surrender, "I'm a botanist, Kirk. All Indians look alike to me as plants do to you."

Through Richardson, Wyeth promised the Pawnees his caravan would camp by the next stream, and welcome the Pawnee there.

The Pawnees left. Wyeth and Richardson rejoined the caravan. Wyeth yelled "Catch it up!" and trotted his outfit hard to the little stream.

Richardson eyed the low ground. "This ain't a place ta defend."

"We'll ride for thunder," Wyeth retorted, sweeping their backtrail with his glass.

"You're gonna jilt the Pawnee?"

"Exactly," Wyeth asserted with an open expression that sought approval.

"You're breedin' hell for the next outfit through here -- an' us if we come back this away."

"No matter, I'm headed north after Rendezvous."

"Ya mean, it makes no matter ta you."

"Isn't that what I said?" Wyeth snapped, telescoping his spyglass shut against his thigh. Wyeth drove his men hard till the moon waned at midnight, making 35 miles -- their best day ever. Aching, Wyeth fell into his blankets Tomorrow he'd retake the lead from Sublette.

*   *   *

Sublette's double columns devoured 30 miles a day till they hit the buffalo on May 21st. Thousands blocked them, grunting, grazing in the dust. Sublette prodded them out of the way with his rifle barrel. He yelled back over his shoulder to Marshall, "Watch their tails. Long as tail's down, they got grass on their mind. Tail goes straight up, better git! They'll gore yer horse fore ya kin spit."

By May 22nd, Wyeth was one hour behind Sublette at noon, but didn't know it because buffalo'd trampled Sublette's tracks. Exasperated by the brutes, Wyeth forded the South Fork of the Platte and camped at noon waiting for the herd to move on.

At dawn of May 23rd, the sky seethed with buffalo gnats. Men of both caravans cursed as bugs bit eyes, noses and throats bloody. Frantic horses screamed, rolling on the ground, tearing free of their packs. Both caravans camped and built fuming buffalo chip fires in tent openings to shunt these fiends the size of a period at the end of a sentence.

With eyes swollen and hands blistered, Marshall penned in his diary:

"*Several of our men have become blind from their poisonous bites. The little devils seem to alight upon you with red-hot feet and billies. They bite, burn and blister you all over. Even my little thoroughbred Black Hawk has been run mad by their unceasing and invisible attacks. His head, neck and breast are swoll to a wonderful degree -- his whole body hot with fever. Even as I burn with him, I long for bread of which we have no more.*"

*   *   *

By May 24th, the gnat swarms vanished driving their buffalo quarry before them, but their pain remained. Wyeth's men caught up strewn packs and gear, but Nathaniel could not. His eyes were swollen shut. His caravan squished through the prairie's fresh buffalo dung, with Richardson leading Nathaniel's horse.

*   *   *

Sublette's pack train pulled away from Wyeth's, passing awesome Chimney Rock May 27th and Scott's Bluff on May 28th. Sublette remembered naming Scott's Bluff after somebody from his caravan'd secretly ditched Hiram Scott there to die from Blackfoot chest wounds. Sublette buried Hiram's bones on the next trip back, but never learned who'd left Ashley's friend to die alone.

May 30th's moon found Sublette camped on the Laramie Fork. True to his plan to establish a trading fort, Sublette staked off building sites near the swirling stream. Marshall joined Sublette. "Wyeth's courier skulked out of camp five minutes ago."

"Thanks. He's waited too long to do us any hurt."

By June 1st the fort's log foundations were laid. Marshall broke out his prized bottle of champagne. "I christen thee Fort Sublette"

Sublette grinned, "It's yer first trip west. Oughta be Fort Anderson."

The caravan clerk Patton chimed in, "All three of us is named William. How bout Fort William?"

"Done, "Sublette answered draining his tin cup. "Patton, pick a dozen men you kin git along with. Build out this fort. We're gonna pin our ears back an' whup Wyeth."

Lightened by leaving their building implements behind, Sublette's 23 man caravan threaded the red rocks in record time, reaching Independence Rock June 7th.

Like a colossal half-buried beast, a mile around the base and 600 feet high, Independence Rock's lower walls carried carvings and messages in buffalo grease and powder. "This here's the trapper's post office," Sublette said to Marshall as his men scanned the names, dates and messages for word from a friend. Sublette grinned, scratching his name and the *wrong date*, "Here's a little sumpthing fer Wyeth ta fret over."

*   *   *

Sight restored to his bloodshot eyes by June 10th, Wyeth read the inscriptions on Independence Rock, startled to see the date beside the newly scratched "W. L. Sublette." Wyeth fingered the date and muttered, "Can't be that far ahead. He's bluffing."

*   *   *

Marshall Anderson had promised himself he'd plant the Star Spangled banner on the brow of the great Rocky Mountains, a compromise of conscience for someone who distrusted Yankees. He tied the flag to his saber and jammed the blade in the ground. "I claim this land for the sovereign state of Kentucky this June 15th, 1834!" he shouted to the winds.

As Marshall savored the flag dancing in the breeze over New Kentucky, four horsemen thundered like Cossacks across the plains shouting, their tattered buckskins flapping. Sublette stood arms out-stretched, grinning like the champion boy runner at the town picnic.

Barely slowing their horses, they leaped off around Sublette, hugging and hollering, as their horses pounded past. With everybody shaking hands and slapping backs, the only words Anderson understood were from the Mountain Man Sublette called Fitz, who yelled in a thick Irish brogue, "Bill, you're the first outfit at Rendezvous!"

CHAPTER 30

DEATH OF ROCKY MOUNTAIN FUR CO.   SUMMER 1834

William Sublette pitched camp beside Rocky Mountain Fur Company. Both camps settled down to hot juicy buffalo ribs around their fires. Nez Percé, Flatheads and Shoshones joined them in joyous reunions and succulent ribs.

Sublette found his Nez Percé friend Bull's Head, a bony fellow known to all as Kentuck for his dismal endeavors to sing *The Hunters of Kentucky*. After excited whispering, Kentuck forked his pony and slipped into the growing dusk.

Soon a bull buffalo thundered through the camp with Kentuck behind on his pony loosing arrows at it. Mountain Men bellered, "Hurrah for Kentuck!" bolted from their path, and fired rifles for the hell of it.

Flatheads howled, "*Oka-hey-trodlum* [Go ahead bull]!" and unleashed arrows. Amid wild gunshots, zipping arrows and flattened tents, spectators whooped as the snorting buffalo plowed into the Green River and paddled off.

Miraculously, injuries were piddling though some near died laughing. Sublette opened sales of alcohol-kicked "wine" at a paltry $3 a pint, and few remembered how the evening ended.

In the-morning-after's frosty dawn, William Sublette shuffled through the wrecked camp's rowdy snores. Bad as his head hurt, Sublette had to grin. Rendezvous was more fun than hell could ever be.

Sublette halted at Fitzpatrick's cockeyed tent. "Hello, the camp!" Sublette yawned.

Friday's bright-eyed little face popped into the opening, "Hello, Big Snake!" he blurted, raising his arms to Sublette.

Sublette grabbed the boy, hugged him and asked, "What's this Big Snake business?"

"Big Snake is what Rocky Mountain Fur men call you when you are not here. They say you strangle the life from them."

The words cut deep, but Sublette smiled, "I'd tell ya why being called Big Snake's not so bad, but yer too young."

"Friday boy, you need to be washin' yerself at the river!" came Fitzpatrick's husky voice from inside the tent.

"Always I am truthful, Big Snake. But truth is not what others want. Let me down, and I will wash."

Sublette watched the fine little feller scamper off, thinking how seldom grown men ever had the guts to tell each other the truth.

Fitz's bleary face showed in the tent opening. "You comin' in, Bill?"

"It's a spritely morning, Fitz. Less take a walk."

Fitz pulled on his boots and his long-tailed settlement shirt. He slipped through the tent flap. "Don't need pants, do I?"

"Lose 'em last night, Fitz?"

"Must have, but no matter. I'll find them pants er they'll find me."

They crunched frosted grass to a clearing and sat down cross-legged in a spot of sunlight. Sublette rubbed his beard stubble. "Truth is, Fitz, I know bout yer deal with Wyeth --"

"I never been comfortable with back-door doings, but you left us no choice. You keep us owin' you blood, bone and marrow."

"Know it seems thataway to ya, Fitz, but I ask ya ta think how business is done."

"Mortal Sins be good business, Bill."

Sublette nodded, "Hear me out."

"To be sure."

"You and me come Up the Mountain in 1823 under Ashley and Henry."

"That we did, haulin' the *Yellow Stone Packet* on cordelle."

"We both turn 35 this year. Been knowing each other a third of our lives."

Fitz pushed his white hair from his eyes. "I look like yer Grandpa since them Gros Ventres turned me hair white at Pierre's Hole."

"Least ya still gotcher hair, Tom. In 1826, Jedediah Smith -- God rest him -- Davie Jackson an' me hocked our souls ta General Ashley ta buy him out. We owed the General more'n Moses owed God fer parting the Red Sea."

"Heard it was big money, Bill."

"While we was still paying down our debt to the General in the fall o' 1830, we sold this same fur business to you, Milt, Jim Bridger, Jean Gervais an' ole Henry Fraeb as the Rocky Mountain Fur Company fer $15,532.23. We tuck yer notes fer it. If you'd paid cash, you'd been debt-free from the outset."

"And we been payin' you ever since. But we never catch up to your charges."

"That's cause I keep letting ya have goods on credit without making ya pay off what ya already owe. I give you boys the zact same credit the General give me. Gotta admit, Tom -- I been with ya through thick and thin without a whimper."

"That's what made me feel so foul about our Wyeth deal. We was tryin' ta get more, while payin' less."

"Sure, but honest business men pay their debts. I got General Ashley paid off last fall -- after SEVEN YEARS o' busting my hump."

"You think we wanted to cheat ya?"

"Finesse is the word, Fitz. You buy Wyeth's goods cheap, run up more debt -- making yer debt ta me shakier -- mebee worthless. You boys gotcher cake an' have a bite on me, cause I'm still owed fer the bakery ya bought 100% on credit."

"Hadn't seen it from your side, Bill."

"Wantcha ta see both sides. I'll be here next year -- and the year after that. Ready ta supply goods and step in when the b'ars bite yer butts, like I done agin John Jacob Astor."

"I knew you and General Ashley was after the old German fer us. What come of that?"

"Ashley read your letter on the floor of Congress bout the Crows robbing you at American Fur's behest. Newspapers taloned Astor like hawks. I jawed with Astor's son, William Backhouse Astor, and eight other fellers till they agreed American Fur boys'd stay outa the Rockies fer a year."

"Name really Backhouse?" Fitz asked through a chuckle.

"Yeah, Backhouse."

"Outa the Rockies fer a year? That's mighty fine, Bill!

"Old man Astor's sold the Upper Missouri Outfit to Ramsey Crooks and exiled Kenneth McKenzie to Europe!"

Fitz slapped his bare thigh. "McKenzie thought God had ta ask him ta let the sun go down at night!"

Sublette looked Fitz in the eyes, "Will Wyeth be here next year ta supply yer goods? Will he buck the richest man in the world ta save yer butts?"

Tears came to Fitz' eyes. "We done you wrong! Whatta we do ta make it right?"

"Ta start with, I'll give you boys the goods fer this season at the prices in Wyeth's contract."

"Won't Wyeth sue us all in St. Lou?"

"Says he will, but I know how ta jump that cow-pie."

"How."

"Rocky Mountain Fur Co. pays all it can agin what it owes me now, then dissolves, so it don't exist when Wyeth demands its contract performance. Can't sue a company that disappeared. You form a new company with a different name and partners and we go on doing business the St. Louie way with Mountain brotherhood stead o' Boston baked beans."

"How we gonna do the legal skullduggery fore Wyeth gets here?"

Sublette pulled papers from his possibles bag. "Got the papers prepared full legal-like by lawyer Henry Geyer."

"How long you been plannin' this, Bill?"

"Ever since I found out the brother I been carrying a cob fer done schemed with Wyeth to ruin me."

"Bill, show me where to sign."

*   *   *

After losing the trail twice more, Wyeth's caravan reached Fitzpatrick's camp at Rendezvous. Wyeth prowled the camp and bearded Fitz while the Irishman was trying to shave with a dull razor and a bad hangover.

"My courier says he gave you my letter begging you not to trade with Sublette, but you did it anyway! I want to hear it from your own faithless lips."

Fitz grimaced, but kept shaving. "Mr. Wyeth, your contract was with Rocky Mountain Fur Co. Rocky Mountain Fur's dissolved and buried in a legal grave."

"I suppose you think you don't have to pay the $500 forfeit for refusing the goods."

"It's the debt of a ghost. But as a gentlemen I'll pay it, Mr. Wyeth."

"What about the $500 William Sublette bullied me out of before he'd let his brother Milton leave St. Louis?"

"Was Milt's a legal debt?"

"Past due note. I paid it, but Milton still didn't have the guts to finish the trip!"

Fitzpatrick nicked himself and showed the blood on his razor to Wyeth. "We'll pay that $500 too, sir. But if Milt heard your talk, you'd not live to spend it."

"Milton isn't here, is he?"

Fitz flicked the bloody soap off his razor. "No sir, he's not. Wouldn't you be havin' somethin' better to do with yourself than ruinin' me shave?"

Wyeth shook his fist at Fitz and started to speak, but thought better of it and returned to his tent, cursing every step of the way.

Seizing his pen, Wyeth scratched a letter to Milton Sublette:

"I arrived at Rendezvous at the mouth of Sandy on the 17th June. Fitzpatrick refused to receive the goods; he paid however, the forfeit and the cash advance I made to you. This however, is no satisfaction to me. I do not accuse you or him of injuring me in this manner when you made the contract, but I think he has been bribed to sacrifice my interests by better offers from your brother.

Now, Milton, business is closed between us, but you will find that you have only bound yourself over to receive your supplies at such prices as may be inflicted and that all you will ever make in the country will go to pay for your goods. You will be kept as a mere slave to catch beaver for others.

I sincerely wish you well and believe had you been here these things would not have been done. I hope that your leg is better and that you will yet be able to go whole footed in all respects."

Wyeth broke his pen and ground the pieces into the dirt with his boot heel. "I will roll a rock into their garden that none of these scoundrels will ever forget!"

CHAPTER 31

CHANGING FACES OF RENDEZVOUS   SUMMER 1834

Mountain Men and Tribesmen drifted into Rendezvous until the camps of 600 trappers and 1,500 Indians adorned the cottonwood groves for 10 miles along the Green River. Business, frolic and debauchery mingled through the hot days and chill starry nights with each camper seeing a different face of Rendezvous.

"Rotten-belly!" William Sublette hollered at the tall Nez Percé strolling past Sublette's trading tent. Sublette aborted his line-up of anxious customers to hug his old friend.

"Cutface!" Rotten-belly grinned, feigning scalping Sublette's long hair. "What prize, this yellow hair! I should take when you is shot at Pierre Hole by Blackfoot devils."

"You couldn't with the Blackfoot rifle ball in the gut that give ya yer name!" Sublette jabbed his finger in the deep dimple in his friend's belly. "If ya wasn't Nez Percé, I'd offer ya a free drink."

Rotten-belly grinned, showing two front teeth busted off in his gums. "Offer anyway!"

Sublette dropped his tent flap, waving off his grumbling customers. "Business is done fer the day! What'll it be Rotten-belly -- fist fighting, horse racing, squaws er lying?"

"We try all, Cutface. We find Flathead Coughing Snake. Drink and cuss Blackfeet devils with hands on our hearts!"

*   *   *

Wyeth's second in command, Captain Joseph Thing, steered wide of Wyeth's disputes with other mountain firms. Thing ciphered his sextant sightings into map computations. Amid the clamor he wrote:

"The mountain men are all assembled on this river this season for Rendezvous and as crazy a set of men as I ever saw. Drinking is the order of the day . . . two or three glasses of grog is the best introduction to trade -- for that is the time men feel the richest and can buy all the world in thirty minutes. . . ."

*   *   *

William Marshall Anderson's 27th birthday was at hand, but he was too deep in discourse with the Nez Percé and Flatheads to celebrate. He cogitated long and hard on how to capture the essence of their pure spirits, then penned in his diary:

"These tribes are remarkable for their more than Christian practice of honesty, veracity and every moral virtue which every philosopher & professor so much laud and so little practice. There are four Christian missionaries now ready to instruct these gentle people. . . it would be charity for these messengers of civilization to desist. . . these are the only people on the globe [by] whom [such] virtues are generally practiced realities -- not Utopian dreams."

*   *   *

Lying sick abed on June 22nd, John Kirk Townsend wrote shakily:

"These people with their obstreperous mirth, their whooping, howling and quarrelling, added to the mounted Indians constantly dashing through our camp yelling like fiends above the barking and baying of savage wolf-dogs and incessant cracking of rifles render our camp a nightmarish bedlam. A more unpleasant situation for an invalid could scarcely be conceived. I am compelled all day to suffer the hiccoughing jargon of drunken traders, the sacre and foutre of Frenchmen run wild, and the swearing and screaming of our own men, scarcely less savage than the savages. . . . smoldering in hell must be preferable to this -- unless of course that is exactly where I am."

*   *   *

Disillusioned Reverend Jason Lee, reluctantly penned a letter to the most devout of Methodists, Dr. Fisk in New England :

". . . Capt. [Wyeth] is a perfect infidel as it respects his revealed religion. This I mistrusted some time since, but

recently, of his own accord, he avowed his infidelity. You probably remember what was said in Boston concerning the roughness of the men, and the promise he made of saving us as much as possible from being annoyed by their profaneness; so far from fulfilling his promise, he indulges freely in the habit himself, though he says he is ashamed of it, not on moral principles, but on those of good breeding. Hence you may judge what kind of society we have been obliged to mingle with on our journey."

*   *   *

At daylight on June 25th, William Sublette, his head throbbing, tried to shave. A pimple reddened the hawkish nose in his broken mirror -- no doubt the result of trying to out drink two righteous fellers like Rotten-belly and Coughing Snake. He could hear some outfit riding into Rendezvous. He hoped it wasn't the Blackfeet. Blackfeet loved to come out of the morning sun to raid a Rendezvous. He checked his boot pistols, grabbed his big bore Hawken rifle and loped into the cottonwoods for cover.

As Sublette peered around a tree trunk, Jim Bridger twanged, "Now there's a feller don't know whether ta shoot er shave!" Men behind Bridger burst out laughing, and all rode down upon Sublette whooping and waving weapons.

Sublette pulled his boot pistols and aimed one straight at Bridger while he fired the other into the ground. Bridger tumbled from his horse, screeching with laughter, and Sublette flopped on him. They rolled in the dirt till another husky man piled on them with a banshee yell. Sublette was amazed to see who that was. The rogue Scottish nobleman William Drummond Stewart, his bearded face tanned near black, roughed up Sublette's hair and whooped louder than Bridger at the bottom of the pile. Sublette gasped, "By God, Captain Stewart, yer a Mountain Man!"

Stewart growled, "That I am."

After getting his cook to fix Bridger and Stewart sizzling bacon, corn batter cakes, hominy and Cheyenne venison, Sublette pawed through his St. Louis mail bag. As usual, illiterate Jim Bridger got none, but he dug out three crumpled envelopes for Captain Stewart. "When you've read these, come back an' we'll tipple with nectar o' the Gods -- metheglin -- wild honey stung with alkyhol!"

Stewart retreated to the cottonwoods. As next in line for the titles and estates, it was his duty to keep abreast of affairs in Scotland. But just remembering Scotland robbed him of the essence of these savage mountain spirits, who epitomized what all Scotsmen longed to be -- wildly free. He dirked wife Christina's letter open. Her fragile script about their son George was reassuring. Stewart's mother gave them enough behind brother John's back to meet their needs. George was a bright lad who mirrored his father, mien and deed. She hoped her husband of so few years would return to her for many. She said nothing of his creditors.

His lawyer's stiff missive enclosed a pittance draft of less than half the interest due from his trust brother John administered. It mentioned naught of creditors. Then he read brother George Stewart's blitherings. Lord Bredalbane's lavish improvements to Taymouth Castle made it Scotland's showplace. But brother John Stewart, never outshone, was expanding New Murthly Castle, already costing a million pounds, putting Lord Bredalbane's efforts to shame. Stewart'd hie into the wilderness and forget his vain brother -- before he revisited Cain's solution for Abel.

*　　　　　*　　　　　*

Swarthy Lucien Fontenelle and his long time partner Andrew Drips lead their outfit into Rendezvous on June 28th and made camp, elated to hear their old foe Rocky Mountain Fur Company was no more. With a bottle of French brandy, Fontenelle enticed Fitzpatrick to leave his Old Sledge card game. Fitzpatrick took a pungent pull off the bell shaped bottle and grunted, "What'd you American Fur boys be doin' here, Lucifer? Bill Sublette said AFC agreed to stay outa the Rockies this whole year."

Fontenelle enjoyed Satanic comparisons. He stroked his devil's goatee, then replied unctuously, "Concessions were made for Rocky Mountain Fur Company -- now extinct. With RMF's end, AFC's pledge to avoid the Rockies died. What'd you name yer new outfit?"

"Fitzpatrick, Bridger & Sublette."

"Must be Milt Sublette. You'd not give blood to the leech who bled RMF dry."

"'Tis Milt, though he doesn't know it. Bad leg's his master. Strays no further from St. Louie than it'll let him."

"Devil has a leash on all of us. Milt's is just plainer to see. Nothing's stronger than new bonds between old enemies who know each other's faults. Your boys know the Rockies and AFC has the money. What *power* we could share! William Sublette would lie helpless before us. We'll talk again before Rendezvous's done." Fontenelle shook Fitzpatrick's hand and walked between the tethered horses into the lush meadow.

Grasshoppers rattled into flight in Fontenelle's path. He took no joy in the privations of mountain life. Never should have come out here at all. He adored the South's culture. But today was tolerable! He'd watched Fitzpatrick's eyes at the hint of power over Bill Sublette. The devil's in every man. What a conquest t'woud be to subjugate an age-old foe without firing a shot!

*   *   *

Still outraged on July 2nd, Nathaniel Wyeth mustered his men and ordered, "Move out!" Wyeth rode from his Rendezvous defeat like a triumphant knight homing from the Crusades with a Saracen's head on his pommel. He'd lost money and many men at Rendezvous. But he'd acquired the services of a Scottish nobleman hunter, who'd unwittingly help Wyeth put his corrupt competitors out of business.

Thirty-some Nez Percé and Flatheads with wives, children and dogs, would follow Wyeth's caravan to their homes in the Snake River region. A Blackfoot renegade rode among them, promising to keep Wyeth's caravan safe from his marauding kin.

*   *   *

Jason Lee didn't share Wyeth's contempt for William Sublette. Rather, Jason'd taken tea with Sublette often. Sublette gave Lee an article from the Western Colonization Society on founding missions and suggested Fort William on the Laramie as a site. Lee even entrusted letters to Sublette to mail in St. Louis, and thanked him for his gracious conduct before riding hard to catch up with Wyeth.

*   *   *

With a gloomy heart at the thought this might be his last Rendezvous, on July 9th William Sublette led his caravan hauling 40 packs of beaver from the valley of the Green River, now trampled and torn.   A lone Indian pup sat wagging its tail. Sublette didn't look back.   The lump in his throat wouldn't let him.

Sublette was anxious to see if the corn he'd planted in the stone-hard ground at Fort William had come up.   He was even more hopeful that Robert Campbell would be at their new fort when William got there.   They'd have a good time going back to the Settlements together.

*   *   *

Not ready to return to civilization's palling confines, Marshall Anderson joined Fitzpatrick's crew, commenting on William Sublette in his July 9th journal entry:

". . . *I shall feel his absence very sensibly. Never have I seen a man in whose skill, prudence and courage I have more confidence . . . a good and brave man.*"

Fitzpatrick combined his camp with Fontenelle's on July 19th, and went into serious talks with Fontenelle.   Marshall Anderson wrote of this:

"[They] *negotiate an affair of business yet "sub rosa."   The sceptre is passing from Judah.*"

Fontenelle dogged Fitzpatrick daily for two weeks. Ultimately, he inveigled Fitz to merge his firm into The Fontenelle & Fitzpatrick Company.   Milt Sublette, Jim Bridger and Andy Drips were given quiet interests.   After dead Rocky Mountain Fur Company's body parts had been devoured by its old enemy American Fur Company, Fontenelle wrote Pierre Chouteau Jr.:

". . . *Messrs. Fitzpatrick, Milton Sublette and others concluded not to have anything more to do with William Sublette and it will surprise me very much if he takes more than ten packs [of beaver] down next year. I have entered into a partnership with the others and the whole of the beaver caught by them is to be turned over to us by agreement made with them in concluding the arrangement.*"

CHAPTER 32

THE AMERICAN BOARD'S DECISION   SUMMER 1834

Crotchety Doctor B.B. Wisner composed his letters for the American Board of Commissioners for Foreign Missions in a closet of a room in the Boston office where the elfin window peeped dim light. Perhaps this cluttered room with its dusty files and yellowing newspapers was a sanctuary only he and God dared enter.

Doctor Wisner seldom wore spectacles in public, and even when on were too weak to show more than blurs. Here, he perused the printed word with his great glass, seeing like a boy again. Unfortunately just reading the letters was scant help in answering them. The Marcus Whitman thing had come up again.

He inched his magnifying glass over the Whitman letters to reconstruct the course of the matter. Whitman still wasn't married, despite Wisner's pointed remarks on that in his May 1, 1834 letter. Whitman's obtuse admission that he didn't even have a present arrangement to get married appeared in his June 3rd reply.

Even Whitman partisans said the man was crude in appearance. So were his letters. Their shortcomings had caused Wisner to write Reverend Strong on June 14th that Whitman's preparatory education was quite deficient. On the same day Wisner'd written Whitman for fuller information of his health. Wisner wheezed the dust off the scrawled copy of his June 14th letter to Whitman and waved his withered hand to clear the particles out of the bleary sunlight shaft illuminating the close air.

Wisner coughed, then located Whitman's June 27th reply. If Whitman had pains, you'd think he'd be sophisticated enough to keep quiet about them or skilled enough as a Medical Doctor to cure them. But Whitman's letter blatantly stated:

"I have not used remidies but in some few instances since and except for the last two or three weeks I have had but trifling inconvenience and nothing of organic or functional deranges. I have not been for any length of time without a slight pain and for the last two or three weeks there has been an agravation of pain and soreness so that I have used remidies and shall have to use more skill. I have thought for the last year or more that my health was nearly restored and I am in hopes that I shall still find my expectation realized in this respect."

Wisner knew his own journal was here someplace. It was under his desk and still showed a page for June. He turned to July, calculated the date from his sermons to be July 17, 1834 and wrote a firm reply to Doctor Marcus Whitman.

*   *   *

Marcus Whitman's new log cabin, very like the hut of his early boyhood, lay midway between Wheeler and Prattsburg. Construction was complete except for chinking the cracks between the logs. Marcus recalled the cathedral-like barn built by Jane Prentiss's father over in Amity and shook his head. The Prentiss barn was square and plumb in every direction. Marcus's logs were crooked, notched and stacked generally on top of each other. Nothing about his cabin was square or plumb, but it'd do.

It had taken every cent Marcus'd hoarded and a formidable note to buy these 150 acres from the Pulteney Estate. He'd built everything himself, spending scarce money only for the window glass and nails. Saving money was demanded of a young doctor of 32 with a budding practice and many patients that paid in chickens and eggs.

At least Marcus had waited till the logs parched before he chinked the cracks. They would've dried quicker if he'd peeled their bark, but then he'd have to paint them. He mixed cement mortar for the chinking in a flat trough with a hoe near his new well. He had to get this chinking done, in time to harvest his grain crops.

His practice ate the lion's share of his time, but if he was ever going to land a mission to Oregon from the American Board, he first had to find a wife. Jane Prentiss was most desirable, but she had no interest in leaving her warm family to prowl the wilderness ministering to heathens. Besides, Jane Prentiss always foisted her unseen sister Narcissa between them. Every New York family harbored at least one old maid school teacher. There had to be good reason why Narcissa wasn't spoken for at 26.

Marcus wiped stinging sweat from his eyes with his wadded shirt. His side pain was such a familiar visitor, it throbbed unheeded. He troweled mortar into the cracks, but it was too dry to stick. He cranked a couple buckets of water up from his well and wet the mud enough to cling well to the logs.

His husky body ached in new places by the time he finished chinking the cabin in the chilly twilight. His icy shirt gave little comfort. Squealing night birds swooped after chirping crickets. Marcus saddled up and galloped to Wheeler to meet several farmer patients who worked during the day and didn't want to pay the extra 25¢ and 6¼¢ a mile for a house call to their farms.

Arriving at his Wheeler office, Marcus stabled his horse, then went in minutes ahead of his seven o'clock patient. A letter lay on the floor. Even in the dark, he could see it was from the American Board. Anxiously, he struck flint until he got his lamp lit. He scalpeled the letter open and read Dr. B.B. Wisner's July 17th letter:

"On the whole, I feel constrained to conclude that duty to the cause requires me to advise you to give up, or at least to defer, till it shall be certain that your health is restored and established, the plan of going on a foreign mission."

A tear wet Wisner's letter, then spread to blur a word. Marcus hadn't cried since he was a boy of eight when his father Beza died. Now he was even more alone. Even God didn't want him. Wisner's words shoveled him out like manure from the barn. Surely, God would not deny Marcus's destiny to save the heathens from descent into hell. Marcus grasped his head in his hands, moaning, "O Lord, what can I do now?"

CHAPTER 33

BIRTH OF FORT HALL   SUMMER 1834

Vengeful Nathaniel Wyeth led 41 men and 126 horses northwest toward the Snake River country hauling goods shunned by Rocky Mountain Fur Company. To bury the urge to kill his brother John in the wilderness, Captain William Drummond Stewart went along and hunted for Wyeth. Thirty-five Flatheads and Nez Percé followed their new savior, giant black-bearded Reverend Jason Lee.

Encamped on July 3rd, Reverend Lee was summoned to the Indian fires, bringing Chief *Insillah* who spoke English. Among the firelight's eerie shadows, Nez Percé Chief *Tackensuatis* spoke of an odyssey so moving Lee gasped as *Insillah* translated.

"Two summers ago Nez Percé and Flatheads want see God. We send four spirit men to St. Louis to bring us teacher of white man's God. Man-of-the-Morning, Black Eagle, Rabbit-Skin-Leggings and No-Horns-on-His-Head are shunned in streets. Hearts of Man-of-the-Morning and Black Eagle are hurt and they die. Other two find *Hi-Hi-Suks-Tooah* [Red-head Chief] you call General William Clark. He keeps them at his fires through the snows, then puts two left on fire-canoe *Yellowstone*, saying God teachers will come next summer."

The Chief's eyes grew large. "Medicine man Catlin on fire-canoe makes faces of Rabbit-Skin-Leggings and No-Horn-on-His-Head live on wood! Fire-canoe swims to Fort Pierre at place Sioux call Dakota. Sioux give God-Seekers feast. But No-Horns-on-His-Head dies. Rabbit-Skin-Leggings runs through forest, until he finds us. He tells *Hi-Hi-Suks-Tooah*'s words that God's man will come. None come. Heart of Rabbit-Skin-Leggings hurts with shame of lying. He dies. Now, you come! We want meet God!"

Reverend Jason Lee rose in the firelight, grieving for four men who'd died searching for a God they never knew. The Indians hugged him, then knelt about him, but he was too overcome by their pure devotion to speak and wept with them.

*　　　　*　　　　*

Fourth of July found Wyeth's band at Muddy Creek. Wyeth addressed his men. "I'm too much a Yankee to ignore our nation's birthday! Liquor will flow!"

Amid cheering Mountain Men, Captain Thing retreated disgustedly to his tent with scientists Townsend and Nuttal, where Townsend penned:

"This being a memorable day, the liquor kegs were opened, and the men allowed an abundance. We, therefore, soon had a renewal of the coarse and brutal scenes of the rendezvous. Some of the bacchanals called for a volley in honor of the day, and in obedience to the order, some twenty or thirty "happy" ones reeled into line with their muzzles directed to every point of the compass, and when the word "fire" was given, we who were not "happy" had to lie flat upon the ground to avoid the bullets careering through the camp."

On July 5th Wyeth's hungover party forded the Bear River and pressed on till their horses were more spent than the men. Reaching the western channel of the Bear River where it doubled back, Wyeth camped, observing to Stewart, "No matter how exhausted men are, they're never too tired to fish." Men cut saplings and tied hooks on any string they could find, baiting with snails, insects and frog parts. Squaws speared theirs. Trout, grayling and char soon roasted over many fires.

Nuttal waddled into camp, his glasses askew and his shirt tied in a great pregnancy of gooseberries and currants.

For several days, they tracked the Bear River north. The alluvial plain evolved from grasses to jagged lava sheets, flanked by towering basalt pillars. Sage brush and cedars provided distasteful forage for the stock. At the Bear River's White Clay pits, they found carbonated springs bubbling through chalky soil. Wyeth asked Richardson, "You think this water's safe to drink?"

Richardson grunted, "Tis if the fizz don't tickle ya ta death."

Wyeth tin-cupped a fizzy drink, then enjoyed its effervescence. Remembering the money he'd made with his patented ice-cutting machines, he tried to calculate how much he could make selling this water. But -- since there was no one here to buy it, he drank another cupful down for the noncommercial joy of it.

Since they weren't racing anybody this trip, Wyeth rested their faltering horses on July 9th. He sent Captain Stewart and Richardson to hunt buffalo. By nightfall they returned with meat and marrow bones of two bulls.

As fragrant meat sizzled over many fires, a tall half-breed in blood red sash and crimson-trimmed buckskins sauntered into camp. At Wyeth's approach, he said, "I'm Tom McKay, son of Dr. McLoughlin, chief factor at Fort Vancouver. My Canadians hunt south of here."

"I'm Nathaniel Wyeth, leader of this expedition. Most gratified to make your acquaintance, Mr. McKay. Please partake of our fine buffalo repast!"

"You're more formal than my father! I'll squat and chew on a rib!"

*   *   *

On July 10th, Wyeth's party stumbled onto Bonneville's camp on a lava plain. Bonneville's men played cards and snored on the stove-hot ground. Wyeth and Captain Stewart sought Bonneville, while their caravan continued onward.

Bonneville rubbed his sleepy eyes and welcomed them into his suffocating lodge. He patted down the sparse hairs on his pate and told his squaw to bring metheglin. Bonneville confided, "Metheglin is my most precious possession." The dark-faced squaw set demitasses before them and spooned paltry portions of the alcohol-honey concoction from her vat.

Wyeth exclaimed, "This is enchanting!"

"Rome's mead couldn't match it," Stewart confirmed, irritated at how much Bonneville put him in mind of his piggish brother John Stewart.

When the squaw poised her delicate ladle over their glasses, Stewart declined to Bonneville's obvious pleasure.

Stewart hated himself when he became boorish, but he unthreaded the tin cup from his belt and dragged it through the thick beverage.

The dismayed Bonneville groaned, "I beg you help yourselves, gentlemen."

Wyeth unlimbered his tin cup and draught after draught of the precious fluid disappeared down the visitors' throats as they regaled the liquor's virtues.

"Falstaff himself could not have adored metheglin more!" Stewart proclaimed.

"Nor held any more," Bonneville added, his urbanity flagging.

Wyeth asserted, "This'll turn Boston Catholics to beekeepers."

When mere drops remained, Stewart ran his forefinger around the vat securing the last of them. He toasted, "Here's to my brother John, High Potentate of all north of London and champion wastrel of the world," noisily licking off the drops amid groans of gusto at the ghastly look on Bonneville's face."

With that Captains Stewart and Wyeth arose unsteadily, swept their hats in great arcs and bowed out of Bonneville's tent. Floundering onto his horse, Wyeth slurred, "Did we say thank you?"

"Not as I recall, but I must advise against going back just now."

*   *   *

In Wyeth's absence, his expedition wended between quagmires reaching a willow grove on the margin of a river. A bull grizzly bolted into the caravan, scattering terror stricken horses and men. Rifle balls popping into the bear infuriated him all the more. Snapping at each wound as if to remove an arrow, the grizzly chased a panicked hunter till another ball veered him among the horses. Shod hooves thumped the grizzly as kicks landed from all quarters.

The grizzly ripped a horse's pack off in its monstrous mouth. With a shake of its head, coffee and bolts of yard goods exploded everywhere. The bloodied bear lunged for a braying pack mule thrashing up a hillside, but her head kick tumbled him down the hill.

The bewildered behemoth stood up, blood flowing from his maw and took six more rifle balls in the chest. Far from dead, he roared, plunged into the water and began to swim powerfully toward horses marooned on the other bank's strip-shore.

Richardson rode up, took aim and fired a single ball into the back of the bear's head, killing him instantly.

Four men roped and dragged the sopping bear from the water, counting 30 bullet holes in his corpse. Townsend measured the bruin's front pad at ten inches across and his claws at seven inches long.

Richardson rod-tamped the new load in his rifle. "Two things you boys gotta learn. Gotta quit practicin' an' jist go ahead an' kill the dang bear."

"What's the other thing?" the shaken Nuttal inquired.

"Nothin's better eatin' than sumpthin' that wants ta eat you!"

*   *   *

July 14th dawned on Nathaniel Wyeth and Richardson scouting the plain bordered by the Snake and Portneuf Rivers. Wyeth warmed to the south side of the Portneuf with its grass and rich soil. "We'll build the fort here," he said simply, mindful of all that had preceded this spiritual moment.

Next morning Wyeth sent 12 men to make meat while he completed the layout of the 80' by 80' fort. Then axes bit cottonwoods. The first crackled and crashed to the ground in a cloud of ancient dust that had been slumbering loam. They stood trunks in holes leaving 15 feet above ground for a perimeter wall. Wyeth loved the aroma of fresh cut wood. He felt building this fort was the crowning accomplishment of his life!

Wyeth knew this fort would attract multitudes to trade. Its permanence would drain all trade from those nomadic St. Louis scoundrels and their willy-nilly summer fiascoes. Though it lay 150 miles from the Green River, Wyeth was certain it would convert Rendezvous to a relic. This fort was the stone he was rolling into their garden.

On July 25th, Wyeth's hunting party returned, startling fort site workers by firing their rifles like Blackfeet. After presenting Wyeth with welcome meat, Captain Stewart said, "We've seen plenty of tracks, but no Blackfeet. Fort looks singularly sturdy. It's no castle, but then it didn't cost a million pounds." Wyeth didn't grasp Stewart's meaning, and blended the hunters into his construction crew after they'd dried the excess buffalo meat.

On July 26th, Captain Wyeth, Thomas Nuttal, Kirk Townsend and Captain Stewart supped with Thomas McKay in one of the many tipis his colorfully dressed Canadians had raised near the new fort. McKay's dark eyes, hair and skin left no doubt of his Indian blood, but he combined the open frankness of the Mountain Man with the affability and grace of a gentleman. Wyeth listened carefully as McKay told how he maintained discipline in his force, using floggings in serious cases. McKay added, "The Indian is the most difficult to subdue; but perseverance and rigid self example makes him clay in my hands."

Neither Wyeth nor the others thought McKay exaggerated, for his men were regimented like the European soldiers, and McKay was worshipped by the half-breeds and Indians who followed him.

After supper, McKay's Indians blessed the new fort with a ritual ceremony and reverent songs no whites understood, but haunting sounds none would ever forget.

At Wyeth's request, Reverend Jason Lee conducted a traditional Methodist service. Even the Indians who understood nothing Lee said, knelt with him, put their hands together and prayed as a sign of their deep respect.

Next morning, Wyeth doffed his sweaty shirt and yelled to his workers gouging the grass with cottonwood poles behind their mules, "Drop those poles along the west side. We've got a fort to finish!"

He centered the front gate in the west wall, building bastions in two corners. The outer fortifications completed, Wyeth erected a log store with living quarters inside the north stockade wall. The fort was finished the night of August 4, 1834.

Wyeth gathered his men at sunrise on August 5th. "Hoist the flag!" he commanded. The hand sewn Star Spangled

Banner rose against the brilliant dawn sky. It was Wyeth's coming of age, as if he were born anew with all his hopes for the fresh fort. As the flag pinnacled its pole, Wyeth dropped his arm. Rifles fired a 12 gun salute that combined into a cannon's roar.

Wyeth pried the top off a whiskey keg and welcomed his 40 men to dip their tin cups and battered pans. Raising his own bail of liquor, Nathaniel Wyeth yelled, "I Christen thee Fort Hall in honor of Henry Hall, far-seeing partner of the Boston firm of Tucker, Williams and Hall, my backers in this heroic trading effort!"

He looked about him at his rabble force. He wanted to address them as *Gentlemen* but could not lie on such an auspicious occasion. "We've done a great thing here in the wilderness -- for ourselves and for mankind. May we all live to feel the warmth of our own hearths again when Fort Hall has served its noble purpose!"

Leaving Mr. Evans in charge of 11 men, 14 horses and 3 cows, Wyeth lead his men across the Snake River on August 6th, and down the lava plain to the Boise River.

At Walla Walla, he was handsomely received by Pierre Pambrun, but continued onward to an even warmer reception on September 14th at Fort Vancouver for himself and Thomas McKay, step-son of its factor.

The brig *May Dacre* arrived the next day, delayed for repair of lightning damage and too late for the salmon season. Wyeth shook his head, muttering, "Another damnable financial disaster to explain to that pig-headed Henry Hall."

CHAPTER 34

THE SILK HAT AND THE MISSIONARIES   FALL 1834

"What're we doing inna dry goods store, Bobbie?"

"Lookin' for a hat, Mr. S."

"We're in St. Louis inna cholera epidemic looking fer a hat?
We could be sitting behind a couple o' beers at the Green Tree."

"No' joost any hat, Mr. S. That hat."

William Sublette eyed the gleaming silk hat squatting over a prim post in the front window. "Hell, I'd never wear that -- too slick 'n harder'n a brick. Beaver hats're soft as a rabbit. Keeps yer head warm."

"Mr. S, you're na lookin' at a silk hat. You're lookin' at the end o' our way o' life."

Campbell picked up the glimmering hat. "Mah brother Hugh writes me silk's in and beaver is oot in New York."

A dapper young clerk with a stiff white collar swaggered across the squeaky floor. "May I interest you in that stylish new hat, gentlemen? Just came in Wednesday!"

"Not on yer life, Mister!" Sublette growled, seizing the hated hat from Campbell and dropping it like a horse shoe on its little post. Cutface Bill Sublette had just seen his own ghost. He shouldered past the clerk and squawked the pine floor with its foot-worn, shiny nail-head islands all the way out the door. Campbell shrugged at the offended clerk and followed in quick squeaks.

Sublette slouched along the street shaking his head. "Knew the silk hat was coming, but seeing it hurt. Think o' all them men still Up the Mountain risking their own pelts to trap beaver. Going agin blizzards, Blackfeet, bad whiskey an' busted bones -- all fer nothing cause of a hat made by a buncha worms."

"Moost remember, Mister S. It started wi' a hat. Only fittin', it should end wi' one."

"Always seemed like it was more'n a hat, didn't it, Bobbie?"

Campbell's short legs churned to keep pace with his angry 6'2" partner's strides. "It did. It did at that, Mister S."

*   *   *

Asiatic Cholera prowling St. Louis flushed the Sublettes from E. Town's comfortable *City Hotel* to the crude cabins at Sulphur Springs. If anything worried William Sublette more than cholera or the silk hat, it was his brother Milt.

The brotherly reunion William planned all the way back from the summer Rendezvous misfired. Ever since Milt'd learned his own brother'd kilt the pride of his life -- the Rocky Mountain Fur Company -- he'd sulked.

William watched ole hound dog Doc Bernard Farrar waddle from Milt's cabin and head for his buggy. "Wait!" William hollered and headed Doc Farrar off.

"You glide like a big cat, Bill!"

"Shoulda seen Milt run before rot got his leg, Doc. Wind was clumsy beside Milt."

"If you're gonna beg me to save Milton's leg again, I got no miracles in my black bag. These poultices are worthless as trying to heal the red off a brick wall. Osteomyelitis has chewed up into his *tibia*."

"*Tibia*?"

"Shin bone. Disease's a boll weevil. Leave it alone, it'll bore up to his knee. Once the knee's ruint, Milton's chances of walking half-normal on a wood leg're gone. Lower leg's gotta come off soon."

"Can it wait till after Christmas?"

"Didn't we have this talk last year?"

"Doc, 12 years ago I promised my dying Mama Isabella I'd take care o' my brothers an' sisters. Words weren't outa my mouth when baby Sally died. Polly follered her inta the grave. I tuck young Pinckney Up the Mountain when he's 15 an' Blackfeet kilt him. Now it's Milt. Not easy fer a man who worships honor, ta be lying ta his dead mother, Doc!"

Farrar snorted, "You protecting Milt from me?   That leg's killing him. You better get another Doctor!"

"Wait, Doc.   Give Milt this last Christmas an' I'll personally help ya cut his leg off."

"You can't do that, Bill. Two strong field hands're all I'll need."

Sublette shook his head and walked away.   "Swear ta God, I'll do it, Doc."

*   *   *

With the coming of the holidays, William Sublette jumped at General Ashley's invitation to a political fund raiser to duck the dogfights with his drunken brother. In his best suit and Beau Brummel beaver hat, William rode his thoroughbred, Hellfire. He couldn't help comparing his stiff outfit to his torn buckskins and floppy hat. But he couldn't show up in them ole duds on a mule at the General's!

William seldom rode past the lofty estates of the Biddles, O'Fallons and Lindells at their fashionable northern edge of St. Louis where General Ashley'd built his mansion among the Indian Mounds.

Ashley's home was a breath-taker at sunset. The front lawn slanted toward the Mississippi. The north side overlooked the Missouri. The south faced St. Louis, and the rear opened on the summit of an ancient Indian Mound serving as a terrace. But the front yard fountain bubbling fresh water was the Ace in the deck. Nobody else had anything like it in St. Louis.

A well-liveried Negro took Sublette's horse, and General Ashley met William on the front porch. As ever, the General's chin was out in front of the rest of him and his hair still didn't stay combed across his bald spot. But in his dapper clothes, he looked tolerable for a man of 56. "Come in, Bill. You're an hour early. Come in and we'll wait for the minnows!"

Sublette stepped nervously onto his first rung of the social ladder. "Wife here?"

The General opened his worn gold watch. "Elizabeth and girls are out with the carriage fetching floral arrangements. Let's grab a bracer in my study before the stuffed shirts pop in. I'll take your hat."

THE SILK HAT AND THE MISSIONARIES   FALL 1834

If William'd thought Washington's *Indian Queen Hotel* carpets were the world's plushiest, it was cause he hadn't trod Ashleys' living room. But the study, strewn with newspapers and books, was downright grim.

While Ashley trickled their brandies from a crystal decanter, William scanned clippings about Elizabeth Moss Ashley. One said she was *an immediate sensation in Washington, queenlike, charming, fascinating and possessing exquisite tact, affable, having a melodious voice.* Another described *her remarkable beauty and grace -- a special favorite in the most refined and intellectual circles -- with versatility to adapt equally to all ranks and conditions.*

"General, I never seen the beat o' yer second wife, Eliza. By the looks o' this, you've matched her!"

Ashley's steel eyes warmed. "Papers don't mention Elizabeth's two young daughters -- solid sterling. I've adopted them. Elizabeth's given me a heart. I don't see things as coldly as I did. To my family's health, sir!"

They clinked their fragile glasses dangerously. While the General savored the bouquet of the costly French brandy, Sublette tossed his down in a gulp.

"How's Milt's leg, Bill?"

Sublette felt himself stiffen. "Gotta come off after Christmas."

"Milt's not taking it well, is he?"

"Milt's taking it like a man, General. That's all anybody could ask of somebody who growed up the fastest boy in Kentucky."

"How's Andrew?"

"Sent Drew to the Upper Missouri with the paperwork to turn our forts over ta AFC. He's gonna swing by our new fort on the Laramie ta make sure it's built-out right. Hope he stays a spell. Our Uncle Solomon Whitley raised Drew.   He's on his deathbed in St. Charles."

"Have a young brother named Solomon too?"

"Yup. Solomon's 19 -- specializes in drinking, gambling and running everybody else's life. How's things in Washington, General?"

"Nastiest problem's the Seminole uprising in Florida."

"Uprising?"

"Seminoles agreed by an 1832 treaty to leave Florida but Chief Osceola refused. Andy Jackson sent Wiley Thompson down there to cart the Seminoles out. Jackson says if he could conquer the whole infernal state in *two* weeks in 1819, Thompson ought to roust out a few Seminoles in *three* weeks! Thompson resented the Chief's swaggering, so he jailed Osceola for one day to show him who's boss. Osceola's still killing settlers. Washington papers call it the *Three Week War*. For the real story without the Washington veneer, read Carlos Hamsa's piece in *The Kentucky Palladium.*"

"Who?"

"Reporter named Carlos Hamsa from Potosi where I lease out my lead mines. Travels as a correspondent. Way Hamsa plays the squeezebox'd make Angels dance. Writes better than he plays. Hamsa says Wiley Thompson won't subdue the Seminoles in *three years*. So much for the *Three Week War.*" General Ashley laid the *Palladium* on his "to clip" stack.

"Whatta ya make o' the silk hat, General?"

"Beaver trade's death song. Grand as your coup was over Astor, silk hat's what ran John Jacob out of the fur trade. Buffalo robes still strong, but beaver's on borrowed time. That's not the worst of it for the West."

"What's worse?"

"Missionaries are coming, Bill. Last month I sent information on Oregon to the American Board of Commissioners for Foreign Missions. They're sending a Reverend Parker out here from upstate New York. Likely to see you, because I gave them your name."

"Methodists already sent Jason an' Daniel Lee. Them boys was at the summer Rendezvous seeking sites fer their missions. You see missionaries as the end o' the Mountain Men?"

"Like TB. Not fatal right off, but snuffs you in the long run. You've talked of coming down the Mountain for years. Now's the time, Bill."

"Bleeve what you say, General, but a man don't always do what's good fer hisself."

"We've all got the scars to prove that, Bill."

"I wanta leave the mountains, but I don't wanta leave the mountains."

"Went through that same torment in '26 when I sold you my fur business. Once a man's been Up the Mountain, he's never the same as other men. When you've shared a mountain top with God, you despise being a mortal. Wild craving for freedom never dies.   All you can do is hobble it and give in to respectability."

"Respectablility's harder'n a grizzly ta face, General. How bout another swig o' brandy?"

"Fine, Bill." The General poured another glass of high-priced brandy. "This isn't beer to be swilled. It's French brandy to be savored."

Sublette grinned and tossed his brandy against the back of his throat. "Ya can civilize me after Christmas, General!"

*   *   *

Fat Uncle Solomon Whitley died during the first fall snow.   William despised the St. Charles cemetery where his Mama Isabella, Papa Phillip and little sisters Polly and Sally lay beneath the dazzling snow, but helped carry the old man's coffin anyway. Andrew Sublette was still Up the Mountain.   Milt refused to get near the place because it spooked him.   Uncle Solomon's funeral was mobbed. Milt's absence went unnoted.

Strangely, Solomon's funeral clinched William Sublette's decision to withdraw from the Indian Country. Out there a man died hard, with body parts hacked off for doodads. Wolves cracked his bones for marrow, and buzzards gorged on leftovers. At least in the settlements, friends lied to yer corpse about how good you was, and you met your maker whole instead of in installments.

*   *   *

Uncle Solomon's funeral made William realize he didn't have forever to do things. William promptly negotiated three contracts for buildings on his 770 acre farm at Sulphur Springs. Lindsay Lewis agreed to build four cabins 14' by 16' for field hands with Sublette furnishing floor planking and shingles. The second contract called for Lindsay's brother John to build two larger cabins 16' by 24'.

Sublette met Lindsay and Sam Lewis at Sulphur Springs two days before Christmas and went over the mansion plans and contract inch by inch. "Boys, 'cept fer filling a inside straight with my next two years pay on the table at the Green Tree Tavern in '28, building this house's bout the most important thing I ever done."

"As a passel, these three contracts outshines any job we ever had," Lindsay said in his Bayou drawl.

Sublette nodded, "House'll be stone with white lime grout on a 45 by 55 foot plot, with the left front corner at that stake."

Wind-driven rain spattered the house plans, but Sublette continued, "Full under-basement and two upper stories done in six months."

"Plans are ketchin' hell, Bill."

"So's my shirt, but I'm only gonna chew this cabbage once, boys. Two foot outer walls'll enclose three basement rooms. Six groundfloor fireplaces, stone caps over each door and window an' a broad arch right there over the main entrance. Building contract calls fer the structure ta be architecturally attractive ta the eye. Gotta be built good as my Grandpa Whitley's mansion in Kentucky."

"Ain't goin' off on one o' yer mountain sprees while we're buildin' these out, are ya Bill?" Samuel asked, shielding diagonal rain from his eyes. "Might need approvals."

Sublette turned west and watched jagged lighting bolts jousting among the towering thunderheads. Sublette's shoulders drooped. He shoved his hands in his pockets. "No gentlemen. I guess I'm not."

CHAPTER 35

Reverend Samuel Parker whip-snicked Resurrection on the hip, sending his spattered buggy careening around a curve on the snow-patched road wending through Allegany County, New York. There was no excuse for the snail-gaited horses the American Board kept pawning off on him. Parker's buggy was buried under fossilized mud because he hadn't found anybody devout enough to chisel it off.

Parker raised his buffalo coat collar to keep mud-meteors out of his shirt. He gave Resurrection another lick with the buggy whip. "They should've named you Lazarus! It'd take the Lord Himself to raise you from the dead! Couldn't hold a candle to Sally!" he shouted, then spat out the mud that interrupted his diatribe. He missed Sally -- Salvation -- who'd gotten skinny and died the fortnight past. Penny -- Penitence -- had lasted one week, then foundered in her stall. Nothing repentant about that lazy wench!

In front of the meeting house in Angelica, New York, Reverend Parker yanked the lathered Resurrection to a stop and bolted inside without blanketing the wheezing horse or even unhitching him. "Sorry I'm late," he hawked to the impatient group in the large room with sweating windows. "Let us pray!"

After his rousing sermon, Reverend Parker accepted the tearful conversions of four sinners -- a paltry number for this size gathering -- but Parker'd started late with an irate flock.

Narcissa Prentiss, garbed in black, approached Reverend Parker by the smoky fireplace. "I do so want to become a missionary in the West. Is there any place for an unmarried female in my Lord's vineyard?"

"Not sure," the purse-mouthed Parker muttered. "Use that bonnet and take up a collection from these people. If that red-gold hair won't open their pocketbooks to the Lord -- nothing will, Sister --"

"Prentiss. Narcissa Prentiss."

"Of course. You're from Amity -- huge house -- where Reverend Rudd holds revivals. Like to preach a sermon er two there myself. Get along now and collect God's bounty. Missions cost money. Nobody goes west if we're broke!"

"Could you write a missionary letter to the American Board for me, Reverend Parker. They've heeded me little."

"Course I will, Sister --"

"Prentiss."

"Soon as you've harvested the offerings -- I'll pen a note -- a persuasive note -- to the Board. Had a shake-up there. Dr. Wisner's abed awaiting his Maker. Think Reverend Greene's the prime Secretary -- go on now, Sister -- bring in the sheaves!"

When Narcissa returned with $22.29 in her black lace bonnet, Reverend Parker borrowed pen, ink and paper from the perspiring hostess and wrote:

"December 17, 1834

Are females wanted? A Miss Narcissa Prentiss of Amity is very anxious to go to the heathen. Her education is good -- piety conspicuous -- her influence good. She will offer herself if -- is needed."

As Reverend Parker was about to embellish his plea for Narcissa, a sullen farmer yelled, "Preacher -- your horse hangs dead in the traces!"

"Get me a horse!" Parker screeched. "I'm due in Wheeler by nightfall."

"I can't git a horse outa thin air on Sunday!" the irritated hand hollered back.

"Do take my horse, Reverend," Narcissa pleaded.

*   *   *

After Reverend Parker finished his Wheeler Revival in blowing snow on the village square, he spied lamplight in Dr. Marcus Whitman's office. Without so much as a knock, Parker burst into Marcus's office, catching the young Doctor sprawled asleep in his chair. "Is this how God wants you to twaddle away His time, Brother Whitman?"

Hair more tousled than usual, Marcus fisted his sleepy eyes. In his cavernously deep voice, Marcus grunted, "Delivered two babies, Reverend. Last one took all night. Lady tried to hold it back so it'd be born on Jesus's birthday."

"What a noble aim! And did she?"

"No!"

"Why didn't you hold it back for her, Brother?"

"Lord wanted it borned at 4:45 this morning. You sick again?"

"No -- thank God -- I won't need you bleeding my poor arm. Hasn't the Board appointed you so we can go to Oregon?"

"Dr. Wisner wrote me in July to give it up!"

"Why in God's name?"

"My poor health."

"Poor health -- piffle! You're a Doctor! You must abide by Luke 4:23!

"Don't recollect that scripture, Reverend."

"*Physician, heal thy self!* Besides, you want to go to Oregon and learn the answer to that riddle on your father's tombstone we talked about at Fairfield! Get up out of that chair!"

Reverend Parker barely missed sitting on Marcus, seized a pen and angrily tried to dip it into rigid ink. "What's wrong with your ink?"

"Frozen."

"Here, I'll thaw it over your lamp while you kindle a fire. Get to it, Brother -- the Lord's work waits for no man! What's your fee for delivering babies?"

"$2 per birth."

"That's $4 last night, Brother Whitman -- half must go to the church. Put $2 right here by the lamp."

Marcus had bills to pay, but counted out the $2 in change. This wasn't the time to vex Parker sitting there with that pen.

Dating the letter Christmas day for divine effect -- though it be two days away -- Reverend Parker mangled a brace of pens before the ink thawed enough to write Reverend Greene:

"I wrote you in regard to Doct. Marcus Whitman whatever may be the fulness -- or want of fulness -- in the testimonials which may accompany his offer of himself to your Board -- his general reputation in regard to all the particulars required and into which I have made particular inquiry -- I think place his case beyond any particular doubt. He wishes to accompany me in my expected tour."

"Brother Whitman -- post this letter at once -- I've got a slackard horse down outside. Get me another. Wife'll pull out what little hair I have left if I'm not home for Christmas!"

Marcus braved the Arctic darkness. In minutes, he exploded into his office wrapped in frosty air and thrust his bluish hands into the fireplace's feeble flames.

"Horse dead?" Parker whined.

"Dreadful sick. Horse'll go nowhere but my barn tonight!"

"No wonder that young woman parted with her jaded nag so readily."

"What woman?"

"Narcissa something."

"Narcissa Prentiss from Amity?"

Parker nodded knowingly. "Since you know her, you can hitch your horse to my buggy -- and take hers back when the lazy thing will move."

"I'm a one horse Doctor, Reverend. What'll become of my patients if I can't git to them?"

"Probably get well -- that bleeding you do's worthless. Don't try it on the Indians. They'll show you what real bleeding's all about. Now hitch up your horse to my rig, Brother!"

Marcus held his hand up. "I know -- the Lord's work waits for no mortals."

"No *man*, Marcus. I want to see a willing horse and a lotta road."

"It's pitch dark, Reverend."

"Only if you have no inner fire, Brother. Git!"

Samuel Parker returned from his whirlwind revival tour to his West Groton Presbyterian church barely in time to preach

Christmas services, but was heaped with bountiful collections for his trip west.

Shortly after the Christmas flurry, Reverend Parker received the December 24th reply about Narcissa from the American Board's Reverend Greene:

"I don't think that we have missions among the Indians where unmarried females are valuable just now . . . ."

Parker lighted his white clay pipe and puffed it as he mulled over Greene's reply. "Drat. Thought Greene'd be wiser than old man Wisner. This Board thinks people willing to risk death and dismemberment abound behind every bush! Where do they get off rejecting everybody? Do they think I've nothing better to do than deliver them the daft?"

"Did you want something, Dear?" Parker's dutiful little wife queried from the front room.

Parker thought about this wife. She was much sturdier than his first wife, who'd just died on him for no apparent reason. "Yes, Dear -- a miracle -- even if I have to make it myself!"

*   *   *

Henry Spalding had wed his dear Eliza Hart in the quietest of ceremonies at the Chapel of South College after evening services on September 14, 1833. Not only devoutly in love, Henry and Eliza cherished each other as companions. The newlyweds rented a cramped house at Walnut Hills near Lane Theological Seminary of Cincinnati and packed it with boarders to defray Henry's expensive education.

Henry bought an offbreed cow to put milk on a table offering meager fare free of tea, coffee or sweetbreads. When two of their boarders bolted their lodgings, Eliza begged Henry to let her teach to make up the deficit, but he proclaimed, "My management will make up the difference." And it did, for while studying at Lane, Henry acquired a $150 library and still donated $30 annually to benevolent causes.

Ministering to the heathens in the West was ever in their thoughts. Henry sat at their stark kitchen table after his nightly stint at the printers and opened the American Board's letter about the Spaldings' offered mission to the Osage Indians:

"January 2, 1835

Female teachers, our missionaries have all along supposed, could not be employed usefully, except at boarding schools. I am not certain that their opinion is correct, even at the present time; and I am quite confident that the way may be opened for them in a year or two, if the Osages should become sufficiently settled. . . ."

Henry Spalding put his aching head down on Reverend Greene's ambivalent missive.   Could the American Board possibly think he would leave his precious Eliza in limbo *for two years* while he ministered *alone* to the Osage Indians?   "What possesses these fools?" Henry railed.

*   *   *

Shortly after New Years Day, Marcus Whitman received the American Board's letter.   He scurried to his barn where Narcissa Prentiss's horse was repairing daily.   Hers was a fine animal even if its breed was anybody's guess.   It was warmer near the heavy breathing horse, so Marcus hovered there and ripped the letter open.

"January 6, 1835

On such a tour as this, as well as in missionary labors among any of the wandering tribes of our continent, great patience, fortitude & perseverance are necessary. You must be willing to encounter hardship, dangers, self-denials in almost every shape & discouragement's without being moved by them from your purpose. Nothing but an unquenchable desire to do good to the souls of the Indians, originating in and cherished by a supreme love of Christ and a firm faith in the promises can sustain you and carry you through."

Marcus was jubilant!   But he wondered if the Board's cautions were to prepare him for the hardships of the frontier -- or Reverend Samuel Parker.   Whatever the cost, Marcus would be serving the Lord at last!   He hugged the horse's head. "What's your mistress Narcissa really like? So be silent! I'll find out for myself soon enough!"

CHAPTER 36

A MATTER FOR THE SUBLETTES   FEBRUARY 1835

Andrew Sublette's snores filled Sulphur Springs' most primitive cabin with wolfish snorts.

"Drew! You gotta help me," William urged from the cockeyed doorway.

"Jesus, it's freezing! What time is it, Bill?"

"Dawn."

"Didn't get my buffalo robes into your warehouse till three."

"Yeah. Three in the afternoon. Then you closed every saloon in St. Louie!"

"Had to howl, Bill. First time I ever brought in my own peltry."

"Ya could do a lot worse than partnering up with Lou Vasquez. That ole boy knows where the b'ar sleeps."

"Bill, why didn't you tell me Uncle Solomon died?"

"Sent ya a letter bout his death to Fort William, Drew."

"I hauled the robes down from Lou's and my fort."

"Fort Convenience?"

"How'd you know the name, Bill?"

"Trappers' talk."

"Drew, we got the sorriest chore inna world."

"What's that?"

"Gotta help Doc Farrar cut Milt's leg off!"

Andrew Sublette sat up, his eyes agape. "Not me, Bill! I can't do that! Get somebody else!"

"There isn't nobody else, Drew."

"Get Robert Campbell."

"Bobbie's in Philadelphia buying supplies for Fort William. Milt isn't gonna sit still fer this. Can't have nobody seeing Milt like that. This's a family affair."

"You think you and me can hold Milt down? I've seen him stack a saloon full o' river men into cord wood without breaking a sweat."

"He's not the old Milt. Been boozing fer months. Throwed up on hisself at sister Sophronia's Christmas dinner table."

"He's the old Milt to me. Can't do it, Bill. Not everybody's as cold blooded as you are!"

"Doing what's gotta be done don't make a man cold-blooded, Drew. Higher up his leg this disease crawls, more it's likely ta kill 'im. You wanta let Milt die?"

"I'm getting up. Whatta you wear to your own brother's amputation, Bill?"

"Guts."

*   *   *

"Why you wanna see the mansion's construction site before the operation, Doc?"

"Need boards to strap to Milton's legs with a foot or so of overhang, so both legs'll be hog tied."

Numbly, William selected a couple 2 x 6s. "Need belts to strap them boards to his legs?"

"Or harness straps -- and that saw over there if its sharp. Try it on a board. Is Milton sober?"

"Left him a quart of brandy. Any other morning, he'd be head-shot, but he knows what we're up to. Gonna fight like a grizzly."

Suddenly, Andrew Sublette stalked behind them shirtless in buckskin breeches. Andrew snicked off a 1 x 2 with the saw. "Plenty sharp, Doc."

"Drew, why don't you round up three of the stoutest field hands you can find?" Doc Farrar asked.

Andrew gave Doc Farrar a steely look. "This is a matter for the Sublettes, Doc. Let's be done with it!"

"Get this laudanum down him, boys."

"Then what?" William asked.

"Put Milton face down on his bed, both legs strapped to the boards," the gray-haired Doctor Farrar muttered, unwrapping his smelly amputating knives with sweaty hands.

"Operation take long, Doc?" William asked, his face pale.

"Five minutes amputating. Three to cauterize the stump -- couple minutes for bandages. I'll cut the calf muscle a few inches below where the thigh muscle anchors to the top of the *fibula* and just above where the *popliteal* artery branches into the *posterior tibial* and *peroneal* arteries. That way I'll only have one big vessel to choke off stead o' two. That'll leave Milton a sound stump below his knee for a peg leg.

"Ready, Drew?" William asked.

Andrew nodded and trotted to the kitchen, returning with two glasses. "Hit this one with the laudanum, Doc."

Andrew slipped into Milt's gamy cabin, "Hey big man, time for a drink."

Even in the dimness, the puffy-faced Milt looked a decade older than Andrew remembered him. Bill was right. This sodden hulk wasn't the same old Milt.

"You jist wanna git me drunk, so's that butcher kin hack my leg off."

"Nobody fools you, Milt. You can drink this dope and dream or see how long you can choke back a holler."

"This is my leg we're talkin' about, Drew. My honest-to-God flesh 'n blood leg. You ain't dressin' out a buffalo now -- though you smell like a skinner."

"Sweet talk'll get you no place, Milt."

"How old're you now, Drew?" Milt asked.

"Twenty-seven."

"Ya look jist like me when I was your age."

Andrew nodded, "Near gets me killed every now and again."

Milt laughed, "Least ya can't say I never left ya nuthin'."

"Here, Milt. Let's drink to the smiles you left on the faces of the lucky women of this world."

"Now that -- by God -- is worth drinkin' to, Drew!"

Andrew held the laudanum to Milt's lips till he swilled it all down.

Milt drifted off. They rolled him face down on top of the boards and strapped his legs to them -- then Milt woke up screaming, "No, by God NO! GIT THE HELL OUTA HERE!" William straddled Milt's back yelling, "Milt, we *ain't* gonna letchu die! Yer leg's gonna come off!" As an afterthought, William realized he'd said his banned word *ain't* for the first time in over three years.

"You always wanted ta do this, ain't chu, Bill? Always green jealous 'cause I could outrun you."

"You was the fastest boy in Kentucky Milt, but now you're gonna act like a 33 year old man while the Doc gits this done!"

"Bill, I ain't never gonna fergit whatchu done here."

"None o' the Sublettes will," Drew growled with sweat streaming down his face.

Milt gritted his teeth through the slicing of his calf muscle, but when Doc Farrar sawed into his leg bones, Milt shrieked like a woman in childbirth. Still straddling Milton, William leaned close to Milt's ear and said, "Don't let *Umentucken* hear ya carry on!"

"She here?" Milt gasped.

"Yeah!" William lied.

Milt choked a scream into a gurgle and went limp.

William whirled his head to Doc Farrar, "Oh God, is he dead?"

Farrar, his face dripping sweat, sawed through the last of Milt's *tibia*, then loosened the ligature on the leg stump. "Artery spurts. He's alive." Gore to his elbows, Farrar snugged the ligature. "Soon's I cauterize the stump and bandage it, we're done." Farrar toweled the handle of the hot running iron in the fireplace and seared the raw flesh of Milton's stump.

William had the fleeting thought the burning flesh smelled like buffalo sizzling over a camp fire.

Fararr bandaged the blackened stump with sheet strips starkly whiter than the blood soaked sheets on the bed.

William Sublette burst out into the icy air and wiped the scalding sweat from his eyes. What if Milt died? Another dead brother? Another busted promise to Mama Isabella? William gasped, "There's ten minutes that took a lifetime."

Andrew Sublette stood with his hands on his hips, his sweaty face steaming in the morning mist. "It was a lifetime, and none of us'll ever be the same for living it, Bill." Sunrise turned the mists golden as Andrew sang in a tormented tenor:

"I'm just a poor wayfaring stranger
a travelin' through this world of woe.
But there's no sickness, toil or danger
in that bright world to which I go."

William growled, "Fer God's sake, Drew! This is no time fer singing."

Drew snarled, "It is for me," and disappeared into the fiery mist, his powerful voice rising into the bloody sun:

"I'm goin' there to see my mother.
I'm goin' there, no more to roam.
I'm just a goin' over Jordan.
I'm just a goin' over home."

CHAPTER 37

SOME KIND OF A PROPOSAL   FEBRUARY 1835

Narcissa Prentiss's healthy carriage horse plodded through the sleepy village of Amity, New York with a sweating Marcus Whitman astride him. Marcus was an infinitely cautious man, who lived life inch-by-inch. Since he'd fallen in with Reverend Samuel Parker, he was a leaf in a tornado. Now there was Narcissa.

The American Board'd said Marcus could go west with Reverend Parker to locate mission sites and see if female missionaries could abide the wilderness. But to get permanently appointed as a missionary in Oregon, Marcus must be married. What if he wed a woman, then discovered she wouldn't go west? He'd be shackled to a stranger for life and further than ever from serving the Lord in Oregon.

Marcus had shared this Sabbath morning with Reverend and Mrs. O.S. Powell of Amity, themselves recently appointed missionaries. Mrs. Powell understood Marcus's predicament and spent ten uncomfortable minutes massaging goose grease into his unruly hair to quieten it down some.

Marcus winced at the perfectly plumb Prentiss home. What would somebody living in a place with 90° corners think of his cockeyed cabin? He wanted to gallop back to Rushville, but this was Narcissa's horse and she had his. Could he stall her horse in the barn and slip away on his? Marcus's shaking hands said that was the answer, but he knew he had to see Narcissa or perish of curiosity.

Somehow Marcus expected Narcissa to meet him in the backyard, as Jane Prentiss had on his last trip. But she didn't, so he stalled her horse in the huge-beamed barn, curried it and forked sweet smelling hay into its manger. His gelding wasn't in the barn, so he lugged his saddle, blanket and bridle back toward the road with the pain in his side acting up. Perhaps the Prentisses were at church.

As Marcus neared the house, a mellow voice said, "Thank you for bringing my Toby home. I'm Narcissa. How is he, Doctor?"

Marcus spied a sincere face between lacy curtains in the open side window and stared. The curtains made Narcissa an angelic halo. Her features were larger than Jane's. She was more direct -- almost manly in her speech. He wondered what the rest of Narcissa looked like. He wished Jane was inspired by the Lord to go among the heathens, but she wasn't.

Standing about six feet, Dr. Marcus Whitman was the strangest looking man Narcissa had ever seen. As Jane said, he resembled their burly Irish Wolfhound *Shamrock* with humped nose and strong stance. His eyes were blue enough to be called purple. As she watched, sprigs of his greasy hair popped up like bug antennae. He was not the Mountain Man she'd prayed for! Narcissa repeated, "How is Toby, Doctor?"

He cleared his throat and said in his deepest base tones, "Your horse was colicked, but he's well now. May not wanta go back in the traces after being free under saddle." He felt foolish and lowered his gaze. "I know I'm not much to look at."

Narcissa realized her face had cruelly sold her thoughts, but rallied, "The devout put more stock in a man's soul than his hide." This was not going to be a girlish love affair. Did his looks really matter, as long as he was decent to her? Her duty was to God, not her unworthy prurience. "Won't you come in for tea?"

Marcus stammered, "I gotta git back to Reverend Powell's in time for dinner."

Narcissa laughed louder than any woman he'd ever heard before.

"What's so funny?"

"Doctor, if you threw a stone over our barn's weathervane, you'd hit Reverend Powell's house. It's only 12 minutes after two. We'll not harvest the tea, just drink it!"

Marcus chuckled. Narcissa Prentiss was the wittiest woman he'd ever met. She had him chortling like an imp in knee pants. "I'll leave my horse tack outside an' take tea."

"You will not! Tack's as welcome in this house as you are! Plenty of room in the vestibule. If you don't run, I'll beat you to our front door."

He nodded and started around the front of her impressive home. She laughed and joked like a man! More direct than the roughest rogue he'd met, Narcissa Prentiss was a woman a man could be friends with.

She swung the great door open and extended her hand. "I'm Narcissa -- but I guess I told you that."

Narcissa wasn't the feminine vision that her sister Jane was, but she was symmetrically formed although at least 5'7" and quite buxom. He shifted his horse gear to one hand and shook her small hand. "I'm Marcus Whitman of Rushville." Her touch didn't thrill him like Jane's did, but it was pleasant.

She turned Marcus's hand over. "Your palm's callused. Not the hand I'd expect on a Medical Doctor. Doctoring's what you do, isn't it?"

Her smile, though quite impious, warmed the spirit. "It is when I'm not building a cabin or shoeing my horse."

"Speaking of horses, your gelding's in the back corral. Reverend Parker left it there last week."

"Can it walk?"

"Certainly, why do you ask?"

"Reverend Parker's easier on scriptures than he is on horses."

"You must be pretty stout to hold your equipage in one hand forever. Put it in here." She pointed to a spot on the shining hardwood floor between the hat and umbrella stands. "Have a seat in the parlor. I'll bring the tea cart."

The Prentiss parlor was the most refined room he'd seen outside New York City. When she left the room, Marcus got up and checked his pants to be sure he wasn't getting anything on their velvet sofa.

Narcissa pushed a cherry wood tea cart with flower petals painted around the tray. Marcus had never seen metal tea ware before, but he lifted the pot.

She rescued the ornate tea pot. "Hostess pours, Marcus. Sugar and cream?"

"Spoon o' both," he nodded and watched how smartly she handled the utensils.

"When did you graduate from Medical School?"

"Three years ago, this spring."

"Did you study chemistry?"

"Needed it to mix medicines for my patients."

"Did you take chemistry or pharmacology?"

"Both at Fairfield Medical College." He hoped that would impress her as he risked balancing his china cup and saucer on his knee. It chattered, so he steadied it. The aromatic tea was tarter than he expected, but tasty.

"You're not a risk taker, are you, Marcus?"

"Sometimes. You interested in chemistry? Might be something I could help you with."

"I dabble in it," she smiled, not letting on she'd taught chemistry at several finishing schools.

"My best subject," Marcus grinned.

She liked his crooked smile and the way his skin crinkled around those blue-purple eyes. "Did you agree with Sir Humphry Davy's assessment of chlorine as an element in 1810?"

Marcus tongued the inside of his cheek. "Didn't Davy just confirm Karl Wilhelm Scheele's 1780 findings?"

Narcissa couldn't resist grabbing his hands. "Why that's wonderful, Marcus! I've never met a man with any depth in this field! I noticed you hefting the tea pot. It really is solid Ag [Silver]!"

"Thought it might be Fe [iron] plated with Ag. Tea's fine as long as you didn't load it with As [Arsenic]!"

They laughed till they remembered they barely knew each other. She dropped his hands, and he fidgeted.

"Marcus, you know we share a higher calling than chemistry."

"That's why I'm here. The American Board's appointed me to see if the West is suitable for females."

"I'd die for such an appointment, Marcus."

"It's not what you think. Nothing but a scout now. Board won't appoint me as a missionary till I'm married or have some arrangement along those lines."

Narcissa rose and left the parlor. Returning, she handed Marcus a letter. "I don't know how Reverend Greene could have rejected me so coldly on the eve of our Savior's birth just because I'm unmarried. I'm only 27, you know."

Marcus sympathized with the woe in this good woman's face. "Solution's in our chemistry."

"I don't follow you."

"Element's a substance that can't be reduced to simpler substances. A compound's matter with two or more elements in the same proportions throughout. We need to combine as a compound to serve the Lord."

Narcissa's face went through a series of changes like the sky during a storm. "Marcus Whitman, is this some kind of a proposal?"

"Should I have spoken to your father, first?"

"Oh no! He's the last person you need to speak with now! Can you see me telling Judge Stephen Prentiss -- this afternoon, a man I never saw before dropped by and proposed to me -- and I accepted."

"Do you accept, Narcissa?"

"Sort of. Just what is your proposal?"

"Call it a compound of convenience, Cc by symbol. If I can honestly tell the Board upon my return from the West, it's suitable for females, we combine. If not, we have a compound that breaks down to its pre-combined elements."

"Fair enough. What if we assume your report's positive, Marcus?"

"Grand leap of faith -- that assumption. No white woman's ever crossed the Rockies. If the Gospel Truth be it's feasible for females, we'll combine under my name and serve the heathen as two separate elements."

"Both a compound and a marriage of convenience?"

"If it be the Lord's will."

"Is it your will, Marcus?"

He nodded nervously. "Will it be yours, Narcissa?"

"As long as you never disclose our real arrangement."

"What about your parents?"

"How long before you get back from the West?"

"Maybe by Christmas -- sooner if possible."

"I could have them used to the idea by then."

Vastly relieved, Marcus rose to go.

"One thing about this was far too subtle for me, Marcus."

"What was that?"

"Our courtship. I didn't even notice it."

Marcus wanted to laugh, but there was something so very sad about all this that tears welled in his eyes. Narcissa was clearly about to cry. He picked up his saddle, bridle and blanket in the vestibule and clutched them against his chest as he walked onto the porch.

Narcissa wanted to kiss Marcus to seal the Satanic bargain they'd made to serve the Lord. She looked into his eyes as she felt a woman just engaged would, and he only raised the saddle higher and left without a word. She went inside and watched him out a back window walking to get his horse from the Prentiss corral. "What in God's name have I done? I've freed the Prisoner of Prattsburg -- Amity. That's what I've done."

Narcissa climbed the stairs to her room. Her fiancé Marcus Whitman would be leaving for St. Louis tomorrow -- February 23rd without even saying good-bye. She reached into her desk for a sheet of her pale green letter paper. She dated it the 23rd so it wouldn't violate the Sabbath, then wrote the American Board with the inner assurance that she had finally solved their simultaneous quadratic equation in four unknowns:

"To the Secretaries of the A.B.C.F.M.

Dear Brethren

Permit an unworthy sister to address you. Having obtained favour of the Lord and desiring to live for the conversion of the world I now offer myself to the American Board to be employed in their service among the heathen, if counted worthy. As it is requested of me to make some statements concerning myself I shall endeavour to be brief as possible knowing the value of your time especially under the late afflictive bereavement [Death of Dr. Wisner]. . . .

Feeling it more my privilege than my duty to labour for the conversion of the heathen, I respectfully submit myself to your direction and subscribe

Your unworthy sister in the Lord,

Narcissa Prentiss"

Narcissa would make certain that when Reverend O.S. Powell, affixed his recommendation to her letter of the 23rd, he would unveil her engagement to the Board's emissary beyond the Shining Mountains, Dr. Marcus Whitman.

Narcissa got down on her knees. She opened her New Testament to *I Corinthians* 4:10 and read:

"We are fools for Christ's sake, but ye are wise in Christ; we are weak, but ye are strong; ye are honorable, but we are despised."

CHAPTER 38

BITTEREST OF MEN   SPRING 1835

It was Tom Fitzpatrick's first time at Sulphur Springs. After a savory roast beef meal from a homegrown steer, Fitz and William Sublette wandered its 770 acres. "Now I've seen yer fiefdom, sure I don't feel so bad about you gougin' us all these years, Bill. I'm almost of a mind it was worth it," Fitz groaned with an Irish twinkle.

Sublette smiled, "Where's little Friday the Arapaho?"

"In school bout six miles from here in St. Louie. In another week, that boy'll be smarter'n me!"

"That Arapaho's been smarter'n you since the day he hornswoggled you on the Santa Fe Trail! What become o' that young lawyer Anderson I tuck out ta the '34 Rendezvous?"

"Minute we got back to St. Louie the night of -- I think it was last September 29th -- Anderson like to had a fit gittin' hisself off to Chillicothe, Ohio to court that Governor's daughter Eliza McArthur! Marshall must o' been a shock to her. He gained 50 pounds and looked more a Mountain Man than I did. But she musta got over it, for he just sent me a clipping about their weddin' last February. I kept it if ya wanta read it."

"Sure would. Anderson's a fine young feller."

"And smart enough to leave the mountains and never go back."

"Fitz, you think Milt'll ever go back Up the Mountain?"

"Milt's the bitterest of men, he is! Bitter at you fer killin' the Rocky Mountain Fur Company. Bitter fer your cuttin' his leg off. Can't see him goin' Up the Mountain in that wheel chair.

It don't seem to help none that we fixed him with a quiet interest in Fontenelle, Fitzpatrick & Co. All Milt wanted to know from me was what happened to that hellion *Umentucken Tukutsey Undewatsey.* Sure if Milt knew she'd taken up with Joe Meek, he'd be out ta kill Joe. Them recent operations on the stump o' his leg have fastened his lips to the bottle. Might be best if ya kin bring yourself to toss 'im out, Bill. Milt's dyin' here."

At the new mansion's building site, William scooped up some curly wood beam shavings. "Fancied the smell o' fresh cut wood ever since I split rails in the summer o' 1820." William blew the shavings from his hand and watched the wind roll them along the barren ground. "Milt's not the only one dying here, Fitz."

Knowing far more about Sublette's personal affairs than he wanted to Fitz said, "To be sure, we got business to do this day, Bill."

They retired to one of the solid new cabins and agreed on terms for Sublette & Campbell to sell Fort William on the Laramie to Fontenelle, Fitzpatrick & Co. The deal'd be consummated later in the spring when Fitz and Robert Campbell went out to the Fort.

"Maybe Milt can manage at the Fort, since he'll be a part owner, Fitz."

"Don't bet the farm on it, Bill. Milt's too all-fired busy broodin'."

CHAPTER 39

THE GOTHS AND THE GOSPEL   SPRING 1835

Dr. Marcus Whitman reached St. Louis sitting on a sore backside on April 1st, after riding his roan gelding cross country from New York. Surprised Reverend Parker's steamboat still hadn't docked, Whitman prowled the levee. Sodom and Gomorrah were sacred shrines compared to St. Louis. Dock workers bellered obscenities so vile Marcus knelt often to pray for deliverance.

Checking another dock, Marcus saw *Sublette & Campbell* scrawled on several bales of goods and copied down their address. A dapper young fellow strolled up to Marcus. "Ah'm Robert Campbell. What's your interest in our goods?" he asked, trilling his *R*s with his Scottish tongue.

Marcus nodded, "I'm Dr. Marcus Whitman, emissary of the American Board of Commissioners for Foreign Missions, headed west with Fontenelle's expedition. Board told me to contact Mr. Sublette about mission sites, so I took your address."

Campbell thumbed Marcus into the shade of a steamboat rasping up and down on its hawser. "Reverend --"

"Sir, I'm a Medical Doctor. Reverend Parker's due here any minute."

"You missionary?"

"Hope to be."

"Then ye need friendly warning about Lucien Fontenelle."

"Sounds dire."

"Aye, indeed it is. Many call him *Lucifer* and swear he's devil's kin."

"You know Fontenelle?"

"Been Up the Mountain wi' him for years, and ah'm oon mah way ta the American Fur Company office ta buy a share in Fontenelle's expedition for Sublette & Campbell."

"If he's so wicked, why would you buy into his venture?"

Campbell laughed, "Doctor, every mon in business sells a bit o' his soul ta the devil!"

*   *   *

Reverend Parker arrived in St. Louis in his schoolmaster's garb with a white stock and stovepipe hat on April 4th. He pounded down the gangway, "How was your trip, Brother Whitman?"

"All right till I reached St. Louis."

"What happened?"

"Night before last my precious roan and saddle burnt up in a livery stable. Yesterday, a cutpurse snatched my wallet."

"Money in the wallet?"

"Seven dollars."

Parker fanned his face with his hat. "That's outrageous, Brother!"

"That's what I thought."

"No, Brother Whitman, *you* are outrageous to lose so much through mismanagement! I raised the money to get us out here. I'll not see it frittered away by you!"

Marcus wanted to argue he was the one who saved an entire boat passage fare by riding his horse all the way from New York, but Parker's livid face said he was ready to send Marcus back.

"Dr. Whitman!"

"I'll find some way to atone."

"No, I will! I'll save back your burnt horse by buying one mule instead of two, and you will carry any excess baggage yourself. Don't tarry now. I need directions to the American Fur Company's office, so we can arrange to join their summer caravan at Liberty, Missouri."

"I got the directions Reverend, and I been assured you'll be impressed with their caravan leader."

*   *   *

On April 9th, Robert Campbell left St. Louis with Andrew Sublette, Thomas Fitzpatrick and Friday the Arapaho for Fort William on the Laramie. Experienced Mountain Men traveling light in a small band, they covered ground like a high wind, resting only a few hours around midnight of each day. As they approached Fort William surrounded by a forest of Sioux lodges, Campbell turned to Fitz, "Recall ah told ye we sent runners to the Ogalala and Bull Bear's Sioux in the Black Hills invitin' them ta Fort William ta trade?"

"That you did, Bobbie!"

"Well, here they be!"

"Sure and I've never had reason to doubt you or Bill Sublette!" Fitz mused.

Drew wedged his horse between Campbell and Fitz. "Then you never played poker with Bill. He's won enough on four card flushes to buy a blue blanket for every Sioux down there."

After Fort William was surrendered to Fontenelle, Fitzpatrick & Co., Andrew Sublette called Fitz aside. "Bad blood's come between the Sublettes. Fitz, you gotta get Milt up to this Fort. He's primed to murder, and Bill doesn't see it coming."

Overhearing this conversation, Robert Campbell was jolted. He hadn't seen a killing coming either. Campbell vowed to stop it, if he had to kill Milt himself.

"I told Bill to kick Milt out, but I couldn't tell him why. Bill woulda *Constable One-Punched* me. I'll do all I can," Fitz groaned.

Their job finished on the Laramie, Robert Campbell and Andrew Sublette assembled the dozen men returning to the settlements. They launched their bull boats loaded with bales of buffalo robes for their 1,000 mile river trip to St. Louis. Campbell only hoped Milt hadn't murdered Bill Sublette.

*   *   *

From the steamboat *Siam's* upper deck, Marcus and Reverend Parker watched the brigade men sticking their poles into the bottom and walking their clumsy keelboats upstream into the Missouri. Other keelboats inched up river on cordelles hauled by chanting men slogging the muddy banks. Parker said, "See what I've spared you from?"

Because of flooding thunderstorms, the eight day trip to Liberty stretched into two weeks, spurring Parker to ridicule Captain and crew relentlessly.

At Liberty, Missouri Parker made his threat good, buying two saddle horses but only one pack mule. Incredibly, Parker demanded that Marcus limit their total baggage to 50 pounds. Deluges stalled their caravan's departure from Liberty three more weeks, but neither Parker nor Whitman bothered to learn how to pack a mule.

Reverend Parker made some use of the time cultivating Baptist missionary, Reverend Moses Merrill, about to embark upon the same journey. But Parker confided to Marcus, "A Presbyterian trusts a Baptist only as far as he can throw his own head."

At the May 14th departure of the caravan's 60 men, 6 wagons and 200 horses, Parker piled all 50 pounds of baggage on their single mule to the jeers of bystanders, already amused by his get-up. That left Marcus toting their clothing, cooking utensils, bedding, tent and an ax draped all over his horse. Once on the trail, Parker's mule pack unraveled. To the glee of the Mountain Men, Parker shouted at Marcus, "This is another example of your pathetic mismanagement!"

As the caravan filed past, Marcus repacked their mule. His effort was no better than the Reverend's, lasting about a quarter of a mile before the pack disintegrated again. Reverend Parker's hissing reminded Marcus of a convulsing cat. Lucien Fontenelle's wagon creaked to a stop beside them. The swarthy Fontenelle mulled over the predicament of these pious pilgrims.

Fontenelle had his own problems. Fontenelle's Omaha wife *Me-um-ba-ne* had split an Iowa brave's skull with her ax for killing her brother. As soon as the caravan reached Iowa country, she'd have to hide inside their wagon because of a two horse bounty on her head. The pilgrims' equipage would come in handy to ransom her life if the Iowas unearthed her. Fontenelle grunted, "Load your excess goods in the back o' my wagon."

Marcus joyfully piled their overage into Fontenelle's wagon, wondering how Robert Campbell could condemn a fine fellow like Fontenelle. Their mule pack fell apart twice more before they retrieved their goods from Fontenelle's wagon and made camp.

Two days later, as Marcus loaded their excess items into Fontenelle's wagon, he was startled to see their items plopping into the mud. "What have we done, Mr. Fontenelle?" Marcus asked incredulously.

"I don't give a cow pie if the Iowas butcher this Omaha ax murderer!" Fontenelle slurred, fastening the canvas flap shut inside his wagon.

Marcus gasped to Parker, "Fontenelle's dumped our equipage. We must buy another mule."

Incensed, Parker snorted, "How dare he?"

"It's his wagon."

"Plead with Fontenelle. Be cheaper than a mule."

"Man's blind drunk, Reverend."

Parker leered, "I'll prevail upon the Baptist preacher."

The Reverend Moses Merrill weathered the rain beside his wagon. He'd just jettisoned supplies he'd hauled all the way from St. Louis for the Otoes at his mission. "As you can see Brother Parker, I've lightened my own load so my oxen can cope with this May mud. I'm not persuaded to add your goods in their place and cripple myself again."

"Dr. Whitman's a man's salvation when you're sick, Brother Merrill."

"But we're quite well, Brother Parker."

Parker stepped closer, shielding his Bible from the sheeting rain and asked, "Have you read *Matthew 9:12?*"

"Not since the rains came."

"In the Savior's own words it warns, *They that be whole need not a physician, but they that are sick do.*"

"All right, I'll haul half your goods, but if I get half a sniffle, I'll expect the good Doctor at my side like a Siamese Twin -- Brother Parker."

"We speak not of half way measures in this full blown deluge."

"Putcher equipage in my wagon, but I bog down, that husky Doctor'll be pushing more than powders and pills."

"So be it, Brother Merrill," Reverend Parker said, sheathing his trusty Bible under his coat after besting the Baptist at his own game.

Marcus Whitman paid for Parker's Pyrrhic victory every time Merrill's oxen had to have their load lightened or a wheel wrestled from a quagmire.

Reverend Parker spurred his horse so hard up a mud bank that its back went out. He abandoned the crippled beast and bought another horse. Marcus pleaded, "Why can't we buy two horses, so we can pack our own goods. Merrill wagon's more work than the whole trip shoulda been."

"Reflect, Brother Marcus. 'Twas you that let your first horse burn up. Atonement builds character."

"If that be true, Brother Parker, why don't you return the horse you just bought and walk."

Parker turned on Marcus with fire in his eyes, "Never use such insurrective tones, Marcus Whitman, or you'll never reach Oregon this trip or any other!" Parker screwed his plug hat down tighter against the wind and rode off growling other things Marcus was privileged not to hear.

Merrill exacted his revenge as well. Every time the Baptist preacher's oxen slowed, Marcus was forced to hoist his tent and all their bedding to his own back. Marcus fought to free his mind of anger staggering under the ponderous load, but it was a losing battle until he soothed his wrath with the 37th Psalm's 7th verse:

"Rest in the Lord, and wait patiently for him: fret not thyself because of him who prospereth in his way, or because a man bringeth wicked devices to pass."

When Marcus wasn't muling his mammoth load, he helped build rafts at deep river crossings and bridges across smaller streams. At every crossing Mountain Men shivering from the icy water prescribed whiskey for themselves. After a fowl fording they camped and a fierce Mountain Man called Big Dog ordered Dr. Whitman, "Swig up with the rest 'o us, er I'll boot yer butt inna river an' step on yer head when ya comes up ta blow."

Marcus was not a mild man by nature. Only his faith separated him from the savages. He looked Big Dog in the eye. "That bottle will not touch my lips though you hold me under till the second coming of the Lord Jesus Christ."

Both preachers came forward amid jeers and cat calls. Merrill said, "Brother Whitman is a man of conscience and piety -- who means harm to no man, Big Dog."

"Leave them stinkin' Psalm singers be!" yelled a wiry Italian Mountain Man. Rotten eggs splattered the three men of God. The Mountain Men slogged back to their tents howling and slapping each other on the back.

Marcus knelt, tears coursing his cheeks and asked Merrill, "Pray for my soul. These brutes have me ready to kill. I came to guide heathens to the pathway of the Lord. Am I now to lose my own path and become a barbarian?"

Reverend Moses Merrill laid his hand in the fetid egg-slime atop Marcus Whitman's bowed head. "In the third century Goths invaded Rome, then a heathen state.   But Emperor Constantine the First repulsed the barbarians, saluting the Christian God as his protector and Savior of Rome. Constantine declared Christianity Rome's religion. Thus the Goths fell to the Gospel and that too shall come to pass here in this barbarous land if we do not lose our faith. Remember, the meek shall inherit the earth."

A sulfurous egg splatted on Marcus's chest. Marcus looked up to see Fontenelle joining the revelers and asked, "Must we wait till the barbarians are through with it?"

CHAPTER 40

THE BELLEVUE CALAMITY   JUNE 1835

      Bellevue's distant image beckoned to Fontenelle's caravan. Amid fields of maize with rolling hills behind it, Bellevue lay like a petulant maiden along the west bank of the Missouri River in the shadow of the powerful Omahas. Bellevue'd belonged to Lucien Fontenelle since 1824.   Lying in what many called Nebraska territory, Bellevue was the only semblance of a home Lucien Fontenelle'd known since running away from his caustic aunt's home in New Orleans as a boy of 15. Like himself, Bellevue had many facets. When Fontenelle was sober, he found it adequate.   When he was drunk, he loathed Bellevue like the world in general and New Orleans in particular.

      In 1824 then young and alluring, *Me-um-ba-ne* [Bright Sun] had become his woman at Bellevue and birthed him fine son Logan there ten years ago. One day Logan would be Chief of the Omahas, like his grandfather Big Elk. Logan was smarter and stronger than his three younger brothers and sister away at boarding school in St. Louis. Fontenelle's Bellevue reverie was interrupted by icy canister shot from the heavens pelting his wagon canvas. Startled, *Me-um-ba-ne* raised the blanket over her hideout to see if bullets were striking the wagon. Her broad coppery face had fewer bruises than usual. He calmed her with a shake of his hand.

      The fierce hail launched a flight of pelicans with snowy bodies and black wings flapping from their roost on the river. They spiraled upward into the foreboding clouds in an awesome *rond de jambe en l'air* that Fontenelle'd idolized as a youthful patron of the New Orleans ballet.

He waved his outriders tighter to keep the horses from stampeding in the hail. Fontenelle's hands turned blue and cold. He clamped the reins between his knees, and slipped his hands into the warmth of his armpits. But they grew icier.

Fontenelle could see pious pilgrims Parker and Whitman cowering in the hail on horseback. The mountains were no place for fools who couldn't pack a mule. He'd ship that pair of deuces back to St. Louie on the next steamer docking at Bellevue.

Fontenelle's stomach retched so hard he nearly pitched from the wagon seat. He forced back a surge of vomit. "Treacherous shrew!" he screamed at *Me-um-ba-ne*. "Have you poisoned me?"

Fontenelle toppled across the butt of the right horse and flopped to the hail strewn ground, narrowly avoiding the ice-popping front wheel of his wagon. He lay puking. Fontenelle's horses shied then halted, leaving him retching behind the wagon. *Me-um-ba-ne* began to wail as it hailed all the harder.

Dr. Marcus Whitman, so exhausted he could barely hold his own head up, dismounted and crouched over the shivering Fontenelle.

Reverend Parker rode up shielding his eyes.   "Is he shot?"

"Could be cholera -- maybe poison."

"What did you say?"

"CHOLERA!" Marcus yelled back, amazed to see Reverend Parker boot his horse in the flanks and gallop through the hail with his elbows flopping. Wagons and horses rumbled past abandoning Marcus and the fallen Fontenelle with his wife wailing his Omaha Death Song from the wagon.

Between Marcus and the stocky *Me-um-ba-ne* they hoisted the shivering Fontenelle into the back of his wagon. "Keep him bundled warm while I drive the wagon," Dr. Whitman instructed as the hail warmed to sheeting rain.

She wiped the rain from her wide face. "Him think I poison. I not get in back of wagon with he," *Me-um-ba-ne* cried.

"Don't be afraid. He's too sick to hurt you."

"I afraid get in wagon because I want kill he."

"Did you poison him with arsenic?"

"I not poison he. Where I get arsenic?"

"If it wasn't arsenic, was it some Indian poison?"

"Omahas fighters. No poison."

"Head for that trading post over there. You know what it's called?"

"Bellevue -- my house."

As quickly as the storm had come, it left. Marcus drove the jolting wagon. Sun rays stabbed through the breaks in the clouds, but none struck Bellevue. Fontenelle gasped, "Doc, . . ." but fainted before he could finish.

Marcus asked Fontenelle's squaw, "Why are all those men in front of the fort?"

"Not good. Give reins. I drive."

As *Me-um-ba-ne* tried to drive the wagon into the post, the men surged forward. Big Dog yelled, "Ya ain't cartin' no cholera case in here. Take Fontenelle on to Cabanne's er Council Bluffs."

Marcus shook his head.

Big Dog shoved his rifle in Marcus's face. Marcus said, "Before nightfall, you'll all be down with cholera. If you kill me, you're standing in your grave."

"Whatta you gonna do, beg God ta save us?"

"That's Reverend Parker's chore. I'm a poor physician -- a poor physician who saved Wheeler, New York from cholera three years ago. Marcus yelled, "I see dead men. If I do nothing, 40 of you will be corpses by morning. Do what I tell you, before you're too sick to move, 20 -- maybe less -- will die. Cholera's beasties littler than lice are on us. We gotta kill 'em, before they kill us."

Big Dog yelled, "Whatta we do?"

"Lay out blankets for those who collapse first.   Then strip and burn your clothes right there by the river. Jump in and lather with lye soap. Where you don't lather, you're leaving beasties. Dry well. Keep warm. Draw clear water -- no pond scum or sewage -- from the river and boil out the beasties for drinking. Eat boiled broth for strength and nothing else. Pour out your liquor!"

"Izzat liquor part fer the preacher, er fer you, Doc?"

"For you! Liquor makes you too weak to fight off the beasties."

Somebody said, "That's why Lucien come down with it first!"

Marcus added, "Sleep outside if it don't rain."

"That it?"

Marcus nodded. "Start NOW while you still can -- and pray to Almighty God that you can do something to save your fellow man from this calamity."

Men who hadn't bathed in a year weren't good at scrubbing but they tried as their fouled buckskins burned on the river bank. The Omahas watched the madness from a distance, pronounced it a curse and went hunting. Except for Fontenelle's muscular ten year old boy Logan. Logan shook Marcus's hand as his second in command, and was suddenly everywhere at once helping the men who hated half-breeds as they hated psalm-singers like Marcus.

By dark, every caravaner at Bellevue was down with Asiatic Cholera. *Me-um-ba-ne*, Logan and Marcus tended all they could until after midnight when Marcus came down with cholera and couldn't move -- even to save a dying man 20 feet from him. Reverend Parker appeared and carried on in Marcus's place feeding boiled broth and blanketing the shivering throughout the night -- the Lord having resurrected his courage -- and his respect for Dr. Marcus Whitman and the littlest soldier against the forces of darkness, Logan Fontenelle.

At dawn Marcus staggered about, tending everyone he could while he fought off the cholera. He found little Logan collapsed, but it was from fatigue. He let the boy sleep, thinking how he was really a small, pure copy of Lucien Fontenelle.

For ten more days Marcus tended fallen Mountain Men, adding to his work force of Parker, Logan and *Me-um-ba-ne* as men recovered. The pain in Marcus's side had never been worse, but when only three of the 60 stricken men died, Marcus was thankful God had given him the wisdom to change a calamity to the Miracle of Bellevue.

And the second Miracle of Bellevue followed on June 21st. Reverend Samuel Parker bought Marcus another pack mule.

CHAPTER 41

HERO TO HOUND DOG   SUMMER 1835

Though June 21st was the Sabbath, Fontenelle braced Reverend Parker and Dr. Whitman, "Suppose I swore on an Angel's -- elbow -- it was Monday? Could you travel then?"

"We will not violate the Lord's day to save ourselves from hardship," Marcus Whitman answered quietly.

The swarthy Fontenelle might have recalled that Whitman had hauled him and his men out of their graves, but for the whiskey riling his blood. "Caravan's two weeks late! We don't get to Rendezvous, we'll be hauling these goods back broke to face creditors from hell. We're leaving. Catch up if you can!" What Fontenelle left unsaid was the Iowa Nation at war with the Omahas would butcher this pair of deuces just for camping at Bellevue.

Marcus watched the caravan's 60 men passing by. Knowing they might never see Whitman alive again, the cholera-weakened Mountain Men dropped their gaze. Dust billowing from under a thousand hooves choked the gritty air. Wagons lurched through the trail's chuck holes. Three yokes of oxen set to lowing.

Parker grated, "Betrayal angers a devout man -- even on the Sabbath."

"True, but these wagons moving west say women could make the trip."

Reverend Parker grumbled, "You know this wagon trail doesn't reach to Oregon."

"One day it will, Reverend."

"Aspirations are no substitute for accomplishment, Brother. Let us pray!"

Marcus nodded, "Pray for them who leave us for their hearts are heaviest."

Next day, Marcus struggled to ride hard after the caravan, but dysentery sapped him till he rode at a walk. Intolerant of the plodding, Parker rode on, leaving Marcus alone on the prairie like a sick hound bellying after his master. Marcus wondered if his cholera had relapsed. He'd killed cholera in others. Would it kill him for revenge?

Using his last iota of strength, Marcus overtook Parker on June 27th near the Elkhorn's banks, so Parker made Marcus set up their tent during a deluge. Once inside, Marcus collapsed in a rivulet swirling under their tent, while Parker waited petulantly for Marcus to cook them a meal. Both were stiffened by voices right outside.

"Hello, the camp!" shouted a Scottish voice Marcus recognized from St. Louis.

Marcus raised on his sodden elbow, "Join us, Mr. Campbell!"

Campbell's bearded face pushed through the flap, falling from a smile to a frown in the failing light. "Back in a mooment, gentleman!"

Shovels scraped and clanged on rocks. The stream through their soggy tent choked to a dribble, dying in lilly pad-sized puddles.

Campbell re-entered in his dripping buffalo coat. "Too many o' us to get in here. Rain's slackened. Coom oot and meet mah men! We'll make supper." Seeing Marcus couldn't get up, Campbell hoisted him to his feet. "Wrap these blankets around ye, Doctor! And you moost be Reverend Parker."

Parker nodded his head, his empty stomach growling impolitely.

"Coom along and help us wi' the fire."

"I do no menial work."

"Good. This'll not be a *menial* fire, boot no one eats till it's hot enough to roast a rack o' hump ribs. We have a doozen men, but soom hafta stay wi' the boats. Ye do wanta eat, doon't ye Reverend?"

Parker nodded angrily.

"Then coom wi' me. Dry wood's in our boats lyin' off a ways from here."

His eyes afire in protest, Reverend Parker slouched behind Campbell.

The rain slackened to sprays wetting the wind. Somehow the Mountain Men had coaxed a fire smaller than a man's hand in the night's blackness. A powerful fellow with his handsome face swathed in dark whiskers extended his square hand. "Doctor, I'm Andrew Sublette. Found the rest of Fontenelle's party up river. Said you saved 'em all from cholera. Thousands died of cholera in St. Louis. How'd you do it?"

"Didn't save 'em all. We morn three Brothers in the ground."

"Three outa 60! That's a miracle! In St. Louis, they were lucky to save two in ten. How'd you do it?"

"Some came from the Edinburgh papers -- the rest experience I gained treating it in New York. With cholera, cleanliness *is* Godliness! You the Sublette that took wagons to the Rockies in 1830?"

"My brother Bill Sublette was in charge of those ten wagons and two Dearborns. I was along -- and greener than day-old hay."

"We don't think our people can make it to Oregon without wagons."

"Wagons haven't been past the Rockies. Takes master skinners to drive freight wagon mules and strong men to muscle wagons up and down river banks."

"What'd your wagons weigh?"

"About 1,800 pounds empty. A ton more loaded."

Marcus shook his head. "Wagons that big are too much for us to manage with no road. What's a Dearborn?"

"Light coach -- like a buggy."

"Will a Dearborn go where a wagon won't?"

Andrew nodded, "But won't haul much more'n a couple of mules can pack. Ours used one mule to pull it. Breaks down if it hits anything bigger'n a walnut."

"Could you make a wagon road with a Dearborn?"

"Not one that'd amount to much."

"Somebody's got to finish the road to Oregon so our women folk can get there."

"You're not going to try that, are you Doctor? Road's not a disease with research papers to read. Beyond hell itself! No bridges over rivers. Blackfeet everywhere, like those killed my brother Pinckney. Many'll die before that road reaches Oregon country."

"Like to help, Mr. Sublette?"

"Name's Drew. And no I wouldn't. Mountain Men travel light, live fast and die young. Wagon roads are for married men that hoard nickels and like outstaring the wrong end of a mule."

Robert Campbell fed dry wood to the flickering blaze. Reverend Parker dropped his sack of buffalo meat, then collapsed gasping beside it. Campbell said, "Speakin' o' the wrong end of a mule, I'll be joompin' Fontenelle aboot leavin' ye behind. Tis a sad way ta treat a blude enemy -- and a loathsome way ta treat your savior!"

Reverend Parker chimed in, "Like Lord Jesus when Pontius Pilate allowed Him scourged and beaten before his crucifixion!"

Andrew growled, "Sober man wouldn't leave a hound alone out here."

"Doc, don't ye remember mah warnin' ye boot Fontenelle oon the docks April Fool's day?"

Marcus lowered his gaze. "I'm unworthy to be mentioned in the same breath with Lord Jesus, even in jest. Be merciful to Fontenelle for he is the unhappiest man on earth."

"Not yet he isn't, Doctor. But that's coomin' at dawn before we head doon the river for St. Louie!"

Campbell's men and the missionaries ate and bedded down. Marcus dreamed of flying over fields of flowers to Oregon where Narcissa kissed him on both cheeks and ran to play near a stream that turned to blood.

At mid-morning Reverend Parker left a sickly Marcus Whitman to pull down the tent and break camp, as he galloped off to catch Fontenelle's caravan. Marcus pulled the tent stakes but was too weak to roll up the tent. A man rode briskly toward him like a buzzard swooping from the horizon. Marcus tried to remember where his rifle was in this tangle of gear.

*   *   *

Captain William Drummond Stewart basked in the flowery meadow adjoining Horse Creek's juncture with the Green River, his fingers laced behind his head. He'd dawdled here a month, occasionally trysting with ladies from the 2,000 Snakes, 40 lodges of Nez Percé and smattering of Utes waiting endlessly for Rendezvous. They'd even flung their own Rendezvous, using the bank notes of the mountains, beaver plews and buffalo robes. The gambling, horse racing and loving had spiced their dreary lives momentarily, but then swooned without the liquor.

To escape the epidemic boredom, Captain Stewart'd hunted. Camp this size needed massive meat supply. His Manton made his shots lethal from ranges others groaned at. He'd accumulated meat payments in beaver and buffalo peltry outnumbering the paltry skins he'd trapped in Oregon country with poor Wyeth.

Wyeth'd given Captain Stewart a letter to go to St. Louis with the summer caravan. As his boredom bloomed, Wyeth's letter grew hotter in his pouch. A gentleman never read another's mail, but what could Wyeth possibly say this time to assuage his Boston backers? Had he told the truth? What was the truth for old Nat?

Captain Stewart flicked a biting deer fly from his wrist and pondered his trip with Wyeth to Fort Vancouver after Fort Hall's completion last summer. Had Wyeth written a dazzling account of Fort Vancouver rising like a castle -- where the Columbia River rushed like another raging ocean to crash into the Pacific tide surging upriver?

They'd arrived at Fort Vancouver in mid-September 1834 in the wide pirogue carrying Stewart, Wyeth, balmy scientists Nuttal and Townsend and Methodists Jason and Daniel Lee. Hudson's Bay dignitaries in dark suits and kilts had met them like an affair of state. White-haired Dr. John McLoughlin posed before his grand stockade like a potentate with the Union Jack whipping overhead -- more prepossessing in the verdant forest than any real King could ever muster in England.

Their feast among Fort Vancouver's European paintings and precious books seemed more regal than any given by Lord Wellington or Stewart's own noble family. The 40 foot table's white linen was bastioned with silver candelabras showering golden lights on silver utensils and crystal goblets.

With McLoughlin like a white lion at table's head, subordinates diminished in direct proportion to their importance toward the inconsequential at the table's furthest reaches. Aromas of roast duck and puddings piqued the air with promise as sublime courses of roast beef, caribou steaks, sugar-cured ham, baked vegetables and delicately flavored apple duff passed in review like old line regiments with impeccable records.

Realizing that Captain Stewart was of noble lineage, Dr. McLoughlin had sequestered him and Wyeth in his study for a gentlemanly chat over delicious candies and brandy -- which the Chief Factor never touched except on the first hunt of each year.

When Dr. McLoughlin discovered that Captain Stewart fought in the battle that brought down the "little Corsican genius," he could talk of nothing else -- as a Scottish piper marched about the hall piping pibrochs. For that night, Captain Stewart's glory as a martial hero and Nathaniel Wyeth's as a visiting inventor from Boston had flourished. But as Dr. McLoughlin had so wisely commented, "Sorrow is the only promise fate always keeps."

In Captain Stewart's subsequent fall and winter, he reverted to being a penniless hunter hiding in the wilderness while his brother John blatantly squandered millions of pounds on a castle in Scotland with the pathetic purpose of putting down a peer.

Surely, Wyeth's letter would not mention the Sandwich Islanders deserting from Fort Hall after sacking its valuables. Would it divulge how Dr. McLoughlin's step-son Tom McKay deliberately built a Hudson's Bay fort on the Boise River seizing trade before it reached Fort Hall? Certainly, Wyeth's letter would not touch upon the failed salmon fishing punctured by arrows from the forests.

Captain Stewart recalled Townsend saying the principal business of Wyeth's Columbia River Fishing and Trading

Company appeared to be its own destruction. Would self indictment pervade the letter?

Just before receiving the letter that now sought to seduce his honor, Stewart found Wyeth bilious from some illness this June. Stewart'd tried to explain that though Hudson's Bay Company guised itself most benevolent, it was smothering Wyeth. Wyeth rejected that -- or perhaps he hadn't. Stewart was compelled to read Wyeth's letter.

Alone in the meadow a good hundred yards from the encampments, Stewart saw that it was addressed to Leonard Jarvis. Stewart slid his butcher knife delicately along under the flap without cutting the paper, unfolded it and read:

"I am surrounded with difficulties beyond any former period of my life and without the health and spirit to support them. In this situation you can judge if memory brings to me the warnings of those wiser and older who advised a course which would at least have resulted in quietness. Yes, memory lends its powers for torment. A few days ago she told a tale which carried me back to early life, led me through the varying shades of days and years, while at every step the tale grew darker and at last delivered me to the horrors of the present time. What at that moment they were you may imagine -- a business scattered over half the deserts of the earth, and myself a powerless lump of matter in the extremity of mortal pain with little hope of surviving a day; and if it could have been said, 'he never existed,' glad to go down with the sun."

Wyeth's letter brought Captain Stewart's own pain searing him. He'd been punished beyond all measure for violating the letter's content, for he was sure he could honestly have penned every word about himself.

CHAPTER 42

FRONTIER DOCTOR'S LOT   SUMMER 1835

When the skeletal rider in buckskins got close enough for Dr. Marcus Whitman to see it wasn't an Indian, Marcus lowered his rusty rifle, yelling in his deep baritone, "Don't come closer. I may have cholera."

But the reedy fellow hollered back, "You didn't shy away none when I had it, Doc!"

Marcus recognized Fontenelle's clerk they called "Pins." Pins slid off his horse and pushed Marcus's rifle downward. "You learnt me bout cholera. I'll learn you bout rifles while I'm shaggin' ya ta the caravan."

As Pins expertly stowed the tent on a pack animal, he rasped, "Out here rifle's a tool like a shovel. Gotta scrape rust off an' oil it." He seized Marcus's rifle, aimed it at Marcus and pulled the trigger.

Marcus gasped through the dry click of the hammer.

"Empty guns kills more people out here'n anythin' but hostiles." "Here, give this rifle a lick an' a promise while I pack your dunnage."

"Could you load this gun for me?"

"Not till you clean it! Cleanin' a loaded gun's like kissin' a rattler's teeth !"

Pins helped Marcus mount and dismount whenever nature forced it. With Pins' dried buffalo meat and benevolence, Marcus regained strength. As Fontenelle's caravan hove into view next day, Marcus asked, "What's your real name? Want it for my journal."

Pins grinned, "Mountain Name's Pins. Plenty Mountain Men never give real names. Goin' past a Mountain Name's like kissin' the rattler. Jist write me down as yer grateful Apostle." Pins loped his pony into the caravan's dust cloud.

*   *   *

When Fontenelle's caravan reached the North Fork of the Laramie on July 26th, Reverend Parker and Marcus Whitman met the Ogalala Sioux. Their parley with the Chief and four braves around the fire in the Chief's smoky tipi was eery. They didn't speak Sioux, so Fontenelle sent for a mountaineer to sign. Waiting for their interpreter, Parker and Marcus were terrified when the Chief repeated a hand sign like he was cutting his throat. Was he ordering their throats slit?

But when thickset Charles Compo squeezed in, he said, "That throat cuttin' sign's the Sioux name. I'm signin' back all men are Sioux at heart."

The Sioux chanted, smoking the calumet by turns. Parker and Whitman pretended to smoke, then Parker asked, "What's the Chief mean when he holds two fingers to his mouth and moves them around in circles?"

"Chief wants you to sing now," Compo grinned.

Marcus announced in his bullfrog voice, "If I sing, they'll attack."

"Then I'll do it, but it's too smoky in here," Parker rasped.

Compo signed for all to troop out beneath stars twinkling like bright signal fires. Parker was inspired to sing John Bowring's decade old hymn, *Watchman, Tell Us of the Night,* and unleashed his quavering falsetto toward God's stars:
"Watchman, tell us of the night, what it's signs of promise are.
Traveler o'er yon mountain's height, see that glory beaming star.
Watchman, does its beauteous ray Aught of joy or hope foretell?
Traveler, Yes; it brings the day, promised day of Is-ra-el!"

The Sioux Chief repeated his singing sign and many Sioux left their fires to crowd around Reverend Parker, who stood wrinkling his nose at their smell.

Compo marveled, "Them Sioux don't understand a word o' that, but likes a white man a-singin' to 'em. Wanchu ta sing more -- though I cain't see why."

Parker removed his stovepipe hat and cleared his throat, but the Chief signed for him to put the hat back on, so he did, launching the second verse in a higher voice than the first:

"Watchman, tell us of the night, higher yet that star ascends.

Traveler, blessedness and light, peace and truth its course portends.

Watchman, will its beams alone gild the spot that gave them birth?

Traveler, ages are its own; see, it bursts oe'r all the earth."

The Sioux Chief put Parker's hand to his own chest, and the other Sioux pointed to the stars. Parker stood deeply moved, sure he could see the face of God in the stars, smiling down on him and his new flock.

Later, after Parker and Marcus bedded down in their tent, Parker wrote in their campfire's dim light flowing through the canvas:

". . . . It moved my heart, and it would have moved the hearts of the Christians of the east, had they witnessed the scene. Can they not now be moved, and send missionaries to teach these very interesting people the way of salvation? Are there no young men who are willing to take up the cross and come?"

        *   *   *

Next day their caravan reached Fort William on the Laramie, called Fort Laramie by many. Angered by Fontenelle's drunkenness, Irish Thomas Fitzpatrick cornered his swarthy French partner in their garrison's black powder shed, "Every day ain't Rendezvous, Lucien!"

"Tom, you realize Fontenelle, Fitzpatrick & Co is this minute $40,000 in the red?

"Well if ya drink enough booze fer a new sea, it won't float us inta the black, now will it?"

Fontenelle shook his head, "Makes the trip to the bottom more bearable."

Fitz shook Fontenelle by the shoulders. "We been enemies many years and friends but a few. Git sober er git out!"

Fontenelle flailed his hands weakly, "To be sure," he mocked Fitz' brogue and grinned stupidly.

"You're two months late. Where ya been?"

"Outfit came down with cholera at Bellevue. The missionary -- Doc Whitman -- saved all but three of 60. I've written a letter to Andy Drips for delivery at Rendezvous about cutting our expenses and giving special care to the Doc who's been of great service to us."

"You won't be going ?"

Fontenelle patted his chest. "Still sick. Take the goods and sell 'em high as you can."

"Last year wasn't that you harpin' how God-awful greedy Bill Sublette was? Vowed you'd never gouge another trapper."

"After a few pints, they crave being gouged. We're desperate!"

Fitz stormed from the powder room. He ordered the wagons' goods repacked on mules because cloud bursts had streams over their banks.

Little Friday the Arapaho found Fitzpatrick packing mules and begged, "Take me to Rendezvous, father. Mr. Fontenelle says I am a waste of time. I do not understand that, so I cannot please him."

"Nobody pleases Mr. Fontenelle, least of all -- him."

"Can I ride beside you?"

"To be sure my boy, but keep your eyes open for Blackfeet. They live to wreck a Rendezvous."

"Father, I'll watch for the Gros Ventres who stole the color from your hair and the Crows who robbed us."

Fitzpatrick knelt beside Friday. "The Crows only robbed us at behest o' American Fur Company. Now I am a partisan of American Fur Company."

"How did we come to work for robbers, father?"

Mystified himself, Fitz turned his palms up, then yelled, "Snug them packs tight, boys. These mules'll be bull boats afore this trip's done."

*   *   *

On August 10th Fitzpatrick's mule brigade scaled the Continental Divide at South Pass. Though Presbyterians were known foes of Catholics, Fitzpatrick found it in his heart to befriend Dr. Marcus Whitman . Whitman's wheezing nag gulped icy thin air. Marcus rasped "I'm baffled at it being this cold in August."

Fitzpatrick squinted at the thermometer from his possibles bag. "Twenty-three degrees Fahrenheit. Would that be 9 degrees below freezing?"

"It would in New York!"

Fitz reminisced, "Sure now, you're not the first New Yorker over South Pass. In the spring o' '24 Jedediah Smith late of New York, Bill Sublette, Jim Clyman and me stood right there -- snow driftin' over our horses. Jedediah -- he was a Methodist -- thanked God fer findin' South Pass agin after it bein' lost fer years. But I daresay you be the first American doctor to cross the Rockies."

"Other nation's doctors been up here?"

Fitz laughed, "Crows, Snakes, Blackfeet and Utes. Mebbee more."

"Indians have doctors?"

"Medicine men -- they call spirits to heal the sick. They got it worse'n American doctors."

"Why?"

"Important patient dies, they're usually sacrificed."

Marcus mused, "Not all that different, Mr. Fitzpatrick!"

They rode in silence, horses and men clouding the air with their breaths. Marcus, awed by the splendor of the Rockies called the Shining Mountains by easterners, observed, "With a rock-free pass this wide, wagons could roll over it."

Fitz looked away. "Our Jedediah's gone now, but I read his poetic letter to General Ashley about this pass back in '24. He said -- *through South Pass the gateway to the West lies open so that one day wagonloads of families may join us here among the snow capped towers of God.*"

Marcus heard the catch of emotion in Fitzpatrick's voice and said reverently, "I will fulfill Jedediah's prophecy -- you have my oath to God on it."

*   *   *

Fitzpatrick trotted his caravan into Rendezvous the afternoon of August 12th, and before nightfall, a sober man was hard to find. Reverend Parker and Dr. Whitman had never seen anything so debauched. Finally, Marcus said, "Nothing's gained fleeing the devil. We must make a stand for God."

"Of your multitudes of idiotic utterances, that's your most harebrained, Marcus Whitman! These savages'll kill you for sport!"

Marcus walked up to the nearest campfire, determined to come to grips with evil. Tom Fitzpatrick yelled, "Doc Whitman, come set a spell. This here's my partner, Jim Bridger!" Marcus crouched beside Bridger, a lean man with abundant brown hair and mild gray eyes. They shook hands, both surprised at the other's strength.

Bridger howled, "We's laughin' bout the doctorin' ole Tom done on mah foot up in the Three Forks country in '32! Shoved a Blackfoot arrow clean through my moccasin. Wanted ta do the same thing ta the arrow in mah back, but ah tole Tom mah belly waren't gonna stand fer bein' spitted!"

"He get the arrow out?" Marcus asked, dodging a drunken Indian kicking sparks as he danced through the fire.

"Busted the shaft off an' left the head in mah back. Likes to itch me crazy inna summer a-settin' there agin mah back bone."

"Won't say that next summer!" Marcus laughed.

"How come?"

"Arrowhead's coming out soon's you sober up."

Bridger pulled his Green River butcher knife. "Gitter now, Doc while I'm flyin' inna dark!"

"My scalpel's sharper. Eyes will be too in the daylight. Nighttime may be good for knifing a man in the back, but not if you want him as a friend for life."

"See ya at dawn, Doc. Bring a few ole boys ta hold me down. I ain't no hero!"

*   *   *

A crowd of drunks that should have passed out before dawn braved the frosty morning air around the camp's only table where Dr. Whitman had Bridger laid stripped to the waist and as close to sober as Bridger got at a Rendezvous.

Fitzpatrick whispered, "Don't be killin' Jim now, Doc. Jim's Injin friends're watchin' and you know what becomes o' medicine men who let the patient snuff it."

Nervously, Marcus grated, "Give him a bullet to bite."

Fitzpatrick offered Bridger a small bore bullet, but Captain Stewart shoved a Manton slug between Bridger's teeth, smiling, "Cookie sends you his biggest biscuit at twelve to the pound!"

Bridger bit the big bullet. Marcus palpated Bridger's firm back muscles. Just below the entry scar, he felt a bulge an inch to the right of spinal *lumbar* number one. Marcus saw small risk of severing the spinal cord or the descending *aorta* or *vena cava*. Since muscle fibers in all five layers of back muscles ran longitudinally, his incision would be parallel to the spine. To minimize risk of cutting the *lumbar ganglia*, Marcus would go in slowly and shallow, set his forceps around the arrowhead and extract it.

Marcus's sweaty face steamed in the freezing air. The only time he'd incised back muscles was dissecting a cadaver at Fairfield Medical College the same year Bridger'd caught the arrowhead. He centered his scalpel over the bulge, and made his incision into the *latissimus dorsi*. Onlookers groaned, but Bridger didn't. Marcus forcepped the slippery black arrowhead, but couldn't budge it. Marcus yanked, snapping one axis of his forceps.

An angry drunk blurted, "What kinda butcherin' izzat, Doc?"

But Captain Stewart handed Marcus a sturdy bullet mold. "Use this. It won't break."

The plier-type bullet mold was strong, but the arrowhead still wouldn't let go. Marcus didn't like the mean growls from surrounding men, but inserted his scalpel and sliced down the side of the arrowhead all the way to the *vertebra* where it hooked into the bone with a cartilaginous sheath around it. Once he cut away the gristle, the three inch arrowhead came free, and Marcus waved it over his head. Trappers and Indians tossed their hats in the air. Marcus tamped a towel into the wound and let out a grand sigh.

Wiping his sweaty face on his sleeve, Marcus confided to Jim Bridger, "I'm surprised there was no pus around this arrow head."

Bridger spit the bullet into his hand. "Well now Doc, meat don't spile when yer Up the Mountain! Now I jist wanta give that back ache a little whiskey to swim in."

Marcus was astounded to see men lining up behind him at the makeshift surgical table. "What's this?"

Bridger gasped, "It's the Mountain way, Doc. First feller lives, they all gotta try it. Lotta boys been packin' unwelcome presents fer years. Few of 'em probably jist wanta git cut on fer the hell of it -- cause they ain't got nobody else what gives a damn about 'em."

CHAPTER 43

RENDEZVOUS ON THE GREEN   SUMMER 1835

Thomas Fitzpatrick's summer caravan muled in letters from St. Louis. Fitz dumped the letters in Friday's lap. Little Friday adored bringing happiness to men's faces and read letters aloud for illiterates, learning much about the whites. Friday handed Captain William Drummond Stewart two letters, asking "You can read?" Stewart nodded and the boy darted off.

Brother George Stewart's artless letter prated about the bejeweled roof on brother John's new castle, but mentioned nothing of Captain Stewart's wife or son. Captain Stewart crumpled the letter and hurled it into the morning breeze.

The British Consul's letter from New Orleans said Stewart came highly recommended by Fort Vancouver's Dr. McLoughlin and urged Stewart to become a cotton broker for English mills needing raw cotton to survive. Money's scent so captivated Stewart he was startled by Reverend Parker and Dr. Whitman. Ever the gentleman, Stewart rose. "Surgeries over?"

Whitman nodded, returning Stewart's bullet mold. "Blacksmith welded my forceps. Took out two bullets, two arrowheads and a broken fork. These men exalt in mutual destruction."

Parker leaned close to Stewart, "Nez Percé say Jason and Daniel Lee abandoned their Oregon mission."

"Lees went into the real estate business in Willamette Valley!"

Parker's hiss startled Stewart. Marcus reddened with anger at the betrayal of the noble Nez Percé. "Captain, you know a good Oregon mission site near water and trails?"

"Near Fort Walla Walla. Ground's rich and well watered."

Parker asked, "Doesn't Hudson's Bay Company thwart American settlement?"

Stewart confided, "Trade's the key to the British soul. Buy from them, they warm to you. Since you pose no trapping threat you'll do better than some -- like Nathaniel Wyeth."

"What'd the British do to him?"

"Beguiled him!" Stewart groaned.

Friday scampered up. "Come quick, Doctor!" Marcus ran toward the roars of men rising into the crisp morning air.

Chouinard, a monster the trappers called Shunar, flung another French trapper over his horse, rushed around and booted him in the face. Bodies of two others scarecrowed in the grass. His black beard dripping spittle, Shunar bellered, "Pussycats! Must I take a switch to you Americans to make you fight?" He charged the crowd that shrank from him like a prairie fire -- except for one small man.

Marcus assessed the stoop-shouldered fellow with plastered down reddish hair, freckled face and soft blue eyes as a dead man "Who's he?" Marcus panted to Friday.

"He is Kit Carson. He cannot read."

"Literacy's the least of his problems now, boy!"

Kit Carson growled, "I'm the worst American in camp. Shut yer mouth, er I'll rip your guts!"

Shunar laughed, "A rampant mouse!"   Seizing a bystander's rifle, he vaulted onto a trapper's horse.

Kit Carson leaped on a bare-backed paint horse, yanking the pistol from his belt. Carson rammed his horse into Shunar's. Their weapons fired in a single smoky blast. Shunar's bullet snicked a white path through Carson's red hair and the blast singed his eye. But Shunar sprawled in the grass, Carson's pistol ball having broken his left hand, wrist and upper arm.

Carson rubbed his scorched eye. "Gimme another pistol!"

"Leave me be, little man! When I sober up, we will get drunk together and fight some more."

Carson slid off his horse. "You plant a big kiss right on my butt an' I'll pass on scatterin' yer guts out to the Three Tetons."   Shunar shunned Carson's rump.   Carson cracked, "Always knowed you Frenchies was fickle."   Carson's face

246

lighted in a grin. "We're the luckiest two fools ever lived!" He strolled away to a chorus of cheers and waving bottles.

*   *   *

When Jim Bridger's back surgery let him stand, he asked Parker, "You marry folks up?"

Parker replied, "That'll cost you one beaver pelt."

Bridger grinned, "Make it two! We want big doin's!"

In the meadow where Shunar'd been dethroned, Jim Bridger held tiny Cora's hand. Daughter of Flathead Chief *Insillah,* Cora wore a golden buckskin dress, wild flowers in her raven braids and yellow ochre on her cheeks. Her midget father, grinning bigger than any man there, basked in the friendship of 1,000 Indians and 200 trappers.

Parker stood tall in his stovepipe hat, Bible in one hand and two beaver plews in the other. Wedding music was by meadow larks, and a bugling elk accompanied by a woodpecker. After Parker pronounced Jim and Cora man and wife, they were carried off by their friends. Parker turned to Marcus, still flecked with other men's blood. "Why you suppose they're called Flatheads, Brother Whitman? Their heads are not flat."

"For the same reason we are called righteous, Reverend."

*   *   *

Early in the evening of August 16th, Reverend Parker shook Whitman awake in his blankets. "Brother Whitman!"

Marcus gasped, "Where's the emergency?"

"Right here."

"You shot?"

"Only with the revelation that if we go to Oregon together, it'll be 1838 before we get back to open a mission. The Methodists have betrayed the Nez Percé! Will they wait longer or call in the Black Robes to open a mission in our place?"

Marcus yawned, "Let's ask 'em."

"It's too late!"

Marcus retorted "They got no clocks." He sent Friday to get the Nez Percé Chiefs with somebody who talked their tongue. Stocky Charles Compo, who'd signed to the Sioux for them, came with three Chiefs.

Compo said, "Wife's Nez Percé. I talk it good."

247

One Chief fumed that trappers had sold them "Bibles" that turned out to be decks of cards for devil games. Through Compo, Parker pledged to give real Bibles, then asked if the Nez Percé could wait another year for a mission.

The outraged Chiefs reminded Compo all four men they'd sent to St. Louis had died trying to get the white God here and still, they waited since Black Beard [Jason Lee] had deserted them. A Chief snarled that Parker had a turtle's head to ask. Both Marcus and Parker were moved by the Chiefs' tears.

Parker told Compo he needed a Nez Percé to learn English and become an interpreter so he could relay God's word to their people. The tattooed Chief volunteered son *Tackitonitis* and Marcus promised to take him to New York for one winter.

Parker snapped to Compo that the meeting was over. The Chiefs filed out dejectedly. Parker hissed, "What possessed you to tell them we'd take a heathen home to unsuspecting New York Presbyterians? What'll you do when he builds fires on the floor and shoots stock from the windows?"

Marcus throttled his anger. "Teach him our ways, as I must learn theirs. These earnest men are not the problem. We are the problem! We see nothing the same. I should return home and bring missionaries back next spring while you locate suitable Oregon sites and wait there to show them to us."

Parker grated, "I do no menial work."

"Ask Compo."

Parker snapped, "I'll take the pack horses and this tent."

Marcus was bewildered. "And what'll I do, Reverend?"

"I'll give you $5 to buy a pack horse."

"They cost $100 at Rendezvous."

"The Lord will test you, Brother Whitman."

"The Lord is already testing me, Brother Parker."

         *   *   *

Charles Compo reluctantly agreed to accompany Parker as interpreter. That no sooner done, Parker said, "Someone must cook and pack for me on the way to Fort Walla Walla."

"We sposed to do all this fer nothin'? "Compo asked.

"You'll all be properly paid."

Compo agreed in spite of the warning voice in his head.

Jim Bridger said Parker and the Indians could ride with his brigade as far as Jackson's Hole.   Bridger'd go north from there and Parker could continue west with the Indians.

On August 22nd, Marcus bought a sore-backed horse for $5. Parker counted out the coins to Fitzpatrick from his change purse.

"I need money for the homeward journey too."

"Start with that $7 you squandered in St. Louis. If you'd demanded payment for medical services at this devil's revelry you'd be mounted like a potentate. As penitence for your profligacy, you must ask the Lord to provide a way."

Marcus asked, "What's the answer to the riddle on my father's tombstone? You promised back at Fairfield Medical College to tell me if I went to Oregon with you."

"But you're not going to Oregon with me, are you Brother Whitman?" Parker mounted up and rode after Bridger's brigade, buzzing bees and bright butterflies rising about him.

Catholic Fitzpatrick spit in disgust at stinginess of such Presbyterian proportions.

Reverend Parker fell in beside Joe Meek, marveling at the striking Indian woman riding behind him on a sleek horse with elegant saddle, ribbons braided into its mane and tiny tinkling bells all over it. Rings adorned all her fingers and one thumb and a $22 blue blanket embraced her comely shoulders.

"Who's she?" Parker asked the handsome Joe Meek noticing that Meek's buckskins were ragged and filthy.

Meek answered proudly, *"Umentucken Tukutsey Unde-watsey."* Then he added, "Yer lookin' at my *last* two years pay."

"At least you didn't drink it all away," Parker observed.

"Drinkin' tuck my *next* two years pay!" Meek grinned, "Watch whatchu say. *Umentucken* unnerstands everythin'. Wife ta my ole crony Milt Sublette fore his leg quit 'im."

Umentucken shook her fist over disclosure of her personal business.

Meek grinned, "I tole ya she unnerstands!"

Bridger's brigade reached Jackson Hole on the Sabbath. Reverend Parker's sermon lambasted the Mountain Men for selling decks of cards to the Indians as Bibles and condemned them as drink-besotted. In the midst of his preaching, a band of

249

buffalo appeared. The Mountain Men thundered off with rifles blazing while the Nez Percé remained with bowed heads listening devoutly to unfamiliar white words.

When the hunters returned with choice cuts of buffalo meat, Reverend Parker rebuked the Sabbath-breakers, yelling they were going straight to hell. But when the juicy tenderloin was cooked, Parker ate with the coarser men till *Umentucken* braced him. "Hunters go to hell for shooting meat -- you go to hell for eating meat!"

Joe Meek exploded, "I tole ya she unnerstands!"

*   *   *

After Parker left, the tentless Marcus slept under the stars, praying for forgiveness of his anger at the Reverend. He continued to tend combatants in ceaseless brawls, and something odd happened. Each morning more goods appeared around his blanket.

While Marcus marveled at his growing supplies, a Nez Percé Chief brought his son *Ais.* Unable to speak the white tongue, he patted *Ais* on the head, pointed upward, then east, poking Marcus. He touched *Ais's* horse packed with provisions. Marcus put his arm around the strapping lad with tattoos of mountains on his chest, saying, "I'll call you John, for the Gospel where Jesus turned water into wine." He tapped the young man's head, "You are John." Then his own. "Marcus."

Before sunset another Chief brought slender son *Tackitonitis,* who looked past everyone to the horizon. Marcus thought the young man was blind till he took the hand Marcus extended. Before Marcus could say more, the Chief brought two supply laden ponies and handed their lead ropes to Marcus. Marcus touched *Tackitonitis.* "I'll call you Richard since you've brought riches to take us home. We must thank God, for the bounty he has provided." They knelt together, heads bowed.

Fitzpatrick walked up behind them and grinned, "Pack up, Doc! We're headed for the settlements!" He'd never tell this stranded Presbyterian that a scorned Catholic Booshway had pressured the Mountain Men into paying up for their patching up and made the Nez Percé buy their sons' passage to New York.

CHAPTER 44

HEARTACHE AND A DEARBORN WAGON   SUMMER 1835

Disgusted by the American Board's refusal to let Eliza accompany him on the mission to the Osages, Henry Spalding applied to the U.S. government for both to teach the Choctaws. A bureaucrat's favorable reply convinced Henry to leave Lane Theological Seminary at Cincinnati, Ohio a year short of graduation.

They left Lane to see relatives and friends in New York before their perilous journey to the heathens who'd dismembered their last teacher. Reaching the home of Eliza's parents near Holland Patent, New York, they vowed not to mention agonies they might suffer at the hands of the Choctaws.

After an uplifting few weeks with Martha and Levi Hart, things got edgy between Henry and Eliza's father. Opinionated Levi was neither Christian nor diplomat. Levi's fierce opposition to their mission among heathens endangered the serenity of the Hart home.

Never one for polite nuances himself, Henry took long twilight walks to cool his ardent desire to lash out at his father-in-law's obtuse refusal to accept Eliza's missionary calling. Just when bloodshed seemed imminent, things changed suddenly.

Levi Hart escorted his daughter and son-in-law to the barn one hot afternoon. Inside the barn, creaking with summer heat, dwelt a new Dearborn. "Consider this my peace offering."

"This is phenomenal, father!" Eliza exclaimed in her scratchy voice.

Levi stared at the barn wall and delivered his qualified surrender, "I realize you'll live your lives according to the dictates of your own perceptions -- however misguided they appear to me." Levi added, "It comes with one horse, a harness, $100, some warm clothing and our love. What do you think of this little beauty, Henry?"

"I'm grateful beyond words. I'm 31 years old and no one's ever given me anything bigger than a hairbrush. I've earned what we have laboring in a print shop for 6¼¢ an hour. I'd work a decade for this fancy rig with the horse and all."

Levi clawed his beard with both hands as he always did when tense. "Well as you know Eliza's birthday is August 11th. It's really her birthday present."

Henry felt the stinging lash of the gift's re-direction, but suffered in silence. Eliza quickly hugged her father, cajoling, "Let's leave Henry to savor our mutual good fortune, father!" She took Levi's thin arm and escorted him from the barn.

Stunned, Henry studied the Dearborn wagon. Its hard wood springs extended from one axle to the other. The bed was a practical dark brown that wouldn't show scratches. Its wheels were jonquil yellow with a sincere blue pinstripe down each spoke. The seat had no springs, but they could sit on their baggage on rough roads and never be the worse for wear. He felt the wagon wanted to address him. Henry ran his fingers over its glistening paint and listened, but it said nothing. So Henry spoke for it, "I want a top!"

"And you shall have one!" Henry answered himself as he left the barn listing the items he'd buy to make the Dearborn's sheltering top.

Levi Hart resented Henry's disfiguring the pristine wagon with his makeshift top. Eliza placated her father, confiding the top was Henry's gift to her because she sunburned so easily. She had more trouble convincing her mother they had to leave earlier than planned for Bath, New York for Henry's ordination as a minister of the Presbyterian Church. She was secretly crushed that her parents didn't ask to attend.

In late July, the Spaldings loaded their scant belongings on their dazzling Dearborn and rode 140 proud miles behind their high-stepping horse to Prattsburg, eager to pick up their governmental appointment to the Choctaws. Henry couldn't hide his exhilaration at people's faces envying his new Dearborn wagon. But when Henry left the Prattsburg Postmaster's cubicle, he stumbled back into their Dearborn in a daze.

His devastation told Eliza the government had dashed their dream. She pulled Henry's head down and murmured,

"We didn't need to get dissected by those Choctaws. We'll just renew our American Board application and go to the Osages. The Osages are dissolute, but they don't practice vivisection!" Henry kissed Eliza's hair, then her warm mouth. She could make him smile when his heart was broken.

Henry began gathering references from old friends. He'd even sought one from Stephen Prentiss because the Judge was so influential, but found the Prentisses had relocated somewhere in Amity.

Henry's prized recommendation was the August 14th missive of Reverend Artemas Bullard of Cincinnati. It praised Henry as a man of strong physique and unquestioned devotion to the Christian cause, ending: "*Few men are willing to labor more abundantly or endure more fatigue, or make greater sacrifices than he.*" Reverend Bullard lauded Eliza too, writing, "*She is one of the best women for a missionary's wife with whom I am acquainted.*"

Henry Spalding was ordained on August 27, 1835 in the most memorable event of his life -- except for marrying Eliza -- and receiving the Dearborn wagon. Although the somber ceremony went exactly as expected, it endowed him with something unexpected -- tangible respectability. Now the cast-out illegitimate shunned in boyhood was ever so legitimate, belonging to a ministry the envy of all New York.

To Henry's amazement the American Board of Commissioners for Foreign Missions had forgotten its earlier stated concerns about women teachers and promptly appointed both him and Eliza to the Boudinot station among the Osage Indians in western Missouri.

Henry rushed into their room, "Here's our seraphic appointment to serve the tribes!"

Eliza smiled earnestly, but placed his hand on her distended abdomen. "The Spalding tribe's having a child appointed to it around Thanksgiving, so the Osages will have to wait till spring, Henry!"

Reverend Henry Spalding had never been so deliriously happy nor so abjectly heart broken. What would the American Board do with the Spaldings now?

CHAPTER 45

BACK TO CIVILIZATION   FALL 1835

Captain William Drummond Stewart watched Fitzpatrick's pack train parading across the valley floor toward the settlements. He'd been Up the Mountain three summers and two winters. His urge to attack the New Orleans cotton business goaded him. His hounding creditors must have lost his scent by now. With shoulder-length hair and curly beard, he was unrecognizable except by other savages. Worse, he approached a milestone no man should face alone -- he'd turn forty the day after Christmas! He spurred his horse and charged after the pack train. His braying pack mule floundered through the trampled grass. The Captain laughed raucously at what *Old Spit and Polish* Lord Wellington would say of him now.

Dr. Marcus Whitman felt like the pack train was frozen in place. Certain he could lead a party out here and build a mission, he had no time to squander. He wanted to gallop his horse -- to soar home on the wings of the eagles. And what of Narcissa? Was she still willing to marry the homely stranger who'd popped in one day to propose?

Marcus blessed Richard's efforts to soak up English. The Nez Percé boy'd memorized four Bible verses, though he didn't understand all their words. In that, Richard was like many whites who parroted the precious phrases -- including himself. Richard and John kept eyeing their back trail with sorrowful eyes. Marcus mourned his decision to uproot them.

Marcus made notes on mundane trail routines. It was one thing to follow orders. It was another to give them. His and Parker's pathetic packing of their first mule at Liberty, Missouri was still humiliating. Marcus's disciples -- if he ever got any -- would not follow a fool. Marcus couldn't afford a Mountain Man guide so he must become one to lead his people west.

On September 8th, Marcus sighted Fort William, known to trappers as Fort Laramie. An American flag with 24 stars wafted from a its courtyard pole. Tipis of Sioux and Snakes surrounded the fort. Richard and John wanted to pick the clusters of crimson berries ripening to luscious tartness on nearby currant bushes, so Marcus let them. He wondered if they'd ride wildly back to their noble people.

Fort William had gotten shabby since Marcus'd been there in mid-July. Slabs of bark were missing off the log rooms lining the stockade wall. The cannon above the gate festered with rusty scabs. The smithy was cold, and the storehouse a tomb. Fitzpatrick, Friday and his caravaners went to work on Fort William to rejuvenate it.

When the caravan was ready to leave for the settlements, swarthy Lucien Fontenelle resumed command of its 120 packs of beaver, 80 bundles of buffalo robes and 85 men -- many of whom were quitting the mountains. Fontenelle knew all this peltry wouldn't make Fontenelle, Fitzpatrick & Co. solvent. They'd still be in hock for Fort William and other old debts to Sublette & Campbell after the furs sold. Beaver prices were dismal. It was a cruel joke that men risked their lives to slog backwards into bankruptcy.

At Bellevue, Fontenelle squeezed the furs aboard a steamer so glutted with goods and passengers its safe water mark lay submerged in its master's greed. Marcus begged to book passage but the purser growled, "Men has offered me their women, worldly goods and souls fer passage to St. Louie. Ain't no passage on this river with ever'body scattin' south fore it ices over. Git them Injuns offa this boat! We're makin' steam!"

About the 10th of October Marcus rejoiced with Reverend John Dunbar and Samuel Allis at their Pawnee Mission near Council Bluffs in the land some called Iowa country. They spoke optimistically of relations with the Pawnee, and hung on Marcus's vivid account of wilderness life, lauding his plan to lead missionaries to Oregon in the spring -- once he was married. Also engaged, Dunbar and Allis urged Marcus to escort their fiancées to Liberty on his return trip. Word of American colonists fighting the Mexican Army in Texas alarmed Marcus. What if war broke out across the West?

Fontenelle's caravan reached Fort Leavenworth the last week of October.   Dr. Whitman was summoned to Colonel Henry Dodge's quarters. The bronzed Colonel'd lost his hair but not his sense of humor.   "Understand you wanta take two Indians to New York. The migratory trend seemed to be strong in the other direction."

Marcus smiled, "Training these Nez Percé boys in English to interpret for the missionary party going back to Oregon in the spring."

"Who'll lead that party?"

Marcus grappled the Colonel's steely eyes with his own. "I will, Colonel."

Dodge inspected Marcus.   "You'll do.   But the Indians need papers. Fill out our blasted forms, an' I'll see you get them. Taking white women over the Rockies?"

Marcus nodded.

"No white woman's ever been across the Rockies."

"Said no American Doctor'd ever crossed the Rockies, but can't say that no more."

"Do lotsa amputations out there, Doc?"

"None."

"Never make it in this man's Army. *Sawbones's* gotta be a Doc's job description in some Army medical manual."

"New York Doctors make sinful jokes about another $10 leg having to come off -- it being the most expensive medical treatment."

"All Army Doctors get is a cast-off boot or a couple useless sleeve buttons."

"You think wagons can go over the Rockies, Colonel?"

"Trapper named Sublette took wagons out there five years ago."

"Ten wagons and two Dearborns," Marcus amplified. "I spoke to his brother, but wondered if the Army'd taken wagons farther."

"Just rolled wheeled cannon into the Rockies and back, but I don't recommend it."

"Why?"

"More trouble than putting your maiden aunt on latrine duty."

"We heard Americans battled the Mexican Army at Gonzales in Texas. Think that war'll spread?"

Colonel Dodge walked to the window and checked his sentries in the moonlight. "Men who predict how wars'll go aren't the fools who fight them. Last Christmas, newspapers said the Seminole War in Florida'd be over in three weeks."

"When will it be over?"

"Your grandsons'll be asking that."

*   *   *

Light snow frosted the St. Louis roof tops as the caravan reached the outskirts on November 4th. Fontenelle put a flunky in charge and headed for the levee to get drunk.

Captain Stewart looked forward to sharing his rite of passage into his forties with Bill Sublette, his finest friend in Missouri. "Doctor Whitman, Bill Sublette has forgotten more about taking wagons into the wilderness than any other man ever knew."

"I'll consult Mr. Sublette upon my return to St. Louis in the spring, but now I have God's interests to serve -- and some of my own -- with a woman in western New York."

Marcus hustled the Nez Percé boys along to catch the steamer, charmed at how much more charitable the face of St. Louis had become since he last saw it so many centuries ago.

CHAPTER 46

THE LEG OF FREEDOM   FALL 1835

William and Andrew Sublette were no strangers to the Green Tree Tavern, but it'd become a stranger to them. They sat at what used to be the "Sublette" table against the back wall of the bar room. "Place's not the same since Tom Eddy traded it fer that farm. Maggie oughta be slapping my boot off the table," William lamented.

"I'll do it for her!" Andrew popped his palm on William's boot, then blew the foam off his beer and reminisced. "Remember when you hired me in here in the spring of '30 for your big wagon trip out to the Rockies?"

William grinned. "Didn't wanta hire you cause the Blackfeet'd killed our brother Pinckney. Tole you I didn't have it in me ta kill another Sublette. Then you center-shot the Ace of Spades with my boot pistol out inna wagon yard and got the job cause I couldn't beat your shot."

Andrew's smile faded. "You couldn't kill another Sublette, but Milt could."

"What're you gitting at?"

"Milt blames you for cutting his leg off."

"I set on him while Doc Farrar butchered it off."

"Bill, Milt blames you for losing *Umentucken* -- and for killing his Rocky Mountain Fur Company. Milt's gonna kill you."

William Sublette's crushing grip shattered his beer mug, drenching them with beer. He dropped the pieces and watched his hand bleed.

Putting his forefingers in his mouth, Andrew whistled shrilly for the waiter.

The wide-eyed waiter wrapped William's bloody hand with his only towel and went after another for the table.

William groaned, "Can't toss Milt out in his wheelchair. Can't leave Sulphur Springs myself, cause Bobbie Campbell's been laid up sick out there ever since you boys come back from turning Fort William over to Fontenelle. Gotta see the mansion's built right. I can't kill my own brother -- though the thought's tempting."

"Come up to Colorado country with me. Lou Vasquez and I are gonna build another fort on the South Platte."

"Milt actually say he's gonna kill me?"

"Every time he gets soused. Drives Bobbie so crazy, he's going to Philadelphia to stay with his brother Hugh. Bobbie wants you out of Sulphur Springs. Says Lindsay and Sam Lewis can finish your house without you pestering them."

"What's Bobbie up to?"

"Won't say, but no man ever had a better friend than Bobbie Campbell."

"Don't think Bobbie'd kill Milt, do ya Drew?"

Andrew Sublette forefingered a question mark in the beer drying on their table.

*   *   *

General Ashley asked no questions when William Sublette said he was out seeing relatives and old friends. He just invited Sublette to stay with him while his wife and girls were in the East. The General's office was still a barren lair away from the lace and frills. After they got past the small talk of William's recent stay with his sister Sophronia in Callaway County, Ashley stuck his chin out and chased his addiction -- politics.

"Guess you thought I should have whipped George Strother more decisively for my House seat, but I got no party support."

A staunch Jackson man, William grated, "Can't have it both ways with Jacksonian Democrats, General. Man's either with Andy or agin him."

Ashley's face reddened. "General Jackson doesn't have a forgiving bone in his body. Davy Crockett served under him in the Creek War, but when Davy bucked Jackson's Indian removal policy, Andy shot Davy's re-election right out of the saddle."

"Shouldn't you git on the safe end o' Andy's guns?"

"Jackson's opposition to re-charter of the U.S. Bank is suicidal for this country! He's provided no alternative. If Jackson buries the U.S. Bank, he'll bury us with it in a depression."

"Hard to see a depression coming when emigrants flood the levee every day an' a carpenter won't build a goat pen fer less'n what a corral around the south 40 oughta cost."

General Ashley thrust out his chin. "Bank goes down -- the country goes down."

Sublette realized how pigheaded he was to argue finances with the man whose advice'd made sure William wouldn't die broke like all the other Mountain Men. Sublette asked, "Gonna run fer Governor of Missouri agin, General?"

"Can I count on your support?"

"General, you backed my fight agin Astor -- the richest man in America. Reckon I can stand with you agin Andy -- the toughest. We'll start the Salmon Party! Our motto'll be *Our heads are busted, but we still swim upstream!*"

Their laughter broke the tension. They shook hands as only two old friends can.

"What's the real story on the war in Texas, General?"

"Mexicans lodged a diplomatic protest demanding we recall all Americans from Texas. But for the real story, I read Carlos Hamsa, correspondent for *The Kentucky Palladium*," patting the stack of papers beside his desk.

"What's Hamsa say?"

"Says Steven Austin proclaims himself Commander in Chief of the independent Republic of Texas. Says Davy Crockett and other great Americans are coming to help Austin free an enslaved Texas from Mexican tyranny."

"Whatta you think?"

"Another independent country in North America's against our national interests. I don't want the U.States going to war with Mexico just to midwife another rival for North American territory. We've still got British and Russians blocking our expansion to the northwest and Mexicans blocking us to the west. Mexicans have even lodged protests over American piracy in California. Bill, what've you heard about Beckwourth and Pegleg Smith's horse raid out there?"

"Jist Ole Boy talk at the Green Tree."

"What's the Mountain version?"

"Jim Beckwourth and Peg-Leg Smith headed fer California ta trade furs fer horses. They run inta Ute Chief Walkara with 60 braves and a passel o' Shoshone slaves. They talk Walkara inta going along, but they git 'tacked by the Shoshones. Peg-leg's horse spooks and Peg-leg can't help but lead the charge that scatters the Shoshones. Walkara says Smith can have as many Indian women as he wants fer a reward, and Smith being modest only takes three!"

The General chuckled, "You know that's a lie. Peg-leg Smith'd never settle for only three squaws!"

"Beckwourth, Peg-leg and Walkara's boys take the ole Spanish Trail to some place called Los Angeles. Their slaves sell fast, but some Spanish Don won't bargain right fer his horses so Walkara thieves 600 head and they all high-tail it back to Salt Lake valley."

"Mexican Protest says renegades pirated 1,000 horses!"

"Them extry 400 horses is Mexican Interest. I run into that in Santa Fe."

General Ashley poured them another brandy. "Didn't your brother Milton cut Peg-Leg Smith's leg off with a butcher knife?"

Sublette stopped sipping his brandy remembering Milt's gory tale. "Milt an' Tom Smith was trapping the Platte in the summer o' '27. A Crow bullet busted both bones in Smith's leg. Smith lunged fer his rifle an' his leg bones stuck in the mud. Smith cut away most o' his own leg flesh, but Milt had ta slice the big tendon. Milt and a big French Negro lugged Smith fer days till they got away."

"You just had to help cut Milt's leg off too. How's Milt doing?"

Sublette tossed his brandy down with a shiver. He sat staring into the empty snifter, a watery hint of tears in his eyes.

General Ashley'd never seen Bill Sublette so wretched.

"Milt's fine, General. Jist fine."

"So fine you can't go home, Bill?"
Sublette couldn't answer.

*   *   *

Milton Green Sublette took the package from the courier, wrestled it into his lap and rolled his infernal wheel chair toward his cabin. He hated the sight of the new mansion -- that should have been his for all Rocky Mountain Fur paid Bill Sublette before he killed it. Milt parked his wheel chair beside the cabin he called *Milt's Saloon*.

The jute cords around the box were too stout. Milt rolled through the propped-open door, torn between grabbing his butcher knife and his bottle. What'd Hugh Campbell be sending Milt from Philadelphia? Barely knew the man. No love lost between Milt and Hugh's brother Bobbie who was back east someplace.

Milt butcher-knifed the cords and ripped off the paper, revealing a wooden box with painted-over black powder markings on it. Was this a joke? Maybe he oughta have that drink now. Hell with the drink. Milt probed a crack with his knife and hit something firm. He twisted his knife under the box top till its squawking nails let go.

Blue flannel cloth wrapped some weird shape. Milt unwrapped it. He exploded, "It's a cork leg -- foot an' all!"

Milt launched himself from the chair, crashed to the ground and ripped his pants off. Breathing like he'd run a foot race, Milt strapped the cork leg to his stump and leaped up like a man on fire. "It works! The leg works! I'm FREE!"

He kicked his wheel chair over with his real foot and strode inside to pack. He was going to raise himself some pure hell in western Missouri!

CHAPTER 47

MERCURIAL MISSION**WINTER 1835-36**

Feeling peaked, Narcissa'd declined the Prentiss family's pre-Christmas rounds in their grand sleigh. One ember blinked like a red eye in the ashes of her upstairs bedroom's fireplace. She draped her red and blue goose-down comforter over her head for the trip downstairs to the wood box. Who'd pound their front door like that? Narcissa unlatched her window and leaned out, but couldn't see who was on the porch. Arctic air flooded her flannel night gown like ice water. She snugged the comforter tighter around her head and shoulders. "Yes?"

Three men in buffalo coats backed off the porch, squinting up at her. The largest asked in a rumbling bass voice, "This the Prentiss home?"

It was Marcus Whitman! Narcissa lowered her own voice, "If you'll wait, I'll find Narcissa!" She slammed her window and raced to her wardrobe that reeked of cedar. "Who are those other men?" she asked her long dresses hanging so primly in a row.

In fifteen frantic minutes, Narcissa transformed herself from a frump to a proper chemistry professor, outwardly composed but inwardly jangling. She opened the front door to find the three men hugging in a circle, their breaths rising like smoke. "Please come in."

Coppery faces and straight black hair of the smaller men left no doubt they were Indians, but it was Marcus that astounded her in his buffalo coat with his buckskin shirt showing at his neck and bronzed face. Only his violet eyes and shaggy, gray-streaked hair were reminiscent of the New Yorker she once knew. Narcissa asked, "Are these young men heathens from the West?"

"No, Christians from the place of the *Saapten*," Richard answered, looking past Narcissa as he did all others he did not know.

"I follow you into great lodge, *Waipitish*," John said, flexing his cold fingers.

Marcus introduced them, "This is Richard and this is John."

"I am Narcissa," she said placing her hand near the ivory broach at her throat.

Marcus enjoyed the fresh scent of soap on her face and its exhilarating effect after a year among bathless men. "Tried your home at Amity, but you'd left."

"We moved here to Angelica last spring so the Judge could enlarge his home building business." Narcissa reached to help Richard remove his reeking coat, but the Indian lad shrank from her hand.

"You can't touch Richard till he knows you," Marcus explained.

They ambled into the plush living room. Marcus and Narcissa sat well apart on the same velvet sofa where he'd proposed to her. Richard and John squatted on the thick carpets near the cold fireplace and conversed in their Nez Percé tongue.

"What is it John calls you, Doctor?"

"*Waipitish* -- Gray Eagle."

Marcus asked anxiously, "American Board appoint you to go west?"

"Last March -- subject of course to our marriage."

"You still willing to combine into our Compound of Convenience?"

She studied Marcus. He'd changed so, she wouldn't have known him but for his bass voice -- but his changes intrigued her. "You left as an upstate New York Doctor. Now you look like the paintings of the Mountain Men."

"Still got plenty to learn about the wilderness. You look pale. Want me to bleed you?"

"No."

His face fell.

"I meant I don't want you to bleed me. I'm willing to combine into the *Cc* compound, depending on your report to the American Board. Is Oregon suitable for females?"

"I don't know."

"What?"

"Crossed the Rockies, but I never got to Oregon."

"You couldn't get to Oregon?"

"Reverend Parker went on to scout Oregon country for our mission sites. I turned back so we could start west a year sooner."

Narcissa clasped her hands to her bosom joyfully. "This mean we're going?"

"Not sure."

"What's wrong?"

"My report to the American Board's favorable to females, but our fate's uncertain."

"Why?"

"The Board's rules are like *Hg*."

"Mercury. Why?"

"Board spills off in a new direction with every letter."

Narcissa's quizzical expression became a frown. "Why?"

Marcus held out his hands with their shockingly callused palms up.

*   *   *

The American Board's Reverend David C. Greene hadn't ventured west of Boston. The slender, graying theologian had never met one of the missionary applicants he corresponded with. He was forced to interpret them from letters and reports like the one in hand from Doctor Marcus Whitman. It was terse with execrable spelling, but credible. He wondered how the Board would react to it.

Reverend Greene considered lighting his lamp, but didn't. He removed his glasses, wondering how dear departed Dr. Wisner'd weathered this weathervane job. Greene had to float every decision based on the flow of money from the Presbyterian, Congregational and Dutch Reform churches, often after settling their inter-denominational squabbles over candidates. Some decisions died in the arms of the Prudential

Committee -- pious unpredictable bankers, merchants and manufacturers of the New England breed.   They professed commitment to saving souls of the savages in the West, but smirked at the spirit that drove men to the frontier -- as if Boston wasn't good enough for *anybody*!

Letters and reports came to hand by the hundreds each week. Few could go unanswered. Brothers accused brothers of foul acts. The Board made sweeping moral judgments based on a few bitter words that may have sweetened in contrition if the writer'd waited an hour before commencing his scrawl.

Reverend Greene questioned the Board's policy of sending only married couples into foreign fields.   Forcing Dr. Whitman to drag a woman over the Rockies, when he'd done so well alone was doctrinal rather than practical. The Board's new edict that TWO married couples must amalgamate to save expenses to Oregon may have doomed two women to death instead of one.   The candidate list for Oregon missions had shriveled.

Reverend Greene checked his pocket for the list of groceries he was to buy on his way home. He rejoiced there were still some decisions beyond the fickle Board's purview -- such as whether it would be haddock or flounder for dinner.

*   *   *

Feeling less awkward than at their meeting before Christmas, Marcus took Narcissa for a ride in a borrowed sleigh in early February to discuss strategy.   Brisk air pinked her cheeks.   Her laughter blended with the sleigh bells.   Clouds threatened snow but sharing the lap robe with Narcissa was pleasurable.

Marcus blinked in the icy wind. "The Board's making me find another couple for our Oregon trip. Reverend and Eliza Spalding have been assigned to the Osages in western Missouri, but I've written them about going to Oregon."

"You've what?" Narcissa snapped.

"Something wrong with the Spaldings?"

"Eliza's baby girl was born dead in October.   Eliza's crushed."

"Can't Mrs. Spalding overcome that?"

"Perhaps, but it gets worse."

"Oh?"

"In 1831 Henry Spalding proposed to me at Franklin Academy, and I rejected him."

"Narcissa, that was five years ago. He's married to Eliza now."

"Henry was enraged. He called me a harlot and vowed to hate me till I die! Last year, Henry told others I have no judgment and he'd never serve at a mission with me!"

"Can't you find it in your heart as a Christian to forgive Reverend Spalding?"

Narcissa was incensed that Marcus Whitman could tolerate such vile affronts to his own fiancée. She couldn't look at Marcus, but said, "Judge Prentiss knows Henry has remarked on my bad judgment. But if the Judge ever hears that Henry Harmon Spalding called me harlot -- he'll kill him!"

"Who else knows Henry called you a harlot?"

"One student was near when Henry shouted it, but I didn't see who it was."

Marcus reined in the dappled horse that steamed in the frigid air. "Henry's words burn me till I can barely talk, but I strive for the greater good. Read this part of the American Board's letter. *The outlook is dark for you. Only six weeks remain before you must be going, and no one else is to be found.*"

Still galled that Marcus was not mad enough to beat the slander out of Henry Harmon Spalding, Narcissa read the pious plea in Marcus's face. Marcus was right, and that was more vexing. She grated, "Do what you must to get us to Oregon."

Marcus held her gloved hand. "I thank you Sister Narcissa, and God thanks you for your forgiving spirit."

Narcissa mellowed, "You are a truly good man, Marcus Whitman -- but please don't call me Sister, now. It's disconcerting."

*   *   *

Throughout February 12th, Marcus rode in a blizzard to Prattsburg. He hoped to find the Spaldings saying good-bye to friends before departing for the Osage tribe in western Missouri. Marcus worried he was killing his horse the way Reverend Parker would. In deepening dusk, Marcus searched out the house the Spaldings last visited, but the craggy-faced man there yelled above the noise of his crackling fire, "Henry bolted runners on their new Dearborn wagon, pitched the wheels in the back and lit out for Howard -- that's 25 miles southwest of here."

Marcus yelled, "Thanks!" He crawled back on his horse, wrapped his muffler about his freezing face and rode helter-skelter into the shrieking blizzard. Even if he caught the Spaldings, Judge Prentiss had given Marcus a cross to bear that Reverend Spalding would never lift.

CHAPTER 48

IN HEATHEN LANDS TO DWELL?   FEBRUARY 1836

Roads fell into the blizzard's screaming maw before Marcus's horse staggered into Rushville. Marcus sheltered with relatives in his old village. The gale imprisoned him there until slain by the sun on the February 14th Sabbath. Marcus prayed for forgiveness for traveling on the Lord's day then galloped through snow mounded in smooth drifts. He spied a sleigh ahead. The finger of Providence had settled on the Spaldings! Marcus yelled, "We want you for Oregon!"

The new Dearborn wagon on runners halted, and sure enough bearded Henry Spalding huddled under blankets with his pale wife Eliza.

"I'm Doctor Marcus Whitman."

Henry growled, "I told you in my letter we'd go to Oregon, but Eliza's failing health won't let her labor across the continent. We're going to the Osages in Missouri."

Marcus eyed the white sky where the sun was a blurry smear and prayed for help. Henry flicked the horse with the reins and the sleigh hissed away. Oddly, it occurred to Marcus the Spaldings had no sleigh bells, as his horse skirted a drift to catch them. "Reverend Spalding, shouldn't the Lord's wishes guide your decision?"

"Indubitably, but how has He shown us what His wishes be?" Henry inquired as Marcus rode beside the Dearborn.

"The Lord inspired the Nez Percé to send four Chiefs -- like the Wise Men -- to St. Louis. They begged in the streets for God's ministers to go to Oregon. General Clark promised ministers would follow if they'd return home. Three died along the way, but the Chief who reached Oregon promised his people God's men would come. Methodists came, but faithlessly aborted their mission to sell land. I brought two Nez Percé boys back with me. They burn for God's merciful word. Will you shun Nez Percé beseeching God's guidance to go where dissolute Osages scorn God's word?"

Eliza screeched weakly, "We'll stop at Howard to pray for guidance." Henry nodded, realizing his bitterness against Narcissa Prentiss was vehement as the day she'd spat on his soul at Franklin Academy.

The Spaldings rented a room at Howard's inn. The three of them knelt together and prayed for God's benevolent intervention. Henry asked Marcus to absent himself, then asked Eliza, "Has God come to you?"

Frail Eliza gazed up at Henry. Prayer had brought the wild spirit to Henry's lustrous brown eyes she'd seen in the eyes of Calvin and Farel in the old engravings. She rose and said, "God's command says *Go ye into all the world* with no excuse for poor health. I take the command as it stands. Let us go to Oregon." Their embrace was delicate but meaningfully deep.

Henry opened the door and summoned, "Marcus!"

Marcus read the *yes* in Henry's eyes and said, "Please join me under God's roof."

Henry trudged into the crystalline snow. Marcus rested his hand on Henry's shoulder. "Let us pray." They knelt together in the melting snow. Marcus recollected the horror in Narcissa's face when stolid Judge Prentiss demanded that Henry Spalding personally apologize for demeaning her judgment before the Judge would consent to Narcissa's marriage or her mission to Oregon. Narcissa'd confided to Marcus, "Our mission is doomed before it's begun. Bull-headed Henry Spalding will never apologize."

Marcus asked, "Do you pray now, Brother Spalding that our Oregon trip will be blessed?"

"I do, Brother Whitman."

"Wilt thou Reverend Spalding do all in thy power to bring this trip to Oregon about, no matter the personal cost to yourself?"

Eyes closed, Henry whispered, "Yea I will, for I go for the Glory of God and not to shrink from harm."

"Then please deliver your apology to Judge Prentiss for questioning Narcissa's judgment, so we can begin our blessed journey."

"Please WHAT???"

"It's only two words, Henry. Believe me you will endure more severe hardships before we reach Oregon. Amen."

*   *   *

To Narcissa's astonishment, Judge Prentiss asked her to leave their home so he could confer with Henry Spalding. Eliza didn't come, but Narcissa watched Henry shamble into her house. She prayed Henry'd have the good sense to forego all mention of his "harlot" insult. She awaited Henry's exit to make her own amends with him. But an hour languished, then died. Narcissa slipped away from her vantage point with a new sense of joy. She prayed her lightheartedness was untinged by surfeited revenge -- but admitted this prayer was frivolous.

*   *   *

February 18th found Narcissa pacing the vestry of the Angelica Presbyterian Church. Narcissa's mother Clarissa and sisters, all in black, primped as Narcissa walked the floor in her black bombazine dress. Marcus was out scouring the countryside for laborers to accompany them on their Oregon mission. She made fists and fumed.

If Marcus Whitman didn't arrive soon, she was not going through with this sham of a wedding to appease a gaggle of Bostonian geese who wouldn't dream of dirtying their feathers -- no matter how noble the cause.

The church clamored with arriving guests. Reverend Leverett Hull opened the door to the vestry and adjusted his tiny glasses. "Sister Prentiss are you sure you told Brother Whitman the time for these ceremonies?"

"I did, but Marcus knows Judge Prentiss is to be ordained as an Elder with Brothers Schoonover and Patrick before our wedding. He's scouring for craftsmen for our Oregon mission and may miss the ordinations. Begin when you wish."

As the other Prentiss women trooped out behind Reverend Hull, Narcissa fervently wished she was as comfortable with her explanation as Reverend Hull was. She clenched her fists, "Dear God, will this farce end before it begins?" She tip-toed to the back of the church and watched Judge Prentiss ordained as an Elder, perspiring more than he ever did hammering a house.

271

She felt a breeze at her side. Marcus Whitman, his hair plastered with goose grease, stood stiffly beside her in a borrowed black suit that would have fit a smaller man. The Indian Richard, garbed in hand-me-downs, gawked with the only smile she'd ever seen on his face. She rushed in tears into the vestry.

When the wedding began, Narcissa didn't listen to their lying vows exchanged before God. What seemed pure in the planning had soured to vile vinegar. Marcus wished Narcissa's sweet sister Jane stood by his side -- and she might have but for rejecting the missionary calling. Their counterfeit kiss sealed their blasphemous bargain.

Disillusioned at how empty their first kiss had been, Marcus Whitman retreated to the rear of the church to join Richard for want of room in the Prentiss pew. He watched Narcissa, finding it impossible to accept her as "Mrs. Whitman."

Reverend Hull's sermon was of joy, but Narcissa felt only shame. Her only true act of the evening was about to begin. Reverend Hull announced, "As the closing event of this glorious night, the bride will lead us in singing *Missionary Farewell.*"

Narcissa faced the smiling congregation and waited for Judge Prentiss to sound his pitch-pipe for the choir. At that plaintive note, all began to sing from their hymnals:

"Yes, my native land, I love thee, All thy scenes I love them well;
Friends, connexions, happy country; Can I bid you all farewell?
Can I leave you, Can I leave you Far in heathen lands to dwell?
Can I leave you, can I leave you, Far in heathen lands to dwell?

Home! thy joys are passing lovely, Joys no stranger heart can tell!
Happy home! 'tis sure I love thee! Can I, can I say farewell?
Can I leave thee, can I leave thee, Far in heathen lands to dwell?
Can I leave thee, can I leave thee, Far in heathen lands to dwell?

Scenes of sacred peace and pleasure, Holy days and Sabbath-bell,
Richest, brightest, sweetest treasure! Can I say a last farewell?
Can I leave you -- Far in heathen lands to dwell?
Can I leave you -- Far in heathen lands to dwell?"

Jane Prentiss clutched the ribbon-tied lock of Narcissa's precious hair. Jane knew in her heart she'd never see Narcissa again. One by one the members of the choir and congregation found their throats too full of sorrow to sing, tears streaking their cheeks. But a few quavering voices joined Narcissa's powerful soprano in the fourth stanza:

"Yes! I hasten from you gladly, From the scenes I loved so well!
Far away, ye billows bear me; Lovely native land, farewell!
Pleased I leave thee -- Far in heathen lands to dwell!
Pleased I leave thee -- Far in heathen lands to dwell!"

Sobs racked every pew. Even Judge Prentiss and Reverend Leverett Hull wept openly as Narcissa's sweet soprano rose alone like the bell of God, chiming the fifth verse:

"In the deserts let me labour, On the mountains let me tell
How He died -- the blessed Saviour -- To redeem a world from hell!
Let me hasten, Far in heathen lands to dwell.
Let me hasten, Far in heathen lands to dwell."

CHAPTER 49

BELLERING SPRING   SPRING 1836

Captain William Drummond Stewart's first visit with British Consul Crawford in New Orleans gave off the delightful scent of fresh-killed money. To keep diplomatic doors ajar, Stewart made a quiet partnership with Crawford. Crawford arranged for Stewart to meet cotton broker E.B. Nichols in a New Orleans bistro. While Stewart awaited Nichols, he supped on spicy gumbo, Creole shrimp and dangerous flirting with escorted women of quality who flashed glances he understood.

When the classic string trio took their break, the crowd cajoled Squeezebox, a gray-bearded fellow with a dangling red wool cap, into playing his concertina. His tunes were spicier than the gumbo. Snobbish patrons clapped, whooped and stomped their feet like rabble in a waterfront dive. The trio resumed the stage, and Squeezebox withdrew to the table beside Stewart's amid riotous cheers.

Eavesdropping Squeezebox's conversation, Stewart learned that Captain Benjamin Bonneville, whom he'd met Up the Mountain, was an Army deserter. Squeezebox-- actually newspaper reporter Carlos Hamsa -- confided, "Bonneville took two years leave from the Army, supposedly to engage in the fur trade. Wrote for leave extension, but his letter got lost. Returning east last fall, he was dumbfounded at being a listed *deserter* and petitioned for restoration. Officers of his outfit protested, but ole Andy Jackson rammed Bonneville's reinstatement through the Senate like a saber through sackcloth. Anybody smart enough to hit the floor after falling outa his chair can see Bonneville was an Army spy, performing services not politically expedient to reveal."

E.B. Nichols shook hands with Stewart, then sat down. He sparkled younger than Stewart anticipated, but his elegant clothing murmured *money*.

Stewart recognized the accent he'd heard in New York as Nichols said, "Captain we stand to reap enormous profits. I have the cotton cornered. You have lucrative markets with the diplomatic entrée to the ravenous mills of Scotland and England. What more could we possibly want?"

"Myself, I've been fancying that buxom beauty over there with the nodding old sot. Her eyes beg for rescue."

Nichols laughed, "Precisely why dueling is so revered in New Orleans, sir. But it's like the essence of business -- the precarious balancing of risk and reward -- one every bit as delicious as the other."

*   *   *

The Green Tree Tavern's new owners saved lamp oil, darkening it to a bat cave at night, but William Sublette still made out Tom Fitzpatrick's mangled left hand. "How'd ya bust yer hand up like that, Fitz?"

"Blackfeet jumped little Friday and me right after we left Fort William in January. Rode like banshees fer the river, not seeing in dim light -- like in here -- that we be ridin' off a 40 foot cliff. Took a fearful plunge! Lucky we was that the river warn't froze over. Blackfeet fired at us. We splashed ashore. Whilst pulling the cover off me rifle, I shot me own hand. Friday reloaded fer me. Rested me rifle on his shoulder. Downed two that away. Dogged us fer a week 'fore we lost 'em. This Irishman kin use a drink!"

"I'll buy ya one, but I'll not be buyin' one fer yer partner Fontenelle."

Fitz squinted. "Fontenelle paying our debts to you?"

"Fontenelle's still sleigh riding and won't leave off frolicking. Hasn't drawn a sober breath since the boar hog died. American Fur honored one of the notes to me, but I think they jist want Fontenelle outa their road."

"Looks like Bridger, me and Milt fell outa the frying pan into the flames when we went in business with him. Partnership's done with Fontenelle. Soon's we sell Fort William, ya have my word I'll pay our company's debts ta ya."

"Agreed, Fitz. Ya want Doc Farrar ta tend yer hand? Tuck Milt's leg off good."

"Hand's bad healed, but not that bad. What's Milt up to?"

"Milt's high-stepping his cork leg in his ole stomping grounds. American Fur says Milt's going ta summer Rendezvous with you."

"Glad ta have 'im. Milt Sublette with one leg's good as a ordinary man with two."

Sublette stared into his beer. "Milt's no ordinary man an' nis is no ordinary spring. It's bellering like a bull calf at nut-cutting time!"

"How zat, Bill?"

"Davy Crockett, Jim Bowie and couple hundred Texans forted up in the Alamo. Held off 6,000 Mexicans fer two weeks till all was kilt. Other Texans're vowing ta fight ta the death. Little brother Solomon wanted ta go down nere. Put a stop ta that by setting him up inna clothing store. Glad Andrew's buffaloing in Colorado or he'd be in Texas."

"Heard the Seminoles and the Creeks are pillagin' the South."

"Two wars down nere. Florida Seminoles ambushed Major Dade's hundred men, massacreeing all but four. Same day some renegade -- Osceola -- scalped General Wiley Thompson and tuck off. Creeks're slaughtering settlers in Georgia and Alabama with General Winfield Scott on their tails."

"Ain't the Florida War the one that was gonna be over in three weeks, Bill?"

"Fitz, remember back in '23 when Arikaras kilt all them horses we jist bought from 'em and a dozen men ta boot?"

"That I do."

"Then General Ashley sent for the Army an' 220 soldiers come. On the march, them soldiers sounded like a rock slide. Now they're barging around them swamps like a buffalo herd trying to sneak up on a bobcat."

Fitz agreed, "Looks like war's the way o' things in the U. States."

"Fitz if all three o' them wars spread outa the South, we'll hafta move back ta Blackfoot country fer some peace and quiet."

CHAPTER 50

HAUNTED HONEYMOON   SPRING 1836

Marcus Whitman relished the Ohio River's bow wind on the cruising steamer *Siam's* upper deck because it was cleaner than the boat's dirty odors astern. Breezes tossed Narcissa's red-gold hair as she leaned her ample bosom on the railing. Outwardly, she was his mate, but he'd never seen her unclad. He knew more about his patients than his wife.

Marcus regretted not claiming his marital right on their wedding night at the Prentiss home. Because their marriage was "purely business," he'd slept on the floor. After that, clusters of church appearances, cloying Nez Percé boys and lodging in homes of well-wishers exiled intimacies. He wanted to explore Narcissa more than the Oregon country. But he had no idea how to start, so he turned to lesser matters.

"Narcissa, our baggage grows by the day. Each church adds to our burden. If we don't stop, our mules'll die before we're out of western Missouri. You sure you need your Little Trunk with your wedding dress in it?"

Her eyes said he'd shed his kindly mantle, to stand ugly naked. "If I sacrifice other things, will you spare Little Trunk?"

"I'll give away the white shirts forced on me in Rushville. They'll be useless in the wilderness."

She answered, "You know best, Husband," but her inflection belied her words.

"As you asked, I've brought your *lobelia* and cayenne pepper hot drops."

"That was most kind of you, Husband."

Marcus mused, "Didn't dream you'd be a Thomsonian with your knowledge of chemistry."

"My chemistry's the reason I shun the calomel you dose so freely."

"Why, Narcissa?"

"It's poisonous."

"Where'd you get such a cockeyed idea?"

"Chemistry texts. Calomel is mercurous chloride, $HgCl$, used quite lethally by deliberate poisoners as early as the 14th century."

Marcus fought his rising temper. "Samuel Thomson's an uneducated farmer -- made a fortune selling mail-order Botanic Physician kits and never treated a patient. Making people puke doesn't make them well."

Narcissa smiled sternly, "But he doesn't poison them. I do hope you won't give calomel to poor Martha Satterlee. She's barely clinging to life as it is, Husband."

Marcus gritted his teeth and retreated to their cabin. He'd tried to draw closer and she'd attacked him professionally! Marcus fell on the rigid bunk in their cramped cabin. He felt like a rat was chewing its way out of his side. In spite of his pain, he dosed no calomel. Narcissa called him "Husband." What a mockery!

But missionary Martha Satterlee, whom they'd rescued from the snow near Williamsport with her new groom Dr. Benedict Satterlee, did lay deathly sick in the next cabin from a malady neither Marcus nor her husband could diagnose. Companion Emeline Palmer kept cool compresses on Martha's head and prayed for her. Marcus prayed Emeline wouldn't get the deadly affliction, for he'd promised her fiancé Samuel Allis last year to deliver her to Liberty, Missouri.

During Narcissa's sheltered life as a school teacher, she'd never seen anything to match the riverboat's sights as exotic as its name. She wandered the *Siam's* throbbing decks among all manner of men -- a grimy gambler with frayed collar, a showy speculator in a moth-eaten beaver hat, a dark foreigner with red stars on a yellow silk shirt, a peddler with rope-threaded pans clanking and a tawdry woman using her painted face like a fishing net.

The way the men stared at Narcissa both reviled and excited her. A handsome scoundrel lurched against her and muttered, "I'm half horse and half alligator, but you could do worse'n me on this river, little lady." She shoved him away, angered by his outrage -- and furious with herself because it was the most arousing moment of her life.

Narcissa shunned bumpkins who scratched too proudly. She wanted none of their passengers. She dreaded meeting Marcus again after their first fight and didn't return to their stuffy cabin until dark.

She entered and locked their door. Marcus lay on his side facing the wall -- or bulkhead as rivermen called them. Glad he didn't look around, she crawled under the covers in her petticoat. She had no intention of making their business relationship more intimate. Of course, neither did Marcus -- and that *really* incensed her!

*   *   *

Leaving Cincinnati on March 22nd, Narcissa tried to keep herself even more businesslike with Henry Spalding than with Marcus. She avoided eye contact with the shambling man. Henry's first words were, "Won't be room for all that baggage in the Dearborn," and there wasn't. Henry and pale Eliza rode stiffly in the front seat. Narcissa and Marcus perched tensely on their baggage in the back.

The Nez Percé boys drove the rickety wagon behind them hauling the Satterlees, Miss Palmer and excess baggage.

Marcus checked often to see how the boys managed the wagon through the mud. There was no small talk. Silence far outweighed their baggage. The snow'd melted to swampy mud. They halted for the men to exchange the Dearborn's runners for wheels.

Eliza and Narcissa waded muck to the shambles of a wooden fence and leaned against it. Narcissa said, "I'm glad I had these gentlemen's boots made in Rushville."

Eliza finger-scraped the mud off her stockings. "I'll buy boots if Brother Henry spares the funds."

Narcissa confided, "My parents were distraught at my leaving for Oregon -- sure they'll never see me again. Each time we stop at a city, I check for letters. I've written them religiously, but received nothing."

Eliza shook her head. "When father found out Brother Henry and I were going to Oregon instead of western Missouri, he told me I'd be disinherited if I proceeded. I don't check for mail from home."

Narcissa wanted to hug the other new orphan's frail shoulders, but didn't know her well enough. "At least we've got our very own mud," she smiled.

Eliza frowned wanly at Narcissa. "Mud's the least of our crosses to bear, Sister Narcissa."

Thankful to converse with someone, Narcissa asked, "Oh?"

Eliza screeched, "Brother Henry and I read about Artist George Catlin's wilderness journey painting savages, so we found him in Pittsburgh and asked if he thought white women could travel into the West."

"What'd Mr. Catlin say?"

Eliza wilted against the creaking fence, "It was appalling."

"Sister Eliza, what did he say?"

Eliza's pale face flushed. "George Catlin said he wouldn't take a white female into that country for the whole continent of America." Eliza sobbed, "Catlin said the rigors of the journey will destroy any white woman!"

"Was there nothing good?"

"Good? I guess not! Catlin said it's unthinkable that any but a savage female could travel 1,400 miles from the mouth of the Platte -- with rivers to swim, scorching sun and fierce storms to endure -- subsisting on buffalo meat and sleeping in the dirt like wolves. Mr. Catlin said red men lusting for a white woman would be their ruin. It looks like my father was right!"

Narcissa comforted the woman's bony hand in both of hers, stifling her own terror. "Husband has been much further West than George Catlin. He would not be taking us there to be despoiled by the land or its peoples. Mr. Catlin sounds like a very excitable Easterner. When we reach St. Louis, we will consult Mountain Man William Sublette. He's sure to give us good advice."

Trembling like a treed kitten, Eliza groaned, "I do so hope you're right, Sister Whitman. I'll allay my fears till we see Mr. Sublette."

CHAPTER 51

THE MIRACLE   SPRING 1836

Landing in St. Louis on March 30th, the Whitmans and Spaldings found it more depraved than expected. Besides its atrocious, brawling waterfront, it boasted the most ostentatious Catholic Cathedral west of Boston. They skulked into the vast edifice during High Mass. The idol worship offended Narcissa, but not as much as seeing a grown man in a dress meandering about with his purse on fire. Narcissa and Marcus escaped the echoing vault for their meeting with William Sublette.

In his best suit, Sublette showed his shockingly white teeth in a grin under a shade oak on Church Street. Narcissa's jaw dropped at sight of this strapping stallion of a man with eagle eyes, hooked nose, cut chin and wavy saffron hair to his shoulders.

Sublette extended a monstrous hand with a newly scarred palm to Marcus. She'd dreamed of this meeting with "her Mountain Man" since she'd read of his "impossible" wagon trip in the 1830 newspapers. She expected Sublette's voice to be deeper than Husband's, but it wasn't.

"I'm Bill Sublette. Heard how ya saved Fontenelle's boys from cholera and cut hardware outa Jim Bridger's back. Felt I owed ya, before I even metchu and this purty lady. What's yer pleasure, Doc?"

"This is my wife, Narcissa."

Sublette bowed to her showing her his lustrous locks.

"We're going to Oregon and wondered if you'd guide us there."

Sublette's face remained impassive, but his eyes said he'd met a mad man. Sublette cleared his throat. "I come Down the Mountain in '34. I'll not be going back. Gonna git respectable like my Grandpa Whitley."

Narcissa smiled, "Aren't you pretty spry for retirement?"

Sublette held up his massive palm to them. "My advice is ta turn back."

Marcus and Narcissa recoiled. Narcissa grated, "God sent us to save the heathen in Oregon, Mr. Sublette. Good day, sir!"

"Hold on, Mrs. Whitman. I was Up the Mountain nigh 12 years. Most Mountain Men're dead in four. By 1830 Injuns had kilt 94 men in my fur company and 20 more's never been heard of agin. Grizzlies, snow and bad whiskey kilt a bunch more. Inna Sublette family, Blackfeet butchered Pinckney, Apaches crippled Milt, and Blackfoot bullet busted my arm. You Pilgrims go up there, Blackfeet're gonna kill ya slow, but they'll likely cutcher eyelids off first so ya won't miss how they do it."

For years, Narcissa'd dreamed of a Mountain Man leading her into the sunset to save the heathens. Now this Sublette was sentencing her to death on a back street of this sin den.

Before she could protest, Marcus spoke calmly. "We respect your word, Mr. Sublette. But we respect God's Word more. We *are* going to Oregon, Sir."

Sublette shook his head. "Then ya better hook on with the American Fur caravan. My brother Milt's taking it ta Rendezvous. I'll ask Milt ta watch over ya. So long!" Sublette padded soundlessly toward the Green Tree Tavern, muttering under his breath and shaking his head.

As distraught as Narcissa, Marcus pressed her hand into both of his. "My dear Narcissa, I'll not Judas you to your death. You wanta turn back?"

"Not if the devil himself is digging my grave this minute!"

*   *   *

The steamer *Chariton's* rhythmic paddle wheel slapped the water. Its hull shuddered as it yawed from the placid Mississippi to buck the burly Missouri. The Spaldings huddled in heavy coats against the brisk evening breeze, but Marcus and Narcissa paid the chill air little mind.

Henry said "This War Department certificate was in our St. Louis mail. Says here, the government 'approved the design of the American Board,' giving you and me permission to settle in Oregon. It asks the Army and Indian Agents to assist -- but makes no mention of our women folk. What do you make of that, Marcus?"

"Bureaucrats. God will fill in the gaps."

Eliza asked, "What did Mr. Sublette say, Narcissa?"

Pretending not to hear Narcissa asked, "What did you think of the Catholic Cathedral?"

Eliza screeched, "My diary entry speaks my disgust." Opening it, she read, "*The unpleasant sensations we experienced on witnessing their heartless forms and ceremonies, induced us soon to leave, rejoicing that we had never been left to embrace such delusions.*" She closed her diary. "What did Mr. Sublette say, Narcissa?"

Narcissa confided to Eliza, "Mr. Sublette's retired from the mountains, but you'll be pleased to know he's having his trusted brother Milton watch over our journey."

Eliza stood on tiptoes and hugged Narcissa, "How glorious! Henry let's rest before Evening Prayers." The Spaldings went below as the moon rose dancing on the waves.

Marcus whispered, "Didn't you evade Eliza?"

Narcissa watched the moonbeams play about the deck. She saw Marcus in a new light after he'd stood up so resolutely to Mountain Man Bill Sublette. "Perhaps, but Eliza's state of mind demands delicacy, and I spoke the truth."

Marcus laughed raucously for the first time in her presence. "You served Eliza rabbit stew, but you left out the rabbit!" Narcissa's tinkling laughter was lost in his thunderous bellering.

She laid her soft cheek against his stubbly chin and pointed down the moon's bright watery path, "There's our way to adventure and a new life together."

Before Marcus could reply, Reverend Spalding bulled on deck, shouting, "You're late for Evening Prayers! Don't apologize to me. Ask forgiveness from your Maker."

*   *   *

Though it was the first week of April, sugary hoar frost glazed Liberty's wharf as the missionary party crunched ashore from the *Chariton*, Doctors Whitman and Satterlee supporting Satterlee's helpless 23 year old wife. While their wagons and baggage were off loaded, Marcus addressed the others. "Made arrangements with American Fur Company to come this far on their *Chariton*. Their steamer *Diana's* beached for repairs, but in three weeks we're to board her here for passage to Bellevue. There, we'll join their overland caravan to Rendezvous. Plenty to do here, so please don't ignore your duties. Let us pray for Martha Satterlee's recovery."

While Marcus bowed his head, Reverend Spalding rasped, "I'm in charge, Marcus. I'll make announcements and conduct prayers. You're my assistant."

"Then you'll be showing everybody how to pack a mule, won't you Reverend?"

"Don't sass! I'm spiritually in charge. You'll continue in charge of chores."

*   *   *

Marcus had the women make a spacious conical tent of oiled bed ticking. Marcus purchased the minimum of utensils required for life on the trail. He outfitted each person with one tin plate, one iron spoon and a knife in a sheath to be worn at the belt. A tin basin doubled as tea cup and each got a pan for meat and milk.

Since Henry had knowledge of stock, he joined Marcus in the dicey business of buying 12 horses, 6 mules and 17 head of cattle from greenhorn-wise frontiersmen for the staggering price of $1,000. They bought food, a heavy farm wagon, harness and saddles, including sidesaddles for Narcissa and Eliza.

With spending done, Marcus wrote Reverend Greene they'd spent $2,800 of the American Board's funds for which he would render a full accounting from Oregon.

Henry verged on apoplexy over their squandering. "We buy not one thing more if we must starve ourselves to wraiths! You'll not make me the prodigal before the American Board. You'll be doctoring in Oregon, but I'm in their business for life!"

As Henry sat ciphering to slash their budget, William Gray arrived from the American Board on the *St. Charles* with credentials naming him a teacher, a cabinet maker and house joiner. Gray was tall, of spare build with peculiar hair, half brown and half white. His dull blue eyes made Henry wonder if there was any fire in the loose-lipped man's lantern. Directing Gray to grease the heavy wagon's wheels, Henry muttered, "Another mouth to feed -- and a big one at that!" Then Henry yelled irritably at Gray, "Hang a full grease bucket from the back axle of both wagons!"

Henry chided Marcus. "Your profligacy's run us broke. To save steamer freight bills for wagons and livestock, I'm hauling everything but the women's baggage and horses 250 miles overland to the Otoe Agency near Bellevue. It'll only take two more wranglers. I leave tomorrow. Make Narcissa watch over Eliza instead of frittering her time away in frivolous gaiety."

Reverend Parker's penury last trip had nearly killed Marcus. He wondered if preachers were just born cheap. "Narcissa watches Sister Eliza like a red hen. You said you'd wed Sam Allis and Emeline Palmer."

"I'll marry them before I go. They're Presbyterians!"

*   *   *

On May 1st, Martha Satterlee lay dead in a rude box at the edge of the Missouri River. As Martha received her last rites, the steamer *Diana* rounded the bend. To the mourners' dismay, *Diana* did not veer toward the landing. They shouted frantically at the American Fur Company steamer.

The Captain leaned out of the pilot house yelling, "Can't take nobody else aboard!" He tooted the whistle and steamed on, churning the brown spring flood waters.

Narcissa grabbed Marcus's arm. "Marcus, whatever will we do now?"

*   *   *

At his May 2nd fording of the Missouri, Henry Spalding whipped a reluctant mule into the shallow water. The mule's hooves exploded from the water, striking his chest and tumbling him backward into the foaming river. He came up coughing as

William Gray splashed in. Together, they yanked the mule till she dog-paddled across.

Since the cows foundered, Henry opted to ferry them across the river. No sooner had the ferry lurched into the current than a fractious cow kicked Henry overboard. Henry floundered across, hobbled to their camp and collapsed in their tent. As he lay gasping, the howling wind tore the tent pegs from the ground and ripped away Henry's blankets. Henry lay wheezing in the lightning storm that followed, and finally entreated, "What have I done to displease you so, Lord? Send me a sign."

The words barely out of his mouth, a hot horrid wetness smothered his face. He grabbed at it, but it was too slippery. Henry heard a laughing voice, "Mister, you done been licked by a salt hungry cow!" followed by a slap on the cow's hip.

Dawn's meager wisps lighted a grinning boy of 19 in a torn straw hat, a threadbare fustian coat, buckskins worn thin enough to read through and one moccasin. His rusty rifle lay in the crook of his arm. "I'm Miles Goodyear. Come to jine up with you Mountain Men."

Henry sleeved the cow slobber from his face. "We're missionaries. I'm Reverend Spalding. I'll pay $5 a month and a horse to ride for as far as you want to go west."

"Make it $6 an' I'll do it -- long as I don't hafta pray."

*   *   *

Marcus gently wrested his arm free of Narcissa's desperate clutches and helped Dr. Satterlee lower Martha's rough-board coffin into her grave. Kneeling mourners shoved stony dirt rattling atop Martha's coffin. Dr. Satterlee sobbed, "Don't anyone step on her grave." Narcissa tried not to cry aloud like Eliza, letting her tears flow silently.

Marcus comforted, "Ben -- Martha's in the wind soaring toward the Shining Mountains. She beckons us to follow. And we will."

Sam Allis asked, "How? Without a caravan's protection against Indian attack, we're stranded, and spring rains are nigh."

Marcus replied, "We'll use our last few dollars to hire a wagon and overtake Reverend Spalding. Pray as you've never prayed before. But we'll not violate the Sabbath, so be ready at dawn!"

At dawn on May 2nd the missionaries launched the most quixotic expedition ever seen leaving Liberty. Medical Doctors Whitman and Satterlee pranced their horses in circles to keep from outdistancing Sam Allis and new bride Emeline in their wagon drawn by snail-paced oxen with the Nez Percé hopping behind. Narcissa and Eliza meandered aimlessly on unfamiliar sidesaddles. Frontiersmen who made their living scavenging outfits off the prairie exchanged knowing grins.

After a week of glacial travel, they failed to glimpse the Spalding contingent. After falling from her side saddle for the fifth time, Eliza moaned, "Don't put me on that horse again -- just tell my mother I died!"

The following dawn, Marcus woke Allis and exhorted the sleepy man, "Sister Eliza can not abide her sidesaddle another day. You must overtake Reverend Spalding and return with their Dearborn for her." Emeline begged him not to leave, but Sam Allis thundered northward across the prairie.

Marcus's party inched over bleak country with sparse grass toward the Otoe Agency, where they hoped to overtake the American Fur Caravan before hostiles cut their odd tracks.

On May 12th, a sickly Henry Spalding came bounding over the clump-grass in the Dearborn behind a lathered pony. Henry and Eliza wilted into the Dearborn clinging to each other. Marcus bled Henry and dosed him with calomel in spite of Narcissa's glowering. That night, the Spaldings, Whitmans and Allis newlyweds bedded down on their India Rubber tarps in the conical tent, soon filled with snorings and snufflings of exhausted sleepers. The following day with hugs, high hopes, and happy good-byes the Allises headed for their Pawnee mission.

The usually placid Platte was roaring in flood stage when they reached the Otoe Agency crossing. The Otoes were off on a hunt. After another fitful night in the tent, they began fording at first light. The Otoes' leaky buffalo skin bull boat had been chewed by their dogs. For three days, Marcus swam, hauling the soggy 600 pound bull boat back and forth across the Platte.

All the while his mind saw the American Fur caravan pulling 15 miles further away each day.

Exhausted, Marcus slipped under the foaming waters. Narcissa dived in screaming, "Marcus! Save yourself! Let the boat go!" But Marcus coughed out water and doggedly pushed the boat until she dragged him from the water, amazed at her strength. Once ashore she hugged his shivering hulk, giving him the warmth of her body. Something divine happened in that quivering embrace. Narcissa found her Mountain Man, and his heart found her. They kissed hungrily until they heard Henry yelling at them -- then they kissed even more hungrily.

Henry was too weak to yell more at their wanton sacrilege, so he rolled over and simmered, vowing to make them atone.

That night amid all the snoring people in the tent, Marcus slumbered, but Narcissa lay smiling beside her Mountain Man who'd once seemed such an odd duck. She wanted to touch him again to savor the exquisite new thrill, but she didn't and just murmured, "Oh thank you, God."

After Gray repaired the wagon tongue the next morning, Marcus spoke hoarsely, "We must reduce our baggage, or fail our next fording. We'll leave our things here with a letter telling the Otoes they're for their boat that sank."

Marcus watched their pained faces as they lovingly laid their valuables on the pile. He made Eliza keep her watercolors and brushes and forced Narcissa to retain Little Trunk. Henry tearfully placed his heavy books in neat stacks, muttering about Marcus's short sightedness. Marcus put clothes on the pile he'd had since boyhood, and discarded his new white shirts from Rushville. But Narcissa stuffed his white shirts under her skirt and secreted them in her saddle bags.

They turned west toward the Loup Fork and stopped to noon. Marcus opined, "American Fur brigade's at least four days -- 50 to 60 miles -- ahead of us in hostile Indian country. If we stop for the Sabbath, we're not likely to catch them. We'll either die at the hands of savages or slink home as shamed failures to beg that willy-nilly American Board for another try next year. I think we should travel the Sabbath. What say you?"

Narcissa saw Henry's face growing turgid and interjected, "You'll recall we asked Dr. Lyman Beecher's advice on this in Cincinnati. He said if he took an ocean voyage, he'd not jump overboard on Sundays."

Henry snarled, "We all know what a liberal fool that Beecher is!"

Narcissa argued, "He was President of Lane where you matriculated. Surely Brother Spalding, you'll not admit to having been educated by fools."

Eliza was furious at Narcissa's impudence. But she astounded everyone, including herself, blurting, "If I must slink back to New York in shame because we could not agree how many Angels can stand on the head of a pin, I'm never signing up to come back out here. That'd only prove I am the champion fool in all this world." All exploded in laughter that launched tears down their cheeks.

Sunday started their forced march toward the Elkhorn. On Monday the Lord punished them by making them watch three naked Indians waddle along the river bank holding a skin canoe above their heads. On Tuesday, Marcus struck their camp at three in the morning. After their prayers, their wagons devoured the incredible distance of 60 miles, reaching the Loup Fork just after midnight. Richard and John straggled behind with the cattle, so Marcus and Narcissa circled back to comfort their Nez Percé boys. Narcissa enthralled them by singing hymns into the dark bowl of the night sky.

After her songs, Narcissa whispered to Marcus, "Ours is a marriage to please God, however we might fail to please ourselves." Dead tired, Marcus tried to solve her meaning, but couldn't fathom it.

The following night, Marcus, Narcissa, the boys and their stodgy cattle still hadn't caught their wagons. They rode horses over land that had never felt the plow under a sky so full of stars there was barely room for darkness. Marcus suddenly solved Narcissa's remark of the night before and called a halt. John and Richard hobbled the horses and let the cattle graze the sparse grass of the Loup country.

Marcus untied a tin basin from his saddle and milked a grazing cow for their warm supper. The steaming milk was perfect nectar. The exhausted Indian lads soon slumbered among the cud chewing cows. Narcissa spread their India Rubber ponchos and mackinaw blankets on the yielding ground. She kept expecting the sky to cloud over, but the stars were even brighter once the campfire burned to popping embers.

They lay down alone together under the sky for the first time on the entire journey -- in fact for the first time in their lives. The thrill of touching was more intense than the day she'd pulled Marcus out of the Platte. There was no time for all the wondrous things they wanted to say to each other. Their kisses were out of control and so were they.

*   *   *

Tom Fitzpatrick fumed. Fontenelle's drunkenness and one freak disaster after another had delayed their American Fur brigade. If they were late to Rendezvous, he'd go home penniless -- if he wasn't already.

Fitzpatrick recognized his friend Dr. Whitman riding in on his horse still wet from a fording. Fitzpatrick asked, "Would ye be travelin' with that circus with the striped tent behind us now, Doctor?"

Whitman knocked water from his ear with the heel of his hand. "We need a favor, Mr. Fitzpatrick."

"Want to hire a clown? You've found yer man, you have!"

"Please wait for our party to catch up."

"I see yer the better candidate fer the clown job. That's the funniest thing I've heard since I left County Cavan. We be near a month behind schedule! The way things are goin', you'll beat us to Rendezvous."

"I'm serious, Tom. This is hostile country. American Fur Company promised us protection."

"You catch up, Doc and we'll pertect you."

"From the looks of your left hand, you could use some protection."

"From meself. Blackfeet jumped me and I shot me own fist, but you're lookin' far too content fer a desperate man. What've you been up to?"

"We'll start after your caravan in the morning."

"God Speed!" Fitz turned and walked off.

Next day, the missionaries rolled out at sunup and forded the Loup Fork by noon. They ate on the move, but still hadn't caught the caravan by sundown. In horror they realized they could never catch up. Marcus walked his horse to a hilltop, hoping to see the caravan's fires, but saw only gray sky blackening into night. Marcus bowed his head and prayed for a miracle.

*   *   *

The American Fur caravan was a village in motion. Moses "Black" Harris scouted ahead on his favorite buckskin horse with its strange mottled "moon" eye. Milton Sublette bumped along ahead of the main party in his two-mule cart. The wagons squeaked and squawked behind him. Four hundred horses and mules behind the wagons left a trail of dust clouds that blinded the sun. An hour after nooning, the caravan squawked to a standstill. Wagon axles were so dry the wheel hubs seized up, spewing smoke -- but no one brought any axle grease.

Fitzpatrick bellered, "Kill two oxen and render tallow!" The oxen's throats were cut, but the treeless prairie yielded no wood. Harvested sunflower stalks burned hot but far too fast. Finally, they rendered some runny fat. They were thickening the tallow with ashes when the missionary party hove into sight. But instead of joining the caravan at once, they knelt in a circle and gave thanks to God.

CHAPTER 52

BEHOLD THE SHINING MOUNTAINS   SUMMER 1836

Shouts of "Arise, arise!" shattered dawn's stillness. Men burst from tents into the yellow-pink light as darting shadows. Tents turned to tarps and blankets to bedrolls. Cooks fanned night fire embers alive. While the missionaries choked cold biscuits down, calls of "Catch up, catch up!" rang about them. Suddenly, the camp vanished.

Henry Spalding yelled, "We follow madmen!"

Marcus waved for the Indian boys to start the cattle, and Miles Goodyear whacked their horses with his rope. William Gray kicked the brake off their wagon and creaked into the man-made dust storm. Still ailing, Henry clambered onto the Dearborn's seat, hauling cadaverous Eliza up beside him. Mindless that the Whitmans were still loading the Dearborn, Henry whipped the mules, forcing them to scramble aboard.

"Sight of dust rising to the heavens takes your breath away," Narcissa gasped.

"Henry wheezed. "If our slew-footed cows didn't hold us back, we'd be in front of the caravan!"

Marcus grated, "Before this journey's done, you'll bless the day you saw those nurturing beasts."

They passed a Pawnee village of domed huts. Spying their first white women, Pawnee braves thundered out on horses. Narcissa waved, and several waved back. "Surely, the caravan will send men back to help us," Narcissa murmured, flashing a frightened smile at the savages riding nearest the Dearborn.

"Henry snarled. "Some protection you arranged for us, Doctor. All we can hope is that these Indians can't stand dust."

A bony Pawnee reached toward Narcissa. She grasped the knife sheathed at her side, but he handed her an eagle plume and motioned for a return gift. Narcissa slipped off her hair ribbon, freeing her red-gold tresses to cascade in the wind. She wafted the ribbon toward the Pawnee, but in a flashing move, he knifed a lock of her hair and rode off shrieking laughter.

*   *   *

Each sunrise the caravan sprang from the darkness like an antelope. It fled across the ground till noon, paused to eat, collected itself and dashed onward till dark. But the missionaries' cows and heavy farm wagon couldn't keep pace. They straggled into camp around midnight. Henry wanted to confront Fitzpatrick, but Narcissa said, "We'll give a tea party."

"That's outlandish!" Henry snorted.

Narcissa invited scout Moses "Black" Harris, caravan leader Fitzpatrick, chivalrous Captain William Stewart, and the Captain's German friend from New Orleans, Mr. Sellem. Narcissa smiled, "Husband, please sacrifice a cow."

Marcus did and built a buffalo chip fire. Narcissa's guests approached the missionary camp dreading a sermon only to be aroused by the aroma of roasting beef.

Moses Harris arrived in a carefree walk, and Narcissa seated him by the fire. Tom Fitzpatrick, white haired with a broken hand, trooped in and sat down cross-legged.

Handsome Captain Stewart in new buckskins with his small mustache curled up on the ends kissed Narcissa's hand and said, "Mr. Sellem's English is worse than my German, but I think he says he's amazed to be here!" Stewart sat the stocky blond German beside him. Nods and names were exchanged when Eliza, Henry, Marcus and William Gray took their places around the fire with its hissing roast juices.

No one spoke. Finally Narcissa said, "Mr. Harris, I hear you're quite the hunter."

"Dat I is -- argh -- one time I shot de strangest ting inna world."

Eager to show what an enlightened abolitionist she was, Narcissa said, "Tell us about it, Mr. Harris."

"Well, I done -- argh -- shot a song."

Everyone but Henry, a Colonizationist not given to hobnobbing with Negroes, laughed.

Marcus asked, "How'd you shoot a song?"

Moses answered, "In dem Black Hills we -- argh -- come across a putrefied forest. De place -- argh -- was all made o' rock -- trees, logs, eberting! Seen a putrefied bird a-settin' -- argh -- on a tree an' fired a shot at his haid. Done missed dat bird's haid, but -- argh -- knocked off what he's holdin' in his beak. Picked it up -- argh -- an' listen to it! It was -- argh -- his putrefied song!"

Even Henry joined the laughter.

Captain Stewart wiped his eyes and said, "You'll relish Oregon. Soil's so fertile there it revived a fresh-buried trapper's corpse and he lived another 30 years!" More laughter.

Not to be outdone, Fitzpatrick said, "Jedediah Smith tole me Californy's climate's so mild, if a man gets a chill, people will ride 20 miles jist ta see him shake!"

Though Fitzpatrick's yarn wasn't the equal of the others, Narcissa laughed all the louder because he could slow the caravan down. Fitzpatrick tossed buffalo chips on the fire. "Buffalo chips, but no buffalo. They be fickle beasts. Don't see any fer days, then you can't plow through 'em. My men're powerful hungry an' so be meself!"

Narcissa filled everyone's tin cup with steaming tea, then asked, "Husband, would you favor our guests with some of our hot roast cow?"

Marcus carved a juicy slice onto each tin plate around the fire. Before Henry could say Grace, Narcissa interjected, "Cows are pitiful slow, but I'm sure that won't keep you from helping us eat this one, will it gentlemen?"

*   *   *

The slowed pace of the caravan likely saved Eliza's life. She'd fallen from her horse again and now could only ride in the Dearborn. She'd resolved to go as far west as the Lord would let her, often asking Him to admit her to Heaven's refuge.

Their flour gone, the missionaries sustained themselves on cows' milk through most of June, until herds of buffalo blotted out the earth about them. The meat of "God's Cattle" relished well for Narcissa, but Eliza could abide it only as broth. Marcus boiled the tongue, roasted the hump and fried it as steak, but it was still repulsive to Eliza. Narcissa tried to cheer her, "Just think! We have tea and buffalo for breakfast, and buffalo and tea for lunch!"

Eliza languished in the rumbling wagon, brooding over Martha Satterlee's frantic burial. Would her colleagues spare her corpse five minutes to accustom itself to a prairie grave 2,000 miles from home? She knew the dust would still be settling when the others bolted west, leaving Henry behind to grieve and perhaps to join her in eternity as they'd been together in life. Eliza prayed for a thoughtful burial.

On June 13th the caravan reached the place most called Fort Laramie, where exhaustion forced all to rest a week. Eliza's strength returned. She rejoiced in washing clothes with Narcissa -- even though the Mountain Men clustered about Narcissa making hopeless fools of themselves. Eliza never thought she could worship a hide-strung chair, but she finally had to admit God had a reason for creating buffalo.

*   *   *

Having just turned 46 in May, Joshua Pilcher was still vain in dress and manner. Pilcher'd come on behalf of the American fur Company to buy the Fort on the Laramie River and the fur business of Fontenelle, Fitzpatrick & Co.

"Well me fort ain't fer sale, and neither is me fur business," Fitzpatrick lied tactfully.

"We oughta git some stronger numbers outa this claim jumper 'fore we run him the hell off," Milt Sublette argued as though Pilcher wasn't even there.

"The man cain't buy what ain't bein' sold," Fitz retorted.

"We'll talk more at Rendezvous," Pilcher intoned. "Meanwhile, I want to liberate that white mule in your forward corral."

Milt leered, "Snowball'd go right purty with them white buckskins o' yers, Joshua. Looks like about a $250 match up ta me."

"Tom, you going to stand by while I'm robbed in your post? You yelled all the way to Congress when the American Fur Company supposedly had the Crows rob you!"

"Crows admitted robbin' me and the boy fer you louts. Snowball's yers fer $249! Man bright enough ta buy Snowball would be close to me heart, he would."

"Can't say that's my life's ambition, but I fancy myself leaving here on that mule." Pilcher paid his $249 and left to claim his prize.

"Tom, ya let the fatted calf walk off!"

"No, I'm gittin' even.   White mule's only half broke to saddle.   We both know this fort's makin' a graveyard outa their Fort Pierre.   Joshua gits drunk at Rendezvous, he'll pay twice the money.   We'll git enuff ta pay our debts to yer brother Bill and keep a Hidatsa squaw apiece fer a fortnight."

"Bill kilt the Rocky Mountain Fur Company.   Our debts ta him don't mean squat ta me."

"I give Bill Sublette, me word.   We'll head fer Rendezvous at daylight."

*   *   *

Andrew Sublette cached his buffalo hides near Fort William, hoping he'd reached there in time to ride to Rendezvous with brother Milt.   He wondered if Milt'd had to turn back to St. Louis like he did two years ago.   Andrew sauntered into the fort.   He spied a knot of Mountain Men unloading a farm wagon and packing the goods on mules while Milt watched from a two wheeled cart.   Andrew asked, "Heading for Rendezvous, Milt?"

It always surprised Milt that looking at Andrew was like a mirror.   "Soon's we git this stuff loaded on mules for these missionaries. They're leavin' this big wagon here."

"Missionaries! How'd the Devil's Own get tangled up with Psalm Singers?"

"You kin thank Ole Bill Sublette. He asked me ta see after them."

Narcissa seemed drawn across the fort's quadrangle to the Sublettes. "I'm one of the Psalm Singers," she smiled. We're most grateful for your help." Her eyes met Andrew's, and a shock coursed through her body.   This pagan in his dirty buckskins with his curly beard and dancing eyes released primitive urges no Christian woman should ever feel.

"You all right, lady?" Andrew asked, raising his heavy eyebrows.

To Andrew's surprise, Narcissa turned on him. "I'm no older than you. Don't call me *lady*." She flounced off, her skirts crackling with tiny sparks in the dryness.

Milt guffawed and slapped his good leg.

"What're you cackling about?"

"It's called quiet lightnin', Drew. Ya cain't hear it, but it starts fires nobody kin put out."

"You drunk?"

"Not so's you'd notice. Catch up a horse, Drew. We're goin' ta Rendezvous!"

* * *

After traveling but a fourth of the 400 miles to Rendezvous, Milton Sublette lurched forward in his bumping cart to clutch his screaming leg.

Andrew frowned, "Want me to shadow you back to the Laramie, Milt?"

Milt shook his head. He wheeled his mules and waved as he bounced over the sage clumps on his way back to Fort William on the Laramie.

Andrew watched Milt disappear in the dusk. Milt'd been shot, stabbed, kicked and frozen. But being eaten by his own leg was a mean way for a Mountain Man to die. Andrew wondered if Milt'd end it sooner. Andrew spurred his mount to catch Milt, then hauled up. Milt Sublette wasn't a man you could take by the hand and tell bedtime stories.

* * *

To Narcissa riding her sidesaddle at dawn, this journey was the realization of a childhood dream. God's vivid landscape extended over endless prairies to violet hills, then muted to hazy shadows against the sky in the west. She wondered if those dark smudges at the horizon were the Shining Mountains she'd longed to see for a decade. She'd know when the sun rose.

But as the sun came up, the caravan's dust choked the sky. They nooned on buffalo jerky in a valley smelling of sage while the caravan's grit settled on them. After filling their canteens in the brook, Narcissa climbed to the brow of a hill to stand awed.

All the poetic words she'd ever read met in the towering snowy mountains outlined against the cobalt sky. The sun flashed on crags of ice, arches of gold and silver, pyramids and crystal palaces frosted with purity white as virgin souls. Marcus joined her as she raised her arms toward the splendor and murmured, "Behold the Shining Mountains."

CHAPTER 53

SOUTH PASS AND ONWARD   SUMMER 1836

A week out on the trail, the half-broke and thirsty Snowball smelled water. With Joshua Pilcher cursing, the milk-white mule seized the bit in her teeth, bolted into a swamp, reared, bucked and tumbled in a mudhole dunking Pilcher and his fine white buckskins. Mountain Men chuckled at first, but William Gray rolled on the ground in glee. Finally, a bear-bodied Buckskinner growled, "Whatta hell are you laughin' at, Pilgrim?" Gray wiped his eyes and sidled into the crowd.

After catching Pilcher's runaway mule, Andrew Sublette rode his nostril-flaring stallion beside the Dearborn carrying the Spaldings. "Name's Andrew Sublette. Brother Milt asked me to keep an eye on you folks before he turned back. You got guns?"

Henry Spalding's head whipped around. "We're people of God. We don't rely on guns except for game!"

"God don't bail you outa trouble right away, I'll have a fling at it!"

Before Henry Spalding could lecture Andrew again, Narcissa urged her slender mare up beside Andrew's snorting stud. "The Sublettes are men of their word. We're thankful."

Henry skewered Narcissa with his eyes, "*And the Lord shall deliver them from the wicked because they trust in him!* Psalms 37:40."

Unflinchingly Narcissa replied, "*And whosoever remaineth in any place where he sojourneth, let the men of this place help him....* Ezra 1:4"

With that, she dropped back behind the Dearborn and watched Andrew thunder away. Narcissa wondered what'd happened to the bookish old maid chemistry teacher from New York. One thing for sure -- there were wild elements loose in the mountains

         *   *   *

After carving their names into Independence Rock, the pack train headed for South Pass, the gateway through the Rocky Mountains. Fitzpatrick sent a rider to alert the Rendezvous his caravan was coming.

They labored atop the Continental Divide at South Pass on July 4th and paused to noon. Narcissa and Eliza knelt with their Bibles and a small, faded American Flag. Both wanted to quote scripture to crown their achievement as the first white women ever to cross the Rocky Mountains, but awed by their surroundings, opted for silent prayers. Andrew Sublette halted his horse beside them out of respect. Narcissa saw him and her heart quickened, but she vowed to adore Marcus all the more and never to let herself be alone with Sublette for a second. Andrew spurred his stallion and was gone.

The pack train descended and camped on the Little Sandy. Fires were barely sparked when Nez Percé and Flatheads stormed up on their horses clamoring in *Saapten* and *Saalish* to see the God-men. Somehow they knew the Spaldings were of the white God, honoring Henry and Eliza with warm pats. Whitman's two Nez Percé charges mingled with their people, but oddly insisted on shaking hands like white men while their tribesmen tried to hug them.

Tall dignified Chief Rotten-belly found Marcus Whitman. "God-man Parker begs me put his letter on you." Rotten-belly tongued the gaps where two of his front teeth were broken off, while Marcus read Parker's letter. Marcus turned livid.

Narcissa rushed to him. "What's wrong?"

"Reverend Parker promised to pick our mission sites, but dawdles at Fort Vancouver. Instead of meeting us as he pledged, he's taking a ship around the horn."

Narcissa comforted him with a hug. "Didn't Captain Stewart say he'd found the perfect site for our mission at *Waiilatpu?*"

"Yes, but the Spaldings have to have a place. We need Parker's blessings on two sites for the American Board. We gotta know where to go after the Rendezvous."

Henry Spalding growled, "As protégés of this Parker, I hold you both responsible for this debacle! Samuel Parker has left our future blank at the very moment we desperately needed him to give it meaning!"

Marcus cautioned, "Don't air soiled linens, Brother Spalding."

"You mean before this heathen?"

"I mean Chief Rotten-belly of the Nez Percé."

Recognizing his name, Rotten-belly tapped Marcus. "You know Cutface Bill Sublette? Him give brandy for good doings!"

Marcus nodded. "I'm handing you something better -- your very own Bible."

Rotten-belly mused, "No got brandy?"

Marcus opened the Bible to Revelations 16:19. "*Cities and nations fell. Great Babylon came before God and he gave her a cup of wine -- the fierceness of his wrath.*"

"Your God gives wine, but you not give?"

"God's telling you wine is a destroyer!"

Rotten-belly nodded. "God right. Brandy better."

*   *   *

As they approached the junction of Horse Creek with the Green River, savages surrounded the pack train, firing and yipping.   The Whitmans and Spaldings dived under their Dearborn wagon.   But their mules bolted, leaving them shelterless in the dry grass.

Mountain Man Joe Meek vaulted from his running horse. Sliding to a halt by the missionaries, Meek war-hooped.

Andrew Sublette flew from his horse, tackling Meek to the sod. Once Andrew recognized his old pal through the war paint, they grappled in the grass until they laughed their breath away. Andrew gasped, "Don't worry about Milt catching you with *Umentucken*. Milt's not coming."

Meek looked stricken. "*Umentucken* ain't comin' neither. Bannocks shot her off that $300 dapple gray I bought her. Musta put eight arrows through her. Got a Nez Percé squaw now. Jist borned me a baby girl. Least I think it's mine. Named her Helen Mar after the lass in Miss Jane Porter's *Scottish Chiefs.*"

The Whitmans and Spaldings walked toward their Dearborn with its standing mules, but the Nez Percé squaws, never having seen white women, mobbed them. The squaws shook their soft hands and kissed their white faces. Many felt Narcissa's hair. Several tried to wipe off the red-gold color.

When the squaws left, Narcissa was ashen and wobbly. She hobbled behind Eliza toward the Dearborn. Eliza asked, "Too much excitement, Sister Narcissa?"

Narcissa shook her head. "I'm pregnant."

CHAPTER 54

BACCHANALIAN RITUAL   SUMMER 1836

On July 7th, Dr. Marcus Whitman walked the Rendezvous visiting old surgical patients from last summer's celebration on the Green. Near Fitzpatrick's trading post in Bonneville's old Fort Nonsense, Marcus spied Jim Bridger. They crashed together in a rough hug. Bridger led Dr. Whitman to a shade tree. "Lotta water's done gone down the Green since I seen ya, Doc! Member little Cora yer friend Parker married me to last year? She jist borned a girl we're a-callin' Mary Ann. Say, Cora's gone dry. I'll pay good plews fer some o' yer cow's milk fer baby Mary Ann."

"Richard or John -- our Nez Percé boys'll milk a cow for your baby. No need for plews. Go in God's good graces, friend Jim."

"Doc, when ya gitchur mission, me an' Cora wanchu ta edicate Mary Ann. Me an' Cora don't read none an' we gotta grow somebody inna family what does."

"Narcissa and I'll be honored to teach little Mary Ann reading and the Lord's way."

Bridger shook the Doctor's callused hand, then examined it. This here's a workin' man's hand, Doc."

"I am a working man, Jim."

"I'm plumb glad ta have ya, Doc. Some here sees comin' o' missionaries as the end o' the Mountain Man. They don't cotton to you none."

"We meet each of God's children in Christian love. They'll learn to accept us for what we are."

"You tuck hardware outa some of 'em last year. They wancher help, but don't wanchu here. Don't that beat all?

*   *   *

Captain Stewart lay panting on the ground in the shade of his lathered gelding after losing a horse race to skinny trapper John Hawkins. The Captain recognized old chum Nathaniel Wyeth wandering by and called out, "I'm getting too old for this, Nat. How're things at Fort Hall?"

Wyeth plopped down beside him looking dazed. "It's gone."

Stewart propped up on his elbows. "Burnt, captured, what?"

"Sold it to Hudson's Bay Company for a fraction of its worth. I'm a failure at 34."

"What brought that on?"

"I got caught between Bill and Milt Sublette at the '34 Rendezvous and lost my shirt. My Boston backers blanched at every minor loss. We couldn't harvest salmon with the Indians picking off our men from the trees. I got the fever. My litany of disasters is endless."

"It's a wise campaigner who knows when to retreat."

Wyeth laughed sardonically. "Even a fool knows when he's ruined."

"HBC built Fort Boise to beat you! Because they didn't rain cannon shells into your fort, didn't make them your ally."

"Dr. McLoughlin and I are fast friends."

Stewart sighed, "Most assuredly. Aren't you an inventor back in Boston?"

"Cambridge. Horse drawn ice-cutting machines."

"And you were successful at that?"

"Quite!"

"Doesn't that tell you something?"

"It tells me you've been a friend. Of course I'm retreating to my own bailiwick. Frederic Tudor will be ecstatic when I concoct some new royalty grubbing contraption. How's it going for you?"

"My brother John choked off my trust fund, leaving me destitute. The cotton brokerage business landed in my lap last spring quite by chance. I'm making money even as I tell you this

303

improbable tale. There's such a subtle difference between success and failure. We're puppets of the Fates. As I recall, Clotho spins the thread of life, Lachesis determines its length and Atropos cuts it."

"They tie knots in my thread every time they're bored. Could you tell the Whitmans that two HBC men have agreed to guide them to Fort Walla Walla?"

"Tell them yourself. When you see Whitman's wife, you'll exult at thought of returning to the land of civilized women."

*   *   *

Mud-stained Joshua Pilcher spent most of Saturday trying to out drink Tom Fitzpatrick. When they couldn't get past a tie, they set to serious dickering over the sale of Fort William on the Laramie and the assets of Fontenelle, Fitzpatrick & Co.

After sale terms were agreed, Pilcher pointed at the mud blotches on his once white buckskins with their red and blue cloth cuffs and embroidered porcupine quill patterns. "Tom, I want you to -- hiccough -- take back that wild bitch mule you pawned off on me and give my money back!"

Fitzpatrick swigged the jug and passed it back to Pilcher. "Will under one condition."

"What's that?"

"You keep us all but Fontenelle on Chouteau's payroll."

"That include Milt Sublette?"

"Expecially includes Milt Sublette."

"What kin Milt do?"

"He kin drive ya crazy same's he's done the rest of us, but he kin do it runnin' Fort William. Milt ain't gonna live ferever, Josh."

"I don't believe this! To get shed of one mule, I gotta take on a wolf pack?"

"Hell Josh, couple of us is even housebroke!"

*   *   *

Although hooting and shooting all night was the rule in most Rendezvous camps, the Mountain Men acted like gentlemen around the Whitman enclave out of respect for the religious women. Still, some who hadn't been home in years sauntered back and forth in front of Narcissa's tent in the hopes of garnering a nod from her.

Henry Spalding lost patience. He roared, "All still here in five minutes will take part in church services!" The promenading backwoodsmen evaporated.

Henry blamed Narcissa. "Amidst this Bacchanalian revelry, you've become their Bacchante! Have you no shame?"

"Henry Spalding, you've lambasted me with perverted Greek metaphors since we were at Franklin Academy. You slandered me as a harlot! Now I'm a drunkard addicted to revelry. My only shame is that I've put up with you! It ends here, Henry. Right here!" With that she slapped his face soundly and stormed back into her tent.

"Hold on thar!" somebody shouted from the trees. Narcissa peered from her tent at a hot-tempered mountaineer aiming his rifle at Henry. Narcissa held up her hand to forestall the shooting. "It's only the Reverend's Bacchanalian ritual!"

CHAPTER 55

THE ODYSSEY   FALL 1836

Marcus Whitman saw all his patients before leaving the Rendezvous. A forlorn Negro Marcus knew only as Mr. Hinds clung to his hand. "Doctor, God tells me to follow you, for you are de first white man ever cared if I lived or died."

"Mr. Hinds, you have dropsy. I can't cure it."

"I do God's work if you tend me till He calls me home."

"Pack up, Mr. Hinds. Hudson's Bay men say it's 600 miles to Fort Walla Walla. May the Lord bless every mile of it for you."

"Wearin' all I own an' He already has."

Marcus spied Tom Fitzpatrick. "Where's your bill for tending us on the trail."

Fitzpatrick smiled nervously. "Where be yer bill fer medical services."

"God has already paid it, Tom."

"Funny thing. He paid yers too. Doc, you be a fine feller -- fer a odd talkin' New Yorker!"

"And you're not half bad for a mackerel-snapping Irish Catholic!"

*   *   *

Hudson's Bay men John McLeod and Tom Mckay led the missionaries west from the Rendezvous. Henry hadn't spoken to Narcissa since the slap. Sick as she was, Eliza exchanged pleasantries from the scarred Dearborn wagon, but she'd become the focus of Narcissa's doubts. Although trappers fawned over Narcissa, the Indians idolized Eliza. Eliza mastered their tongues quicker than Narcissa.

Narcissa knew the Nez Percé and Flatheads following them argued over which tribe would get Eliza. Narcissa wondered if her whole life spent yearning to help the heathens had been self delusion. Was this God's revenge for her clandestine lust for Andrew Sublette? Whatever she felt for Andrew was already withering along with her morning sickness.

Because the Indians scorned noon breaks, caravaning became an endurance ordeal. Eliza had to resume her side saddle because the Dearborn's skinny wheels mired at stream crossings, and it often flipped over. At last the Dearborn's front axletree splintered.

Disgusted to death with the Dearborn, Miles Goodyear muttered, "Bout time we junked this junk."

But Henry disdained discarding the only new wagon he'd ever had. He and Marcus sawed the Dearborn into a two-wheeled cart and lashed the front wheels aboard it. Henry announced, "This will be the first wagon ever to reach Oregon if only as a cart. Pilgrims will thank us for leaving them a track to follow."

Marcus replied, "Hope so, Henry cause nobody here's going to thank us."

They thanked God for reaching Fort Hall without encountering hostile Bannocks or Blackfeet. HBC's Fort Hall factor Joseph Thing, who'd come west with Wyeth to measure distances by sextant, was preoccupied with his desiccated garden. Touring it with Narcissa, Thing lamented, "Turnips've all gone to tops, and the prairie mice have eaten the peas. Onions're going to seed because nothing out here likes them."

Narcissa hoped she wasn't an onion. What would she do if the heathens hated her?

Next morning, their expedition unraveled outside Fort Hall. Miles Goodyear twanged, "If that Dearborn's agoin' west, I'm agoin' south."

Marcus lamented, "We'll miss you, Miles. Since you crossed the U. States from Connecticut to Fort Leavenworth, you proved you can make it on your own now. We'll stake you to two horses and an outfit as your pay."

Henry argued, "I only promised him $6 a month!"

"Samuel Parker'd knight you, Henry, but we'll set no boy afoot in Bannock country!"

The Nez Percé and Flatheads begged the missionaries to go with them, but the Hudson's Bay men assessed the Indians' route to Fort Walla Walla as twice as long. Only Chief Rotten-belly and Kentuck staid with the evangelists to help Richard and John drive their 16 head of cattle. Then the Hudson's Bay men delegated a substitute guide and went on ahead.

A few days out from Fort Hall, the substitute guide led them into swamps where ravenous mosquitoes blackened the air. Cattle bitten bloody went berserk. Rotten-belly and Kentuck couldn't keep them from bolting. Marcus, Narcissa and John rounded up the cows, driving them through biting swarms to the Portneuf River. After building bonfires that lured and cremated mosquitoes, Marcus justified their ordeal. "Hudson's Bay sells no cattle to settlers. Without this bull and these cows, we'll never have a herd."

Henry spat, "Cattle cost $700 -- plenty reason to brave a few bugs."

As they penetrated Snake River country, trees shrank to sage brush and finally sweltering sand. The Snake's cliff walls fenced them off from water. Narcissa moaned through parched lips, "The heavens over us are brass and the earth's an iron skillet under foot."

Again they jettisoned precious possessions to lighten their loads. Henry and Marcus removed the wagon box from the Dearborn. Ashamedly, Marcus asked Narcissa to abandon her Little Trunk, and she did, but HBC man Tom McKay was so touched by her tears that he packed it on one of his mules.

The Dearborn capsized in the Snake River crossing, tangling the mules in their harness. Marcus untangled the mules and wrestled the Dearborn ashore. Fresh horses hauled the Dearborn's skeletal remains to Fort Boise, where they agreed it could go no further. McKay, in charge of Fort Boise, couldn't be persuaded to go on either.

At Division Creek HBC man McLeod elected to guide the Whitmans, Gray and the Nez Percé boys over the faster mountainous route to Fort Walla Walla. Chief Rotten-belly led the Spaldings with the bedticking tent, hired men, Indians and cattle across the flatter terrain.

Naturalist John Kirk Townsend greeted the weary Whitmans at Fort Walla Walla. Having just pilfered the perfectly preserved mummy of an Indian girl from a tree trunk, Townsend felt far too guilty to make small talk with missionaries.

Fort Walla Walla was a wilderness castle. Cannon glowered from its towering bastions, but inside the Pambrun family was most gracious. Kitty Pambrun was half Cree and all heart. She spoke French and Cree, but her English consisted of nodding pleasantly.

Kitty seated them in cushioned armchairs around a real table replete with smiling children. Kitty and two older children served ample portions of pork, potatoes, beets, cabbage, turnips, bread, butter and tea. Dapper little 43 year old Pierre Pambrun presided. He smiled, "As a Canadian, I fought Americans in your War of 1812. But to show how much we've come to trust you, you're sleeping in the bastion with two loaded cannon!"

*   *   *

After the Spaldings reached Fort Walla Walla, Marcus and Henry decided to proceed to Fort Vancouver to arrange credit with Dr. John McLoughlin for their venture.

Surprisingly, Eliza's health was the best it'd been on her seven month journey from New York. William Gray confided to Eliza, "You're proof that if women of the U. States would get off their sofas and try rugged life in the wilds, they'd rid themselves of the vapors."

Eliza eyed Gray, mentally reviewing her odyssey, then replied, "You know Mr. Gray, you are unquestionably -- out of your mind."

*   *   *

Pierre Pambrun steered his 30 foot *bateau* with five stout oarsmen and the missionaries down the Columbia River toward Fort Vancouver. After they cleared the Twin Sister Rocks, the *voyageurs* chanted, "*Rouli, roulant, ma boule rolant. En roulant, ma boule rolant...*"

During their lurching run through The Dalles' rapids, Indians fishing for salmon appeared along the Columbia's banks. Narcissa began shaking her dress and petticoats frantically.

Pambrun beached the *bateau* on a sandbar, confiding, "*Madame* need not be affrighted. These Indians never attack when they fish."

Narcissa still clawed her skirts, "Then I wish these fleas were fishing, Mr. Pambrun! She seized her Little Trunk, rushed behind an outcropping and changed to her black wedding dress to rid herself of stowaways.

Still 160 miles from the Pacific, Dr. Whitman felt the boat shudder. "What was that?" he asked Pambrun.

"We crashed through the ocean tide, Doctor."

At a waterfall, savages materialized to carry the upturned *bateau* on the portage trail. Narcissa gaped at a squaw, horrified by her infant. The squaw proudly unbound the baby's head from the press board showing the purplish bruise around its fashionably flattened cranium.

After paying off each of the Indians with a twist of tobacco, Pambrun told Narcissa, "That Flathead fashion's fading, but not soon enough." He pointed to a squadron of tiny canoe-coffins crowding the river island's treetops. Narcissa's baby kicked inside her as if frightened by the sight of so much infant death. Narcissa tried to shake off the sinister omen as she clambered cautiously into the boat.

They glided around a bend, and Fort Vancouver materialized out of the mist on the north bank. The sea-going *Columbia* and the British man-o'-war *Neriade* moored there like misplaced dreams. A flag emblazoned with stags and beavers fluttered over the fort, the standard of the Hudson's Bay Company some called the "Old Lady of the North."

A double gate opened into the mighty log palisade jutting above the bluff. A glance inside from their landing revealed a massive courtyard sporting a cannon beside a pyramid of ammunition surrounded by buildings.

Marcus recognized John Kirk Townsend on the landing and shouted, "Where's Reverend Parker?"

"Gone home," Townsend yelled.

Before Marcus could voice his bitter disappointment, a white-haired giant strode toward them with the bearing of the patriarch of a vast domain. With Old World charm, he bowed to Narcissa and Eliza, offering each an arm.   "I'm Dr. John

McLoughlin and you're the most courageous women ever to grace our fort. Townsend tells me you're teachers who crossed the Rockies -- an unheard of journey!"

Eliza nodded, "We liked everything till Narcissa got fleas."

*   *   *

Overwhelmed by Fort Vancouver's vast fields, orchards and lavish meals, the missionaries couldn't compliment it enough. But when they learned McLoughlin and his crew were Roman Catholics with a Reverend Beaver as Chaplain from the Church of England, they said dreadful things covertly as well.

The dinners were lavish beyond anything they ever imagined, but Narcissa was puzzled why none of the officials' wives dined with their husbands. After she assessed the blue and white Copeland and Garrett platters, the late Spode dishes, the delicate jade green cups and underglazed porcelain from China, Narcissa praised, "Doctor, you preside over the New York of the Pacific!"

Dr. McLoughlin toasted her then inquired, "Will you tutor our children while your husbands are off selecting mission sites?"

"Our Presbyterian pleasure, Doctor McLoughlin."

*   *   *

After purchasing supplies on credit from Dr. McLoughlin, Marcus and Henry probed the wilderness for mission sites. In spite of Chief Rotten-belly's warnings about the evil Cayuse Indians, Marcus elected to serve them, while Henry selected the noble Nez Percé for his congregation.

Marcus chose an enchanting site in the area Captain Stewart suggested at *Waiilatpu* a day's ride from Fort Walla Walla. By October 12th, Henry finally picked his mission's location on Lapwai Creek.

*   *   *

Narcissa tutored 18 year old Eloisa Maria McLoughlin and her 15 year old brother David.

Mrs. McLoughlin revealed that she was Marguerite Wadin, daughter of a Swiss-Canadian father and Cree mother. Her first husband Alexander McKay'd been massacred with his crew on the ship *Tonquin*, leaving Marguerite widowed with son

311

Tom McKay, now the HBC factor at Fort Boise. Mrs. McLoughlin also confided that her husband was feuding with the fort Chaplain, Reverend Herbert Beaver.

Narcissa daintily changed the subject, telling her hostess how she respected Tom McKay and finally asked the question burning inside her, "Why don't officials' wives dine in the great hall with their husbands?"

Marguerite whispered, "They say only men of high rank can eat in there, but it's cause us half-breed wives don't got table manners."

In the following weeks Narcissa taught the half-breed wives sitting, folding napkins, using silverware from the outside inward and general etiquette. Narcissa closed one session by cautioning, "Never smack your lips or throw bones over your shoulder."

Marguerite asked, "Is it good to make the belch?"

Narcissa smiled, "Only if looks like you can get away with blaming it on the person next to you!"

*   *   *

Henry Spalding returned to Fort Vancouver to take the women back to Fort Walla Walla while Whitman, Gray and Hinds commenced building a shelter at *Waiilatpu*.

Henry motioned imperiously for Narcissa to board the boat with him and Eliza, but something inside her rebelled. Henry'd spewed his senseless bitterness on her at every turn for the five years since she'd spurned his marriage proposal. She boarded John McLeod's boat, savoring Henry's furious expression. McLeod presented Narcissa with a puppy named Trapper to cuddle on the 18 day trip against the Columbia's current to Walla Walla.

Narcissa met her Marcus at the Pambrun home in Fort Walla Walla on November 18th. Once safely in their bastion bedroom, she said, "Husband, I know I've gotten over-plump. I fell into gluttony because I missed you so much."

Marcus held her in his arms, "I think it's because I have two people to love in this one sweet body."

Marcus soon left to resume work on the shelter at *Waiilatpu*. After only four days at Fort Walla Walla, the Spaldings took William Gray, 125 Nez Percé and the stock to

Lapwai.   Narcissa still loved Eliza like a sister, each understanding that Henry could not be allowed to alienate them from one another. Narcissa wrote of Eliza in her diary:

"This dear Sister goes very cheerfully, expecting to live in a skin lodge until her house is completed and this too in the dead of winter. But she prefers it to remaining here away from her husband, and so should I."

Narcissa watched the trail until the sun set in a peach and purple haze. Although the Pambruns treated her royally because of her obvious favor with Dr. McLoughlin and her tutoring of Mrs. Pambrun and the children in English, she couldn't wait to begin the life's work she'd dreamt of since girlhood. She'd just die if Marcus didn't come for her ever so soon.

CHAPTER 56

RESPECTABILITY   FALL 1836

Captain William Drummond Stewart's first chore after his luxurious bath at St. Louis' fashionable *City Hotel* was to pick up his mail. He bought a bottle of French brandy on the way back to his plush room. He laid his letters in a row on his bed, nestled into its softness and began to read. The first letter from cotton broker Nichols was sinfully lucrative. His emaciated finances were gaining weight fast.

The second letter was from one of the gentle "leddies o' Logie." Aunt Mary's fine script from Logiealmond sympathized with his penniless plight and offered to send him £100 for the journey home to Scotland. William's brother Thomas, now in line to become a Cardinal, was visiting Aunt Mary. He'd been made a Knight of Malta and would soon return to Rome.

William's hand trembled angrily as he read brother George's letter lauding brother John for progressing so famously on New Murthly Castle, soon to be the show place of Scotland. George wasted a page describing the turrets and towers rising majestically at the foot of Birnam Hill to overlook the gentle Tay. Brother John'd frittered away enough to buy down town St. Louis on a fourth castle the family didn't need, while refusing to send William a farthing. William wadded the missive into a tight ball and bounced it off the wall. He noticed a letter on the carpet and retrieved it.

The parchment envelope bore no return. He tore the end off, blew into the envelope and plucked the letter out. Wife Christina's words were as cold as their spent love, but set fire to him. He leapt up with a Mountain Man whoop. Its two lines said, "*John Stewart, 18th Lord of Grandtully, Sixth Baronet of Murthly and cadet of the Earls of Perth, now lies stricken abed with a fatal illness in Paris. Shouldn't you come home to claim your inheritance?*"

A knock sounded on Stewart's door. A muffled voice asked, "Did you call, sir?"

"Not unless you are Atropos!"

"Don't understand, sir."

Jubilantly, Captain Stewart flung the door open. "Atropos is the Fate who cuts the thread of life. Do you provide that service in Paris?"

The hotelman muttered, "We don't even serve food in the bar, sir."

Captain Stewart couldn't wait to ensconce his bastard son George in Sir John's suite at Murthly Castle, but wondered if he really wanted the responsibility of running four castles and 32,000 acres in Scotland. Perhaps he'd just put their jester, Jamie the Dwarf, in charge and go right on raising royal hell in America.

*   *   *

William Sublette aimed a forefinger at the safe squatting like a yard-square, steel dice in the corner of his new office, "That come today."

General Ashley bent forward to examine the workmanship on the safe with the maker's name in yellow script across it. The gray hair combed over Ashley's bald spot opened like a door showing its pink secret. "Trouble with having anything valuable in the city is right off people start plotting how to rob you."

Sublette nodded and rested his boots on his new desk. "Have a seegar, General."

Ashley fingered a cigar from the aromatic box and settled in the stiff leather chair. "If Andy Jackson hadn't killed the U.S. Bank that used to sit across the street, you wouldn't need that safe. How big's your lot here, Bill?"

"Bout 38 x 160 feet."

"What's your capital outlay for this building?"

"Paid $12,833."

"You and Bobbie still full partners?"

Sublette nodded. "Renewed our partnership for another three years last January. I knew my ole life was over when I signed that agreement."

"I don't understand," Ashley mouthed around his unlit cigar.

Sublette stared out the window at the small tree in the back. Its leaves were splotched with red from the first fall frost. "Partnership agreement said we'd be merchants stead of engaging in the fur trade."

"Still grieving over coming Down the Mountain?"

"When I come in nis store this morning and smelled them new leather shoes and checked our dry goods -- hats and such, I wasn't. But when I look out this winder at that spindly tree there, I git worried. It's the only living thing I kin see from this office. Feel like I been tuck hostage. I wanta saddle a horse and ride west till he can't run no more."

"You went Up the Mountain with my expedition in the spring of '23. You came down about this time of year in '34. You were Up the Mountain almost a dozen years -- three times as long as most men live up there. How's Andrew doing?"

"Him and Lou Vasquez built some forts up in Colorado country. He's due here in St. Louie any day ta store their buffalo robes an' furs in our warehouses."

"Milt?"

Sublette scraped his boots across his new desk, sprang up and paced his small office. "Had breakfast with Chouteau Tuesday. Milt's writing him crazy letters. Fort William's fulla robes an' beaver, but Indian lodges're all gone cause Milt's got no goods ta trade. Blames Fitzpatrick and wants nothing more ta do with him. General, Milt wouldn't have a job if it wasn't fer Fitz. Been fighting the notion I oughta bring Milt home."

"Milt's more out o' place in the settlements than you are. I remember Milt and Fontenelle playing poker on a dead trapper's chest while they ate raw buffalo guts. Milt went savage years ago. Bill, some men can't come home. Milt's dying. Let him die free."

Sublette frowned and rubbed a knuckle under his eye. "How's yer Governor campaign going, General?"

"Opponent Boggs is blaming me for everything gone wrong in Washington."

"You holding yer House seat whilst you're running fer Governor here?"

Ashley nodded. "Can you believe Boggs blaming me for killing the U.S. Bank? I sacrificed party affiliations and relations with Andy Jackson trying to keep that bank alive. But since Andy issued the Specie Circular banning payment of debts to the U. States in paper money, financial panic's swept the east. Boggs says panic's on its way out here, and he's right. But it's none of my doing! I told you it'd happen, didn't I?"

"Thatchu did! Think St. Louie banks'll start calling their loans?"

"I hope to God they don't before the November election. I came within a whisker of being Governor in '24, Bill. I really want it this time!"

"I'll do all I kin, General. Boggs blaming you fer the Florida War?"

"Of course! Says it's my fault it wasn't over in three weeks."

"Think it'll be over by the election?"

"Bill, I don't think it'll be over by the second coming of Christ!"

"Way the papers talked when General Scott routed the Creeks an' started relocating them west, I figured the Seminoles'd go quiet."

"Seminoles will quit warring when Milt Sublette forms a temperance movement."

"You think Texas'll give the U. States trouble now that it's a separate country?"

"I've read communiqués from Sam Houston since they captured Santa Anna at San Jacinto, and I feel better. Houston's averted full scale war with Mexico. In spite of his blustering, he wants Texas to join the U. States down stream. Boggs must think so too, because he's made no issue of Texas."

"Abolitionists backing Boggs?"

"Don't know why they would on his record, but that issue's been snuffed for the time being by our House resolution gagging slavery debates. How's things at Sulphur Springs?"

"Mansion's done, modeled after Colonel Johnson's house on 5th street. Bought the Gratiot land next to Sulphur Springs and sold some off. Leaves me 990 acres."

"Wouldn't buy more land till we see what this bank panic does, Bill."

"Hadn't planned to. World's Smartest Mule Bluegrass died last week."

"What killed her?"

"Couldn't stand being respectable. Jist upped and died on a full belly."

CHAPTER 57

PLACE OF THE RYE GRASS   DECEMBER 1836

After Marcus Whitman returned to *Waiilatpu* on November 20th, he sweat from sunup to sundown every day but the Sabbath with two Hawaiians loaned to him by HBC and dropsy-slowed Mr. Hinds. They chopped trees, hand-sawing beams and planks out of the trunks. The resulting green cottonwood lumber changed shapes like frying bacon as it dried in the weak winter sun.

The 30 x 36 mission plan was laid out for two bedchambers, a kitchen and pantry. When they couldn't enclose the structure to hold out heavy snows, Mr. Hinds pledged, "I make a closed-in lean-to for Mrs. Whitman, if it be the last ting I ever do."

Walking itself was a battle for Mr. Hinds, but he nailed the last board on the lean-to just before sunset. Next morning Marcus found his loyal friend had gone home to God in the night. Marcus prayed fervently for the black man's soul as he dug a grave in the rich black dirt.

Marcus's funeral prayers were heartfelt. "Mr. Hinds endeared himself to each of us. A man this righteous must have been loved by many. May God bless and keep Mr. Hinds for eternity. We never knew his first name, but we didn't need to. *Mister* paid our respects to this loving and simple child of God -- the first American to die at our infant mission." Marcus kissed Mr. Hinds on the forehead, and they lowered him into the ground.

*   *   *

On December 9th, Marcus returned to Fort Walla Walla. A Narcissa-tutored Mrs. Pambrun greeted, "Good afternoon. How are you!"

Marcus smiled, "Ever so grateful to you and your esteemed husband for your gracious hospitality."

When Marcus saw Mrs. Pambrun's mystified expression, he grasped her hand and bowed to her. She beamed and called out, "Narcissa, your Mister's here!"

Marcus was gladdened by Narcissa's enormous abdomen. They hugged, then strolled into a misting rain, ignoring the rooting hogs and cooing pigeons in the Fort's courtyard. "Narcissa, please stay here till our child is birthed."

Narcissa's eyes pleaded. "Husband, I'll leave my puppy here till we have a yard for him, but I've waited since I was 16 to see where the Lord would have me serve the heathen. For the love of God, take me there now."

Marcus relented, "At dawn tomorrow."

"How long's the trip?"

"One day in good weather."

"That's an eternity for me, Husband!"

As the bleak sun rose, the Whitmans traded tearful good-byes with the Pambruns. Marcus hefted Narcissa ever so delicately onto her horse, then climbed on his own sturdy mount. They rode out together, waving nostalgically to the wonderful Pambruns.

Their horses occasionally slipping in patches of light snow, they rode side by side into the glorious Walla Walla River valley. The river's limpid waters murmured along a channel of sand and gravel 50 feet wide and two feet deep with lace-ice at its edges.

"Is the mission going well, Husband?"

"Mr. Hinds passed away, so the two Hawaiians and I will finish it."

"How sad that Mr. Hinds is gone, but can't you get the Cayuse to help?"

"Chief Rotten-belly begged the Cayuse, but their men consider work as slavery. Cayuse women also refused to become slaves of the whites."

"Did he tell the Cayuse we'd pay and bring them precious teachings of God?"

"Pay does not change work from slavery. As to our God's word, they care not."

"What are you saying, Husband?"

"They have their own Gods everywhere and will honor them."

"Perhaps we should have gone to the Nez Percé, Husband."

"Perhaps, but that's not the worst of it."

"What could be worse than bull-headed heathens?"

"Rotten-belly says Parker, the most penurious Presbyterian of our time, promised we'd pay the Cayuse for the mission site and fields. Rotten-belly says the Cayuse Chief told him we could not finish the mission till we paid 20 horses and 15 cows -- paying more horses and cows each year we stay."

"What did you say to that?"

"I had Rotten-belly tell them that our God does not pay men to use their lands any more than their Gods do, and that we'd come to save their souls from hell."

"How did the Cayuse take that?"

"The Cayuse Chief shouted so fast Rotten-belly said he couldn't understand. I think he did, but was too terrified to tell me."

"God will watch over us here as He did on our journey, Husband."

Marcus nodded in the ominous dusk.

"I've never seen land more enchanting than this valley," Narcissa whispered, praying they had not entered the valley of the shadow of death. "Is it much further to our mission, Husband?"

"Over the next hummock."

As the daughter of New York's finest carpenter, Narcissa was appalled by the skeletal mission's misshapen framing, but bit her tongue. Darkness would brook no broad exploration this night. They groped through the primitive lean-to's inky shadows.

"Mr. Hinds died finishing this for you, Narcissa. Let us bless him before we sleep." Shivering in the chill wind, they held each other and blessed Mr. Hinds.

"Where are the Hawaiians, Husband?"

"They are will-o-the wisp. Never know when they'll come or go."

Marcus brought blanket rolls from their horses, then kindled a fire on the unfinished hearth. He stalled their horses inside the roofless dwelling to conceal them from the Cayuse. Soon, they sipped simmering tea from tin basins that scalded their lips, but warmed their hearts. This hovel was hardly the idyllic realm of her girlhood longings, but Narcissa set her jaw and vowed never to abandon her dreams.

Narcissa spread their blankets close to the fire, then lay down and held her arms out to Marcus. He eased a green log into the dying fire, then burrowed under the blankets with her. They hugged and kissed with a spirituality that lost them in the timelessness of each other's devotion. They slept ever so soundly after their tiring ride from Fort Walla Walla.

Still stiff after their night on the frosty ground, they bundled in their blankets till the sun's warming rays crept into their squalid lean-to. When they ventured into the icy air, a hill covered with yellow-tan rye grass cast its long shadow across *Waiilatpu*. "Let's climb that hill for a view of our lands, Husband!"

Without waiting for him, she ascended through dry knee high grass rolling in wind-waves like a golden ocean. When he overtook her, Marcus grasped her arm to steady her climb. She panted, "What does *Waiilatpu* mean?"

Marcus breathed, "Place of the Rye Grass."

"How poetic!"

They knelt together at the summit, awed by the majesty of the lands surrounding them. A range of snowy mountains towered into wispy clouds to the east and mountains lay to the west. Narcissa asked, "Husband, which of these vast ranges are the real Shining Mountains?"

Marcus laid his hand gently to her cheek. "Those you carry in your heart, my sweet Narcissa."

BIBLIOGRAPHY FOR *BEHOLD THE SHINING MOUNTAINS*
by Gary H. Wiles and Delores M. Brown

Alter, J. Cecil. *James Bridger, Trapper, Frontiersman, Scout and Guide.*
    Shepard Book Co.Salt Lake City 1925
Anderson, William Marshall. *The Rocky Mountain Journals of William
    Marshall Anderson.* Edited by Dale L. Morgan and Eleanor T.
    Harris. Huntington Library. San Marino 1967
Axelrod, Alan. *Art of the Golden West, An Illustrated History.*
    Cross River Press, Ltd. New York 1990
Bancroft, Hubert Howe. *History of Arizona and New Mexico 1530 - 1888.*
    Horn & Wallace. Albuquerque 1962
Bancroft, Hubert Howe. *History of Oregon.* [Volumes 1 & 2]
    The History Co. San Francisco 1886
Beaver Club of Lafayette. *Cajun Men Cook - Recipes, Stories and Food
    from Louisiana.* Beaver Club of Lafayette. Louisiana 1994
Beckwourth, James P. *The Life Adventures of James P. Beckwourth* as told
    to Thomas D. Bonner. University of Nebraska Press 1972
Birch, William Russell. *Birch's Views of Philadelphia in 1800s.*
    University of Pennsylvania Press 1983
Bradley, William Aspenwall. *William Cullen Bryant.*
    Macmillan. New York 1905
Bryan, William Smith and Rose, Robert. *A History of the Pioneer Families
    of Missouri.* Genealogical Publishing Co. Baltimore 1977
Bureau Developments, Inc. *U.S. History on CD - ROM.*
    IBM Version [using 85 of 102 Volumes] 1991
Burnett, Peter Hardeman. *Recollections and Opinions of an Old Pioneer.*
    Da Capo Press. New York 1969 Reprint of 1880 Edition
Carson, Kit. *Kit Carson's Autobiography.* Edited by Milo Milton Quaife.
    University of Nebraska Press. Lincoln, Nebraska 1935.
Campbell, Robert. *The Rocky Mountain Letters of Robert Campbell.*
    Printed for Frederick W. Beinecke. New York 1923
Catlin, George. *Letters and Notes on the Manners, Customs of the North
    American Indians.* [Vol. 1 & 2.] Ross & Haines.Minneapolis 1965
Chittenden, Hiram M. *History of Early Steamboat Navigation on the
    Missouri River.* [Vol. 1 & 2.] Ross & Haines. Minneapolis 1962
Chittenden, Hiram M. *The American Fur Trade of the Far West.*
    [Vol. 1 & 2] University of Nebraska Press. Lincoln, NE 1986
Christ-Janer, Albert; Hughes, Charles W.; Smith, Carleton Sprague. *Amer-
    ican Hymns -- Old and New.* Columbia Press. New York 1980
Clokey, Richard M. *William H. Ashley - Enterprise and Politics in the
    Trans-Mississippi West.* University of Oklahoma Press 1980
Clyman, James. *Journal of a Mountain Man.* Edited by Linda Hasselstrom.
    Mountain Press Publishing Co. Missoula, Montana 1984
Coman, Katharine. *Economic Beginnings of Far West: How We Won the
    Land Beyond the Mississippi.* [Vol. 1 & 2.] Kelley. New York 1969

Coutant, C.G. *The History of Wyoming from the Earliest Known Discoveries.* Chapin, Spafford & Mathison. Laramie 1899

Dale, Harrison *TheAshley-Smith Explorations and Discovery of a Central Route to the Pacific.* The Arthur H. Clark Co. Glendale, CA 1941

Daugherty, James. *Marcus and Narcissa Whitman - Pioneers of Oregon.* Viking Press. New York 1953

Dossenbach, Monique & Hans. *The Noble Horse.* Portland House. New York 1987

Drury, Clifford Merrill, *First White Women Over The Rockies.* [Vol. I, II & III.] The Arthur H. Clark Co. Glendale, CA 1963-1966

Drury, Clifford Merrill. *Marcus Whitman, M.D. Pioneer and Martyr.* Caxton Printers, Ltd. Caldwell, Idaho 1937

Drury, Clifford Merrill. *The Diaries and Letters of Henry H. Spalding & Asa Bowen Smith.* Arthur H. Clark Co. Glendale, CA 1958

Estergreen, M. Morgan. *Kit Carson A Portrait in Courage.* University of Oklahoma Press. Norman, Oklahoma 1962

Fife, Austin E. and Alta S. *Cowboy and Western Songs - A Comprehensive Anthology.* Creative Concepts Publishing Corp. Ojai, CA 1969

Franzwa, Gregory M. *The Oregon Trail Revisited.* 4th Edition. The Patrice Press. Tucson, Arizona 1988

Garrison, William Lloyd. *Selections from the Writings & Speeches of William Lloyd Garrison.* Negro University Press. New York 1968

Gilbert, Bil. *The Trailblazers.* Time-Life Books. New York 1973

Goetzmann, William H. *New Lands, New Men - America And The Second Great Age of Discovery.* Viking. New York 1986

Gordon, Alexander. *The Journal of the 15th Hussars.* Edited by Col. H. C. Wylly. J. Murray. London 1913

Gowans, Fred R and Campbell, Eugene. *Fort Bridger.* Brigham Young University Press. Provo, Utah 1975

Gowans, Fred R. *Mountain Man & Grizzly.* Mountain Grizzly Publications. Orem, Utah 1992

Gowans, Fred R. *Rocky Mountain Rendezvous: A History of the Fur Trade 1825 -1840.* Peregrin Smith Books. Layton, Utah 1985

Gray, Henry, F.R.S. *Anatomy, Descriptive and Surgical.* Edited by T. Pickering Pick & Robt. Howden. Bounty Books, New York 1977

Guild, Thelma S. & Carter, Harvey L. *Kit Carson A Pattern for Heroes.* University of Nebraska Press. Lincoln & London 1984

Hafen, Leroy R. *Broken Hand: The Life of Thomas Fitzpatrick: Mountain Man.* Old West Publishing Co. Denver, CO 1973

Hafen, Leroy R. *The Journal of Captain John R. Bell for the Stephen H. Long Expedition to the Rocky Mountains, 1820.* Edited by Harlin M. Fuller. Arthur Clark Co. Glendale 1957

Hafen, Leroy R. Editor: *The Mountain Men and the Fur Trade of the Far West.* [Vol. I thru X.] Arthur H. Clark Co. Glendale, CA 1965-72

Hafen, Leroy R. and Ann W. *Old Spanish Trail with Extracts from Diaries of Armijo & Pratt*. Arthur H. Clark Co. Glendale, CA 1954

Hafen, Leroy R. Editor. *Trappers of the Far West*.
University of Nebraska Press. Bison Books. Lincoln, NE 1983

Hanson, James A. *The Buckskinner's Cook Book*.
The Fur Press. Chadron, Nebraska 1979

Holy Bible.
King James Version.

Horn, Huston. *The Old West -- The Pioneers*.
Time-Life Books. Alexandria, Virginia 1974

Hulbert, Archer B. and Dorothy P. (Editors) *The Oregon Crusade*.
Denver 1935

Hymns -- Ancient and Modern -- With Notes on Origin.
Clowes & Sons Ltd. London 1909

Irving, Washington. *The Adventures of Captain Bonneville* [Vol. XVI of *Complete Works of Irving*] Twayne Publishers. Boston 1977

Irving, Washington. *The Western Journals of Washington Irving*. Edited by John F. McDermott. University of Oklahoma Press 1944

Janetski, Joel C. *Indians of Yellowstone Park*. Bonneville Books.
University of Utah Press. Salt Lake City, Utah 1987

Jones, Nard. *Marcus Whitman: The Great Command: The Story of Marcus and Narcissa Whitman*. Binsford & Mort. Portland, OR 1968

Lloyd, Trevor Owen. *The British Empire 1558-1983*.
Oxford University Press. New York 1984

Maughan, Ralph W. *Anatomy of the Snake River Plain*.
Idaho State University Press. Pocatello, Idaho 1992

Meigs, William Montgomery. *The Life of Thomas Hart Benton*.
Da Capo Press. New York 1970

Morgan, Dale L. *Jedediah Smith and the Opening of the West*.
Bobbs, Merrill Co. Inc. Indianapolis 1953

Morris, Ralph C. *The Notion of a Great American Desert East of the Rockies*. Mississippi Valley Historical Review [Vol. XIII] 1926-27

Mowry, William A. Ph.D. *Marcus Whitman and the Early Days of Oregon*.
Silver, Burdett & Co.New York 1901

Official Report on The Expedition of Dragoons Under Col. Henry Dodge To The Rocky Mountains in 1835. American State Papers [Vol. VI] No. 624, 24th Congress, 1st Session, 1835.

Official Report of Expedition of Squadron of Dragoons Under Col. Henry Dodge. House Doc. No. 181, 24th Congress, 1st Session, 1836

Parker, Samuel. *Journal of an Exploring Tour Beyond the Rocky Mountains*. Ithaca 1838

Peters, Virginia Bergman. *The Florida Wars*. Archon Books.
The Shoe String Press, Inc. Hamden, Connecticut 1979

Porter, Jane. *The Scottish Chiefs*. Thomas Y. Crowell & Co.
New York 1831 Reprint of 1809 Text with Illustrations

Porter, Kenneth Wiggins. *John Jacob Astor Business Man.* [Volume II.]
Russell & Russell. New York 1966

Porter, Mae Reed and Davenport, Odessa. *Scotsman in Buckskins - Sir
William Drummond Stewart and the Rocky Mountain Fur Trade.*
Hastings House. New York 1963

Pugnetti, Gino. *Guide to Dogs.* Edited by Elizabeth Meriwether Schuler.
Simon & Schuster. New York, London 1980.

Raph, Theodore. *The American Song Treasury - 100 Favorites.*
Dover Publications, Inc. New York 1964

Rawling, Gerald. *The Pathfinder - The History of America's First
Westerners.* Macmillan Company. New York, London 1964

Remini, Robert V. *Andrew Jackson and the Bank War A Study in the
Growth of Presidential Power.* Norton & Co. Inc. New York 1967

Riley, Glenda, *Women and Indians on the Frontier 1825 - 1915.*
University of New Mexico Press. Albuquerque, NM 1984

Rollins, Philip Ashton. *The Discovery of the Oregon Trail.* Robert Stuart's
Narrative. Eberstadt & sons New York 1935

Rosenberg, Charles E. *The Cholera Years -- The United States in 1832,
1849 and 1866.* University of Chicago Press. Chicago 1962

Russell, Osborne. *Journal of a Trapper.* Edited by Aubrey L. Haines.
Bison Books - University of Nebraska Press. Lincoln 1955

Sandoz, Mari. *The Beaver Men - Spearheads of Empire.*
Hastings House. New York 1964

Schlesinger, Arthur M. Jr. *The Age of Jackson.*
Little, Brown & Company. Boston 1953

Schlissel, Lillian. *Women's Diaries of the Westward Journey* Edited by
Gerda Lerner. Schocken Books. New York 1982

Secoy, Frank R. *Changing Military Patterns of the Great Plains Indians.*
University of Nebraska Press. Lincoln, NE 1953

Smith, Arthur D. Howden. *John Jacob Astor Landlord of New York.*
J.B. Lippincott Co.Philadelphia & London 1929

Sullivan, Maurice S. *The Travels of Jedediah Smith Including Journal.*
Fine Arts Press. Santa Ana, California 1934

Sunder, John E. *Bill Sublette: Mountain Man.*
University of Oklahoma Press. Norman, Oklahoma 1959

The Pilgrim Hymnal. The Pilgrim Press.
Boston and Chicago. Revised Edition 1935

The Software Toolworks. *Illustrated Encyclopedia IBM Version 2.0.*
[21 Volumes] on CD- ROM. Grolier, Inc. Danbury, CT 1991

Tomkins, William. *Indian Sign Language.*
Dover Publications, Inc. New York 1969

Townsend, John Kirk. *Narrative of a Journey across the Rocky Mountains.*
Perkins & Marvin. Boston, Philadelphia 1839

Triplett, Frank. *Conquering the Wilderness.*
N.D. Thompson & Co. New York & St. Louis 1895

Twitchell, Ralph Emerson. *Old Santa Fe - The Story of New Mexico's Ancient Capital*. Santa Fe New Mexican Publishing Corp.1925

Unruh, Jr., John D. *The Plains Across -The overland Emigrants and Trans- Mississippi West*. University of Illinois Press. Chicago 1979

Van Every, Dale. *The Final Challenge - The American Frontier 1804 - 1845*. William Morrow and Company. New York 1964

Victor, Frances Fuller. *River of the West: Adventures of Joe Meek*. Winfred Blevins, Editor. Mountain Press Pub. Co. Missoula, MT 1983

Walker, William. The *Southern Harmony, And Musical Companion*. E.W. Miller. Philadelphia 1835

Warren, Eliza Spalding. *Memoirs of the West (Journal of Eliza Spalding)*. Marsh Printing Co. Portland 1916 [?]

Whitman, Narcissa Prentiss. *My Journal*. Ye Galleon Press. Edited by Lawrence L. Dodd. Fairfield, Washington 1982.

Whitman, Narcissa. *The Letters of Narcissa Whitman*. Galleon Press. Fairfield, Washington 1986

Weigley, Russell F: Editor. *Philadelphia - a 300 Year History*. W.W. Norton & Co. New York - London 1982

Weston, Sydney A. *The Pilgrim Hymnal*. The Pilgrim Press. Boston - Chicago. Revised Edition 1935

Wiles, Gary H. and Brown, Delores M. *Ponder The Path*. Photosensitive™ Laguna Niguel, California 1994

Wilson, Elinor. *Jim Beckwourth, Black Man and War Chief of the Crows*. University of Oklahoma Press. Norman, Oklahoma 1972

Wraxall, Sir C.F. Lacelles. *The Backwoodsman*. T.O.H.P. Burnham. Boston. & O.S. Felt. New York 1866.

Wyeth, John B. *Oregon or A Short History of a Long Journey - 1832*. From *Early Western Travels 1748-1846* Edited by Reuben Gold Thwaites, LL.D. AMS Press, Inc. New York 1966

Young, Stanley Paul and Goldman, Edward A. *The Wolves of North America*. Dover Publications. New York 1964

Ziegler, Philip. *King William IV*. Collins. St. James Place, London 1971

INDEX OF PERSONS [With Identifying Data]
Since chapters are exceedingly brief, reference numbers are to chapters rather than pages.

Bridger, Mary Ann [Infant Daughter of Jim & Nez Percé Cora Bridger] 54

Bryant, Dr. Ira [Medical Doctor & Mentor of Marcus Whitman] 4

Bryant, William Cullen [Journalist & Author] 4

Buckner, Alex [U.S. Senator Who Dropped Dead From Cholera on Senate Floor in 1834] 24

Bullard, Reverend Artemas [Recommended Henry Spalding to American Board] 44

Bull's Head [Nez Percé Chief - Also Called Kentuck - Friend of Wm. Sublette] 30, 55

Burr, Aaron [Guest in Wm. Marshall Anderson's Kentucky Home] 28

Cabanne, J. P. [American Fur Co Official Arresting Leclerc For Transporting Liquor] 24, 40

Campbell, Robert [Mountain Man & Partner of Wm. Sublette] 6, 7, 9, 11,12, 14, 15, 16, 17, 18, 19, 21, 23, 24, 31, 34,
36, 38, 39, 41, 46, 56

Campbell, Hugh [Robert's Brother Living In Philadelphia] 24, 34, 46

Carson, Kit [Mountain Man] 3, 7, 43

Cass, Lewis [Secretary of War Who Once Accepted $35,000 "Gift" from Astor] 12, 16, 24

Catlin, George [Famous Painter of Indians] 15, 50

Cayuse Indians 55, 57

Chaves, Jose Antonio [Mexican Governor at Santa Fe in 1831] 3

Chavez, Magistrado [Santa Fe Official in 1831] 3, 17

Choctaw Indians 44

Chouteau, Pierre Jr. [American Fur Co's St. Louis Managing Agent] 12, 24, 31, 54, 56

Christy, Edmund [Mountain Man & Investor in Rocky Mountain Fur Co.] 21

Clark, General Marston [Kaw Indian Agent & Kinsman of Wm. Marshall Anderson] 28

Clark, General William [of Lewis & Clark - St. Louis Agent of Indian Affairs] 6, 23, 24, 33, 48

Clay, Henry [U. S. Congressman] 8, 28

Clyman, Jim [U.S. Army Lieutenant & Friend of Abe Lincoln] 12, 17, 42

Columbia River Fishing & Trading Co. [Wyeth's Firm Owned with Tucker & Williams] 24, 27, 41

Comanche Indians 1, 3, 5, 9

Compo, Charles [Mountain Man & Interpreter in Fontenelle's 1835 Caravan] 42, 43

Cooper, Captain [Monterey Trader] 3

Coughing Snake [Flathead - or Shoshone - Chief] 31

Crawford [British Consul at New Orleans & Business Partner of Captain Stewart] 43, 49

Creek Indians 46, 49, 56

Crockett, Davy [U.S. Congressman & Texas Freedom Fighter] 12, 46, 49

Crooks, Ramsey [Purchaser of American Fur Co's Northern Department in 1834] 26, 30

Crow [Absaroka] Indians 9, 17, 21, 23, 24, 29, 30, 42, 46, 51, 52

Danner [Employee of New York City's Riddle, Forsythe & Co- Brokers for Wm. Sublette] 16

Dade, Major [Leader of 96 U.S. Soldiers Massacred in 1836 Seminole Ambush] 49

Dodge, Colonel Henry [Commandant of Fort Leavenworth in Kansas Territory in 1835] 45

Dodge's Ranger Battalion [Commissioned at Fort Gibson, Arkansas Territory in 1832] 12

Dorian, Baptiste [Iroquois Starting Battle of Pierre's Hole in 1832] 9

Driedopple [German Translator for Prince Maximilian] 18

Drips, Andrew [Mountain Man & American Fur Co. Employee] 7, 9, 10, 31, 42

Dunbar, Reverend John [Presbyterian Missionary to Pawnees] 45

Eddy, Thomas [Former Mountain Man & Owner of Green Tree Tavern] 26, 27, 46

Ermatinger, Francis [Hudson's Bay Co Field Manager] 19, 21

Evans, George Henry [Embroiled in Cholera Debate] 8

Evans, Mr. [Wyeth's Managing Employee of Fort Hall in 1834] 33

Farrar, Dr. Bernard [Surgeon Treating - Then Amputating Milt Sublette's Leg in 1835] 23, 34, 36, 46, 49

Ferris, Warren [American Fur Co. Mountain Man Shot by Blackfeet in 1832] 10

Fisk, Dr. Wilbur [New England Methodist Mentor of Jason Lee] 25, 31

Fitzpatrick, Bridger & Sublette [Short-lived Firm at 1834 Rendezvous] 31

Fitzpatrick, Thomas [Partner in Rocky Mountain Fur Co. & Fontenelle, Fitzpatrick & Co] 1, 3, 7, 9, 10, 11, 17, 18, 21, 23, 24, 26, 28, 29, 30, 31, 38, 39, 42, 43, 45, 49, 51, 52, 53, 54, 55, 56

Flathead [Saalish] Indians 7, 9, 30, 31, 33, 43, 53, 55

Flournoy, Samuel [Wagoneer on Santa Fe Trail] 3

Fontenelle, Fitzpatrick & Co [Partnership Including, Bridger, Drips & Milt Sublette Created at 1834 Rendezvous] 31, 38, 39, 42, 45, 52, 54

Fontenelle, Logan [Heroic 10 Year Old Son of Lucien in 1835 Cholera Attack] 40

Fontenelle, Lucien [American Fur Co. Employee & Fontenelle, Fitzpatrick & Co. Partner] 9, 10, 15, 18, 19, 31, 39, 40, 41, 42, 45, 46, 49, 51, 54, 56

Fontenelle, Me-um-ba-ne [Bright Sun - Omaha Wife of Lucien] 39, 40

Fraeb, Henry [German Mountain Man & Rocky Mountain Fur Co Partner] 18, 21, 30

Friday the Arapaho [Precocious Indian Child Ward of Fitzpatrick] 1, 3, 18, 21, 30, 38, 39, 42, 43, 45, 49

Gannt, Captain John [Bankrupt Booshway of Kit Carson] 7,

Gardner, Johnson [Mountain Man Burned Alive on the Upper Missouri in 1833] 17, 18

Garrison, William Lloyd [Ardent Abolitionist] 2, 13, 24

Gervais, Jean [Mountain Man & Partner of Rocky Mountain Fur Co.] 21, 30

Geyer, Henry Esquire [Lawyer of Wm. Sublette] 1, 12, 24, 26, 30

Glass, Hugh [Mountain Man Burned Alive on the Upper Missouri in 1833] 17, 18

Godin, Antoine [Iroquois Starting Battle of Pierre's Hole in 1832] 9

Goodyear, Miles [19 Year Old Hired Hand on 1836 Trip West with Whitmans] 51, 52

Gray, Rockaway Bill [Stabbed Milt Sublette for Dallying with Gray's Wife] 7

Gray, William [Presbyterian Missionary on 1836 Trip West with Whitmans] 51, 52, 53, 55

Green, Beriah [Abolitionist Pastor of Western Reserve College] 4, 22

Greene, Reverend David [Corresponding Secretary of American Board] 35, 37, 47, 51

Gros Ventres Indians 7, 30, 42

Hall, Henry [Tucker & Williams Partner Backing Wyeth & Namesake of Fort Hall] 24, 33, 54

Hamsa, Carlos [Newspaper Correspondent] 34, 46, 49

Harris, Moses "Black"[Negro Mountain Man & Friend of Wm. Sublette] 18, 19, 23, 26, 28, 29, 51, 52

Harrison, Dr. Benjamin [Son of General Harrison Taken West in 1833 To Cure Drunkenness] 17, 18, 19, 23, 26

Harrison, General William Henry [Future President - Hired Sublette & Campbell to Take Son West] 17

Hart, Eliza [Missionary - See Eliza Spalding After Marriage to Henry in September 1833] 4, 22, 35

Hart, Levi [Father of Eliza Hart] 22, 44, 50

Hart, Martha [Mother of Eliza Hart] 22, 44

Hawken Gunsmiths [Famous St. Louis Gunsmiths] 14

Hawkins, John [True Name Hawken, Jacob - Mountain Man & Nephew of Gunsmith Samuel Hawken] 54

Helen Mar [Infant Daughter of Joe Meek & Nez Percé Wife Named For Heroine in *Scottish Chiefs*] 53

Henry, Major Andrew [Former Ashley & Henry Co. Partner] 17, 23

Herring [Indian Commissioner and Judge in Washington D.C.] 24

Hidatsa Indians 16, 52

Higby, Reverend [Revival Preacher in Prattsburg, New York] 13

Hill, James [Captain of Steamboat *Otto*] 18

Hinds, Mister [Negro Patient of Dr. Whitman & Cherished Laborer on the Whitman Mission] 55, 57

331

McLoughlin, Dr. John [Hudson's Bay Co's Chief Factor of Fort Vancouver] 23, 41, 54, 55

McLoughlin, Marguerite Wadin [Half-breed Wife of Hudson's Bay Co's Chief Factor of Fort Vancouver] 55

Meek, Joseph [Mountain Man Crony of Milt Sublette] 7, 9, 21, 38, 43, 53

Meek, Stephan [Mountain Man & Brother of Joe Meek] 21

Merrill, Reverend Moses [Baptist Missionary] 39

Monroe, President James [Guest in Wm. Marshall Anderson's Kentucky Home] 28

More, George [Nathaniel Wyeth's Employee Who Died in Wilderness] 19

Newell, Robert [Mountain Man at 1832 Battle of Pierre's Hole] 9

Nez Percé [Saapten] Indians 7, 9, 19, 25, 30, 31, 33, 41, 43, 45, 47, 48, 50, 51, 53, 55, 57

Nichols, E.B. [New Orleans Cotton Broker in Business with Captain Stewart in 1836] 49, 56

Nidever, George [Rescuer of Thomas Fitzpatrick at Pierre's Hole in 1832] 7

No-Horns-on-His Head [Messenger of Indians Seeking the White God in St. Louis] 33

Nuttal, Thomas [Botanist Paying to Go with Wyeth's 1834 Caravan] 27, 29, 33, 41

Omaha Indians 39, 40, 41

Osage Indians 35, 44, 47, 48

Osceola [Rampaging Seminole Chief in Florida War] 34, 49

Otoe Indians 28, 39, 51

Paine, Thomas [Patriot & Benefactor of Captain Bonneville's Family] 19

Pakenham, Sir Edward [British General Killed at Battle of New Orleans & Sent Home in Keg of Rum] 6

Palmer, Emeline [Presbyterian Missionary Fiancée of Samuel Allis on 1836 Trip with Whitmans] 50, 51

Pambrun, Kitty [Cree/French Wife of Pierre] 55, 57

Pambrun, Pierre [Hudson's Bay Co Factor of Fort Walla Walla] 33, 55, 57

Parker, Reverend Samuel [Presbyterian Missionary] 4, 8, 25, 34, 35, 37, 39, 40, 41, 42, 43, 45, 47, 51, 53, 54, 55, 57

Parkman, Samuel [Partner of David Jackson] 3

Parsons, Lieutenant [U.S. Army Officer at Fort Leavenworth] 23

Patton, William [Wm. Sublette's Clerk Left To Build Out Fort William in 1834] 29

Pawnee Indians 23, 28, 29, 45, 52

Peabody, Angus [Slaver Driving Artemis onto William Sublette's Land] 5

Peña, Señorita [Santa Fe Enchantress] 3

Pettis, Spencer [U.S. Congressman Killed in 1831 duel with Major Thomas Biddle] 5, 7

Pilcher, Joshua [Mountain Man & American Fur Co. Official in 1836] 52, 53, 54

Pilou [American Fur Co. Mountain Man Killed in 1832 by Blackfeet] 10

Pins [Mountain Man in Fontenelle's 1835 Rendezvous Caravan] 42

Powell, Reverend & Mrs. O.S. [New York Presbyterian Missionaries] 37

Prentiss Choir [8 Presbyterian Prentiss Children Lead by their Father Judge Prentiss] 13, 48

Prentiss, Clarissa [Mother of Narcissa & 8 Other Prentiss Children] 13, 48

Prentiss, Jane [Love Interest of Dr. Marcus Whitman & Sister of Narcissa] 25, 32, 37, 48

Prentiss, Narcissa [Teacher & Presbyterian Missionary - See Whitman, Narcissa After Marriage to Marcus in February 1836] 2, 4, 13, 22, 25, 32, 35, 37, 41, 45, 47, 48

Prentiss, Judge Stephen [Carpenter & Father of Narcissa & Siblings] 2, 4, 13, 25, 32, 37, 44, 47, 48, 57

Rabbit-Skin-Leggings [Messenger of Indians Seeking the White God in St. Louis] 33

Richard [Tackitonitis - Nez Percé Ward of Dr. Whitman in 1835-6] 43, 45, 47, 48, 50, 51, 53, 54, 55

Richardson [Chief Hunter for Wyeth's 1834 Caravan] 27, 28, 29, 33

Riddle, Robert [Pittsburgh Seller of 2 Keelboats to Wm. Sublette in 1833] 16

Rocky Mountain Fur Co. [RMF - Partnership of Bridger, Fitzpatrick, Fraeb, Gervais & M. Sublette] 1, 3, 7, 9, 10, 12, 18, 21, 24, 26, 27, 30, 31, 33, 34, 38, 46, 52

332

PHOTOSENSITIVE™
DEPT. BHS

P.O. Box 7008
Hemet, CA 92545-7008
or ☎Free 1-877-742-6241

BOOK ORDER FORM

Sold To: _____

_____

_____

_____

Telephone _____

LIBRARIES, BOOK STORES & DEALERS CALL FOR VOLUME DISCOUNTS.

Disregard Sales Tax Unless You Are Ordering From California!

BOOK & ½ SHIPPING COSTS	NO.	PRICE EACH	SALES TAX CA ONLY	TOTAL
PONDER THE PATH by Gary Wiles & Delores Brown	____	$12.95	$ .99	$_____
BEHOLD THE SHINING MOUNTAINS by Gary Wiles & Delores Brown	____	$14.95	$1.16	$_____
HOW TO STOP SMOKING WHILE SMOKING* by Gary Wiles [who quit this way over 20 years ago]	____	$ 9.95	$ .77	$_____
You pay ½ shipping @ $1 per book		$ 1.00 Shipping		$_____
		GRAND	**TOTAL**	**$**

* Money-Back Guarantee If You Do What Our Book Says and Don't Stop Smoking!

___Check ___Money Order Payable to PHOTOSENSITIVE™,

___ Visa ___ Mastercard No. _____ Expires _____

Signature of Ordering Party_____

INSTRUCTIONS FOR SHIPPING, AUTOGRAPHING AND FREE AUTHOR PHOTOS:

_____

_____

_____

TEAR OUT AND MAIL TO ADDRESS AT TOP OF THIS PAGE